THE BOOK OF RUTH

THE BOOK OF RUTH

JANE HAMILTON

ANCHOR BOOKS

DOUBLEDAY

NEW YORK LONDON TORONTO SYDNEY AUCKLAND

AN ANCHOR BOOK
PUBLISHED BY DOUBLEDAY
a division of Bantam Doubleday Dell Publishing Group, Inc.
1540 Broadway, New York, New York 10036

ANCHOR BOOKS, DOUBLEDAY, and the portrayal of an anchor are trademarks
of Doubleday, a division of Bantam Doubleday Dell Publishing Group, Inc.

The lyrics from the song "Mandy" on page 271, © 1971 Screen Gems-EMI Music Inc.
and Grahple Music Ltd., are used by permission; all rights reserved.
The line from the poem "The Lake Isle of Innisfree" on page 315 is from *The Poems
of W. B. Yeats: A New Edition*, edited by Richard J. Finneran (New York: Macmillan,
1983).
The lyrics on page 323 from the song "If You Leave Me Now," written and
composed by Peter Cetera, © 1976 Polish Prince Music/Big Elk Music, are used by
permission; all rights reserved.
The lyrics from the song "You're Sixteen (You're Beautiful and You're Mine)," by
Bob Sherman and Dick Sherman, © 1960 Warner-Tamerlane Publishing Corp., are used
by permission; all rights reserved.

The Book of Ruth was originally published in hardcover
by Ticknor & Fields in 1988. The Anchor Books edition is
published by arrangement with Ticknor & Fields.

Library of Congress Cataloging-in-Publication Data
Hamilton, Jane, 1957–
   The book of Ruth / Jane Hamilton.
      p.   cm.
   I. Title.
[PS3558.A4427B66   1990]   89-38241
813′.54—dc20   CIP
ISBN 0-385-26570-0

21   22   23   24   25   26   27   28   29   30

For Bob

One

WHAT it begins with, I know finally, is the kernel of meanness in people's hearts. I don't know exactly how or why
it gets inside us; that's one of the mysteries I haven't solved yet.
I always tried to close my eyes and believe that angels, invisible
in their gossamer dresses, were keeping their loving vigil. I learned,
slowly, that if you don't look at the world with perfect vision,
you're bound to get yourself cooked. Even though I may still be
looking through the dark glass, even though I haven't finished
learning the lessons, I'm the only one who tells the story from
beginning to end. It can't be up to Ruby, because he has been
spirited away and born again. Neither love nor prayer can bring
him back. May can talk herself blue in the face and no one will
hear. By rights this belongs to Justy, because he inherits the earth
for a short time, but he doesn't quite count yet. He'll remember
the taste of pecan balls, exactly how the powdery mash got stuck
on the roof of his mouth, the color black maybe, and the color
and shape of Ruby's teeth. They were rotten with sweets.

I tell myself that it should be simple to see through to the past
now that I'm set loose, now that I can invent my own words,
but nothing much has come my way without a price. I'm not

counting on a free ride. I know the only way to begin to understand is to steal underneath May's skin and look at the world
from behind her small eyes. I shudder when I think about the
inside of Ruby's head, but I know I have to journey there too,
if I'm going to make sense of what's happened.

Sometimes Aunt Sid shocks me into seeing myself in a new
light; she'll speak to me, looking straight into my eyes, and it's
as if she's talking to an adult; and then I realize she is, that I am,
in fact, grown up. The bones in these legs don't get any longer.

She tells me that there has been a grave error, which is actually
how I've felt for a considerable length of time, as if I'm a series
of sums that doesn't come out right. She says she doesn't understand how my clear intelligence went unrecognized, but I
haven't explained to her yet the confines of my mother tongue.
We were the products of our limited vocabulary: we had no words
for savory odors or the colors of the winter sky or the unexpected
compulsion to sing. The language I had to speak to be understood
is not the language of poetry or clear thinking. I only let on once
to May that I had acquired other words for private use.

In the Bible it starts with the spirit of God moving upon the
face of the water, but I don't buy those ideas. You couldn't pay
me to take my story back that far. Everyone's probably heard of
Honey Creek, where I lived with Ruby and May. There isn't
anything fancy about the location, except the iron gate around
the church and the pigeons with their purple breasts.

Mr. Abendroth, the oldest person in town, spends his time
walking through farmers' fields picking up corn and stealing apples, and he shares his loot with the pigeons. Honey Creek is
way up in the very north of Illinois; if you lean over the Aben-
droths' back fence your torso is in Wisconsin.

You will miss the town if you drive through listening to your
favorite song on the radio or telling a story about your neighbor.
The two blocks of white clapboard houses with black trim will
look like nothing more than a cloudy morning. Only Mrs. Crawford's house is blue, like the color eyeshadow my friend Daisy

wears, and she has a red barn in the back. She had her place painted blue after her husband, Bub, died and everyone figured she'd gone crazy with grief. Then for Christmas she put lights all over the trees in her yard, colored lights which flashed on and off. Then everyone watched to see if she would come out one day wearing hotpants and white boots, setting off to marry someone forty years younger.

Every Memorial Day neighbors get together and put on a parade, a parade without a marching band or a fire truck. There are three horses, five old men dressed in uniforms as if they were all set to free the poor slaves, and a hay wagon with the Kraut Queen, if we're lucky. Last year the queen had ringworm on her face and didn't show. Since there isn't an audience to speak of, because everyone in town is in the parade, it snakes back along the same road after a while so the front can view the rear marching by. One year I wanted to be a nurse with a real Red Cross outfit to wear in the parade, but May said stop wishing for the impossible. She cut a paper plate in half and pinned it in my hair, drew a cross on her white apron, and set me walking.

You're supposed to slow down to 35 when you're going through Honey Creek, but most people speed by. There simply are no outskirts to prepare the driver. At the intersection — that's County Road J — you'll see the post office and the grocery store, which doesn't have anything useful except beer and milk, toothpaste and potato chips. Across the road from the Mart is our church, our white church. One of the church committees put up a steeple a few years ago to accommodate the new bell, which plays songs three times a day. It cracks me up going by there when it chimes "Rock of Ages," as if the church has a big old mouth and it's singing to itself. No one ever stops to listen except the Labrador retriever. He's tied up outside of the post office because he belongs to the postmistress, Laverna. He howls to all the songs like he's overflowing with devotion. He sits on his haunches and lets out a long sad moan.

In the block beyond the church there are four more white

houses. All of them have heavy plastic over the windows, meant for winter, which blow and rattle in the summer storms. The pickup trucks, parked outside in every yard, come in handy for deer hunting and cutting wood, plus driving places. If you look in the garages you'll see that they're filled with rusty farm machines, milk cans, large rusted wagon wheels with broken spokes, from the ancestors. People in Honey Creek like to keep junk in the family. You never know if a huge chest of bent nails might not come in handy some time; you can't be too careful. I think folks hold on to metal scraps and furniture because the world is an enormous place, far and wide, but they have never experienced much of it, and they're afraid. They want an anchor so there's no danger of drifting away into outer space, or down under the ground, strange places they aren't too familiar with.

The river comes next. Our town is named after it. It isn't deep or long, but it has water and bloodsuckers and fish. If you cross over the bridge you come to the edge of Honey Creek proper. You see the factory. Everyone in town is proud to have Industry, that's what they call it. It's a cinder block building and it doesn't have windows. Most of the letters fell off the sign that says what it is.

Even with Industry half the town doesn't work in Honey Creek. The other half is practically dead. People go to Stillwater to teach school, sell clothes, work in the factory that makes paper napkins. Honey Creek used to have a mill by the river, but it doesn't function at the present time. It used to grind victuals for humans to eat. I wonder if I'd been born just five miles the other side of town, would I have met Daisy? Would I have known Ruby? Would my story have happened to me or a complete stranger? I'd like to know exactly how much I'm to blame. Was it my character that triggered the events, or chance, that I woke up and found myself in Honey Creek with a big old dog howling to "Rock of Ages"? The ancient saying goes, "None are so blind as they who won't see," and I'm banking on there being truth in it.

Otis Buddle's fields come right up to the parking lot of the factory. There isn't a space between; there isn't a minute to switch gears, get used to the idea. After the factory it's all farms: muddy fields and the smell of someone hauling manure, and the sight of a rusted-out combine sitting in the lane, as dumb and still as a cow. Of course the cemetery is along the highway too. I love walking there in October because the maple trees line the road and they turn crimson and orange and gold, a paper-thin gold. My Aunt Sid says that the trees must be doing a dress rehearsal for their own death, a phrase that has always made me wonder if we rehearse our death, and if we know when we're rehearsing it. There are a lot of dead people in the cemetery, but what you see are the same ten last names, over and over, on the gravestones. I used to be certain that everyone in the whole world was related.

About a half mile out of town is where we live, on a farm. We live in a wooden house, but I wouldn't exactly call it white. It hasn't been painted since May got married the second time, which would take me a long time to calculate, because I'm not, as anyone within twenty miles could tell you, a wizard in math. There are pink granite stone steps up to the porch, similar to palace steps. We go around back to the kitchen door, where the trash and tin cans could trip and kill you if you weren't paying strict attention. May plants purple and red petunias in the planters each year. That's when the washed-out gray house looks drab, compared to the flowers.

When I was small my favorite time of day came at the sight of Wendell Kate driving the cows past our farm into Honey Creek to his barn. It's a gift he gave me. I have the memory of twenty cows stumbling down the road so not one car can get by, and there's Wendell on his big old blue bicycle with the high handlebars. He's a redheaded bachelor. His pants always look like they might slip down from his waist since he doesn't have a rear end to speak of. His crotch is about at his knees. He spent his time in church glancing down the pew and winking at the ladies.

I loved the sight of Wendell on his bike, his red hair so flaming his head looked like a great torch, and the twenty cows, not wanting to walk. You'd hear the squeeze horn he had on his handlebars all the way into Honey Creek. He got killed by a bull a few years ago. He didn't like to use that artificial stuff for breeding. He bled to death.

Sometimes I feel like I'm a hundred years old and I can see clear around the world, and then other times I think how I'm nothing; I don't have one thing on my mind except pictures of bachelors riding their bicycles. I haven't even been out of Illinois. I only spit into Wisconsin. In high school, when I was in all the dumb classes, we learned about the evil man, Hitler, over in Germany, and even though Hitler seems as distant to me as the Romans and their crumbling walls, I feel like I know him, just a little. I have to feel kind of sorry for him, for what he had to do. There was something in him that he couldn't help, that made him more terrible than anyone before or after him. I said those words out loud in my class, to Miss Daken, my teacher. She had a nose like a pelican's mouth, this big old hooked nose that looked like it could catch fish. I said that maybe history books didn't tell about Hitler's good points, and she stepped all over me with her steel-toed eyes. She was so tired of teaching dumb students. I wanted to say that it was the same with the Bible; that the serpent was doomed before he hatched, that something so low and sneaky and slippery wouldn't, by its very nature, be taken for good. It seems as if nobody could really be all bad, although everyone has the meanness in them. Sometimes people choose one person in a crowd to pick at. It makes them feel better to say how there's one entirely rotten person they can blame everything on.

When I grew up I heard about the wars we were having with other people, on television. We watched some of the battles. I knew we were safe from machine gun fire in Honey Creek, where there hadn't ever been wars, if you don't count the Indians. There was only the one Mexican family who lived in the trailer home, and even though they had ten children they were too disorganized to cause trouble outside of their own family. Without putting words to it I recognized the beauty of war; I realized that it was entirely in keeping with ordinary human nature.

It wasn't until I was ten that I realized our family must be the ones with the wrung-out hearts, and that other people's faces shone with a sadness for us. I was ten when my father climbed into the Ford one morning, in the dark. I heard his black boots crunch on the gravel. He was too scared to start the engine so he rolled down the driveway with his foot on the clutch. Goodbye to Illinois, he probably said to himself, because he had lived up here near Honey Creek all his life. I threw off my blankets and ran downstairs and down the road in my nightgown, shouting at him to come back. We learned later that he drove to Texas, to his brother's grapefruit ranch. He lived in a tin shed next to his brother's house and spent his days picking grapefruits the size of my own head. I thought about him at night, reading his paperback books by the light of a smoking kerosene lamp; I couldn't stand the thought of him being happier there, but I had enough sense to know it was true.

Soon after he left we sat in church on Sunday and I could see how sorry people felt for me. I could hear their whisperings about the latest tragedy. I could tell by their faces and their eyes that we were new and strange. They came past us in church, filing out, and I knew suddenly they were the kind of people who would pet me, like I was an animal that didn't have a single chance to survive. The young Mr. Snodgrass bent down to me while May was in the ladies' room and he told me that I was going to be a big strong pretty girl one of these days, and I appreciated his words. But I could tell from the scowl on his wife's face that he was lying. I had heard Aunt Sid telling May she looked pinched once, and I wanted to ask Mr. Snodgrass, right then and there, if I was pinched too. When I got home I took out the mirror to examine my new and strange looks. My eyes are squinched together; they're small and gray and they don't open all the way wide. My mouth isn't too much better off. It's tight like a closed drawstring laundry bag. There's nothing special about my nose: it's small and sits on my face like someone set it down and forgot to come back for it. My hair, my best feature, is nothing more than tight brown curls stuck to my head like I'd taken glue to them, but at least there's room for improvement. When Daisy does my hair over it looks shiny and fluffy, like a soufflé cooked up to perfection. May is very much the same, except she's older and uglier and heavier than I am, and she has a wart by her nose. She has wrinkles too, like she went and slept face down on an oven rack. Sometimes I see her standing by the door, in plain view. She's so clear and radiant she hurts my eyes.

After Elmer disappeared into the wild blue yonder—I always liked the sound of "wild blue yonder," it was somewhere I wanted to go—after he left, May reminded us that Daddy rolled away because we made him. When we asked her, "Is he coming back?" she said, "You made him go with all that fighting you do."

I used to listen to May like she was about one hundred miles away and the only thing I could hear was her thin voice trailing off on the other side of a mountain.

Sometimes, when I played, I pretended I was actually a regular person. I sat out in the yard with the hens, calling each one by their full first names. I gave them confirmation names like the Catholic girls had, such as Prudence Grace and Mary Ellen Maria. They loved me for bringing their mashed corn. I kept wondering why I wasn't a hen or a bug. Even back then I wondered how I got where I was: did I choose to be May's baby girl, or was I like pieces of dust floating around in the wind and then landing any which way? I said to May, "How come I'm your baby girl?" She cocked her head like she was asking herself if I was ready to hear the news. Then she sat me down on her bed and asked me if I recalled how the ram had to do his business in the fall.

I said, "Sure."

I had only seen it about a million times. The ram curls his upper lip and snorts around; he can't help it. I knew how it was with animals but I didn't think the process translated over to people.

She said it did, that we had pretty much the same equipment as animals.

I stared at the floor. I was trying to imagine. I had never seen men, say in the grocery store, simply walking up to ladies, with their lips quivering, and then climbing on top of them. I couldn't remember seeing that kind of behavior so I asked, "But how does it happen with people?"

"It'll happen when someone pushes you down on the bed and lifts up your skirt," May said, laughing. When she saw my scared eyes she said, "I'm teasing you, angel-face, I'm only teasing."

She said almost under her breath as she left the room that it was something crazy adults did for fun, and I'd understand years from now.

I couldn't believe what she was saying. I came after her into the hall. I said, "You mean people do it for entertainment?"

She snickered with her back to me. She tried to act serious as she turned around, but she said, Yeah, she guessed it was all just for fun. She didn't look happy at all, maybe because she didn't have one person who would let her get anywhere near them, or maybe because what she had told me was an enormous fabrication, meant to hide something sad. You can tell the ewes don't like it when the ram curls his lip and rides around with his hooves sunk into their wool. They tolerate it with the patience of saints, but it isn't the greatest experience for them. As soon as he's off they act like nothing happened and wander back to the feeder.

The idea slayed me: here I was on planet earth because May

had one minute of fun. I didn't mind so much the thought of my being a piece of dust. I liked the idea of floating around and then changing into a baby, in the dark, in secret, but I got gloomy when I thought maybe it was my choice that put me in May's belly. I knew she was hiding the truth and really I had a little something to do with the scheme. It meant I made a dumb mistake. I closed my eyes, wishing I had the memory of what all my parts were before they became me. If I hadn't been born I suspect nothing would have happened to us. If I was very smart I could have been Mrs. Crawford's girl, Diane, and lived in a blue house, the color of eyeshadow.

When I got gloomy, when I was ten years old, I sat on the ground with the hens pecking near my feet and I screwed up my face to try and remember the good occasions in my life. Just one thought in a day, to carry me beyond my dark feelings. My favorite memory — the one I went back to the most — happened the year July was so hot you sweated standing still. I was seven. Matt, my brother, and I, and May and Elmer were drinking black cows in the kitchen after supper. Elmer, scooping up refills, missed my glass, and this splat of ice cream landed on my head.

It is crystal clear. We are a family, laughing our heads off, and I'm laughing too, because the ice cream feels cold dripping down my hot skin, and I'm making faces, twisting up my tongue to get the drops. Everyone's howling at me and I'm cracking up because I know I'm funny. I have my eyes crossed. May doesn't try to wipe off my head. The flesh on her bare arms is shaking and she has tears coming down her face. She can't breathe. Elmer stands behind me with his hands on my shoulders, patting me. He has a deep laugh with spaces between, like he has to remind himself every few seconds what's so funny. And the best part is Matt. He reaches out to touch my arm. Suddenly I'm a celebrity.

I wished then, while it was happening, that we could have stayed there at the kitchen table for about five centuries. I could have stood it that long. I wanted to preserve the scene, just as fossils do, keeping rare animals so still in stone. It took me several years to figure out that on that July night we were actually experiencing the gladness some people feel every day, not just once in a summer. I saw how it was with other people, because I watched the children in church, running to their mothers after Sunday school. I saw it every Sunday, week after week, year after year. The mothers swept their children off their feet and kissed them on their cheeks, and both mother and child laughed. They didn't need to say words because they had this gladness inside, just the same as if for a few minutes they all had a splat of ice cream dripping down into their mouths, and it's the hottest day on earth.

Two

I ONLY had to annoy Matt because he was smart. "Delayed," is how May described me to myself. Matt's a year younger than I am, but he learn~d to talk first. He always told me what to do in whole sentences, pointing his finger at me. I couldn't seem to make the words to say "Jump in the lake." I couldn't say words but I noticed that they were all over the place, in your ears, in front of your eyes. I watched *Cheerios* march across the cereal box. I loved how *e*'s looked, so squat and happy. I couldn't say thoughts or insults but I wrote down letters on the walls. I saw the word *bear* and I wrote BEAR all over my room. I printed SILO in green crayon on my white dresser. Elmer practically made an exclamation when he came into my room one morning and there's SILO on my dresser. As far as he knew I didn't have the marbles to say *dog*. He laughed at me under his breath. I could see him knowing he should scold me, possibly with the shoehorn, but deciding against it. He went and got a wet washcloth to scrub the word off. He spoke one of his longer sentences. He said, "Don't tell anyone our secret." I nodded my head with all the sobriety I could muster, although I wanted to scream to the world, WE HAVE A SECRET!

Since Matt talked like an expert he told me what I had to be when we played house. I was always the man in a black top hat. We found the hat squashed flat on the bottom of the trunk in May's bedroom. I was the husband each time, and Matt got to be the bride. He wore a veil on his head, and May's old white high heels. He stumbled over them, fell and bruised his knees. I didn't offer him pity, although we were recently married. I could be the doctor making babies come, and the father, but Matt had to be the lady. When he served me tea in our plastic cups he bawled me out in a high voice. He told me I should hurry up and get back to my chores at the barn. He said there was mud, and other materials I won't mention, on my boots. He reminded me that I was tracking it all over the clean carpet and for punishment I would have to vacuum.

Matt had the words, but my gift was the strong muscles in my arms to put him flat on his face, and when I socked him I had joy in my heart, surging fresh into my vessels and knocking in the core, because I could see blood flowing out of his nose. There was a space where time stopped dead and I listened free to his terrible hurt sounds. It lasted until May made the room come alive with her body in it, yelling the pure strain of noise only she, and rabbits who are dying by the knife, are capable of. She was like sergeants on TV shows, frowning and whistling and pointing. She said she didn't think my brain functioned. She shook her head and wondered why I was retarded. I didn't pay attention to her when she discussed my intelligence. I was waiting to spring on Matt. I was watching for his weak points.

The meanness that some people have in great quantities came to me early, because Matt became a prodigy. The minister says all of us have proud hearts, which helped me understand why I had to clench my fist and hit Matt's knowing eyes. When he and I got into school, I couldn't clobber him quite as easily. He grew taller than me in the space of six months so I had to think of other ways to make his body sting. He understood all math; he was perfect at numerals and digits. He knew about numbers you can't even see on paper, and everyone at grade school said he was truly a phenomenon. I mentioned the circus or the zoo as an ideal spot for viewing him, but May suggested with her hand held high that I shut my flap. Every teacher discussed Matt's brain in the teachers' lounge. The smoke was always seeping up over the folded screen that obscured the doorway, and you could hear the murmur of the teachers' voices as they ripped the youngsters' personalities into twenty pieces. Arthur Crawford said you would die of emphysema instantly if you even set foot in the lounge.

I tripped Matt coming up the road from the school bus and he cried a piercing cry that was out of proportion to the injury. Every now and then it struck me that his tears were the same material as any old human being's, even people who didn't have parabola shapes whizzing through their heads, but I didn't stop capturing bees in paper cups and dumping them inside his sheets. He knew the bites he got were my fault.

He never mentioned the stings to me. He went straight to May to tell. Naturally she petted him — she always wanted to stroke his silky hair that covered up where his quick thoughts were made. Sometimes, when I had to be in my room for the salt I put in Matt's milk, the tacks in his brownie, I cried, because the real punishment was Matt never noticing I'm alive, like the numbers he's always looking at breathe the air and I don't.

When I think about little Matt I hardly see a person there. In my mind he's a rising river filled with leeches; I have one small dry square to stand on, and finally I can barely keep my nose above water. I have to work exceptionally hard to conjure up each one of the features on his face. He had fat cheeks and thin blond hair and brown eyes the shape of pennies. His perfect teeth grew in like they were choir members filing sternly into their pews. He had stomachaches and head colds half the time. May loved nursing him. She'd come out of his room, softly closing the door behind her.

▼

Elmer read stacks of books about the Civil War, the Second World War, and the wars of ancient times. In rare moments, if he didn't know you were crouching in bales of hay watching him do the chores, he mumbled poetry he had learned in high school, ennobling words about cohorts gleaming in purple and gold, and steeds with flaring nostrils, and the Angel of Death — not the stuff of his average argument with May.

He loved historical novels about lands so far away they didn't seem like they belonged in the world. After supper he came to his chair in the living room with his round shiny bald head sticking up, and he sat breathing loudly while he read, until the snoring started. Sometimes he stayed there all night or until May shook him back into this time zone. She yelled at him for falling asleep before he built her a pie safe or mowed the lawn. She probably wasn't crazy about sharing the cornhusk mattress with him, but she got hurt feelings when she realized he'd rather spend the night in an armchair than brush his back against the bristly curlers she put in her hair, to make her curls even tighter and stiffer.

I don't have too many clear memories of Elmer. He stayed out of the way. He didn't come into the house except for supper, to get yelled at, to read his books, and sleep. I could tell he wished he was something desirable, like a cow. When I picture him I see a looming shadow and then a bald shining head. After he left us, when I sat in my room missing his shape and the gleam of his head, and while I felt particularly angry at him, it occurred to me that if they were going to name a song after him it would be called "Silent Night." That's a perfect title for him.

There are just a few memories that come through in one entire piece, events with Elmer and me, together: the one day in March, when the lamb was born the year I turned eight. I used to lie on the floor out in the barn in a heap of straw, to see if the lambs liked me. I told them stories about my life. They climbed on top of me and poked around to see if they could find my milk supply.

I let them paw me and gnaw on my fingers. There was a ewe rolling her eyes around one day and curling up her lips, looking back to her rear end with great agitation, as if she wanted an explanation from her hindquarters. I had seen a lamb born twice before, once when Elmer had to help it come. I understood the mystery taking place under my nose. I sat waiting and pretty soon, with a grunt from the mother, a little white head poked out of her. I loved seeing the quiet face — that lamb didn't even know it was being born.

I waited for an hour. All I could see was the head, stuck, and its pink tongue hanging out of the side of its mouth. Something wasn't right because the mother pawed at the ground and then lay down, dragging her rump right through the dirt. The infant head was getting all muddy. The tiny pink nostrils were going to get clogged with dirt, so I went over finally and said, "Easy, easy," like Elmer did, tenderly, and I wiped off the nose. It was similar to the experience that Alice had in Wonderland: the lamb's front hooves were sticking straight out under the head, and I could hear a small voice whispering, "Pull me." I swear I heard the voice three times. I knew that lamb was having problems getting born. I knew I didn't have a decade to decide whether to dance or to hobble. So I pulled the legs as hard as I could, with both my hands, and the mother gave a terrible groan and then splat, out came the whole wet lamb body, yellow like an egg yolk. It was all slimy, and sneezing. It shook its head as if it had a bug in its long wet ear. The mother naturally began to lick it and grunt, and snack on the afterbirth. She was glad to have the whole works out. I couldn't believe the strength in my hands, what they did. I smelled the yellow color on my fingers. It smelled so raw and new I had to quick close my eyes and wonder.

I kept thinking how the mother didn't put up a fight; she let the pain consume her, without the faintest understanding. She didn't have any idea about her life, from one minute to the next. You could see how much having the baby killed her, the way her eyeballs rolled back into her head. Maybe she was watching the inside of her brain and seeing miles of green alfalfa and acres of trough filled with golden corn. She was awfully brave to merely scream and then lie still while a puny girl yanked at her lamb. I had to spit, to admire all that courage in the mother.

When Elmer appeared I whispered, "I helped it come."

He said, "Well!" He grinned at me for lack of words and then bent down to examine the newborn. When he stood up he said, "Aren't you a good little farmer?" I hugged my own ribs all the way to the house, while Elmer rested his hand on top of my head.

In the spring, when I heard all the frogs down in the marsh singing as if they had urgent thoughts they wanted to speak of, I sat at the table eating, and I had to blurt out how I wanted to know a frog, and know what they talked about down there in the murky water. They made such a racket and they were invisible. I said, "All those frogs singing night and day without stopping. What are they saying?"

May snapped at me. "You just eat, young lady. You get frogs out of your head."

I learned to stay quiet at meals because I usually said sentences of astounding dumbness. May looked at me like I was a stranger, Elmer didn't say anything, perhaps to avoid getting the cold stare that suggests you're a lunatic, and Matt ate delicately and then went straight to his room, leaving piles of food on his plate. May would have loved to feed him with tweezers. She made a sport of seeing he got enough nourishment; she stood over him watching him put the smallest bit of tuna casserole into his mouth and she waited until he screwed up his face. She scrutinized his plate afterwards, to see if she could figure out exactly how many peas he had eaten. If I couldn't help mentioning that it made me sad to see the geese flying south in the fall, how there was something inside of me that felt like cracking, May said, "God for Daniel, ain't you gloomy! You make me want to dig a hole and stick my nose right down in it."

I kept my observations swirling around in my head. Occasionally I spoke with the chickens, and in the spring and summer I planted and tended and talked with carrots and lettuce. They were my special vegetables. I was in charge of them. I spent whole afternoons in the dirt, making my patch of ground flawless. I even cleared the worms away, before I found out that all the tunnels they make give air, and probably other molecules I don't know about yet, to the plants.

I started out in the hole, in school, because of my impression that I was a miracle of stupidity, and because I was afraid of my teacher. Her name was Mrs. Ida Homer and she wore cushiony shoes like nurses', only hers were red, and you could smell stale cigarettes and coffee on her breath. She had thick flabby ears that looked like nice soft pillows decorated with little tiny white hairs. I longed to rest my head on them. Her eyes were gold and I was sure from the first moment I saw her that they were hollow inside. I tried to hold her hand once when we were filing down the hall but she shook me off. I never tried again. I knew even then that she wasn't very fond of children. Her ears were her best feature. Plus her husband's name was Beau. I never saw him but I couldn't help picturing him as an oversized red frilly ribbon you could tack on a birthday present.

Mrs. Ida Homer made me stand in the wastebasket because I wrote on my desk and poked my neighbor, and because I did not follow directions. Instead of drawing pictures, I put words all over the sheets of paper. I loved the shape of letters in a word like *shampoo*. I got into trouble for coloring outside of the lines when we were drawing turkeys for Thanksgiving, and I forgot to put hands on May the time we drew our families. Her hands were just the things I didn't want to think about. Mrs. Ida Homer said I didn't do my coloring right. She said I had to stay in for recess to get the colors inside the lines of the turkey.

I waited for the words she was going to say when I did something wrong; one of these days she was going to tell me that I had to stand in the wastebasket for the next eight grades. I suspected that all the teachers in the whole school were exactly like Mrs. Ida Homer, and I tried to imagine seven more years and then high school with ladies who would watch Arthur Crawford stick a clothespin on the back of my arm so it pinched, and then give me the punishment.

Matt caught up with me in school by the time I was in third grade. He skipped second. He had absolutely no use for that grade. May wanted him to go directly to college, but the counselors said then he wouldn't fit into society. Matt and I weren't in the same class ever; he didn't have to have Mrs. Ida Homer back in first grade. She might have been able to make him feel slightly lacking for a minute or two. He had a math book he did on his own since his brain was at least in junior high. He was leaving his body behind; his head was going to get larger and larger and his arms would shrink to the size and weight of long deflated party balloons, the black ones. His feet would become webbed to support the weight of his calculations. I imagined the president of the U.S. asking Matt for advice. My brother wouldn't be able to see over the desk in that oval office they always speak of, and he'd have to pluck out bee stingers from his hands, which I was responsible for, while he recited figures.

Matt was destined to come home with gold stars pasted on his papers. I didn't have anything to show because I dropped my work in the trash before I got on the bus. I couldn't concentrate on one thing except how everyone said I was ugliest in the class. If boys and girls touched me they thought they were poisoned. Diane Crawford had a special potion in her desk; she said it could cure people if they by accident got too close to me.

In second grade I had a dress with blue and yellow violets covering the fabric. I liked it very much at first, especially because it featured a braided yellow straw belt with a blue leather buckle. The instant Missy Baker saw it she said that the dress used to be her sister's and that it got in the Goodwill box by mistake. Then she changed her story and told everyone that I stole the dress from her house. She said she knew she had heard someone in the laundry room the week before. Therefore I told May I despised the dress. I rolled on the floor kicking, trying to rip it with my bare hands. I sobbed that I wasn't going to wear the dress one more time, even if she smacked me all over my body. May is a saver, like everyone else I know. She fished the dress out of the garbage. She calmly stated that it was in excellent condition, and she laid it out for me to wear again the next day. Every time I wore it Missy Baker said her sister wanted it back, and she was going to personally come to rip it off of me. I'd have to be in school sitting at my desk bare naked.

On the playground a few girls along with Diane Crawford and Missy Baker told me they'd be my best friend if I obeyed them. They took me out behind the hedges and said I had to close my eyes and stand still. I could feel hands lifting up my dress and pulling my underpants down. I could feel people squatting on the ground, staring up at the way I was made. They looked while I shut my eyes tight. I was going to have so many best friends.

When the bell rang to come in there wasn't anyone around me. My underpants sat at my ankles. I knew all the girls were swarming around Diane's desk, getting the potion to purify themselves. After third grade my fame ceased and no one paid any attention to me because Elizabeth Remenchik moved in. She not only came from somewhere near Poland, and had a club foot, but she was also cross-eyed and had to wear thick glasses. When you looked at her eyes you felt as if you were looking way down through the ice on a lake and watching two slow fish trying to keep alive through the winter.

What I waited for were the letters from May's sister, my Aunt Sid. Sid and May weren't the best of friends because they had always squabbled, and because May never forgot past injuries.

There were all sorts of occasions for mistrust, one of the latest being the time the family divided up the spoils from the home farm. May thought Sidney was extra-greedy and grabbing more than her share, taking antiques that were valuable and leaving behind the riffraff for May. Never mind that Sid was responsible for shipping Aunt Marion's portion down to North Carolina. Aunt Sid had learned over the years to ignore May even when May came behind her nipping at her heels like a yapping dog the size of a peanut. Finally, as the last dresser was loaded into the truck, Sid turned on May, told her in a normal speaking voice that she was a sorry excuse for a sister, and that she had never been reasonable. Sid quickly got in the car before May could scratch her eyes out.

Soon after the grab Sid came over to make amends. May didn't serve cookies like you're supposed to for guests, even though it was clear Sidney came with her arms loaded down with olive branches, not to mention proof: she had photos of Aunt Marion's living room that showed where the valuable antiques were located. May said nothing. She averted her eyes from the salt water taffy box, and the basket full of extra-fancy red delicious apples. She mumbled something about requiring charity from no one, and left the room.

I was alone with Aunt Sid. She took a present from her bag and handed it to me. I didn't care about the gift. I wanted nothing but blond hair exactly like hers, sweeping back over her head into a long bun held together with tortoise-shell hairpins. She had brown eyes and lips that were a color I never saw on anyone but Aunt Sid. I had to stare at her mouth, at her moist lips, continuously. Finally she showed me the tube of lipstick in her purse; it said "Coral" on it. She stretched out her hand for me to come closer. I never forgot how her lips parted and she cocked her head and smiled without fear. Although I looked like May, Sid seemed sure I wouldn't tear her nylons with my fingernails or sink my teeth into her thigh. I took her hand and went to her side, without one thought in my head. I couldn't hear what she was saying into my ear because my heart was singing like a frog—a frog calling to her partner down in the marsh, singing through layers of mud. I hung on to her skirt until she left. I watched her drive away. I watched her even after her car disappeared into a cloud of dust and exhaust.

The present was a music box that was intended for jewels. It played "Oh, How Lovely Is the Evening." After Sid was gone May came back into the living room. Her face was puffy. I knew she never cried so I figured she must have gotten stung by several hornets.

"What's that box?" she asked.

"Nothin'," I said, trying to hide it under my dress.

"Give it here," she said, grabbing it from my arms.

She turned it over in her hands, lifted the lid, and heard the song. She bent down and stared at the metal pegs striking the keys for several minutes, completely absorbed by the machinery.

"It's mine," I said in a voice hoarse from the frogs chanting in my chest cavity.

She laid it on the table without saying a word and went to stare out the window. It seems to me that later in the day she smacked me out of the blue. She must have felt that she bungled her chance to make peace with her sister and she was so mad at herself she came at me with her zinging hand. I learned the lesson about justice fairly early on: if the rulers of the kingdom aren't fairminded, then there simply isn't any such thing as fairness or just deserts. I'm not going to tell you how many times in the following weeks I set out for De Kalb, where Aunt Sid lived, before my stomach led me back to the hearth fires. I won't tell you about my dreams starring Aunt Sid, who adopts me, and I happen to look exactly like Shirley Temple.

In the third grade I actually started to know Aunt Sid. We were supposed to write to a pen pal. All the girls in my class picked their best friend, who sat across the aisle from them. I didn't understand the logic of writing someone within reach, so I chose Aunt Sid, who lived forty miles away. We were to write one letter a week to practice our penmanship. We were to ask our parents for stamps, if we wanted to write someone beyond the classroom. I took stamps from Elmer's table, where he paid the bills. I could not believe the miracle of the U.S. postal system: Aunt Sid wrote me back each time, and since it was my task to bring the mail up from the box at the road after school, May never knew of our regular communications.

At first Aunt Sid told me about her childhood, and she wondered if it was still the same there in Honey Creek. She guessed it probably was. She said if she remembered hard enough she would know how it was to be me. She hadn't lived in Honey Creek since she was eighteen, at which time she figured out what was good for her and made a beeline to the teacher's college in Evanston. If you have talents you can get away from Honey Creek fairly easily, but if you don't have anything exceptional to show for yourself you might as well forget it, no questions asked. Once, she told me that I shouldn't use "gonna" in my letters, that the words were actually "going to." I instantly wanted to shape up. My teachers had spent plenty of red ink and cross words correcting me, but I didn't see any use trying to please people such as Mrs. Ida Homer. Aunt Sid was different. I longed to understand what was correct, for her eyes alone; I wanted to write everything as precisely as the Queen might, transcribing from her gold-bound grammar rule book.

It didn't take a high-voltage brain to figure out the best uses for May's harsh talk, that her tools were particularly well suited to describing the varieties of barnyard manure. I didn't want to talk the way May talked but it was everywhere around me. With my hands clamped over my ears I still kept hearing the F-word.

Even after third grade Aunt Sid wrote me once a week. I couldn't understand why she wanted to, but I always wrote her back before the smell of her wore off her heavy beige stationery. I made up stories about how May went to the Sears store in Stillwater and bought me one hundred dresses all in different colors, and girls at school wanted to have clothes just like mine but their parents couldn't pay for so many dresses. I wrote her about how I wished I could be a bloodroot flower — the jewels that come in the spring at the edge of the woods. They are white and clean and in the evening they close up tight as if they're a hand holding something secret in their fist. If you wait too long to find them, all their petals are on the ground and there's nothing but a naked stem. I told Sid she should call me names such as Diane or Missy. They were such beautiful names. To my surprise, Aunt Sid wrote saying that it was nice to own lots of dresses, but she'd rather have a letter from me than have a new outfit, or the sight of a bloodroot. She said things I knew couldn't possibly be true.

What I knew for fact, even then, was that Matt would steal away. I could think only of Matt when I saw a shooting star out of the corner of my eye; always, when I turned to look, it was gone, and I had to imagine a trail left behind the blaze. Teachers had the habit of calling up to take Matt to special classes, show him off. They took him to Chicago, to a museum where he saw a gray submarine. He told me it shot torpedoes through the water. I was afraid, for as far back as I can think, that Matt, with his smartness, would order the sub to come wipe us off the earth, and what's left would be a pile of chicken feathers on the ground.

Three

I'D LIKE to tell you that May told her story to me, but I can't. Everything I know about her I learned from firsthand experience and from Aunt Sid. When I picture May I first have to wonder about the very day she was born. It was the early morning of a dark rainy March day, according to the legend my Aunt Sid grew up with. There was a flood and handfuls of dead worms floated around the yard. Perhaps May got the idea that that's what it all was going to be like, so she never noticed the sun shining, unless it was beating down on her and making her unbearably hot. I love when I'm outside, feeling the sun on my skin. The grass, and the cats on the porch, and myself, all thirsting after the warmth, and finding it, make me know that there's something mighty about our planet and the whole works out there in the universe. May doesn't have curiosity about sunshine, or the very first crocus flowers that come in the spring. Sometimes when there's still snow on the ground, we see purple petals bursting through the white flakes. They have the urge and the will to see the light. But neither heaven nor earth moves May to thought; she says nature is around just because.

Maybe there was a bad omen on her birthday somewhere, and

no one paid attention, like on the worst day of my life I saw a whole slew of birds on a telephone wire, hanging upside down by their feet. They were murdered by the current. They were still and so black, hanging and hanging. It spooked me, but I didn't think it was a warning. I'm not exactly superstitious, but if there's a lurking power I'd like it to know that my eyes are now open and watching.

May was the first baby, out of eight. The second child, Richard, was born deaf. My guess is after all the others starting coming, one after the next, including the boy who couldn't hear and who sat and smiled while everyone pitied him, she turned a little sour on the entire race of man. She fell to the floor, actually hurting herself, and no one ran right to her side to pick her up, or if she banged her head against the wall the hired girls said, "Knock it off," even if they noticed the blood. People were too busy to soothe her scraped knees and her sore head.

When the third child, Marion, came, May was sent away for two months to the great-aunts' house in Stillwater. My grandmother, with the deaf boy and a newborn, couldn't handle little May. The two aunts were proper ladies with dusty velvet couches in rooms with warped floors, and shelves full of china dogs children weren't supposed to touch. May couldn't examine a thing in the house for two months because the aunts were forever screeching "STOP!" They expected her to sit still and never get dirty, and to like to eat stale bread softened by milk, and overcooked peas.

I can imagine wrinkled old Aunt Margaret hovering over May, explaining where she got the china Afghans, the three of them, with rabbit fur coats, all strung together with a golden chain. Her breath was probably like the smell of goats when they are panting and giving birth. She stood close, smacking her thick lips, exhaling into the air that was meant for May to breathe in. And she laughed at everything May said or did in her nervous high-pitched laugh. She laughed before May had finished the sentence. Sid says Aunt Margaret had a flat face, like a pug dog, flat and smashed, and eyes that were too small for her drooping sockets. I can picture May three years old, living away from her parents, waiting, night after night, on her cot in Florence's and Margaret's parlor. After they kissed her with their oily lips and turned out the light, May would have stared at the china mother collie on the top shelf, who she was sure some night was going to come to life, take her neck in its strong white teeth, and bring her home.

When May did come home to the farm, she walked through each room and nothing looked as she had remembered it. The furniture was in different places, without a doubt, and she hadn't recalled the constant sharp ache in her stomach. She wanted to squeeze the baby's hands while it sucked at her mother. It rolled its eyes around and stuck out its tongue every which way. Everyone said it was beautiful, which made May suspect she didn't know the correct definition of the word. She couldn't stand to watch it feed. She looked at it in a basket with a pink satin ribbon strung through the wicker and she poked its cheeks as hard as she could. Her mother slapped her face, back and forth — May couldn't believe how things had changed. She knew she was better than the puking baby and her brother with broken ears, but no one saw her worth. She knew she could get them to see, even though as the months went by her mother was forever saying, "Why can't you be nice like Marion?" I know from experience that that comparison doesn't engender love and kindness. It makes you want to go up to your closet and practice biting people's heads off.

When Richard was six they took him to the deaf school in Humphrey. He had no way of understanding why they were leaving him, or if they were ever coming back. May knew that her parents might leave her next, on the stone doorstep of a yellow brick building, with a leather valise. And when they turned to get in the car she planned to sink her teeth into their ankles and stay there fastened, for the rest of their lives.

Two of May's brothers are already dead, and the rest of the

siblings are spread out over the country. I've never met any of them, except Aunt Sid, since they don't go out of their way to visit Honey Creek. May used to tell her sisters she was going to kill herself. She'd show them the noose, or the knife; she called it a dagger. She terrified the little sisters. They didn't know what to do, or who to tell. She'd get a rock and start tying it to her ankle, saying she was going to walk into Honey Creek and drown, and they'd beg her not to. She'd say, slowly, "Well, maybe I won't *today*; maybe I won't if you treat me good." She made them fetch things for her, and she got their best toys. She was rough and careless and the toys were usually wrecked when she returned the pieces. She was the sort who saved all her Christmas candy until April and then took it out and ate it in front of everyone. She sat at the center of a circle of candy, noisily sucking her peppermint stick.

We go by the farmhouse there on Orchard Road sometimes, where May grew up. It's falling apart, sinking into the ground. The shutters dangle by threads like loose teeth. When May's parents got too old to keep the farm up they sold it. None of the boy children were interested in carrying it on. Will moved to California for his asthma, worked in a factory that made ceramic hands which served as soap dishes, and drank himself to death. Thomas went over to France in World War II and he never came back. He married somebody French and bought a hardware store. I remember when Aunt Sid told me about the hardware store and how it cracked me up, thinking of French people needing wrenches and nails. Then there was Samuel, who passed away of meningitis when he was fifteen. May didn't ever mention him. She probably couldn't stand him until the minute he died. That's when he became the brother who loved her the best and never did one thing to aggravate her. Richard, the deaf brother, works for a newspaper solely for deaf people.

When we drive past the old farmhouse it gives me the chills, seeing it die inch by inch. No one loves it, and I can't help thinking about all the lint floating aimlessly, from clothes washed years before, and the ghosts sitting in wing chairs telling the family secrets. I don't believe in ghosts on most days, but sometimes it seems like there has to be something left over. We can't just die, bam the lights are out, can we? It's strange to think of a house filled up with a whole cast of characters, with all their shoes and hairbrushes and plates of food, and then there it is empty and quiet, insects chewing away at the wood, as if none of the past mattered.

In the old days laundry was May's job. She got all the clothes together on Sunday night and soaked them in the copper tubs, and then on Monday she boiled water on the wood stove in the basement. First she scrubbed linens and the delicate white items and all the underclothes, and then she worked at the rougher things, ending up with the men's coveralls. I'm sure that's how her huge hands got wrinkled and red, going in and out of the tubs with the water so hot. She wrung everything through the wringer; she stood there grinding the crank, watching the shirt buttons pop off as they went through. She went back and forth to the clothesline where the sheets flapped in the wind at her, almost as if they were saying "Nyah, nyah" behind her back. They were trying to tell her that if they got loose they'd flap away and never come back. I imagine May stood at the line holding one end of a sheet that couldn't keep still, and I bet she wished she could be free and high spirited. I wonder if she took whiffs of the clothes, if she noticed that they smelled like they were dancing partners with grass and dew and sunshine.

When they were dry May brought the loads in. She starched and ironed everything: the underwear, the trousers, the sheets, the shirts, the bedspreads. She wasn't done until past supper because she had to clean out the washing pots, fold up the clothes, sew on the buttons. She had to scrub the laundry room floor. She didn't need to be nagged or chided, because it's her nature to be tidy. I've seen pictures of the poor primitive jungle people cleaning their clothes in a river and it seems to me that May wasn't too much better off with the washboard, the wringer, and the clothesline. May must have been glad that someone dreamed up washers and driers. She stepped on Elmer's neck until he bought her one of each. Actually, that's not quite a true story. She did put the pressure on though, and wouldn't you know it, he came through right before Mother's Day, when I was eight years old.

May only went to high school part time because she had to stay home and help with all the babies and the farm work. There wasn't rest; there wasn't one person who could sit around and be lazy. One of May's jobs was to draw the cows in the herd. She drew the way the black and white went on the cows so they'd know who was who by looking at the pictures. I can hardly believe that she drew, pencil in hand, but Sid says it's so. Perhaps she loved the job, sitting on the barn gate, trying to make a likeness. She was probably so tired of her parents having babies that she herself could have invented the operation they have now where they tie up ladies' tubes. There's a photo with May and her littlest sister, that's Aunt Sid. May has Sid on her lap, and how Aunt Sid tells it is May pinched her when they were supposed to be smiling for the picture.

The best thing May could do when she was a youngster, besides laundry and drawing cows, was dance. She went to several dances a year at the church. She could waltz and polka like an expert, and learn new dances just by watching for a few minutes. She was tall and thin and she had hands the size of lobsters, but she knew how to move her bulk. The men couldn't toss her up in the air without straining themselves, but she was light in their arms and led them without their knowing it.

Maybe she was pretty. In the pictures I've seen of her she squints at me through the faded paper with eyes that make me nervous. She's fourteen and she glares out to the world as if she can already tell what's going to happen to her. Her eyes are narrow and dark. Maybe in the moment of the picture she can see me all grown up, and Ruby, and the scenes in our kitchen. She can see baby Justy asking for the pecan balls.

In the old days she had a thin curving mouth that stretched a long way across her face. She had a whole slew of little white teeth inside. I imagine her walking out into the night with her red pruny laundry hands all the while wondering when her real life was going to start. She prayed that someday she wouldn't have to lift one single pail, or stand in a muddy cow yard with cows staring out as if their eyes weren't connected to a brain. She said to herself, standing in the mud with a bucket of feed, "Someday I'm going to find a man who doesn't know one thing about seed corn, and I'll follow him away and never come back to Honey Creek."

Maybe she was exactly like me when she was young. I have to stop and stare, thinking about it: how strange if we really once had the same thoughts. Could May have gone out into the night to watch stars, wondering about the cold and hot planets in the universe, and about God and angels? It doesn't seem possible, but then the idea isn't exactly real to me that May was ever a young girl. I have to get my mind working pretty hard to conjure her up young. Maybe she looked at the glittering points of light shining down on her from out of the darkness and there was a sensation she had never felt before in her heart; it was getting larger and heavier by the minute, and she thought perhaps she was going to burst open. At sixteen she wanted something desperately, only she couldn't figure out exactly what it was. She knew there were so many enormous things yet to come in her life, and she cried for she hardly knew what: boys marching to war, and the hired man across town who got his arm cut off by a threshing machine. She sat on a stump in the sheep yard, and moaned, rocking back and forth, and finally she put her head into her lap. I like to believe May felt how utterly sad and small we are, and that some of the friendly sheep came and put their noses in her ear, as if it's ear wax they love to smell more than anything. They probably stood there sniffing her, and she cried, sticking her hands into their wool, down into their pink skin. She smelled her hands when she got into the house and discovered that the sheep had a good odor, that the lanolin from the wool made her hands feel greasy and nice. I like to think that she sat at the kitchen table drinking cocoa, reviewing the night in her mind, and thinking that it perhaps wasn't all so awful, now that she had the warmth in her stomach and the smell on her hands.

But for the most part, May had the unhappiness to begin with. She was always a long-sufferer — and to top it off the worst happened. She found someone she had been waiting for, all her miserable twenty-one years. Suddenly there was a man bringing her clumps of violets in his dirty hands. He had acres of black hair that grew like grass on top of his head, like it's the Great Plains up there, and eyes the color of forget-me-nots. Aunt Sid said the general opinion of the church ladies was that his piercing blue eyes could get the man a job in the ministry. He came across town through the fields and asked so cordially if he could see May. Then he went down to the basement and sat on the edge of a rickety white chair while she plunged material into the copper tubs. He sat and talked to May, looking right at her. He told her about things and places she had never heard of before, or thought she didn't care to know. He had been away at college for a few years; he had even seen New York City. The whole place is sidewalks, he told her. "There ain't nothin' but cement for a hundred miles."

She didn't want to see cities any more: one hundred miles of cement didn't sound so glamorous. As far as she was concerned he was the world itself. It had come to her doorstep.

May bent down to sort a clump of laundry, old black rags, and when she stood up he was looking at her. She found herself staring into those sensational blue eyes and when she looked down she didn't have more breath left inside of her. There was an absence of something there in her stomach, as if all her organs had turned to fish and swum away. Aunt Sid knows about May's romancing because she was little at the time. She used to hide in closets and spy on everyone. She told me about how Willard Jenson used to get up from the white chair and take May's waist and waltz with her all through the piles of laundry, scattering them over the floor, and how May laughed with her head on his shoulder. She laughed until there were tears trickling into her mouth.

Willard Jenson was a Honey Creek man who knew May from church, knew her to nod and say hello. He had probably seen her at the dances they had. He knew she could create the illusion of lightness. He probably liked the way she did laundry too; he admired her neat and tidy methods. I bet he could smell all the clean clothes even in his sleep. I bet he dreamed of May folding diapers and sheets and denim men's clothes, just his size.

May, with that hard place she has in her which says absolutely no one is going to tell her one thing, ran off into the night with Willard Jenson, on more than one occasion. Aunt Sid didn't speak about how they must have stood against the barn, with May's blouse unbuttoned, her breasts rising and falling, so white in the moonlight, against Willard's dirty hands. May could see the color of his eyes, even in the dark of the haymow.

Just before the whole town exploded with how sinful the two young people were, they saved themselves by getting married. "It's a miracle," the church ladies said under their breath, "that her belly is as flat as an iron." They wondered if there was a baby hid somewhere in a dresser drawer or stashed amongst the bulrushes. I have my theory: I don't think they went all the way. May doesn't seem the type, somehow. Aunt Sid described May's lacy wedding dress, and I didn't interrupt her even though I knew the dress from memory. It's the same one I wore at my wedding, shortened and tucked up. May had a garland of white roses in her curly hair, and bright red lipstick on her mouth. Her eyes were huge, because she didn't have an ounce of fat on her face, due to the way true love affected her appetite. She gazed at Willard Jenson with his patch of hair on his head, fertilized by the good Lord to make it grow double time, and she knew that this day was one of rescue and mercy. She had the feeling that all her years and years of doubting love were over.

They moved into Willard's house, on the other side of town, by Abendroth's farm, the one with the fake deer nuzzling the flamingos, and the Blessed Virgin Mary birdbath. Willard had some of Honey Creek running through his land. Sometimes it comes to me, the name Honey Creek, and I think about what the two words mean. A creek filled with honey, all gold, not even one bee remaining. Thick honey oozing on through the fields. Honey Creek doesn't resemble anything of the sort. It isn't gold. Indians probably named it. It's black in the springtime, from the mud and the farmers' chemicals rushing along the bottom, until it broadens up where the mill used to be. There's an antique store in the building now; it's off the main road so it doesn't do a bit of business. Right down under the store the creek settles into a deep blue pond. All the dogs in town pack and sometimes they end up swimming there in the summer, except the Labrador retriever at the post office, tied up on a two-foot string.

May and Willard Jenson had Brown Swiss milk cows and several thousand barn cats, and Willard did threshing in the fall for neighbors. They weren't going to get rich but they had enough; they didn't have to eat dandelion greens and shoot woodchucks for dinner. Aunt Sid tells the story of May's birthday, the time Willard bought her a radio. May shook her head and said, "I don't believe it," about ten times. After Sidney left they probably went upstairs to bed. May folded her legs around Willard's scrawny hips, the famous bones that stuck up sharp enough to cleave watermelons. May didn't care about getting cut in half. She screamed joyfully, hoping her whole family on the other side of town could hear.

Being married made her fairly kind and charitable toward animals and other people. She stroked the cats and kissed them on their foreheads. She wanted to have a baby, even after washing thousands of diapers every other day of her life. If I erase each one of May's wrinkles and the wart, I see her in the morning, in a wooden bed with four posters, stretching and yawning, remembering the night, closing her eyes to go back to sleep as if she thinks she's the bank president's wife. She's wearing a plain cotton nightgown, and I imagine her pretty. She's waking up and feeling over to Willard's side, although he's been out three hours already, milking, and she thinks how nothing could ever take away her happiness. She feels as full as a big old cow pond where cows come to drink all summer, and it never dries up, because it's fed through the earth by an eternal spring. ·

She gets up and makes breakfast for her husband. She says the word over and over to herself, "husband." When she goes home to all her sisters she tells them, not about Willard, but about "my husband." She says, "My husband got up at two in the morning because a calf was born." Or, "Did you see my husband in town yesterday?" She asks them about "my husband," as if all of a sudden he doesn't have a name; what's good about him is he belongs to her.

I'm not sure whether to be glad or sorry for May, that she was so happy with Willard, that she felt like a spring-fed cow pond. May never thought too much about religion back then, probably, but being married, she knew exactly what she wanted to find in the afterlife. She didn't even care that she wasn't off with some man from Peoria who wore suits and sold hairbrushes door to door. She had the bug that afflicts every part of you, especially your reason. It makes you dream of babies crying out for you in the night.

Aunt Sid says that Willard was a fine upstanding human being, that it wasn't a mystery why May thought he had been sent to her express from God Almighty. On the day after their marriage May burned his toast for breakfast and he said burned toast was just fine, in fact he liked it better charred. So May burned his toast every single day afterwards, and he choked it down with a smile on his face. Aunt Sid told me that finally she felt easy with May; I imagine that they could now chat about underwear without May saying Sid's stunk worse than anyone's in the world since the beginning of time. And she probably loaded Sid up with pure corn; she said, "Sidney, someday a man will come along and make you as happy as Willard is making me right now." If someone said that to me right at the moment I wouldn't know whether to laugh and choke on the bile caught in my throat, or cry. I suspect I'd burst out crying.

The year was 1941 and Pearl Harbor gave President Roosevelt the chance he'd been dying for. War was declared and Willard Jenson got the call. He didn't have ailments that could get him out of it. They were hoping the Japanese would quick get mashed to a black pulp so the men from Honey Creek wouldn't have to fight in major battles, but the president said, in his voice that sounded like he was so far away and lonesome, that we had to make the world safe for democracy. Miss Daken, my history teacher, told us about the greatest lines from the speeches, and then we watched a movie that ended with the mushroom cloud. Willard Jenson had to go down to the South for training camp. There must be letters somewhere in May's things, love letters between them, words that can't describe half of all the yearning in their loins. Someday I'll find the packets all strung up with rotten ribbon, and I'll be able to know her a little better. I've seen shows on television about the war. All I can picture is May standing at the depot waving a white handkerchief at Willard. He's on the train; they just kissed so long it almost pulled away without him. They are like the lovers on a TV show, except we don't have a train depot in Honey Creek or Stillwater.

After Willard went overseas, Marion, May's sister, became engaged to Frank Bane. The couple kissed in the pantry and when May bumped into them she backed out, staring. Marion never mentioned the war. Frank Bane wore thick glasses, and once when they got knocked off by a cow's tail he was found crawling around in the straw. He couldn't go to war because his eyes were too weak. They signed him up to work in a gun factory.

On Marion's wedding day May helped her get dressed. She put the flowers in her sister's hair, never jabbed her with a pin, although she wasn't thinking about anything except the barbed wire you find near trenches. May made lame jokes about wedding nights and how you walk crooked the next day. Every week there was news about how some boy got shot dead over in the Pacific. For the wedding reception there were biscuits and slabs of roast beef, cut thin, because of the war effort. Wild daisies, wilting, stood in pots all over the house. There wasn't anything alcoholic to drink except the wild stuff the men passed around out in the yard. The guests sat on folding chairs in the dining room and wiped up the gravy with their bread.

May had moved back home for the war, with her parents, because Willard Jenson's father took over the farm. She didn't want to live in the same house as her father-in-law. He was so stern, especially when there was weather coming that he didn't like. He called her "young lady." About the only thing he ever said to her, in an accusing voice, was, "Young lady, I don't like the looks of the sky."

May came home, did the laundry, drove tractor, heaved milk cans, and pushed cow rumps from stanchion to pasture. She had to take out her wedding gifts, including the entire china dog collection from her senile aunts, to know that she hadn't merely dreamed of her marriage. Her menstrual period stopped coming because she was lifting eighty-pound milk cans. There wasn't one part of her body that felt alive.

Aunt Sid says that Marion was the beautiful one in the family. She had a braid so thick you could hang or swing from it, and soft brown eyes almost as tender as a dead mouse's in a trap, and small hands that hadn't done one load of wash. Marion had gone to high school and knew Latin; she said words such as *declension*, and probably May looked up at her from the pile of laundry like she was cracked. The dress May wore for Marion's wedding had large white flowers swirling around on a pale blue background. I found it up in the attic when I was in high school. I put it on in my bedroom, and thinking I was alone in the house, went down to May's room to look in the mirror. I stood there admiring myself for a minute, before I realized that she was in bed, staring. I met her eyes in the mirror and I didn't recognize them. Each one looked like a dull gray plug under the bath water. I didn't say anything. I got out of there as fast as I could. I waited for my punishment but it never came, and I began to wonder if the dress had some kind of forgiving power.

There's a picture of May wearing the dress, after Marion's ceremony. She looks like she read instructions in a book about how to make a smile and she was trying it out for the first time. Her little teeth didn't make it into the photo. May had all her teeth pulled when she was forty-nine. I try not to look at her in the morning, when her mouth is empty. The size of her entire body is suddenly diminished without her jaw.

After Marion and Frank Bane drove off for their honeymoon, May sat in the barn and closed her eyes. She stroked the two kittens without thinking they were animals. She imagined the hair on Willard's head. She made a note about how Marion's husband wasn't half as good as Willard, especially with those two-foot glasses he had to wear. She noticed the sun going down, and for once she looked at the sky. She stopped and mentioned to herself how blue it was, how if you could reach up and taste the color of dusk you might turn into something shimmering and silver; you might be transformed into the moon itself.

When the telegram came that night her heart turned to stone.

She wouldn't hear what her parents were telling her. They tried to explain but she blocked her ears. She walked out into the dark field, to the spot where so many years ago she had tied the rock to her ankle and told her sisters she was going to drown in Honey Creek.

Four

Aunt Sid told me that the whole town came to the funeral. There wasn't a casket because the body of Willard Jenson was nowhere to be found. He had been blown up on an island in the Pacific, as brave a soldier, the reports said, as there had ever been. The news was full of accounts of the boys overpowering the yellow devils; the papers said that although the Americans were practically never defeated, when we did have to retreat a mile or two we always begged and pleaded for more Japs to kill. After the funeral the relatives went back to the home place and they had all the leftover food from Marion's wedding: slabs of roast beef warmed up and potatoes made into hash browns. May wore the same dress she had worn at Marion's wedding. She hadn't shed one tear at the church. She sang out the hymns while everyone watched to see what she might do next. They were waiting for her knees to give out; they expected her to keel over and hit the hard pew, and then everyone would swarm around her mopping off her cold brow. When the guests left she wrapped her wedding china in newspaper. We still have it in our attic. The teacups are preserved in memory of Willard.

May figured the officials in the government who had the lists of dead people made a mistake. She told Sid she knew it was a simple mistake and that after the war was over Willard would come home. He was hiding under all the carnage so the enemy wouldn't notice that he was alive. Once, she woke up in the middle of the night screaming. She had dreamed he was dead, and if it was true she knew that wherever she went she would always be a stranger in a foreign country.

May lived at the home place for ten years after Willard died, until she was thirty-five. Her brothers survived the war, and of course Frank Bane never had to go. May couldn't tolerate Marion. She insinuated, by gesture, that Frank wasn't any better than a fop with the thick glasses he had to wear. She bet he could actually see perfectly, he just didn't want to defend his God and his country. Marion and Frank moved to North Carolina. They couldn't stand it in Honey Creek.

It came to me, as a revelation, that May lived through all the history I learned about from Miss Daken. Not of course the Romans and their sewer systems, but to think that May was living and breathing while Nikolai Lenin rode through Russia on the train. If May was around then, it doesn't seem so much like history; it seems like life itself, close and thumping. Still, she never spoke about islands in the Pacific or the European theater. While it was going on she couldn't seem to see farther than the wash hanging out on the clothesline. In those days she didn't have words for one single person. She did all the cooking for the hired men but she didn't speak to them; she served and went straight back to the kitchen. They were such rough, ugly old men, and they always tried to catch her eye. She knew each one's shoes by heart. She promised herself she would never look farther than their ankle bones. She washed and ironed and canned. She kept her hands flying while her mind probably said the same thing over and over: she whispered, "I don't believe this is my life." She watched her enormous hands become chapped and tough. They got so cold when she drove tractor, from the metal steering wheel and the wind cutting through her cloth gloves. She said all her sentences to herself. "Someday I'm going to leave here" was her favorite. But then she'd go up to her room and lie down on her bed and stretch her arms across wondering when her Willard was going to come back. She knew it wouldn't be long now. She knew she'd wake one morning and there he'd be at the door, with a bandage over his burned-up heart. That old hole was just about healed, he'd tell her, while she tried to control the tick in her smile. She believed he'd come back because she couldn't imagine him not in the world. He was probably walking the streets down in Argentina. He was in a park picking flowers that he was going to press and then send to her. There's a stone for Willard over in the Honey Creek cemetery, with nothing below. It says on the stone that he's singing unto the Lord a new song, and that May was his beloved wife.

When May was thirty-five Elmer Grey started coming around by himself. He didn't bring flowers or chocolates. Elmer had a rear end the size and shape of a tractor seat and fingers the thickness of a corn stalk. He had red hair all up and down his arms. Compared to her slim Willard, Elmer was more like a creature someone caught in a trap. Excepting his head, where there wasn't one strand of hair. When he offered to marry May she didn't look up at him. She said to herself, "I'm already married." What occurred to her was the list of items he owned. She had a vision of the long low chicken sheds and his healthy milk cows with their heads bent to the ground eating grass from the lushest pasture in the township. His first wife had cancer and didn't last beyond the third month.

Aunt Sid tried to tell May that something awful happens to every single person somewhere along the line, and that May shouldn't squander her life weeping at Willard's gravestone. "It's a fact," Aunt Sid said, reaching across the table to touch May's sleeve, "that he isn't ever coming back."

"Is that what they teach you at the conservatory?" May said

without a moment's hesitation. "Dead people don't come back, could have fooled me. I'm glad you're so smart after all the years in your short life."

She covered her face with her apron for a minute, as if the effort of being snide was taking its toll. "You'll never know what it's like, Sidney," she said just before she raised her head. "Look at yourself. You look dried up, as if all your life is in your brain. I'd bet a million dollars there ain't one man who knows you're living. If I had the energy after waiting on all of you hand and foot I'd laugh for two hours straight in your face."

It was ten years since Willard's death and May still had the habit of leaving the hall light on, in case he was looking for the place to come home. But whenever she saw Elmer she examined his wide strong back carefully, and since it didn't much matter to her, when he asked her to get married the second time, she said, "Why not?" Perhaps there was something in her that made her sorry for him, the way he didn't have hair growing on his head, and his wife had shrunk to nothing and then died in his bed.

They got married in the courthouse in Freeport. May wore a beige suit and a string of pearls around her neck. In the blurry photos she looks like she's standing in front of a firing squad. She's squinting out to the hateful light. Probably by then her eyes weren't any too big. They were getting narrower and narrower, on account of the way she looked at the world, as if everyone, even each animal in the barnyard, was set on making trouble for her. All the space around her seemed the same, and when she heard the red-winged blackbirds in March, she swore under her breath; she swore saying, "It's that spring time, again."

What I can't picture is May and Elmer coming home to the farm on their wedding night and walking up the stairs to the front bedroom. It makes my insides feel like jelly to think about it. I can't see May taking off her suit and hanging it up as carefully as she can, and then removing her slip, and all that time Elmer is under the covers waiting for her. I don't like to imagine such a thing. May must have told herself while she took her stockings off that anything was better than serving dinner to all the hired men. They looked at her like they were waiting for a chance to catch her on the dark stairway. They didn't do anything but belch to say thank you after breakfast, dinner, and supper. May probably screwed up her eyes and pretended, despite the hair covering Elmer, that he had turned into her smooth and slim Willard. I have a feeling there wasn't a minute of—joy—not for either one of them. Elmer wasn't a prince to start with but May wasn't going to be able to improve him much, if she shut her eyes and wished he were someone else.

One thing I've acquired too late is the habit of stepping into other people's skin. If I pretend to bore a painless hole in May's shoulder and steal into her large frame, stretch myself out to actually fit, and then look out from her dark eyes, I can see things I've never noticed. I can feel May, not long after her second marriage, at home in the everyday world of her kitchen. She made a cake seven days a week, first thing in the morning; she could iron exactly six shirts while it baked. She did all the dishes and made the frosting in the time it cooled. The day was divided up into half-hour segments, each segment time for a specific task. The cake, the shirts, the bed, the hens, the dusting, dinner. The dishes, the mending, the floors, the garden, supper. She planted her feet in front of the sink and scrubbed her copper-bottom pans once a week, her pride. They hung up on the wall, flat and orange, and she saw them as nothing but perfectly scrubbed pans.

She liked to go to the orchard nearby and spend two dollars and fifty cents on a bushel of small red delicious apples. The basket wouldn't budge on the way home, even with the sharp turns, because of her thoughtful planning: she went to the mill first, to get the flour, and she propped the fifty-pound sack against the apples so they wouldn't spill.

She probably was already angry, before she got in the door, thinking about Elmer. She knew he would be sitting in the recliner chair with the stuffing coming out, doing nothing, reading a history book about the Civil War at three in the afternoon. He deserved a rest in the afternoon, he had told her once, and she scowled and then laughed. She had grown up knowing that nobody deserved anything, most of all rest. He might have looked up at her from his comfortable chair, without seeing, and mumbled something about how bad the shocks were on the covered wagons that took the wounded soldiers from Gettysburg. She knew nothing would have made him happier than a whole basket of apples set by the chair, so he could eat when he pleased, but she took them into the kitchen.

I imagine her making clove apples. She sat in the kitchen poking the cloves into the apples and hurting herself, and also feeling sick on the sweet smell of the spice. She turned an entire bushel of red delicious apples into clove apples in three short days, and hung them all from black strings in Elmer's closet, where he had nothing but a checkered suit, one white shirt, and a brown silk smoking jacket his first wife gave him for a wedding present. She hung two hundred clove apples up and down the sides of the closet. Neither of them ever mentioned it. She sometimes mentioned, showing off her red chapped hands at dinner, how the hands indicate how much a person works. They cannot lie. Hers were stung by cloves. But it was her face that reflected the bitterness of being trapped in a world of half-hour segments of time, not one second of which sparked in her a thought of the Civil War or the splendor of the Assyrian coming down like a wolf on the fold.

May was thirty-eight years old when I was born. She probably thought I was going to be retarded since she was over the hill. I wonder if she enjoyed carrying me. I wonder if she ate liver and spinach and drank a quart of milk a day, like they tell you you must. Sometimes, the way I get so tired, I suspect May never ate the right food. I feel like I don't have all the ingredients a person is supposed to have.

I've already described most of the main events that happened to me when we were a family, all together. I didn't mention the one year my job was to bring the cows home from pasture. I had to make sure there were no cars coming, and scoot them across the road. I was a young girl wearing a plaid dress, hollering at the cows to come. I opened the gates and they followed me, not because of my personality; when they saw me they thought of corn. At supper Elmer put a hand on top of my head, those hands that were so heavy I felt he might take my head and crumple it up like a piece of paper. I think he was saying I was a good girl.

There were times in the fall when I had to go look for the cows. The dark would be coming, and as I walked through the pasture and up into the woods searching for them, from far away, if I stood and listened, I'd hear the sound of hooves shuffling through the leaves. It'd get closer and louder and louder until all the cows' feet in the leaves sounded like water thundering over a dam. I loved standing, my cold knees knocking each other, listening. I heard that rush of leaves, and sometimes if I stood still and watched, I might see an owl flying between the trees. Its wide wings beat slow and quiet.

I didn't ever tell about the owl and how you can't hear them flying, even with their beating wings. They mean to go in silence. I didn't say anything about the cows and the racket the leaves made. I stared at May and Elmer and Matt, when they weren't looking, trying to figure out how I was going to explain that the nurse in the hospital made a mistake and I wasn't their baby, that I belonged to my teacher, Miss Pin, and she was coming to fetch me instantly. I also tried to figure out why nobody liked me except Aunt Sid, the minister in church, and Elmer, though he never said. I made up a place in my brain that looked like a tropical jungle and that's where I went when Elmer and May had their spats. They didn't close their door. I pretended I didn't know what their words meant. For the most part it was May shouting at the top of her lungs since Elmer, in her opinion, was the one who needed shaping up. He wasn't big on using his vocal cords but he made use of the time by scratching behind his ears and getting them clean. I knew May didn't have the life she wanted. I guessed what she needed was a nice pen pal who would write her to say what a great person she was.

I started paying close attention in school to the reading lesson, so I could understand Aunt Sid's letters. Aunt Sid was the choir director of a world-class high school chorus, which she told me all about. She took her students to auditoriums around the country and had them sing in their maroon blazers. Naturally she always wore a corsage.

In third grade I brought Sid's letters to school because of the teacher I mentioned, Miss Pin. Miss Pin made me sound out the syllables of all the words I didn't know, and she explained what high school chorus singers do, and she showed me the color maroon. Miss Pin was tall and skinny, and she always wore high heels that made a clacking sound wherever she went. She had a large head surrounded by a ball of teased hair. By coincidence her shape was exactly like a pin. Every night I closed my eyes and first dreamed that I was going to marry her when I grew up. I loved her without reservation. She wore blue dresses—blue was her favorite color—and pink scarves bunched up at her throat, and she smelled like lotion made from roses. She had little blond hairs above her upper lip, which I was dying to touch.

I liked her with such urgency that I was scared to death in her presence. I had to be careful that I didn't do something dumb, which meant I had to watch every move I made. When she smiled at me my heart galloped out of my body and did perky fox trot steps by her desk. I couldn't figure out if my head was still on my shoulders, her smile got me so mixed up. Although

Miss Pin had thirty other students to care for, I imagined that she was watching over me, in particular. In my dream I went up to her when she was fixing her head scarf to go home, and I said, "I love you, Miss Pin." She always kneeled down and hugged me for a long time, rocking back and forth, and crooning. She had breasts just the size of cupcakes. I also worshiped her because she always asked, "Did you get a letter from Aunt Sid?" She called her "Aunt Sid" as if she knew her. My mail was a secret Miss Pin and I had, together.

One of my favorite letters from Aunt Sid that year, one Miss Pin helped me figure out, went like this:

I remember so well when I was a little girl in Honey Creek. Because I was the youngest, I was spoiled, and I used to steal up to the haymow with a good book and not come out all day long. When I got home at night, after supper, I had to do the dishes; they were stacked up from the whole day; thousands of plates, glasses, spoons, pots and pans. But this is a secret — you can't tell anybody — my mother usually shooed me off to bed when no one was looking, even though dishes were my responsibility. She couldn't bear to see me looking so tired.

Now that I live in the city I miss all the smells; I miss the lilac grove in the spring and the carpet of violets on the front lawn. I love how you describe the country — keep writing your thoughts down. After all these years I still haven't really been properly transplanted to the city and your letters make me homesick. Someday you will come to visit me in De Kalb and you'll see the beautiful flowers I have in my yard. We'll sit on my porch — just think of all the things we'll have to talk about. You have a very special place in my heart, my dear, and I think of you every day.

That's what she said, "You have a very special place in my heart, my dear . . ." I almost laughed out loud in front of Miss Pin when we read that sentence. I thought about what that special place must look like in Aunt Sid's heart. I thought it must be a garden with all the kinds of flowers there are in the world, in every color. It would be a place where I could walk and smell the sweet air. I sat picturing the spot, where I could live if I wanted; I thought about it all day long sometimes. I sent her a photo Elmer took of me outside on the front steps. You can't see my face because I'm holding a kitten up to the camera.

I also loved to think about the days when Aunt Sid and I would lounge and talk about our lives from start to finish. We'd sit at a table stocked with food; we wouldn't leave; we'd sit there through day and night, nibbling at desserts. Not for one second were we going to have hunger pangs.

When she stopped to visit that year I was so happy to see her I stood in the hallway trembling, and then I ran out into the yard and hid up a tree. I wanted always to be on the verge of seeing her. She left me silver bracelets, four of them, that hit each other on my wrist and made me dizzy with their clanging. I wrote her and told her I never took the bracelets off. I said we were a great big happy family. I didn't mention that when May got mad she grabbed the dish towel and with her red hands as fierce and large as lobsters she clawed at the towel and wrung it until her hands turned white. It made her feel better to strangle something. I always ended my letter with how happy we were.

Once, when we were in church, all of the little children had to go to the altar for the children's story. It was three weeks before Christmas. The minister — May calls him the Rev — was there in the white robes and his rainbow belt, and he came down and sat with us on the steps going up to the pulpit.

He said, "What is it that makes this time of year so very very special, boys and girls?"

All of us started to think; we wanted to get it right. Susan Abendroth said it was cold and they had to have more blankets on the bed. One boy told about how every single person in his family got the flu. Cassandra Kate said that they went to see Santa at the shopping center. When I heard the word *Santa* I remembered, and I knew what the Rev wanted us to say. I raised my white arm covered with goose flesh and the Rev pointed at me. In a voice no louder than a speck I whispered, "Pretty soon the baby Jesus is going to be born." I mentioned that he was our Savior, come to save all men, and make everyone love each other.

I don't know how I knew all the information; they must have been priming us with the stories in Sunday school. The teachers had us waiting for so long, coloring flocks of sheep with their shepherds. I hit the jackpot with the Rev, make no mistake. I could see him wanting to say *bingo!* He came to my side and kissed my forehead. Then he put his hands on my shoulders and said that I was just right, that that's what was truly going to happen to us. I kept saying the word *truly* to myself, and I thought that if I ever had an infant I'd name it Truly.

Then the Rev sat back down and read from the Bible. He read that a young woman would conceive and bear a son, and that he would eat curds and honey when he knew how to refuse the evil and choose the good. "And in that day," the Rev said, "a man will keep alive a young cow and two sheep, and because of the abundance of milk which they give, he will eat curds and everyone that is left in the land will eat curds and honey."

I wanted the baby Jesus to come in the worst way, with his curds and honey, choosing the good, refusing the evil. It seemed that surely he would come soon. I knew for fact that sheep did the job fairly quickly, but here the teachers had me confused; they said the baby didn't have an earthly father, so I wondered out loud if it was like when the truck comes to the cow barn and the man gets out with his long syringe and then next thing you know the cows are fatter than a pig and groaning with every breath. My teacher started to laugh. Finally she said, "No, it wasn't like that at all," and there I was, left in the dark.

When I wrote Aunt Sid about how I was expecting Jesus to come, and how he was going to whistle for the fly which is at the sources of the streams, Honey Creek, no doubt, and for the bee which is in some other land, she wrote right back and asked did I know what the word *symbol* meant, or the word *myth*? She said the Jesus story was a celebration of life but that an actual flesh and blood child wasn't going to appear. I knew she was a liar then, because the Rev had said to me, "truly."

I wrote Aunt Sid:

Dear Aunt Sid,

You should read that book, *The Bible*, because in there it tells about the baby Jesus, and about the people walking around in the dark and then seeing a great light. We have a teacher in Sunday School, she tells us how to pray and we draw pictures of Jesus, I always put his mother in too, Mary is her name. She's going to have the baby in the stable, and when he learns how to eat curds and honey he'll be all set. The Rev says he has the good news, the baby is coming any day, maybe you didn't get the word yet over there in De Kalb. The Rev wears white robes with a rainbow belt and right above him in church is a giant cross of real gold. I don't know where they got the cross, I never seen ones like that in Coast to Coast. I just know the baby Jesus is coming to save all men. We sing alleluia in church.

Before she could write back it was Christmas Eve. In church they had a pageant, and they acted out the whole story. There in the crèche was the postmistress's baby. That baby was a girl, about three months old. Wouldn't you know it, Laverna had to lift "Jesus" out of the straw because she started crying when the Wise Men came. Laverna had on a blue nightgown and I swear she forgot to take off the rubber thimble she wears on her thumb for sorting mail. Plus she has black hair. I've never seen pictures of the Virgin with black hair. She's always a blonde. I couldn't believe the way everyone in church tittered when the baby cried. It came upon me suddenly that Jesus was in the same league as the tooth fairy and the Easter rabbit, not to mention Santa himself. But with Jesus, for some mysterious reason, you had all the grownups kneeling down, praying to him. I was furious with the deacons and the Rev and the Sunday school teachers and the imaginary God who made the whole story unfold.

I kept getting madder and madder, all the way to Easter. First, they had us waiting for a baby. It was going to be in swaddling clothes, but all I could see was Laverna's baby girl smelling like the mess she had in her pants and howling at the frankincense they stuck near her nose. Then, in an instant, they were talking about Jesus as if he's a full-grown man. They didn't spend time on the pranks he pulled as a youngster or the names of his teachers. A few Sundays later, that baby, who as far as I could see wasn't even born yet, is riding a mule through the streets healing the sick people and everyone's waving branches at him. All the Jewish people want him to wash their feet and cut their toenails down to the bone. His favorite place is leper colonies. Then, the next thing I knew, they're killing him and sticking him up on a cross like the one we have in church. I wanted to get an old dish towel and strangle it when I heard they killed him. And if that isn't enough they throw him in a cave, push a boulder across, and then he isn't in there when they look. He's in heaven. The whole thing sounded very dumb to me, but mostly I felt sad, because I was sure there was going to be a child who would come to me and make the world light. I was sure I would wake up to find jars of honey out on the doorstep.

I wrote Aunt Sid and told her that she was right after all, and that I was going to learn the word *symbol* so I wouldn't make the same mistake twice. Aunt Sid said that Jesus was an example to people and we should try to behave like him, but in her opinion he wasn't divine. I asked Miss Pin what this divine business was about and she said the word meant heavenly. I still didn't understand one bit of it, or why it had been invented in the first place. They said something at church about Jesus coming back in the near future, but I wasn't going to believe it. May herself said a person shouldn't put all the eggs in one basket. It's possible that May was in her usual bad mood all the time, just as I was for months after Christmas, because Willard Jenson had been her savior, and she was banking on his saving powers lasting at least until the end of her life. Instead, he came down to her and made everything seem so dandy, and then poof, he's gone. The world was instantly and permanently spoiled for her. She didn't have one thing left except a couple of teacups that smash if you let go. She didn't care if Hitler took over the world or the Japs invaded California. She wanted Willard back. Probably it was Willard's death that taught May the lesson about having two baskets for the eggs. And it probably didn't help her, living in Honey Creek forever, where everyone knows what you are. They won't let you change even if you feel like it. People were always saying May's first husband, the one she truly loved, got killed, and how sad it made her. There wasn't a single person in the area who didn't know her story. Maybe she couldn't be happy even if she tried, because folks wouldn't know her then. They might think she was haywire.

Five

I T wasn't until I got to eighth grade that I started seeing clearly how different we were from other people. It took Miss Finch to show me all the colors in the world, such as the people who live in jungles without clothes, hunting for berries and nuts.

I had the job, for five years, of running Miss Finch's tapes. She was the blind lady who lived in the stone farmhouse down the road. She had arthritis and was blind on top of it. She couldn't string up a tape recorder so I'd go over there and thread the tapes and turn them on. They have books recorded on them. They were supposed to keep her company. The first time I went over she called me "my dear," just like Aunt Sid, only she said, "My deeah." For the longest time I couldn't figure out what she was saying. I thought she was talking about an idea she had, but it never made sense in the sentence. She said, "My deeah, why don't you stay and listen? This book is one of my favorites."

I didn't want to. I didn't want to spend the entire afternoon sitting in a boiling room that smelled of old age. Her filmy eyes were hard to look at, and she blinked so slowly I had the urge to tell her to hurry up and finish. When I didn't respond she said, "Well then, make yourself comfortable. Is the machine ready?"

I switched it on, thinking I could sneak out of the house after a while, but I couldn't help getting sucked into the book. It was called *Oliver Twist*. Miss Finch said, "I just adore Dickens, don't you?" and again I said nothing. In the story there were evil people and exceptionally good ones also. I figured that must be like life, good and evil, otherwise people wouldn't listen to blind tapes so hard. I wished I could meet Oliver Twist. I knew we'd have a million things to talk over. I pretended I had a cudgel and I beat up Bill Sikes and his little dog, too. Afterwards Nancy and Fagin and all the boys had a party to celebrate. Miss Finch said she meant to listen to new books as well as her old favorites, even the ones that pierced her heart, before she departed this world. After *Oliver Twist* we listened to a book about an artist named Picasso. I daydreamed through some parts, when they were talking about cubism, which I couldn't figure out for the life of me, but I listened when the author, his mistress, talked about how the artist made her feel captive, and how she served him, and felt hollow. I listened when she told about sitting naked on the patio so he could look at her. Miss Finch often murmured that he wasn't a very nice man, but mostly he made me feel small. He made me think about the strangeness of the world, and how very large it must be. I thought about Paris, France, a place full of buildings full of pictures, and I was stumped. Nothing I heard in the Picasso book related to Honey Creek, and yet I couldn't help remembering the people, and how they were tied to each other.

I got off the school bus every afternoon and went straight to Miss Finch's house. There were a couple of people who took care of her, made her meals and gave her baths, and her son came home from his engineering job in the evening, but she was alone in the afternoons, and she got lonesome, you could tell. Her blind filmy eyes even looked excited when she figured I was in her room. She told me she had been a great reader all her life, that she gobbled books like candy, until her eyes went bad. "My deeah," she said, "treasure your eyes and all that you behold." I looked out the window and saw May in the distance cutting the lawn in her curlers and her apron. I thought I saw rocks being thrown up from under the machine; I saw her stop and lift something out of the grass, knowing it was probably a rabbit's nest, or blind baby mice, which she would take inside and put in a warm oven and nurse with a doll's bottle.

At first I felt like I had to be prim around Miss Finch, sit up straight and pull up my socks, make sure I sat like a lady, but then it came to me that she couldn't see one single thing. I stuck my tongue out at her as fast as I could. Nothing. Those eyes of hers were looking in two different directions. She didn't care what I looked like or if I abused her until kingdom come. So I lay on the floor with my head on a pillow, like princesses get to, plus I sucked on the hard candies Miss Finch had by her bed. I tried to get candy out of the jar without Miss Finch hearing, but she always said, "Help yourself," right when I had my greedy hands on the loot. Her ears were extra perked up.

Sometimes I ran all the way from the school bus with my bag over my shoulder slapping my back. I couldn't wait to hear the next chapter. I dreamed about the plots all day long without once touching down to real life. Once, we were listening to a book called *The Mill on the Floss*, and we were finally, after twenty reels, right near the end. I had a terrible feeling about Maggie, that her days were numbered, and that water was going to be responsible. I couldn't bear it. I thought about her constantly at school, hoping the best, although my heart told me she didn't have a chance in the world. I bumped into people in the halls and they pushed me away with their elbows. They didn't know Maggie was the only person on my mind. I was desperate to hear the end. I raced down the school bus stairs and tore along the road while the boys leaned out the windows jeering at me. I took the porch steps by twos; I didn't even call, "Hello, hello." I was out of breath, heaving and gasping. I said, "Hi, Miss Finch." I couldn't keep it straight that she was married once and that her real name was Mrs. Finch.

"Is that you, my deeah?" she asked. She didn't wait for an answer; she said, "I don't feel up to reading today. Why don't you and I have a little chat?"

"Huh?" I said. I couldn't believe it. I stood there staring into her useless eyes. It seemed that every time we got to the juicy part in a book Miss Finch wanted to talk. I wasn't going to listen to her mouth run on. I scowled and flapped my hands with my thumbs sticking in my ears. I hated for her to start in her slow, tired voice about how great it all was back when she was a girl in New England, and how they always ate Boston baked beans and she shoved the beans into a little drawer in the table because she couldn't stand to eat them. I plugged up my ears but I couldn't keep my fingers in my eardrums all afternoon and pretty soon the book magic occurred—that is, I sat there with my mouth hanging open, greedy for what she was talking about. She always said, "My deeah, I'll tell you about the good memories. I don't have any use for the unhappiness I've had in my life." She told me about her husband, Mel, and his massive coronary attack. He was sitting at dinner and he dumped over into his chicken salad. She told me about their trips, all the beautiful islands, and living in the memories made her cry for the lost pleasures. She had a whole set of photo albums. My job was to describe each picture, and then she told about where they took place. There were pictures of lobsters she ate, and girls doing the hula dance. She went all over the world because Mel was a merchant. I'd go to the islands with her, sitting right by the bed, and remember my favorite parts for her.

I started to bring Aunt Sid's letters over to Miss Finch because she liked anything at all from the outside. I think I can imagine how it would be, not seeing a thing except all your past life swirling around in your brain. Any noise would be magnified: the clang of silverware, the mice scratching in the walls, the cats knocking paint cans over on the porch—all vibrations carrying noise long after it's stopped. Miss Finch was always looking alarmed, saying, "What's that?" when I hadn't heard anything at all. So, just as it used to be with Miss Pin, Miss Finch got acquainted with Aunt Sid. Miss Finch, Aunt Sid, and I were a family, always eager to know the news about each other.

Aunt Sid wrote me more about her life, now that I was older. She talked about her job teaching music at the high school in De Kalb. She said sometimes she closed her eyes while she conducted and she saw flocks of blackbirds leaving the basswood tree at the home farm in one gust, and then all of a sudden she had to perk up, because she realized the students were singing their song without mistakes. Sid was more than your average conductor. She had no children of her own since she never did get married—despite her stunning looks. She probably had so many offers she didn't know who to pick. She wrote me about the pale green evening dress she wore for the spring concert, plus the white lily pinned to her chest. She had to stand on a platform with her arms stretched out like a goose flapping its wings right before takeoff. And when she brought her arms up in a certain way all the singers opened their mouths and blasted the audience to pieces. Miss Finch wouldn't have been able to tolerate such a thing. The students usually sang songs by dead composers. Then, after they were finished, Aunt Sid had to turn around and bow to the parents. The entire auditorium rose up clapping and stomping their feet. I asked Aunt Sid to write and tell me every little thing in her life, because I wanted to breathe with her, and Miss Finch did too. She described the time she went to Chicago and heard a singer named Leontyne Price. She said she had dreams that she herself was a black opera star, and when she woke up she was awfully disappointed. I was shocked; I couldn't stand to think of Aunt Sid as a Negro.

I read the letters to Miss Finch and she'd say, "Ask Aunt Sid what her house looks like." So I had to write to Aunt Sid, "Don't send a picture because remember Miss Finch is stone blind. She can't see her own nose." I confessed that I stuck my tongue out at her, just to make sure.

When I got Aunt Sid's letters I ran over and ripped them open, and then I read the news to Miss Finch. There was the one summer Aunt Sid took a group to Europe. They sang songs and people threw flowers at them. Before they left the U.S. they sold thousands of grapefruits to raise money, and it had to make me wonder if the grapefruits were those Elmer picked way down in Texas. It had to make me think that somehow, in a strange way, there are a few binding strands between us. Picture it—Aunt Sid selling Elmer's grapefruits to go to Europe, to sing songs to the communists so she can write me, so I can read the letters to Miss Finch, and add something new to her brain. It's all a big old chain. There isn't one unconnected link.

There were parts of the letters I didn't read to Miss Finch. I'd skip sections like this:

> I know how hard it is to be a teenager. There is so much going on inside a person's head and heart. It is sometimes difficult for me to watch my students struggling through adolescence; I think it's much harder for your generation than it was for mine. You sound as if you have a good friend in Miss Finch, and I'm so glad you can share all the lovely books. I don't think I could have survived if I hadn't discovered the library in Stillwater, and Miss Ogelsvee, the choir director, who told me repeatedly that I had a good voice. Still, it is books that are a key to the wide world; if you can't do anything else, read all that you can.

I didn't have much luck reading to myself because my eyes weren't extra-strong. I needed glasses but May said she didn't have the money for the optician. I wrote to Aunt Sid and said how adolescence, that's what she called it, wasn't so bad. I told her that every minute I could, I was out of the house, at Miss Finch's, and that when May talked to me I pretended I was far away, and then her voice came to me like it was a thin column of smoke from way over on the other side of the mountain. That's what I said, although we don't have mountains in Illinois, except Starved Rock — where some people didn't have food and they died. I wrote Aunt Sid about how I walked out into the night, back through the cow pasture and up into the woods, to the plateau where there are a few cedar trees and long wild grasses. I lay on the ground looking up to the sky and sometimes I got the queerest feeling. I could sense the earth spinning around, and I felt small, probably how a midget feels in a room with regular people. For a split second I had the sensation all through my body that there wasn't a reason for our being on the planet. We were hurtling through space and there wasn't any logic to it. It was all for nothing. Such a thought made me feel so lonesome I had to turn over on my stomach and cry for all the world. I cried for the little lamb we had once that lost its hind leg in a dog attack. It had to hobble around the yard bleating, waiting for someone to feed it corn. I cried for it, and the hungry people on top of Starved Rock, and Miss Finch's blind eyes, and how long and soft the grasses were that I lay in. I cried for the loveliness in the night. I couldn't stop the flow, because I knew if Aunt Sid ever saw me for an extended period of time, not counting her short yearly visits out of duty, she'd change her mind about liking me. "Adolescence, it isn't so bad," I wrote Aunt Sid, even though I could tell she knew I was in all the dumb classes. I had the feeling she knew I cried up on the plateau at night, in the grass, that I felt just as fragile as the tender green shoots.

I didn't mention May's habit of yelling at me. She wasn't actually yelling at me all the time; she only needed someone to blame for how rotten her life was going. I did do stupid things more often than not. The day I made scalloped onions I took the onions out of the bag down the basement, where I thought we kept them, and I cut them up, just as May had taught me, and I got the cheese and bacon and toast together. I read the recipe about four hundred times so as to get it perfectly accurate. Then I put the casserole dish in the 350-degree oven for forty minutes. It was my job to make supper on the nights May worked at the dry cleaners. I dreaded her coming home because she always walked in the door, took her coat off with a terrible slowness, as if her arms were so tired she wouldn't ever get her wraps untangled from her body, and then shuffled into the kitchen to take stock of my disasters. I could tell she was tired by the way her skin hung on her face, and I didn't improve matters with the smell of char coming from the oven. She couldn't help hollering at me sometimes, wringing that dish towel, saying, "Won't you ever learn to get your tasks right?" I always said I didn't know, and she'd tell me she wished she could order me some new brains. She wondered out loud if scientists could figure a way to do brain transplants.

The time I made scalloped onions I took them out of the oven — the top was sizzling and golden — and I set the dish on the table. I stepped back to admire it. May was the first one to take a bite because she was always starved after a day at the dry cleaners. She swallowed without chewing, due to extreme hunger. She sat still for ten seconds and then she spat what was left in her mouth out on her plate.

"You're trying to kill me," she whispered. She couldn't talk too well because she still had food clogged in her throat. She choked, "You're going to poison us."

She took the casserole dish and threw all the onions into the garbage pail. There went the whole supper I had planned so carefully. "You show me where you got them onions from," she said. She made me march down the basement stairs with her right on my tail.

When I pointed them out she laughed uproariously, with her hand to her bosom and her eyes closed. She laughed, not out of happiness, but because what I had done proved to her that I was without one sign of intelligence. Those onions were actually tulip bulbs.

I didn't tell Aunt Sid the scalloped onion story because I thought if she knew how dumb I was she wouldn't write to me. Once though, I got to feeling so sad and useless I had to tell Miss Finch about the tulip bulbs, and other episodes. Miss Finch didn't laugh at me at all. I couldn't believe it. She said it was all right, anyone could make a mistake like that.

"You mean anyone could?" I asked her.

And she said, "Yes, that's correct. It was simply a mistake."

She had a worried look that would come over her blind face when I imitated May snickering at me. Miss Finch said it wasn't right. She shook her head and said, "No, my deeah, that isn't right."

Miss Finch, even though she was blind, made a person believe what she was saying, on account of her high forehead and her soft white hair that started way back on her scalp. She might well have worn a crown since a young age, that didn't let her hair grow in perfectly. She looked like she was reigning over some little kingdom, with her long nose and all her own teeth. She sat up straight in her bed and she always had on a clean night jacket decorated with flowers and lace. And she spoke so confidently, saying things like, "No, my deeah, that isn't right."

Perhaps it was hard for May to see me growing into—a woman. Perhaps I reminded her of how she used to be, of what she lost by getting old. When she watched TV she drooled after Steve McQueen, and maybe she realized all too often, like about every time she looked in the mirror, that Steve McQueen might mistake her for someone dressed up as an ogre for Halloween. It must be strange to keep your strong mind in a body that grows older and weaker and no longer resembles your own image of yourself.

Maybe she was already scared about the future, about being left behind in her kitchen while everyone else went out to the world and never came back. She made sure I didn't get notions. There was only one time when I tried to talk to May like the characters in the books by my favorite author, Charles Dickens. We were cleaning the living room and while I vacuumed I prac-ticed the sentence over and over. When I switched off the machine I said, "This room is excessively bare and disorderly, wouldn't you say?"

May dropped her dust rag and put her hands on her hips. She looked at me like I was a Jap who had snuck up behind her, something she would never tolerate. "Did a bird shit on your brain?" she asked.

When I didn't say anything she said, "Well, did it?"

"No," I said.

"Then don't talk like there's a pile of crap in your head." She picked up her rag and started dusting her china dogs, which meant lifting each one carefully, and gently wiping their bodies.

In Charles Dickens's books I had to admire the way the meanest enemies spoke to each other, with what seemed to me to be the greatest civility.

Sometimes I think that May purposely stopped noticing certain progressions. She never bought me a brassiere at the store. There I am in my second year of high school squeezing into little-girl undershirts, until my nipples showed through. Some of the boys made circles around me, smirking, because of my new tits. They said I was behind the other girls developing, which wasn't news to me. Finally, because of the humiliation I wrote to Aunt Sid. I said,

Dear Aunt Sid,

I have a special favor to ask you. It's all because Miss Finch doesn't ever remember to pay me for the job I do at her house. I don't even mind, we are great friends, but I don't have money I need for certain things, and Ma says if we aren't careful with the funds we're going to go to the poorhouse. It's her birthday coming up and I thought I'd get her a bottle of perfume. She got a whiff of some on a lady at the check-out at the grocery store, and she said she sure wished she could smell so good. Isn't that an ideal present for her? Only a bottle the size of a soup can costs about ten dollars. If I could borrow that money from you I could make Ma's day a real jubilant one. I'll pay you back the minute Miss Finch delivers, I promise. I know you and Ma aren't the best of friends so you might not want to contribute. I'll understand. Ma said she would let me visit you over her dead body when I suggested a trip to De Kalb. She really burns me up. I bet you're going on another journey this summer. Your luggage must have stickers all over saying the places you stayed at. I sure wish I could visit you sometime. Did you ever see pictures by a man called Picasso over in France? He is on my and Miss Finch's bad list.

Aunt Sid wrote right away with twenty dollars inside the envelope. She said to keep ten for myself and to forget paying her back, period. I spent two dollars on some lacy potholders for May's birthday and the rest was going for brassieres. I know brassieres aren't an important subject to talk about, but back then they seemed like the hardest trouble in my life. I didn't pay attention to the world, such as the story of the students who got shot down in Ohio because they didn't like the war we were having in Vietnam. I felt sorrier for me without underwear than I did for the poor dead college people.

The next Saturday I walked to Stillwater. I went to the Sears store and bought myself three brassieres. They were in boxes with young girls standing in mist with nothing on except the item. Each day I stuffed one in my lunch sack and then when I got to school I went into the restroom and put it on. The boys laughed more when they saw I finally had one. They slapped my back to feel it, but I didn't care. I knew I had been smart to get cash from Aunt Sid.

When I got home one day, May saw the strap sticking out of my lunch sack. She said, "Where did you get that brassiere?" I stood up tall and said that I wasn't going to be laughed at in school so I went out and bought it. She didn't even ask me where I got the money. I could tell she was a little impressed.

"Well, ain't you grown up all of a sudden?" she said. There was half a smile on her mouth.

I wanted to say, No, Ma, it ain't all of a sudden. If you'd been watching you could have seen that it's been going on for a year or so. I didn't say anything. I had the feeling I knew what it would be like to be a plant stuck in a pot, with a mistress who every now and then remembered to give it a trickle of water.

If my nose were taken away I would have no memories. When I have lain awake all night and my eyes are finally closing I'll get a whiff of something far off, from another year, another county. Aunt Sid asked me how she could help me sleep and I thought to myself, Nose plugs. Sometimes, there are only smells: the smell of chickens, the smell of Miss Finch's stale breath and the hard candies by her bed, peppermint, all stuck together with the heat of her house; the smell of Matt's math books where you crack the bindings, they're so new; the smell of May in the kitchen frying the onions.

I have smells and also the sound of words. I heard something in church once that made me grin. The Rev declared from his stage, "The dung heap shall smile." I had to crack up in private thinking about a splat of smelly cowpie with a grin on its face. I kept hearing the words "The dung heap shall smile" all day long, and I wondered what kind of miracle it would take to make such a substance happy.

When I'm lying here thinking about our lives and imagining some of the words May could have spoken, and how it was for her when she was young, and the way she got riled on occasions, I think, Maybe May's not so bad, and somehow I got it wrong. It doesn't seem fair: here I am telling it, and she can't come in and say, No, that ain't right. There were the times when I knew she was a good person, struggling with something a little bigger than herself. I remember shortly after Elmer left and she was yelling at me for spilling lemonade on that precious carpet of hers, and then all of a sudden she was in the chair, her long legs, covered with varicose veins, flapping around. I looked and she was crying with her hand over her eyes, gasping for breath. She told me to come over to her that instant, and she got me all wet. I stood leaning into her, stiff, like something dead. She scared me because I had never seen her cry. She didn't say anything except when she choked, "God damn it." She sobbed, and when it was over she removed me from her path and went into the kitchen sniffling and honking. She blew her nose on her apron, she didn't care. She was extremely nice afterwards, as if crying had purged her of the venom.

The funny thing about May was how unpredictable she could be. Every now and then she went out and bought me a dress, even though we were almost in the poorhouse, and she made me put it on to show her. She admired me in it, like she was some kind of fashion expert. I didn't like the dresses; they were slimy material, with flashy checks or flowers, and I felt like I was a sign that said "Road Repairs." But the next minute after the fashion show where I modeled the new dresses and May oohed and aahed, she barked at me to do the dishes. With the weather at least you get storm warnings. Still, I'm probably poisoning the times she was good to me, because of the way things turned out. On some days I can't help thinking she designed my every move. If she was cleaning the bathroom she sent me out to use the woods, even in winter. She woke me up in the morning by taking the blankets off the bed. My memory has replaced her with someone completely warty, no teeth, stiff bristles growing out of her chin.

And I have to say to myself, Think of the happy episodes. Think of your fourteenth birthday. May baked me a cake in the shape of a lamb, and she even made Matt shut up so she could sing "Happy Birthday." She gave me some pink barrettes, and a hat and scarf set that she knit. She kept saying she couldn't believe I was fourteen. She told us exactly how it was when she gave birth. I know the story by heart: they knocked her out, and then when she woke up there I was, a five-pound red wrinkled baby girl. She said they couldn't decide on my name for the longest time and so my wrist bracelet said BABY GIRL GREY. She told me I cried for hours and she never got a wink. I can see May lying on the sofa praying for sleep while the thing in the basket screeches.

May said what she was going to do was give me fourteen kisses for my birthday, and I clamped my teeth down while she did it. I couldn't imagine what possessed her to kiss me. It didn't occur to me that maybe she secretly liked me, but that she couldn't often be enthusiastic because of all the times I let her down. If she got her hopes up it would be one more example of putting her eggs in the one basket.

In grade school I gave her the ultimate disappointment. It happened when by some miracle I made it into the Stillwater All City Spelling Competition. There were three eighth grades in my school. I was to represent my class; Matt and Missy Baker won in their rooms. When I was the only one left up in front of the blackboard during the first elimination, my teacher almost dropped her pants. I was shocked myself and had to look left and right to make sure I was standing alone.

I wrote to Aunt Sid to tell her the good news. I described how we would stand on stage and spell, after repeating the word. I told her Miss Finch wanted to help me study but I said, "Miss Finch, how can you drill me when you can't read?" Miss Finch demanded I leave the word sheets with her, and when I came the next day her son had recorded all fifteen pages on the tape machine. While I sat on the floor the machine spoke, using all the words in a sentence. I spelled, and Miss Finch corrected me. If I misspelled she made me do it right three times in a row. "Let's get this right!" she would say, slapping her hand on the night stand. There were times I practically hated her for making me drill, and she always remembered every single word I had missed and made me spell them at the end of the session.

The day of the spelling bee May washed one of the navy jumpers I loved, and right before we drove to school for the big night she gave me a special pin of hers. I was sitting at the table finishing my macaroni, studying the word lists frantically, when she loomed over me out of the blué. She started dusting off the front of my jumper, like she was cleaning a wall to hang up a masterpiece.

"This is an heirloom pin I'm going to let you wear," she said, holding it up to the light. "Your grandmother had it when she was married, and her mother gave it to her. It's for real rare events." She latched it on me. "There, ain't it pretty?"

She made her shoulders shimmy while she looked at me. She went crazy when her offspring won their way through contests. I didn't know what to say; I didn't know May owned anything so beautiful. I kept touching the brooch on the way to school, feeling the gold and the purple gems. The pin was made in the shape of a daisy and the stones were the petals. I knew the gift was going to make me lucky.

The spelling bee took place in the junior high gym. The thirty contestants were on stage and the audience sat on the bleachers. Matt, naturally, sat right up front on the stage. Everyone expected him to spell the hardest words with the greatest degree of accuracy, but I was what's known as the dark horse — what they call people who are dumb but astonish the public every once in a while. I had to spell *exemplary*. When I heard the word I held my hand over the pin, closed my eyes, thought of the sounds, each one, and spelled. The pin came first; I felt it alive and burning at my throat; next I heard the sounds, and then the picture of all the letters flashed up on a board in front of me in white neon, and I could spell the word correctly. Each time I sat back down in my chair I was breathless with surprise. Other children were falling dead like flies. I had trouble believing I was myself, sitting still in a metal chair, apparently destined to be a winner. When there were seven people left I stroked my pin right before I got the word. It was *devout*. I said, "Please use it in a sentence," and Mrs. Golden said, "The congregation was devout." I spelled it just right, D-E-V-O-U-T. I blew air out of my cheeks on the way back to my seat. I had survived for such a long time. Missy Baker was up next, and I wished on the heirloom pin that she would fall flat on her face and contract permanent scars. They gave her *exercise*. She started to spell it. She lost her place. She was so mad she stamped her foot, like a cow that has insects biting its flanks. She said R in two places. She was down. Mrs. Golden had to say twice that she was sorry, but to please be seated, Missy could try again next year. It wasn't true. Next year we would be in high school.

I wasn't noticing words people got; I was so dizzy, praying to win. Eventually, as a result of my winning, I would become a TV celebrity. They'd send me to Springfield, Illinois, to win the state championship; then I'd go to Washington, D.C., and beat every boy and girl in the nation. The president would kiss my cheek in person and invite me to live in his house. For lunch we'd have deviled eggs and slabs of ham, and root beers so tall you'd have to stand up to suck at the straw. And there Diane Crawford and Missy Baker would always be, following at my heels like hungry pet slugs, waiting for me to feed them some dirt.

When I got up the next time I stroked the pin, of course. My word was *petroleum*. It was a long one. I started out slowly, petting the purple gems. I said, "P————E—T—R—O-L-E-U-M." One false move and I knew it was over. I sent a flashy smile in the direction of Missy Baker. She had her head down in her lap while her mother handled her black braids and tried to tell her it was all right. It wasn't all right, not with me up there just about to take the grand prize.

I pictured fighting it out with Matt. There were only five of us up on stage, if you don't count Diane Crawford. She was the teacher's helper. She kept track of the spelling lists and marked off the students who went down. Mrs. Golden was on stage too, giving out words and making up sentences on the spot. I prayed during the next round that I would cream Matt. I told Jesus that I'd believe in him forever and on into eternity if I could only whop Matt, just this once, I'd never ask for anything again, in Jesus' name I asked it, Amen.

Just as I had gotten my word, *pejorative*, the fire alarm went off. I was so dazed I thought it was someone screaming at me. I stood straight with my eyes closed, watching my red flaming lips make the sounds. When David Cazola bumped into me and said, "Get moving," I scrambled along behind him. I didn't have the slightest idea how to spell *pejorative*. I didn't know I was moving or knocking against people; I was hearing myself say, "Please use it in a sentence." I tripped at the door on my shoelace and went sliding down on all fours as I thought, P-E-J . . .

After waiting ten minutes we were allowed back in. Mrs. Golden announced to the parents that having to stand up while the alarm went off would tangle up anyone's nerves and that I would be awarded a free round. David Cazola immediately went down on *unrequited*. Matt was up next. He had to spell the dangling word. He didn't have to stop to think. My turn came and as I stood up I felt for my pin, for the luck; I felt, my hands went spastic, they flittered all over my chest, my neck, my face — my pin wasn't there any more. My heart instantly shriveled to the size of a raisin. I had to clutch at my throat and croak, "Wait." I had to look all around me back and forth, and back and forth. I was like beagle dogs when they think they smell a squirrel. They don't have control over their body parts or their hoarse yelps.

"Miss Grey, please step up to the center," I heard Mrs. Golden say. It was my turn. The free round was over. I felt the tears streaming down my cheeks and I felt the hole where the pin used to be. I knew my luck couldn't last now. I knew I was being punished, for among other things, wishing Missy Baker a scarred-up face.

Sandwich was my word. It was easy but I stalled for time. I said, "Please use it in a sentence." I held my throat like my head wasn't screwed on tight.

"You have a delicious sandwich for lunch," Mrs. Golden said. I could hear the parents laughing at me for asking for a sentence. "Sandwich." I tried to pronounce it so carefully. There was no hope for me since my vocal cords had decided to change jobs, see if they liked being ear lobes instead. I whispered the letters "S-A-N-D-W-I-T-C-H." For one second I thought I had it right. I wasn't punished after all, but Mrs. Golden said, "I'm sorry, please be seated."

When I got to May way up at the top of the bleachers I was crying so hard it was impossible to stop. She took one look at me and said, "Where's my pin?"

"I don't know," I wailed at her, so that everyone heard me. I was hoping she saw it fall off of me somewhere along the line. The latch on it was too weak for fire alarms and scraping your knees and praying and spelling. I could tell May was dying to get her hands on a dish towel so she could wring it. She picked violently at the knees of the orange slacks she always wore. I couldn't figure out how the pin had fallen off, plus I went down on *sandwich*. I wanted her to strangle me right then, get my life over with.

Afterwards, while everyone cleared out, I sat on the bleacher with my head down and I felt a hand at my back. I didn't recognize the feel of it and I had to look up. It was Aunt Sid, come forty miles to see me spell. When I saw her I burst into tears all over again.

"You were wonderful," she said. If I had had the words I would have told her that lie stank worse than a pig fart.

I couldn't speak to her. I heard nothing she said. When she was gone I noticed that there was a bag on my lap. I picked it up and carried it to the car.

All I wanted was May to be proud of me, to be her smartest daughter, and for Matt to turn a hideous green color at my stardom—and what did I do but go down on the easiest word in the English language and lose May's favorite jewel, worth millions of dollars. Afterwards I had looked everywhere. I only saw Diane Crawford laughing at me, at the way I crawled around, feeling the floor like I didn't have sight. Matt was the first alternate. He went down on *aforementioned*. He must have temporarily slipped a cog. Still, he ended up going to Springfield because the winner busted his collarbone at the last minute. That's the kind of luck Matt has. On the way home May said one thing. She turned around to me at the stop sign and said, "I'm never going to give you nothin' valuable again."

Later that night I went out to the plateau and stared into the sky, thinking how I didn't care about the gems. I didn't care about the cassette recorder Aunt Sid had placed on my lap, including five full tapes. I was going to pin stars on my chest, real ones. I'd walk into the house with a huge shining star on me, it'd blind May, and she would fall to her knees saying how sorry she was.

One Saturday, a year after the spelling bee, I was over at Miss Finch's house, even though I didn't have to visit her on the weekends. There was something about her, with no eyes to see, that made it seem all right to tell her thoughts. We were listening to *Emma*. I started telling Miss Finch I wished I could be in that book; the people were so funny and even the bad characters weren't too terrible. We were talking about their faults a little and I told her that compared to May, with the sharp flat back of her hand, and Elmer, who was about as emotional as a corpse, the English people didn't do anything very terrible. It seemed like having pride was the biggest sin back then, and not knowing yourself through and through. Miss Finch said she wanted to hold my hand so I let her. Hers was all scaly like a fish's back. She said she could tell I had good thoughts—good thoughts, she said—and that I shouldn't ever let people put me down, that I had to try and rise above any meanness I saw. She asked me if I told my Aunt Sid the things I told her, and I said, "Sure," even though I was lying. She put her fingers on my face, and she said that she knew I was beautiful. I felt something far down inside me, the size of a pin point, flicker and then glow for a minute.

Six

I HAVE to go backwards one more time, to a certain Sunday
when the Rev called upon us in church. It was one of the
children's Sundays when Matt and I were small. We had to go
up to the pulpit to hear the words from our Rev. I watched his
brown shoes tapping the green carpet while he sat there with us
discussing how great it is for people to have friends. Better yet,
Best Friends. He had a mustache that didn't amount to anything
and places on his cheeks where it looked like he hurt himself
shaving. He said that sometimes a good friend surprised a person,
with their generosity and kindness. He told us about Lazarus, in
the Holy Bible, and how Lazarus was just a bag of dry bones,
and then bingo, Jesus comes along and puts him back together:
puts skin on him, restores his beard and the creases in his wrists,
and makes him breathe. The Rev said Lazarus was lucky to have
such a good friend in Jesus. He mentioned that the Lord could
be our friend also. For a while after that story I tried to get in
touch with Jesus, but it's not the easiest thing in the world to do.
You have to create him in your mind's eye, and I already had
my mind's eye cluttered with owls flapping their quiet wings and
frogs calling through mud. Still, when I saw bones of sheep out
in the pasture, a whole skeleton picked clean, I imagined it all

of a sudden covered back up with wool and eyeballs and nostrils, and I ached for the Son of God to come on over and do his magic. That old skeleton was Gloria, one of my favorite sheep. Now I'd have to say that the Lazarus story is about the craziest section in the book.

I remember when the Rev was talking about friends, how he looked at Matt and me sitting together like we belonged, like we were supposed to be playmates. The Rev didn't know that my brother lived in an entirely different landscape, that Matt thought he was a handsome oak tree vigorously climbing up toward the light, while May and I were scrawny mulberry bushes.

By the time we were in high school Matt was fairly handsome, according to the girls in my class—despite his outbreaks of pimples. Matt didn't seem to mind having acne. He probably thought each pimple was a national treasure. He played tennis on the team. Doubles was his specialty since he cooperated with the other boys. I always thought the coach must have been hard up for players, because whenever I watched the games all Matt did was shift from foot to foot, leaning over, gripping his racket. I didn't ever see him take a shot. It was always the boy in the back. Nonetheless he was popular, which made May awfully glad. She was thankful he hadn't gone straight to college from kindergarten, because then she couldn't have rooted for him at the tennis match. He was the youngest in our class but you couldn't tell, because of the fancy sports jacket decorated in the school's blue and white. The jacket had a patch on it that meant he was a hot shot. Most of all, however, everyone raved about his math. Our Matt was a wizard. They drove him to Chicago for contests, and it seemed like he was always taking exams so he could go to college at a great distance from Honey Creek. They sent him to a math summer camp at the University of Chicago. You should have seen May mourning him for two months. She gave up putting her hair in rollers and wearing fresh aprons, plus cooking food a human could stand to eat. The principal at our school,

Dr. Heck, was apparently in love with Matt, judging by the number of times he called our home. All of the faculty had plans for my brother.

Matt came home each day with a calculator attached to his belt, in case he needed to figure out something quickly, I guess, like in an emergency. He went into his room, came out for supper, and then went back to his desk. That's my brother Matt: we were supposed to be friends; we were supposed to surprise each other with kindness and generosity. When he looked at my face I turned away, because I could see him scrutinizing me for signs of life. I felt shy around him, because I knew his brains were tremendous. Shy isn't the precise word; I felt smaller and meaner than a bee sting.

May desperately wanted to be his favorite person. She reminded me of our gray cat who never died; she always kept living, and each year she had scores of kittens. There she was every time you looked, with a juicy mouse in her chops, calling to her brood. The kittens were usually playing with their tails or going crazy watching an ant. They couldn't have cared less about their mother and her carefully planned meals. May tried to pet Matt sometimes — she'd get up from the supper table and I could see her wanting to touch his hair, and if she did it, gingerly, he shook his head like she'd spilled hot grease on top of him. He mumbled at her with his mouth full of tuna casserole if she asked him, "How was your day?"

Matt, with the pimples and the jacket, didn't talk to us, and I was quiet because I didn't have usable words on my tongue. I saved them all for Miss Finch. May had to do the talking, solo, if she wanted company. She sat at the head of the table in her extra-large fuzzy green sweater that looked like a bloated zucchini consuming her. She told us about everyone in town and what all their children were doing. Matt and I ate without uttering a sound while May went on about Mrs. Brierly's daughter, Pamela, and her marriage to the banker. The newlyweds went down to a hotel in Rockford with a big old bubbling bathtub in their room. I couldn't imagine Pamela and that pock-faced banker sitting in a boiling hot tub, coming out with their flanks all red.

When we were in high school May worked at the dry cleaners. We had our land rented out, although May and I continued to raise chickens. I fed them and shoveled out the henhouse, and May took the eggs on a route. She sold dozens and dozens to Negroes. She didn't like it if people were a different color. She drove about sixty miles twice a week, taking eggs to feed people she didn't think should live on the earth. It slayed her, serving the black ladies who had more money than she did. We didn't have cows or sheep any more because they were too much work without a man around. Matt didn't do chores. He was busy exploring all the avenues in his head.

I knew one truth about May back then, without putting words to it. She was so lonesome. You could tell it in every movement she made. She never sat still and when she moved she dragged herself from place to place; she couldn't bear to think about how empty she was. She sure needed Jesus to come breathe life into her. There were moments, too, when I could see May feeling sorry for me. I would catch her looking over at me, her head tilted, and her eyes a little wider and sadder than usual. How pitiful I was made her even more lonesome. I averted my eyes when she stared my way. I couldn't stand the hopes she had for me. She told me about the dances and parties at our school. They showed all the queens in the paper, being crowned, and then kissed by their consorts. I knew she wished I was in the paper too. They photographed all the girls in fluffy skirts and fitted tops. If I went to the dances I might be sorely tempted to sink my teeth into their flesh, and then they'd put me in the dog pound.

One fall after supper, when I was a junior, May asked me if I didn't want to go to the homecoming dance, and I got scared because it was within her power to make me do it. I felt myself looking like a cow when it's being led somewhere it doesn't want to go, bugging out its eyes so the bloodshot whites showed. I could see myself in some dress not fitting my top, and no one asking me to dance, not once the whole night, and all the other girls are queen.

"I don't want to go, Ma," I said, "and no one is gonna ask me either."

"That's what every girl thinks," she said, mopping up the table. "You wait, someday someone will beg you to go."

"Never," I said under my breath. I didn't say that I would pass out dead if it ever happened.

Then May started telling me that when she was my age she loved to dance. She wiggled her fanny and took me into the living room by the wrist; she trotted around moving the TV out of the way and pushing the chairs to the side. She grabbed my grandmother's handmade broom, the antique May always said was especially valuable because of the walnut handle. She started waltzing with it. She was graceful, and she smiled at the broom awfully moony. I thought I was going to be embarrassed but she looked so idiotic and happy I had to laugh.

"Teach me to do that, Ma," I said.

I wanted to look moony just like her. So she went and turned the radio on and yanked me into position and said, "OK, one two three, one two three." May told me where to put my feet, how to be light, how to feel my bones dissolve into thin air. We worked at it for a good half hour. When we were taking a breather, she said next we'd learn the fox trot. She said I was getting the hang of dancing. We didn't see Matt standing in the hall watching us. We were concentrating but giggling also. May didn't call me a stupid. She told me I must have her feet because I was catching on so quickly. She said, "You're getting it, now relax your shoulders." We were floating around the living room, skimming the floor. But when May saw the expression on Matt's face she got flustered. When she saw the jacket that says "Varsity," she dropped her hands from my waist. He looked at us like we were a couple of perverts. He didn't need to say one thing. He shook his head, went into the bathroom, slammed the door. May frowned and turned the radio off. She walked upstairs. I heard her bed rattle as she climbed in it and adjusted the covers over her head.

Sometimes I dream we are dancing. We're wearing dresses that look like they're made out of the heads of Q-tips. Our skin is scrubbed clean to perfection; we don't have chapped elbows, and I'm on the homecoming court. After the dance we teach each other hobbies: I show her some of the blind tapes, books I think she'd like, my favorites by the author Charles Dickens. And she can make my feet do steps that aren't invented yet. We don't even touch the floor. We trade secrets and guard them. Sometimes, I feel that I'm only just ready to start my life. I know what I need to, to live it a hundred times better. As far as I can see, no one is out there waiting for me with a ticket that says "Try it again." I'll probably really figure out exactly how to be alive right when I'm gasping for my last breath.

In those days I used to look around myself, trying to see farther than Honey Creek. I couldn't see much beyond the cemetery, and I understood that I wasn't ever going to go anywhere unless something explosive happened, such as a war in our state. I was going to be cooped up in a building with rows and rows of metal lockers and bad light in the halls, and drinking fountains with green gum sitting on the porcelain like toads, for years to come. When I watched the news on TV with May at supper we saw people getting bombed over in Vietnam. They were having battles while we ate our food. I used to imagine Honey Creek going up in flames and smoke and I wondered who would survive and if they would share their food and if the low would still be low or if the bombings would upset the pecking order.

I was still scared of everyone at school. There were two boys who menaced me. I won't say their names; they know who they are. Maybe the teachers kept me in the dumb classes because I never opened my mouth and they forgot I was alive. They didn't know that I was like the mice who come out after dark, squeaking and pattering. About the only time I spoke in school was the time I told Miss Daken I thought Hitler had some good points and she stared me down until I changed my mind. In most cases I couldn't speak about history or math because I was dreaming about blind tapes. I couldn't do math no matter how hard I stared at the page, and everyone thought to themselves, Why aren't you like your brother Matt? When Miss Taylor said that very sentence to me out loud—she was exasperated because I could not do long division—I ripped up my math sheets and bit my tongue so I wouldn't cry. I got an F. When we had to read books in school I never understood them like we were supposed to. My eyes hurt from looking at the pages all the time, and when the teachers asked me what the books were about, I couldn't say in one single sentence. I seemed to feel the meaning with my body, rather than my head. When I got promoted to the regular English class my teacher asked me what I thought were the major themes in *The Great Gatsby*. My face heated up and turned to steam. I saw the rich people floating before me, very fat on being rich, and they were empty, and there was the big old billboard with the glasses watching over the highway like it thought it was Jesus Christ. When Mr. Davidson asked me what the book meant, the only words I heard were "one two three, one two three, now relax your shoulders."

He wrote "See me" on all my school themes. He said I had serious problems with the language. I had to go in at lunch time and sit by him at his desk. I had to smell his perfume and watch the crust of shaving cream behind his ear. He always took his glasses off and wiped his eyes. My themes made him so tired he couldn't stand to think about them. The whole paper was covered with red ink; there wasn't one place to start correcting. Finally he demoted me to my old class. He decided he couldn't save me.

I asked Miss Finch, "What would you think if I joined the army after high school?" I was certain they didn't send girls over to Vietnam because the posters at the post office showed the women at typewriters and switchboards. They spoke of careers and travel. I asked Miss Finch, "Do you think I could get into the U.S. Army?"

She told me the superiors made a person do one thousand sit-ups and push-ups, and run around, and that women as well as men were taught to handle guns. She said the army was a ghastly place, unfit for man or beast. I couldn't imagine what else I might end up doing except wiping eggs and selling them to people who saw the sign on the road. I guessed the best thing I could do was sniff the air and say how good it smelled.

When I was in the last years of high school May got a girlfriend. That's what she called her, only Mrs. Foote was over the hill. She was about forty-eight. She definitely was not a girl. She first came as an egg customer and gradually she got very chummy with May. She lived down the road, in a house that was more run-down than ours, with her three children and her husband. He had weak kidneys so he couldn't work. Mrs. Foote had gray short hair that was so stiff it stuck off the back of her head like a slide. It looked slippery too. She had several black moles on her face and breasts so big if they had hands at the end of them they might be useful. They could wipe silver or sew on buttons. Her teeth had wide black spaces between them. If you were an organism in her mouth you'd have to be able to jump pretty far, going from tooth to tooth. Wherever she went her fat son followed. He bossed everyone around and thought he knew as much as Dr. Heck, the school principal, possibly even more. He had sisters at home who were always getting into trouble stealing and running away. He said his sisters were loose; he told me he whipped them, but he was lying. He was too lazy to hurt people.

Mrs. Foote wore flowered dresses that zipped tight up the front, and an apron with a hammer, her flashlight, and a dust rag in the pocket. Her nylons had runs so wide I couldn't figure out why she even bothered to wear them, and her shoes were holey. I could see her broken soles because she always put her feet up on a chair. She said she had to rest her swollen veins. She had probably the shortest fattest legs in the state of Illinois. If she wasn't a person you'd laugh at the shape you saw out there in nature.

She was a fixture in our kitchen in the afternoons when I came home from stringing up the blind tapes. May didn't ordinarily smoke, but with her girlfriend she lit up about five cigarettes, one after the next. The place smelled like a murky tavern. May exhaled as if she thought she was a knockout — she blew smoke up to the ceiling like a movie star.

Mrs. Foote and May became friends because Mrs. Foote had problems she couldn't solve. She had to tell someone about them. For instance, her girl hurt someone on the road when she was driving around smashed. Mrs. Foote didn't know what to do about her children, so she always cried with her head down on the table. But the beauty of it was May going over to Mrs. Foote, and patting her on the shoulder and saying, "Now, now."

When I was in the living room folding laundry and watching the news I could hear them in there, Mrs. Foote sniffling and May saying, "It's OK, it's OK." Sometimes I got little flashes of understanding. All of a sudden I knew what the Rev had been saying all those years ago when he talked about how friends are people who can surprise you with kindnesses. May was a friend, both ordinary and miraculous. What cracked me up was the way Mrs. Foote thought May had a TV-show life with her smart boy winning science fairs and math games, and a girl who didn't do stunts, such as practically killing people at three in the morning. May didn't say to her best friend, I'm just as miserable as you. Instead, she acted as if she had been guaranteed a trouble-free existence by Mr. J. Christ.

Probably compared to Mrs. Foote's Daisy I was the world's best-behaved high school girl. But Daisy was spectacularly beautiful. She was in my grade and she had dark hair that curled around her face, and big black eyes with thin feathery plucked eyebrows, and she put green makeup on her lids, piles of it with silvery specks, so she looked like she was from somewhere else —the moon, for example. Everybody couldn't help looking at her when she walked straight down the hall, not turning to see a single person. She was two years behind in school, because she didn't care about anything except boys. Some said even the football coach couldn't help himself and that he took Daisy to the Rainbow Motel.

One spring night when I was sixteen I heard banging at the door. I lay stiff and alert in bed. Probably someone was coming to kill us. I listened to May go downstairs and pretty soon there was the noise of Mrs. Foote blabbering. I heard the wind moving out between the wide spaces of her teeth. Naturally she had her son Randall along. He was so fat if he sat on a worm on a rock it would make a fossil in about five minutes. Then scientists wouldn't have to wait a million years. I went downstairs because I couldn't help it; I was curious. No one said anything to me. Randall was the only one who glanced at me standing in my nightgown, shivering. He had a belt about a mile long stretching around his belly, as if he thought his pants could actually fall down. It was impossible, they were so tight. He always stared at me like he was planning to gobble me up.

Daisy was gone. They couldn't find her. It was four in the morning. "Actually," Randall said, "she hasn't been home for two days." Mrs. Foote was having a fit; the flab on her arms was quivering even when the rest of her was quiet. May said, "Sit down, Dee Dee. Here's some whiskey. You just steady yourself. We'll find her."

May spoke in a way that made us all believe her. May would make it come right, make no mistake. Randall kept saying he was going to murder Daisy when she got home, for driving his mother hysterical. Because Mr. Foote's kidneys were on the blink, Randall acted like a big old rooster, watching over his brood of bad girls. May called the sheriff and the Rev while she poured drinks for Mrs. Foote. May was such a good friend, to share her alcohol. Mrs. Foote got loaded on the whiskey, so May put her to bed on the couch. She told Randall to use the recliner. When they woke up at about ten the next morning, Daisy was in our kitchen eating cereal. Daisy wouldn't say much. She told Randall to lay off her. There was something she said about a trucker down at the truck stop near the highway, and how she went clear to Kentucky with him.

Seven

ONCE I got out of high school, where I didn't learn a thing because I dreamed about blind tapes the whole time, I went to work where May worked. I kept trying to keep my eye on the world so I could get to it sometime. I wasn't sure how I was going to get there without money or wits. I spent all my energy keeping track of dirty clothes, and chickens, and all the eggs: every day more eggs. I had dreams where I was shredding newspaper and wadding it into balls to stuff up the hens' bottoms, stop them from laying for a while. Still, I knew the world was out there, another country, with an ocean between us.

It was right around my commencement when Miss Finch had to go to a nursing home. I didn't say goodbye to her. Her family came and packed her up, and took her to a place full of old people strapped into wheelchairs, screaming about the 1920s. It was the Baptist Home, where May's Aunt Margaret had gone, so May was an expert on the subject. She said in that place people die in bunches; there'll be a dry spell for months and then three or four will go in the space of twenty-four hours. Before she left Miss Finch was forgetting everything I told her. She didn't want to hear any more books. They made her so tired, she said. When

I went over in the afternoons she was already angry with me; she'd say, "Where's my lunch? I'm so hungry. Why don't they bring me lunch?" She'd pout and then whimper. I had to take her hands and make her feel her empty lunch tray by her bed. I tried to make her remember the Jell-O with the bananas in it but she said I was pulling the wool over her eyes.

"Miss Finch," I said, "don't tell me I'm a liar."

I had to cry about her lost brain. I took her hands and put them on my wet face and whispered, "Say I'm beautiful, OK?"

"Remember the islands you went to with your husband?" I said, about one hundred times each visit.

"Yes I do, clear as a bell, my deeah, that sweet warm blue water, clear as a bell."

She could remember the details about the islands, but what escaped her was, did she actually eat lunch? and who was I again? I wanted her to at least think of the books she loved. I tried to jostle her thoughts by saying, "Wouldn't it be great if Mr. Darcy walked in here?" He was our favorite, out of all the people on her blind tapes. She was always saying "yes, yes," but she wasn't actually recalling; she was only saying "yes" like a little dog, thinking it might get a snack if it did the right trick.

I watched from our house when they came to take her. It was a silent parade of people and suitcases. Then, when they were gone, I sat on our steps, just sat, thinking over the years I knew Miss Finch, thinking of all the afternoons we spent together. I sat there until it got dark. I sat through May calling me for supper three times. I was living in the books Miss Finch gave me — I couldn't believe how lucky I was to have her for a friend. I couldn't believe how much I was going to miss her blind eyes looking at me with all their tenderness.

Matt and I graduated at the same time because we were in the class of '73 together. He didn't get anything but A's for four years straight, so he made the speech. The girls were supposed to be dressed entirely in white, without flashy jewelry, and the boys had on black suits. We carried a couple of red roses in our arms but when I sniffed them they smelled old, as if they had been piled up in a grocery store for a few weeks. Our school probably got them cheap. I went into shock when the words began flowing from Matt's mouth, because I hadn't heard him say a complete sentence in ten years. He was exemplary, everything a person could wish for in a graduate, except for that complexion of his. He probably broke out because he was nervous, standing up there in front of hundreds of people he didn't like. He knew a great deal of information; he talked about wars we were withdrawing from. He didn't mention any particular place. He probably didn't want to get into trouble with the country, but he did say that wars resulted from the foolish work of the government and that our president would have it on his conscience. He talked about corruption in the highest places, that it was time for new leadership — this is Matt, I kept saying to myself — and that we were trying to be an honest generation. He said he was going to go to college and work to make peace through science; he said that peace was something everyone in our class had to work for, because we lived in a dangerous age. I could tell some of the parents out there in the audience, shifting around, didn't appreciate Matt bad-mouthing the president. I guess commencement speeches usually outline a brilliant future. They don't mention H-bombs that could fall on us and char the little children.

I kept looking at Matt, at the back of his head, while he spoke. And I thought to myself, He's my brother. I couldn't believe that I grew up in the same house with him. We knew nothing about each other. If he said anything in my presence it was to tell me I was a moron. He stood up on stage informing everyone in the town about his plans to make peace on earth with the technology stored in the cavity of his head, and when he got home that night he would, as usual, call his sister a moron, with his eyes, not his voice.

I had a tremendous urge: I was going to burst if I didn't stand up in the spiky white heels May bought for me, and scream to everyone there — I could even see the Rev — GO TO HELL EVERY SINGLE LAST BASTARD! I was going to march down to the microphone, grab it from Matt's smooth freckled hands, and tell the parents the F-word. I was going to turn to Matt and demand that he take me with him when he left Honey Creek. I had to clamp my hands to my chair to make myself sit rigid and not go clumping in my heels to the podium. I had to take deep breaths so I wouldn't spontaneously combust.

May appointed herself guest of honor, because she had made Matt with his fine round face and his clean fingernails. Everyone congratulated her, and she smiled vaguely, as if she were saying, My boy has been a genius for so long . . . why are you shaking my hand *now?*

Daisy graduated also. It was common knowledge that she passed English because Mr. Davidson craved her every inch. He was too shy to take her out, but so in love he forgave her for not turning in her themes. At the ceremony she wore a dress that had holes punched out of it in rows all around her stomach, as if they were windows on a ship. She wore green fingernail polish to match her eyelids, and contrary to instructions, green plastic earrings the size of half dollars. Everyone's heart raced when she pranced across the stage, chewing her gum. She was tall and dark and cared for no one. To me she looked like Mr. Darcy's twin sister. In the book Miss Finch and I read, *Pride and Prejudice,* Mr. Darcy didn't have a twin sister, but you never know, he could have had one they were ashamed of. I had always tried to get in gym class with Daisy so I could see her in the shower, but we were never on the same schedule. She winked at me and waved her diploma when she climbed the risers to find her seat. Her look made the fur on my back stand up all prickly.

Afterwards, Randall shook my hand and said, "Best wishes." He had his little change purse in his clutches. He always carried that thing around with him, as if he thought he was living in some fairy tale where he, the king, has a purse of gold. Randall wasn't my favorite person of all time. He made me want to run away from the sight of his shirt coming out of his pants. Sometimes, when he sat on a stool in our kitchen, if he was straining to reach the potato chips, his pants, even though they were tight, slipped down. You could see his crack.

Mrs. Foote asked May if we wanted to go out with the Foote family, not counting the mister, who was in the hospital hooked up to a kidney machine. May looked at Mrs. Foote as if she'd never laid eyes on her before and said, "We have other engagements." She had her nose in the air as she turned her back. Mrs. Foote was only stupefied for an instant and then she remembered that people always treated her like that. She walked slowly away on her stumpy legs. She didn't even put her head scarf on to keep the rain from ruining the permanent May gave her—the hairdo that made Mrs. Foote look like a bald baby who has one curl on top of its head. It was true that we did have an invitation to go out for ice cream with Mr. Hanson and a few of the other graduates with brains and their parents. Still, in front of all the people at graduation, May had to make it absolutely clear that she was far too good for the Footes.

I would have been happy to be on a date with Randall, compared to the company of the smart graduates, in that one single terrible hour at the ice cream parlor. I'm eating my chocolate sundae as fast as I possibly can in the white dress May borrowed from Mrs. Foote. It's plain except for the puffy short sleeves and a scoop neck, and drops of chocolate running down the front. The salted pecans and the hot fudge don't even taste good but I don't know what else to do except eat. I wish I was a black hole that was swirling through space, suctioning up brilliant young stars. When Dr. Heck, the principal, asks me, "What are you planning to do, young lady, now that you're out of high school?"—and he pats my diploma—I say, turning red like

May's lobster hands, I say fast, "I'm gonna go work at the dry cleaners."

Nobody makes one sound. Matt is wishing an elephant would come over, hook its trunk around me, and carry me off. I can see all of them thinking, How in the world did one family turn out a genius, ready to make peace on earth, and a dry cleaners employee? I have the urge again, it's so fierce in me, to stand up and tell how Matt got a head start because he talked practically the day of his birth and because May was crazy about boy babies. He got all the new clothes from Sears. I want to scream that I'm possibly just as smart as any one of them, except Matt. I want to ask each graduate if they can name all the characters Charles Dickens ever wrote about — then I bet their faces wouldn't gloat too long.

I can't think about the ice cream parlor without feeling my face heat up with the humiliation. In those days I didn't have an ounce of gumption. I only dreamed about standing up and telling Dr. Heck, GO TO HELL, because I knew if I did I'd get put in the clinker, or May would blindfold me and drop me off on someone's doorstep, where she delivers eggs.

Matt told all the ignorant parents what he was going to study when he got to MIT out on the East Coast. It wasn't a secret that the college was paying for him to come and learn science concepts. Diane Crawford was going to be out there too, at Smith College. Dr. Heck made some crazy remark about Diane and Matt getting together in Boston to talk about their alma mater and old times. Diane almost gagged on her cherry. She was probably planning never to think of Honey Creek again once she got beyond the town limits. When I got home I looked at a map to see where Boston was located. It didn't look so far away. Only, I knew it was one thousand miles away, so distant I couldn't imagine the length of those miles.

Right after graduation Matt went off to another one of his summer camps. He lived in a dormitory in New York City and did his math. He got money for doing it. He was probably rich. He never sent May a nickel. He sent her one postcard of the Empire State Building, and that's when I knew Matt was gone for good, as I had predicted, and what's left is May and me in our house, and the job at the dry cleaners. Mrs. Foote came over the day after graduation and she and May picked up where they left off. I could hear May saying, "It'll be all right, Dee Dee, it'll work out good, you'll see."

So there May and I are out at the dry cleaners just at the edge of Stillwater on Highway 12, trying not to breathe. I remember nothing about the early days, except the smell. The smell got into your heart, and your heart pumped poison all over you, up into your brain, so everyone you looked at appeared gray. Still, I thought it might be awfully nice to be a clean coat, underneath the plastic, an orange ticket saying you belong to somebody.

The Trim 'N Tidy dry cleaners is a low square white stucco building with glass windows so you can look out and see the trucks going by. Trim 'N Tidy: it sounds like the perfect place to be. It'd be funny if that's what planet earth were called. There were rows and rows of plastic bags with coats and sweaters, dresses and blankets, men's suits and quilts—everything you could think of that attracted dirt. Every now and then an idiotic girl brought in her bathing suit because it said *Dry Clean Only*. May and I stood at the counter to take the clothes and weigh them and write up the tickets. It was the only place in about four towns for cleaning so we got everybody's dirty—*soiled*, we were supposed to say—garments. After we weighed the clothes we were to look them over and mark the spots, and take off the buttons that could get wrecked by the chemicals. Artie, he's the boss, and Louise, the steamer, and Debra did the work in the back. There were enough clothes in Trim 'N Tidy to make a mountain for people to ski down. After the clothes were clean May and I sewed the buttons back on, wrapped up the articles in plastic, and put the number stickers on so we would know who owned what. We were called the finishers.

At first I thought I'd never get used to the smell. You feel it in your veins. My breath smelled like dry cleaners. I could feel the odor in my mouth and on my teeth. I could taste it in my chicken soup from my thermos at lunch. I could feel that smell behind my eyeballs.

I watched the trucks flashing by the window, taking pop and flour and hogs and junk to places far away. Maybe they were carrying Daisy to see the world, down in Kentucky. I stared at people's faces when they weren't paying attention to me, and I made up stories about their lives. I imagined how the elderly ladies with professional permanents and blue handbags lived alone in three-story houses with their small dogs and their gardens. They were so prim when they came into Trim 'N Tidy. They were doing their spring cleaning all year long, getting their blankets and curtains freshened up. They dabbed their runny eyes with immaculate white handkerchiefs. I watched the farmers come in with their wives. I watched them stand in the doorway, shuffling back and forth in their tall rubber boots. They smelled like cows; they were going to smell like cows even after they were dead. They didn't say anything. They looked big and dumb, like being with a herd their whole lives had made them mute. I saw the little children sniff the air and turn up their noses. I saw all of Stillwater passing by. Nothing escaped my attention. If I didn't keep my hands busy I had to think, Here goes my life; I'm going to spend the rest of my days working at Trim 'N Tidy. I couldn't stand thinking there wasn't anything more left for me so I worked at a frantic pace to keep my mind still.

There were a couple of times when I'd forget and May would bawl me out for not saying things such as "Have a nice day." I laughed so hard to myself when she demanded I say, "Have a nice day." The Rev's words came to me: "The dung heap shall smile." The dung heap shall say, "Have a nice day." I had to tell Aunt Sid about that one, May shouting, "You tell them customers to have a nice day."

Aunt Sid wrote me and said I was resilient. I had to look the

word up. It has something to do with my wanting to laugh at
May when she tells me to say, "Have a nice day." Resilient. I
liked being resilient because it sounded like a jewel glittering in
the light.

Mrs. Foote came into the dry cleaners when Artie, the boss,
wasn't around. She must have known his schedule because she
always came in with her pack of cigarettes just after he'd left,
and she and May chewed the fat while May bagged the clothes
and I washed the windows, swept up, waited on people. Mrs.
Foote had information on everyone in Honey Creek and Stillwater. May would always say, "Is that right? — you don't say.
My God, I can't believe it," as if old Frank Wartman and his
bum liver were the most fascinating news she'd ever heard about
in her life. Sometimes Mrs. Foote told stories about Daisy; that's
when I perked up my ears. I tried to move closer to her big empty
mouth. She said Daisy had a boyfriend from way down in Peoria,
who bought her little tiny bathing suits. Mrs. Foote had found
pictures of Daisy on a motorcycle with a strap as thin as a string
bean around her, "Ahem, ahem." I couldn't stop thinking about
Daisy on a black metal bike with her legs spread apart, and all
that dark hair around her face, and then the little strap. I could
almost imagine how that motorcycle must have felt to her legs.

May and I both worked five days a week from nine to five back
then, at Trim 'N Tidy. When we came home at night May made
supper while I went out to get water for the hens and collect the
eggs. We got along. We were with each other so much we didn't
have a choice. We had to be companions because we were all
each of us had, that's not counting Mrs. Foote. When May did
the grocery shopping on Saturday she bought us movie magazines
and the books that tell what's going on in the soap operas, and
since we both smoked, she bought a carton of Newports. Mrs.
Foote offered me a Camel once, and May didn't say anything,
so I started smoking. Except for a couple of coughs I did it expertly

on the first try. I felt adult, only I wished I had a black holder, the kind Daisy used. May and I sat at the table after supper and while I cleaned the eggs, she smoked and flipped through the magazines. She read me news flashes, slowly, about all the celebrities and their new dates. I liked hearing the stories, and at the end May always held up the pictures so I could examine Farrah Fawcett's big teeth. I'd squint to see; I'd have to make comments, like "wow, look at Liz Taylor's tits." We had to laugh over some of the stars' body parts. We were good friends then, May and I, in a certain way.

Every fall I couldn't help missing the cows and going across to the pasture to hear them shuffling through the leaves. My first September at Trim 'N Tidy I came home and stank in my blood and bones. I had to go outside, at the end of the day, to feel the weak sun on my skin. I walked up to the plateau, knowing I wasn't a youngster any more, because I was out in the work force. I wondered why I went to school all those years, just so I could put clothes in plastic bags. Why had I undergone the torture of long division? Sometimes I couldn't figure it out, what all the living was for.

I did know that I loved autumn even more than spring. There was something about it that made me feel fond and sad, the way the fields turned gold and all the wild apples dropped to the ground, smelling and wasting. The wind screeching around the house told me the year behind us was gone forever. You could see the animals in the woods, and the farmers, gathering up food for the winter, to keep from dying. The men, dwarfed by their machinery, were doing their tasks so urgently, shelling corn by tractor light with pitch dark closing in. I walked out in the early morning to sniff the leaves burning and whisper words to the geese on their way south. I loved how they knew exactly where they were flying.

On payday I handed my check over to May, because she was the banker, and she gave me five or ten dollars she said I could keep for myself. She said that we were barely scraping by: the oil, the taxes, the food, the car, were so expensive. I had a pink plastic pig Elmer gave me when I was six, where I stuffed the dollar bills. Someday, when something enormous was going to happen to me, I'd need the money.

That fall Artie got me to join the Trim 'N Tidy bowling league. He said I didn't need to know how, he was going to teach me. I mumbled, "OK." I thought he might fire me if I said I didn't want to. Our team was made up of May, Artie, Debra, Louise, and me. Sometimes Mrs. Foote came too. She told me I should call her Dee Dee, but I couldn't quite do that, so I just called her nothing. I'd say, "Hi," and stop at that. She brought Randall along, with his change purse. He needed loads of quarters to buy Bit O' Honey bars from the vending machines. He didn't bowl at all; he said he wasn't real athletic, and I murmured, "You can say that again." He got mad at me, so mad he bought a Three Musketeers and tore at it with his teeth right in front of me. I wanted to tell him, Randall, you're fat and useless, and I hate the way you stare at me — but instead I whispered my thoughts to myself because probably somewhere in him he hated how he was, he hated his body. I saw the backs of his legs once when he was in shorts and they were all dimpled like cottage cheese.

Dee Dee tried to get Daisy to come along on the league too, something to perhaps interest her a little. She came a couple of times. I couldn't help gaping at her. I couldn't help observing the way she walked up to take her turn, as if she knew everyone would wait all night for her to first spit on her hands, and then hold them over the drier, and get her thumb in the hole just right, and eyeball the pins. She shook her head so her curls flopped around, and then she licked her lips. When she held the ball in her hands all I could see was a motorcycle and her legs, and the little bathing suit strings hardly covering her up.

When we sat around waiting for our turn she'd ask me how it

was going, and I'd say, "Pretty good. I'm working with Ma down at the cleaners." Like she didn't already know that, because there we were in the cleaners' bowling league. She must have thought I was short on marbles. When she made strikes she said, "*Hot shit!*" and rubbed her hands together. She always wore tight pants and I was afraid her thighs might lose all their circulation and atrophy.

I liked bowling because I was halfway decent at the sport. Matter of fact, I always scored the most points for our team, and May grinned at me through the haze of smoke. She was a lousy bowler but she actually didn't seem to mind being the worst. She smoked her cigarettes and drank whiskey sours and danced around with a butt hanging out of her mouth. She danced in her bowling shoes and her nylons, plus her bowling outfit, her pink-and-white-checkered pants suit. She started to hack too, because of all the nicotine she had in her poor soiled lungs. She could produce a hoarse laugh just like some of the stars on *Hollywood Squares*. I see May, a pink dancing lady with a big old ball on her thumb, blowing smoke rings up to the ceiling. She sure made me laugh, and the beauty of it is she made herself laugh too. We were in our element back then, at the Town Lanes. Daisy said to me, "You bowl fantastic!" It was my bowling skills that made her notice I was alive. If I had been a dud she probably would never have spoken to me. She made me so happy I had to go outside and catch my breath.

Right around Thanksgiving Dee Dee's husband dropped dead. His kidneys gave out one morning and he didn't wake up. They were expecting it for so long it wasn't a great big deal, but of course Dee Dee came over and got trashed on May's liquor. I went to the service they had for him. You could see his body sticking out of the casket. He looked just about the same dead as he did alive, except his mouth was molded into a smile. At the end the whole family walked down the aisle behind the casket—it was on wheels. Randall stared straight ahead while

Dee Dee bawled into his sleeve. Daisy came last. She looked over all the guests as if she had just taken her wedding vows and was counting up how many presents she was going to receive. She didn't seem too sad. I thought you were at least supposed to pretend to be mournful at funerals.

When we got home from the church I said, "Ma, how about you teach me some more dancing?"

I wanted to do something cheerful. May turned on the radio and she started one-two-threeing me. We were going along waltzing. I remembered every step and didn't miss a beat. May spoke the words "Cha cha cha"—she liked getting jazzy—when all of a sudden she saw a ghost. She saw Matt standing in the hall in his high smart judgment. Her feet stopped working. She sank into the chair and started to cry.

"Ma, don't cry, it's OK," I said, hardly patting her shoulder from behind. "Please don't cry, Ma."

She cried while I stood gripping the back of the chair. With the bowling and her whiskey and Dee Dee she sometimes forgot to miss Matt, but when she remembered him there was no one else on earth for her. Perhaps I'm wrong and she cried because she felt sorry for Dee Dee losing Mr. Foote, or she was recalling both her own husbands and how they left her. Since I'm not May I can't be positive what she was thinking, but I'd say that most of all she was upset because Matt wrote her two postcards since he'd left for MIT in September. She had to make up details to tell people, about how he sent her letters three times a week and how popular he was with girls; he took them to dances, he couldn't decide who to ask since they all wanted to go with him. She told about the clubs he belonged to—don't ask her to say which ones, there were so many she couldn't remember. I heard her telling someone at church that pretty soon, if her rheumatism improved, she was going to go visit Matt for a special weekend they had for parents, that Matt had asked her if she could come out. He was sending her cash for the jumbo jet.

After Mr. Foote's funeral we didn't carouse for a while. Sometimes after we ate, and the chickens were fed, the eggs wiped, I went out into the night and stared up at the sky. I wondered if there were someone just like me on another planet, if they had dry cleaners up there, and winters coming on, and the symbol and myth of Jesus Christ. I wanted to find out what she did when her heart grew so heavy not even lying smack on the ground relieved the terrible ache.

Eight

S TILL, those days were kind of like a honeymoon with May. We were just ourselves. We were in the mood to raise a little hell—that's a phrase Dee Dee uses twice a night. It doesn't really apply to us all that much, but we did bowl maybe three, four times a week. May and I had yellow vinyl bowling bags with our initials embossed under the handle, and I owned my own ball. It was a present from the Footes on my birthday. I can't quote you prices, but they aren't exactly cheap. It fit my fingers to perfection. I got the best feeling, knocking all the pins down, and Artie always petted my curls in praise of what he called my "sensational talent." He was an old guy so I bowled far better than either he or his wife.

"Sweetheart," he called to me, "you are a terrific bowler, there ain't no doubt about that. You must have been born making strikes."

I was queen at the Town Lanes, with my big old blackie ball on my thumb and fingers. I'd get crazy sensations when I stood up to take my turn. It must have been all the exhilaration because I was a natural expert that made thoughts and sayings fly through my brain. There I'd be with blackie ball, holding her up in front of me, looking at her like I'm worshiping, and what came to me was the sentence "In the beginning was the WORD, and the word was GOD." And I had to look at blackie very hard for a few seconds, thinking about "In the beginning was the WORD." I love how extraordinary that sounds, nothing in the world but one word, out in the blackness, not even stars. One word. Sometimes I felt so queer, as if I weren't standing on firm ground, to think of it all starting with a couple of letters. Everyone thought I was concentrating or saying a prayer when I stared and then brought my arm down smooth, letting her go, and wham all the pins, all of them tumbling, and a second later they're swept away. You do the damage and bingo, it's gone. Bowling was a fantastic sport for my eyesight back then because it made me focus on faraway objects. When I was mad at something, I said, seeing the pins fall, "There goes Honey Creek. There goes Randall."

After bowling one night I got stuck in the car with Randall while May and Dee Dee went to buy gin at the liquor store. Randall tried to get me to hold hands with him. His hands were short and fat like lizard paws.

"Not on your life, Randall," I said, when he asked me.

"Why not?" he said, leaving his mouth hanging wide open. We were both in the back seat; naturally he took up over half of it. I had to smash myself up to the window. I didn't want to be near him. I didn't want to smell him up close.

I felt as if I were watching myself from way up near the ceiling light. I wasn't used to being in situations like this one. I heard myself sneer, "On account of I don't love you, Randall. I don't even like you."

"A person don't have to be in love to hold hands," he said. "I've touched hundreds of girls. It don't mean I have to marry any of them."

"Why don't you just go touch your other hundred girlfriends, then?" I mumbled. "If you ever mention the subject again I'll make sure Ma never buys sour cream and onion potato chips."

I didn't think about what I was saying. He made my dinner thrash around inside me. I couldn't stand the sight of him gripping his change purse, but after I spoke like a snide prom queen my knees went shaky and I felt a little sorry. But then again I couldn't help thinking that if only Randall had been in my class in school, all the bullying would have gone to him. I had a nightmare that I ended up married to him and all my babies were as big as full-grown Randall when they were born. Randall didn't speak to me after that. He turned his head away as if my presence disgusted him also.

Besides bowling we went for fish fries down at Johnny's on Friday nights. Johnny's has soft red paper that sticks off the wall, inviting you to pet it. May said I should keep my hands to myself. It was all you could eat on Friday nights for $3.99. May and I went down with Dee Dee and Randall and Daisy, and Daisy's younger sister, Lou, and Lou's friends. We'd have a long noisy table, everyone talking at the same time and grabbing for the onion rings and ketchup. None of the Footes had patience when it came to eating. I tried to sit far from Randall because he loved food so much, and because I was afraid he might grab my hand and squeeze it, to spite me.

Daisy didn't have a job and probably spent all day being photographed on different kinds of vehicles. She was supposed to behave, stick around, seriously look for employment, and quit drinking as part of her probation. The police had their eye on her every move because she stole and went driving around when she was smashed. She had hurt Mr. Kirk—a farmer with a wife and three children—so badly his arms and legs will never function. They couldn't absolutely prove it was Daisy's fault because no one saw the accident and Mr. Kirk failed the breath test too. Still, she was not allowed to go out at night unless she was with family members. For me, Johnny's was the special event of the week; for Daisy, spending Friday nights in a greasy restaurant with her family was like being tortured mercilessly. She said, "It takes me a whole week to get the smell of this dump out of my hair."

Sometimes she'd catch my eye and cock her head in the direction of the bar. She made my heart run and scramble just as it used to when I saw Miss Pin, my third-grade teacher. We'd go stand at the bar and talk while everyone else sat in the next room. Daisy said, "How come you don't ever say nothin' and I just jabber away?" She didn't give me time to answer. She said, "I wish everyone was like you, you know, friendly without always giving me the time of day."

I know I blushed at the compliment, before I continued to pant for more details. Daisy always described her favorite boyfriends and where they took her, before she was on probation. She always made them drive her to fancy clubs and restaurants, otherwise she wouldn't bother to date them. Secretly I was glad I wasn't a man of Daisy's, because she bossed them around and spent their money. They came home broke, wondering who she was going to go to next. She didn't ever mention a motorcycle to me, however. Daisy was either going to enroll in broadcasting school so she could be on the news, or beauty college. She couldn't decide which. "I think I'm a natural for communications," she said—but if she graduated a beautician she told me she'd always do me up for free. She said I was lucky to have curls but that a person had to show them to the best advantage. Her good taste made it possible for her to instantly say what could make a girl look beautiful. She tilted her head, inspecting my whole body. She made me feel like I was a frog but that she could almost imagine the fairy princess, if she whipped her brain into working overtime.

She explained that at beauty college she would learn to do stage makeup and facials, so she could go to New York and do makeup for ABC. Either that, or someone would be putting the makeup on her in New York, before she went on the set for the evening news to describe the fires and the murders. When Dee

Dee stuck her head in the bar to see if we had run off, Daisy gave her cold stares, practicing, I supposed, for the looks she'd give the weatherman when he predicted snow and ice.

Daisy told me about the classes she was supposed to attend where they teach you not to drink and drive at the same time. I bet she sat in the back row of the classroom with her arms folded, her feet on the seat in front of her, and stared the teacher down, letting him know she had never been subjected to such a boring human being in her entire life.

I could see both Daisy and Dee Dee in one of the books Charles Dickens wrote, because sometimes it seemed as if they were larger than life, on top of the fact that they were so greedy for trouble. Randall also could fit in the books perfectly. He could be the star boy in the schools Charles Dickens always has, where there are two hundred scrawny starved kids, and one boy who is fat and greasy. That's Randall for you. Daisy is certainly beautiful, but she assumed she didn't have to do one thing; she would always look glamorous and everyone would automatically love her for her looks alone. I did love her; I even worshiped her, but I knew she was no saint. She did hit-and-run accidents and thought nothing of it. She kept saying she was moving to Hollywood, California, one minute, and then New York City the next, to do makeup for famous people, such as soap opera stars, and one of the actors would fall for her and then they'd put her on TV. She said it would be a high-class program about police-women stopping criminals. We had to laugh over that one. I didn't like to tell her, but sometimes I had the feeling Daisy and I were going to be bowling forever right in Stillwater. We'd probably have heart attacks when we were eighty-five, down at the Town Lanes.

On the first anniversary of our commencement from high school May got word from Matt. He said he was planning to spend the summer out in Boston doing research. He wrote that he was sharing an apartment with a person named Virgil King. May looked up at me, worried. She said, "Ain't that a jigaboo name?"

I considered saying yes, to see if Matt's high standing would plummet, but there was a chance May would walk straight into the kitchen and stab herself. So I said, "It's probably just one of them common names out there in Boston."

My remark didn't comfort her any. She frowned, no doubt running over a list of who she might call to ask what black people name their children. It would have to be someone who knew but wouldn't wonder why May wanted such curious information.

She hadn't seen Matt since Christmas — and that time doesn't count. He came home for two days in late December; he didn't spend more than an hour with us, because he had teachers in town he wanted to talk to. It didn't bother me that Matt wasn't coming back for the summer. I already figured I'd never see him again.

It doesn't do one bit of good to say, If only . . . , but if that summer of 1974 hadn't happened to me, I know May and I would still be down at Trim 'N Tidy, rubbing our noses from the odor, polishing up the bowling trophy I won for the team. It was the summer, in the month of July, when we, all of us, weren't ever going to be the same again.

On a scorching night around Independence Day we were restless and irritated by every noise and movement. Even the bugs seemed nervous, due to the sultry weather. The mosquitoes buzzed extra loud in my ears. Daisy drove up in the truck when I wasn't doing anything but slouching on the porch. She had behaved herself and gotten her driving privileges back. She said she was going to go straight through the ceiling if she stayed in the house. It was too hot to do the usual activities she does with men so she was staying miles away from temptations. She said she was going to melt down any minute. All that you'd see if Daisy melted would be a patch of green eyeshadow on the carpet. May was so upset about Matt staying in Boston that she didn't notice what I was up to. She fanned herself with a magazine and flicked her hand at us. She didn't care if we drove to Toledo and back. We went out into the night, Daisy and I, climbed into the Footes' truck, Daisy revved the engine, and we bombed away. She had on lime green shorts with a halter top. Her perfect oval navel looked like someone yawning. Daisy laughed at me and said I looked like Miss Baily, our ex–gym teacher, who always wore shorts past her knees. We got to giggling over what a dried-up homo she was. In fact, I was wearing some prehistoric shorts of May's and a blue T-shirt that didn't show my shape, just the kind of thing Miss Baily wore every single day. We went over to the beach in Stillwater. There's a lake two miles outside of town where you pay fifty cents to get in, unless you wade in from the swamp, which is what Daisy and I did.

That night the full moon lit up a trail on the lake. I almost said out loud that it looked as if you could follow it and actually get somewhere, but I knew Daisy might push me over in the water for remarks of that sort. We didn't see too many people around, because it was a Tuesday, and because even the water looked hot. There was no relief. Probably everyone was at the movies just to feel the cool air and to think about ice and snow and salt on the roads. We couldn't help noticing the orange wooden boats parked upside down on the beach, with their oars tucked away inside. There was something inviting about the line of boat ends touching the hot waves. Daisy went and tipped one of them over; that's how she could be, acting as if everything belonged to her.

"How about a ride?" she said. She pushed the boat into the water and stuck one of her legs over the side. She kept telling me to hurry up, what was I waiting for, hell's half-acre to freeze solid? "Don't we wish, my friend," she said. "Come *on*, you Miss Baily look-alike."

"What are we going to do if we get caught?" I asked, standing in the water ankle deep with my sneakers on, trembling because she had called me "my friend." Also, I didn't like tampering with things that weren't mine.

"We'll get into trouble, but it ain't the worst thing that can happen to a person. It's better than roasting alive. They ain't gonna murder us just for borrowing a beat-up orange boat on a night when you can crack an egg in the water and it poaches. My armpits are soaking wet and stink worse than a piglet. GET IN, I'm gonna shove off."

So, we were out there in the water; I trailed my hands along while Daisy rowed. I stared up at the moon wondering if the man on the moon was as sad as he looked. If I were the moon, all silver, lighting up the water, transforming the earth, I'd feel pretty great about myself. Since we didn't have a light on the boat we couldn't see things as they were. There was an object in the middle of the lake that looked like an enormous piece of litter, as if a giant had wadded up his heavy-duty Kleenex and tossed it in the water. We couldn't figure out what it was. We were one hundred percent sure it wasn't a fishing boat. Daisy, of course, insisted on checking it out. She'd make a much better spy than a broadcaster. She'd have to learn to whisper before her first mission, though. What we came alongside of, after we rowed out, was an ordinary inner tube. A man lay still in it, looking as if he'd been drained of his blood for several weeks. We didn't say anything to him. He had his head resting on one side of the tube and his legs flopped over the other. He didn't have a shirt on. We could see the ivory skin of his moist stomach and chest shining. He was wearing sopping wet blue jeans, and he had a six-pack tied with a string around the tube. His eyes were closed and there was a stub of a cigarette hanging from his lips. There was something about him—the way he soaked up the beams and how serene he was, you could just tell it—that made me want to get in with him, see how it felt. Daisy leaned out of the boat, squinting at him, and then she started to snicker. She took

her oar and splashed him while she shouted, "DING DONG MORN-
ING, DING DONG MORNING."

"Hi, Mr. Ruby," Daisy said sweetly when he shook his head
in slow motion. The water didn't surprise him. He felt refreshed.
He must have been very far away because he had to look around
himself and blink and dunk his head back.

Finally he grinned at her and she splashed him twice more.
"You seen Mr. Party-face lately?" Daisy said to him.

Turns out they were familiar with the same probation officers.

I didn't register the conversation. Daisy did most of the talking
without bothering to introduce us. I couldn't help staring at Ruby,
because he looked as if he lived in the water. The inner tube
was home. He needed nothing to be happy except water, a few
beers, some damp cigarettes, and the moon shining down filling
him with the pure light.

"Don't all the fishes nibble your toes?" Daisy asked him. "Don't
they eat them up for live bait?"

"Yep," Ruby said, grinning at her again, as if he didn't care
if a snapping turtle came and bit his foot off.

I wouldn't have been surprised if he had a smooth black seal's
body under the water, if in a moment he pointed his nose in the
air and let out a hoarse bark. Daisy didn't notice that Ruby was
looking at me. He smiled. He asked me a couple of shy questions
with his grin and the curve of his eyebrows. I didn't know what
those questions were about, but I knew he was asking me. I don't
know what he saw in my face. Maybe the moonlight made me
look like Liz Taylor. I stared at him for more than five seconds,
until I couldn't stand it any longer and I had to quick squint at
the water. The little waves were giggling at my reeling heart. I
studied his reflection because I knew it was going to disappear if
I didn't watch it carefully. Don't ask me what Daisy talked about
because I didn't hear one word. Her loud voice was like a radio
too far off to pick up meaning. I only knew we were peaceful,
drifting in the water, and that after a while she said we had to

shove off, intimating that we had appointments to keep. Ruby stared at me with moonbeams on his teeth while we rowed away — made his incisors look like they were electrified. I could see him smiling, I was sure of it, until we got to shore.

I didn't ask Daisy one question about him. I wanted to make him up from scratch, without one single fact. He was a waterman, that much I knew; perhaps he was also an amphibian. I thought about how a person got cool on such a terrible night, in the water, without clothes.

Daisy put the boat back without turning it upside down as we found it, and she mentioned that I was so quiet, we might just as well get loaded. We drank quite a few tequila drinks and watched Johnny Carson in the bar. I could tell he was wanting to recite dirty jokes. He kept making snide remarks to the movie star he was talking to and snickering into his chest. The liquor we drank made me want to hug something large, such as a continent. Daisy was flirting with the bartender and so I sat squeezing the leather on my chair, feeling my empty arms growing heavier.

Three nights later, on league night, May came down with her quarterly headache. Matt was responsible for them. She knew he had made a new life for himself that was leading him directly into the fire. Perhaps she was wondering how she was going to commute from heaven to hell, if God issues passes so you can visit your children. She told me I should go bowling on account of league night. They'd need me to score. She said, "I'll call Dee Dee and tell her to give you a ride." Even though she couldn't bowl to save her life, it mattered to her that we whip the pants off of all the teams in Stillwater. She celebrated seriously when Trim 'N Tidy destroyed the other teams.

Dee Dee obeyed May's orders and picked me up. She told me about Randall's hemorrhoids on the way. Right there in the parking lot, when I got out of the car at Town Lanes, was the waterman smoking and sniffing the air, perhaps searching the skies for signs of intelligence. My heart took a trip down to my knees, paid vacation. I stood staring until Dee Dee said, "Are you froze to the car door?"

I mumbled no and tripped over the curb.

That was the night we were killing the Red Bell Market. I made strike after strike without sweating a drop. Artie kept saying, "Sweetheart, are you hot!"

Everyone was waiting for me to have my turn to see if I could do it again—they were primed to whoop and stamp. All the check-out girls from the Red Bell looked genuinely glum, because there wasn't a chance in the world for them. Without May to bring our average down our team had the possibility for greatness. After each strike I turned around trying not to smile, and walked coolly down to my seat. Then I couldn't help it; I beat on the table and flashed a smile at my friends. I knew I was doing a spectacular job. I'm crazy about bowling when I score off the charts. I was also noticing my waterman, Ruby. His name is a precious gem. He sat at the bar watching my every move—I know, because I felt his gaze burning through my back when I stood at the line. He stared at me, only it wasn't at all like Randall's look, which made me sure he was going to eat me whole. Ruby stared as if he would never stop searching for my face, because he knew he would find something good there. He stared as if he was compelled to see me. Maybe he had never noticed magazine photos of beautiful people. I swear he admired the way I stood up to bowl, and with each turn I became more and more flamboyant, for him alone. I waltzed after I made points and hollered, trying to mimic Daisy. I knew I could score 300 forever if only he was there observing my form.

In the tenth frame of the third game I cocked my head so I could see him out of the corner of my eye. He was gone. In my two shots he had disappeared. I turned around and scanned the room; then I rushed out to the bar and over to the vending machines. I no longer cared about smearing the Red Bell Market, and as I knocked my empty head against the pay phone I realized that with him gone there was no reason for doing anything any more. The shell of me slumped down on the yellow sofa until Artie came to fetch me for my turn. My streak was over, although we still won hands down.

I didn't see a sign of him for an entire week. I looked for him everywhere I went. I searched the aisles in the grocery store knowing that if I ran into him, within an instant my tongue would dislodge and moss would cover my brain. I wondered if he floated away because he didn't belong to anyone. He lived his life on rivers and lakes. There wasn't a minute when I didn't dream about his coming to find me. He had a silver boat glistening even without moonshine, and we went sailing away. We had delicious fish to eat, boneless, plus we didn't ever get seasick, not once. Finally we turned into swimming creatures and never came back to land. There weren't dry cleaners or chicken manure in the deep sea, and we communicated only by loving gestures.

Then one day, when I was weighing a pile of filthy blankets, I looked up to see him, out of water, coming into Trim 'N Tidy. He stood at the door smiling at me, and I had to smile back, breathless with surprise, at his face in daylight. He stared and grinned, showing all his rotten teeth. Something woke up in me, something that was hiding, although it used to come alive in particular spots of Miss Finch's books, such as the one about Madame Bovary. Miss Finch never knew I ordered the tape from the library. She had told me once that it wasn't an appropriate book for me. I took it home and sweated through most of it. When Madame Emma was in the hotel with one of her men, she locked the door and then her bathrobe fell away from her shoulders, and there she was standing at the door with nothing on, her body calling out for what the man had.

When I saw Ruby shifting back and forth on his feet, looking at me, I wished I had the bathrobe at my shoulders, that I could let it fall. All of a sudden I longed to own a bathing suit that would barely cover me, and I desperately wanted Ruby to first slowly stroke the motorcycle I would of course be sitting on, and then he'd find me with his hands.

He told me he had a sweater he needed clean because he had somewhere special to go. He made his speech deliberately. I could tell he had practiced saying the words. I weighed the sweater without checking the scale. I glanced up at him and looked at the ground, back and forth. Ruby has wide blue eyes that look straight at a person, and he doesn't blink all that much. He smiles to show off his crooked teeth, the dead and the living. His brown hair that day was plastered to his head because he always wore a Cubs baseball hat. It's the team that doesn't ever win. But it was his eyes, reflecting the kindness, and his broad steady smile that had me caught. He wasn't asking me questions; he was saying, "Here I am." When Ruby keeps his mouth shut he's especially handsome. He isn't exactly devoted to his dentist. May, at least, sent us to the dentist every so often so we wouldn't have to have our teeth pulled. She restricted our sugar intake because she said not having her teeth spoiled her pleasure in just about everything. Ruby told me that when he was little his father tied his front tooth to a doorknob and then closed the door. The tooth refused to budge but a few months later it turned black and died. I'm not sure if it's a true story, or if he got it from one of the Three Stooges movies.

At Trim 'N Tidy Ruby and I stared at each other and time stopped. I kept thinking about water, how gently it lapped his inner tube, how peaceful we all were, Daisy talking almost quietly into the night. I shivered and had to look away, and then he said he had never seen a lady bowl so professional before. He was talking about me. I had to laugh, because he complimented me just the way I liked to hear.

When he came to pick up his sweater the next day he said all in a stream, "Do you want to go to the bar across the road for a drink after work?" He had to clear his throat and say it all again, so I could understand him. I had to grin to myself because Ruby swaggered so confidently with the clumsy shoes he wore—they had chunky wooden heels—but when he opened his mouth you could tell his nerves were on edge. I knew that we were two humans, that's all, two humans walking around blindly in the night, looking for a warm hand.

"Hold on," I said. I went to find May to tell her that I had an invitation. I wished I had a better outfit on. I was wearing dark blue stretch pants and a faded sleeveless shirt decorated with rosebuds. Daisy as usual had issued her compliments earlier in the day: she had said my outfit looked like something people in the depression wore. May came out and looked Ruby up and down, mumbling phrases under her breath. Perhaps she was comparing him to her handsome and dead Willard Jenson. She said to him, "Don't be late with her."

We walked across the street watching out for every pebble on the road. We sat down and Ruby ordered a beer and then I did too. We didn't say anything. Finally he asked me, "Do you want some peanuts?" and I said, "Sure." I felt embarrassed even having a mouth to put food in. It didn't seem like a girl should eat; it didn't seem like eating was how dates got to like each other. Then, after hours of grinning and eating, staring at the walls and the ceiling, picking skin around our cuticles, I mentioned how peaceful he looked in the inner tube, and he said, Yeah, he liked it out there in the middle of the lake, only thing that bothered a person was flies, but that was something he could pretty much handle.

"I love being outside more than just about anywhere," I said.

He took a big swallow of beer. His fingers gripping the glass were dirty.

"Yeah," he said.

We grinned at each other some more. It was a nice habit we were getting into.

"I used to get up at six in the morning and fish until night," he said. "I got some fish, sheesh, you wouldn't believe the size of them babies, my old man had to drag me in at night by the ears. I didn't want to stop catching fish."

He told me about his lures and the bait. He loved night crawlers. He'd watch the fish come up, stuck through a bright red and yellow lure. "I'd watch them flap around for a couple of minutes," he said, "and then I'd throw them back. Boy, were they relieved." He laughed a great ha-ha, which sounded like something that didn't quite belong to him. Still, I had a clear picture of little Ruby fishing in a dazzling white T-shirt, with every single white tooth in his mouth. I saw him, by himself for hours, listening to the water and the bees buzzing around him on the bank.

"What did you think about all day long there by the river?" I asked him, putting a peanut in my mouth as primly as I could.

"Stuff," he said. "I looked at the water floating by. I liked being warm and peaceful. Sometimes I didn't even have my line in the water, I just slept on the bank. I sure liked being warm and peaceful."

When he said those words I knew we were meant for each other. There wasn't one doubt in my mind. It happened that quickly.

We were on our third beer when I told Ruby that I had an aunt named Sidney in De Kalb.

"You ever been there?" he asked.

"A couple of times," I lied. I tried to look like I had done that a million and one times, had beers with a man, but my teeth were chattering, and also the undersides of my thighs were quivering against the seat, so I could barely make sense.

"What do you do besides pretend you're a fish out in the middle of the lake?" I whispered, changing the subject. That question made him grin again for at least a minute. He liked my teasing. He told me he worked at the gas station and they were all set to make him manager, but then the boss got mad at him for no reason and shouted, "You're fired."

"That ain't fair," I said, and he shook his head and said he was looking for another job. He said he could get a job at the glass factory they have in Stillwater. Only it got so noisy in there, and he had real fragile ears. He couldn't tolerate too much noise.

"I was born with them that way," he told me, and I felt right then and there like leaning over and kissing his feeble ears.

I couldn't believe I was with the waterman. It was crazy to hear him utter words, after I had seen him in my dreams, a sea animal, without a drop of human blood. To tell the truth—and it probably is not a revelation—I had had fantasy dreams about him ever since I met him: he was a seal, black and shiny, barking at me. We were always swimming together with our legs touching, our stomachs rubbing close when we rolled over—when we were playing games.

Each time I looked up at him I had a jolt. I had to connect the person talking to me with the one my mind had created. I bit my tongue so I'd know here I was in the flesh having romance like I had seen on TV all my life. I didn't think anything like it would ever happen to me. I always put myself in other people's shoes, people such as Emma Bovary or Elizabeth Bennet. I imagined I was them, and then love came to me.

Once I opened my mouth, after the third beer, I couldn't stop talking to Ruby. I told him things I never mentioned to anyone, not even Aunt Sid. He made me tell the secrets because he looked straight into my face and smiled, and because he fished all day long by the river when he was young. I told him about one of my favorite sights in the world: old Wendell Kate riding his bike down the road herding his cows and pumping his horn. Ruby nodded and looked at me with beer foam on his lips, making a mustache, and then I blurted that I loved, almost more than anything, the first spring peepers singing up from the marsh, come April, and how full of longing the little frogs must be, wanting a mate so desperately after being frozen all winter long. I felt my whole head thunk on the floor and glow like an ember when I mentioned the word *mate*. He smiled and gazed at me with his wide blue eyes, hardly blinking. He listened carefully to my words. He listened like Miss Finch used to. I knew he understood my thoughts. I quickly said that I always sniffed the earth and wished on stars and that I knew something powerful was going to take me from Honey Creek. I said it so Ruby would hear me and maybe make my plans come true.

Afterwards, before he took me home, we went up to Andrew's Hill, the hunting grounds outside of Honey Creek, because of what I said about liking to sniff the earth. We stood outside and were quiet together, breathing deeply, and he watched me, as if he had to have lessons in breathing. He watched my chest rise and fall. When we got into the car he spoke slowly, his grin spreading across his face as he moved closer. He said, "Do you want to see my little one-eyed snake?"

"Sure," I said. I didn't mind snakes. They usually had fancy designs on their backs. There must be reasons for the patterns but I didn't know what they could be. I thought maybe Ruby could teach me — maybe he was an expert on nature.

He stretched both his arms around me and started kissing my mouth, first softly on the outside and then he went inside. Our teeth clacked together. For a long time I saw nothing but searing white light with my eyes closed. The whiteness filled me up until in a flash I saw Madame Bovary letting her bathrobe go. The next part happened before I could open my eyes: I felt my slacks down at my knees; he yanked them down, he was saying, "Oh *God*, baby, oh *Christ* in a convertible." He was hurting me with a dagger, reaching under and inside. I cried out but he didn't hear. He had my arm in his grip while he pricked the skin with his teeth. When he let go he laughed one minute and then moaned the next. He kept shouting, "JesusJesusJesusJesus," for a reason I couldn't understand. When he was done—it didn't take more than one long minute—he collapsed on top of me. He shuddered. I could see his half-closed eyes, just the white part. When he opened his eyes he laughed again. He told me to wait, he'd make me feel better. He said he was Mr. Magic Fingers, some friend had told him so. I was whimpering, a sound I hate to think of. Even though he rocked me in his stiff arms I still wanted to cry, because I was so dumb about all the things a person is supposed to know about in life. I cried because Ruby didn't hear my shaking voice. I wanted to escape from him, but there he was holding me in his arms like I'm newly born, saying so jubilantly, "Baby, you'll get to like what we was just doing, take it from expert me. I never met a lady that didn't go crazy in the sack."

I didn't believe anything he said. I sniffed and swallowed and watched a firefly make its way along the floor of the car. He was attentive for a minute; he patted my head with his filthy hands. It wasn't exactly like on some TV shows I've seen where the man breaks into the apartment, takes the girl with a lead pipe at her head, and then dumps her on the sofa.

When I got home May asked me with a queer grin on her face, Was I in one piece? And I sat at the table eating some old stale cake smiling down at it, except I wanted to die right then and there, because I didn't know who the good people were. I ran out of the house, wishing I could crawl into the ground, join the worms. I stumbled up to the plateau where I always go, and I wept.

When I stopped I rolled over on my back, tired and wet. I looked up to the sky, to the Swan constellation. I looked up to all the untroubled stars shining down on me from so far away. Something inside, maybe the part of me that's the best bowler in the universe, whispered faintly that I was more than an animal, and I tried to remember Miss Finch telling me I had good thoughts—good thoughts, she said. And every time the memory came to me, of Ruby and his cruelty, I thought of Aunt Sid, the liar, saying how big the world is, and how, when she conducts her chorus and sees all the wide open mouths and hears the music coming out of them, she knows there's a force, perhaps born of the earth itself, that insists on beauty.

Nine

A COUPLE of days later Daisy came strutting into Trim 'N
Tidy. She leaned way over on the counter, sweeping her
tongue along the outside of her mouth, as if her lips were made
of butterscotch candies. She started singing the song "Love Is a
Many-Splendored Thing," in an opera star voice. I've heard those
singers on TV. They sound scared to death. I turned my back
on Daisy. I stood between the racks, plastic on both sides of me.
She called out, "Does he kiss good?" She knew I didn't know
anything about kissing. She reminded me of Missy Baker and
Diane Crawford, jeering. I was standing between all the plastic
bags that say, "CAUTION — PLASTIC CAN CAUSE SUFFOCATION." I
didn't need plastic. I was smothering in my own skin, and Daisy
thought it was funny. She moved on to a tuneless song, singing
the words "I need you, I want you," over and over.

I felt feverish, and couldn't stop trembling. Finally I had to
turn around and shout, "*Stop it, Daisy.*" Tears streamed down
my cheeks, into my frowning mouth, past my chin. She couldn't
believe the way I looked. She came behind the counter
quickly — regular people aren't supposed to do that — looking so
worried. I loved her wrinkled forehead. She asked, "What's the

matter?" That question uncorked me. I cried my head off on her shoulder. I got her black shirt with the silver letters B-I-T-C-H all wet. Daisy went back and told Artie I had to have a little break; she said I was having my period and I needed to walk to distract myself from the pain.

Daisy and I went up the highway to the Dairy Queen. We sat on the picnic benches and I told her what Ruby had done to me and how I was sure I had been sliced in half. I said I didn't ever want to do that again, and Daisy giggled. She said she couldn't help it. She explained that the first time *is* like sitting on a spike but there is improvement like you wouldn't believe. She put her arm around me and said, "Don't worry, you have that first experience behind you now." She said, "Ruby likes you so much. He was too crazy for you."

"How come he's on probation?" I asked her, blowing my nose on Dairy Queen's napkins. It was the first time I wondered, seriously, if he had done something against the law, but she said, "He ain't on probation. He got a little kooky after his old ma died, and went around smashing stuff, nothin' major. He just goes to that same class I do for drunk drivers. The teacher likes him because he don't mouth off. He sits so quiet. I ain't sure what he did before," she said, handing me another napkin, "but it wasn't anything too terrible."

Drunk driving didn't bother me. I know it isn't responsible, but just about everyone in Honey Creek, including May, drives around smashed now and then. The bars are all out of town so you can't help driving home a little tipsy. Most of all, I was worried that he went around showing hundreds of girls his little one-eyed snake, but Daisy said, "Far as I know he don't have a girlfriend, besides you.

"Don't kill me, OK?" she said, trying not to crack a smile.

"I won't," I said, even though I had the feeling I might want to.

"I told Ruby where you worked, and about league night—

I've never seen a man wanting to know a girl so bad. I told him he should take something into Trim 'N Tidy to get cleaned. I was his coach, see. He really thinks you're a hot little number."

"Thanks, Daisy," I said, trying to scowl.

She bought me an ice cream to make up for it. I didn't mention to her that somewhere inside of me I kept saying the words over and over to myself: "He thinks you're a hot little number." I went into the ladies' room and looked at my face, trying to see it through Ruby's eyes. I had hives all over from crying, and my eyes were puffy. I wasn't exactly at my best.

We walked slowly up the road. I knew I was going to be embarrassed talking to Artie. He thought it was the time of the month for me. He didn't do anything but pat my shoulder once as he rushed by.

All afternoon I pictured Daisy and the girls she told me about who went out with men and let them perform all types of maneuvers on and in their bodies. Daisy described some of the details. She didn't blush. She said on her dates sometimes she kneeled on the floor of the truck and put her mouth places I wouldn't think could taste — good; that's putting it mildly. Still, Daisy and her acquaintances didn't look so happy for the fancy sensations. It isn't nice to say of my best friend, but I knew Daisy was a cheap girl. There wasn't anyone who truly loved her. She didn't have strong attachments to her partners either. She used her men for their money and their certain body parts, and if she was lucky she was finished with them before they got tired of her. She gave herself away to millions; she sucked on them like they were food for life and then she spat it out. Even though I wasn't an expert on men I understood that she didn't have perfect bliss in life. She was restless without knowing why.

It was true that I didn't have experience with men, except for Elmer, and he doesn't count. And Matt, of course, but he never had much of a body; he was a brain stuck on a pole. Artie, my boss, was one man I liked. He called his wife Dumpling — always made me smile to hear it. Also, I tolerated the Rev. He isn't too bad, if you don't consider the crazy stories he believes in.

However, Mr. Darcy was the man I truly admired. I see him clearly. He is exceptionally tall, and his head is covered with black curly hair. He looks serious except when he smiles at you; it knocks you right straight across the room. His smile is that brilliant. He doesn't ever do anything to hurt girls. I longed for him to walk out of his book and reach for my hand.

I didn't see Ruby for the longest time, but I couldn't stop thinking about him. There was something woke up in me — I started saying to myself, in bed, "If Ruby doesn't kiss me by tomorrow night, I'm going to actually die." I reminded myself of the wild dogs who attack and kill sheep. Once the dogs get the taste of blood in their mouths they keep coming back to injure the poor innocent animals. I had learned a new sensation and I had to have some more of it instantly. I wanted terribly to kiss Ruby's mouth, more than eating food, or drinking, or sleeping. It was the craziest predicament, because first I never wanted to see him again, after the trick he played on me, but then he crept into my head, thinking, as he did, that I was a hot number. His opinion of me had to make me see him in a slightly different light. He noticed I had good points. Maybe he liked my nose, it isn't so bad, and the tone of my voice, and the way I teased him a little. Daisy said he couldn't help himself, that he was attracted to me. Far as I know, he was the first man in the history of the universe who noticed that I had a feminine lure.

I ate breakfast with my spoon in the cereal bowl stirring around, not knowing what my hand was up to. All I saw was blue eyes. I had to hope against all hope that Ruby's pizza became my face when he sat down to eat. To tell the truth, I wanted him to think of me, and only me, continuously. I made a big request to the Maker, that this be so. Each night I went up to the plateau to talk, not to the stars or God, but to Ruby. He was listening to me, I knew he was. I repeatedly relived the beers we drank, and the words we said, and the kiss we gave each other in his car — only I didn't go one step farther than the kiss. I re-created history: I had Ruby telling me I was the most beautiful girl he had ever seen; he couldn't keep himself away, he just couldn't help loving me, and then we stared at each other indefinitely — until we almost dropped dead. When he drove me home we met May on the doorstep and we all had to laugh over how stifling the weather was, how miserable the entire summer had been.

In the night I dreamed I was just like Daisy, kneeling on the floor of his car, making him cry out, and he always did the same thing to me with his expert tongue.

Then, about three weeks after our date, he walked into Trim 'N Tidy. The blood drained from my legs, every single last drop. I felt it wanting to seep out my toenails. There I stood like I didn't have limbs, like there was nothing to my body except a fierce heart, thumping out of sync. The Madame Bovary hot juicy flashes came over me. I didn't invite the feelings, but they were present nonetheless. Ruby grinned at me from the door and stared sweetly with his wide eyes. They weren't blinking much. When he started to talk he blinked numerous times, to make up for all the seconds when his eyeballs didn't have moisture washing over them.

"Do you want to get a drink at Mabel's?" he asked, and I murmured weakly, "Sure."

When we sat down at our spot in the bar I looked at him, and even though I wanted to go straight to the back seat of his car and try what he did before, because Daisy said I'd got my first experience out of the way, I mumbled, "I'm not about to handle that one-eyed snake of yours."

It took all my gumption to speak. My teeth were loose and chattering inside my closed mouth.

I think I expected him to grin at me forever, but he didn't. He looked down at his hands and frowned. He couldn't say anything. I tried to peek under, to see his face. His head was bowed so low it practically touched the table.

"What's the matter?" I asked.

"You don't like me no more," he said, turning away.

I had to laugh because he was such a bashful person behind his cocky walk. Without thinking I took his hands in mine. He had long slim fingers that curled around my hand the instant we touched, as if he'd been waiting for something to hold on to for a long time.

"Course I like you, Ruby," I whispered. "I want to know you so bad."

His face changed gradually. He wasn't positive I meant it, but after I said the words again his big old grin came back, like the sun on the rise: first you see a ray of light and it gets brighter until finally there's this burst, and it's morning. I was powerfully strong, capable of making a person feel brilliant and sure. And for the first time I had nerve. For once in my life I wasn't going to let people pull up my dress and look underneath.

I said to Ruby, "I like discussing the river but I just ain't ready for . . ." I couldn't say exactly, but he knew what I was talking about. I said I wanted all the sensations in my body to go slowly. I didn't want to miss out on one feeling. Then I had to whisper in his defective ears, "You can kiss me all you want," and he did, right away, there in the bar. He kissed me all over my face while I sat still and shivered. I loved his face so close to mine.

He said he was sorry for hurting me in the car. He said, "Baby, I thought you maybe done that millions of times!"

"I never had no boyfriend before," I told him.

"I don't believe it." He stared at me and shook his head. "I don't believe it."

"I ain't lying to you—you was my first kiss."

"Which closet you been hiding in?" He was amazed I was such a late bloomer. He said, "Wasn't you ready to explode?" and then he looked bashful again, because of his appetite.

I felt so glad, being together, apologizing. Later, we drove down to Honey Creek, and he sang to me; he sang, "You're sixteen, you're beautiful, and you're mine."

I didn't ask him where he learned about girls. I didn't want to hear how many others he had kissed. Daisy told me Hazel taught him. She's an old bag in Stillwater. She pretends she's a young girl still, but she couldn't fool anyone. She has crimson hair—it isn't her natural color, I can tell you that much. It's in tight curls, looks like her head is killing her, and she wears blouses that are open all the way down to her waist. They lace up the front. She wears them loose so you can see her fake leopard-skin bra. Plus her jeans are too small for her pot belly that wants to pop out of her fly. She's real sensual, all right. You can hear her coming a million miles away in her spike-heeled cowboy boots. The wrinkles on her neck are the giveaway: she's at least fifty years old. I thought females were dried up by then. Daisy said that even though Hazel looked ferocious she was a kitten underneath, that she treated Ruby decently most of the time. She said she saw them hugging outside of Dino's once, after Hazel got mad at him and chased him around the bar with a fly swatter in one hand and a broken beer bottle in the other. I guess Ruby didn't visit her too much any more. She found some other boys she liked better. I didn't ask him questions about her. I didn't want to know anything else about his education.

At supper the next night I asked May if Ruby could come bowling with us, and she said he didn't look like he had too much upstairs—the way he grinned at people, he looked like a fool. I said I had my own eyes and Ruby looked just fine to me.

"Well, if you ain't gonna turn feisty on me, on account of some man with bugged-out eyes and a girl's name."

She didn't look so hot herself. We were eating sweet corn, and she had a bunch of hulls stuck between her teeth. She said, "Don't you know that he wrecked Viola Hanson's car, plus he stole something from the gas station where he worked?" She spoke as if Ruby were a famous bandit, when in fact she had never heard about him before I met him. She got her information from Dee Dee. I looked down at the table and I saw the sweet blue eyes of Ruby's and the way he sniffed the earth and looked out to the universe—and I raised my voice. I said, "Are you perfect?"

"I've seen you loaded and driving too," I mentioned, leaning toward her. "I've seen the way you squished Daddy down so much he left you. He never did anything right in your smart opinion; you was *always* at his heels. That's what you did, Ma, you squished Daddy so much he drove down the road. He likes me and Matt. He sends us ten dollars when he thinks it's our birthday. He don't ever do that for you."

She froze. Her eyes were fixed on my face. "You just ain't no angel," I said slowly, to wrap it up.

She looked at me as if I were a complete stranger. I thought perhaps her head would collapse from the weight of the reprimand, into something akin to a pancake, but the next minute I could tell she wanted to wallop me. She started to raise her hand.

"Don't touch me, Ma," I begged. "I just want to be a little happy. Ruby don't do real bad stuff," I pleaded. "And he likes me—he's good to me."

May snorted. She shoved her chair back and got up to slam some objects around. I didn't say anything more, and after a few crashes, metal on metal, she came back to the kitchen and sank into her seat. She stared at the table. Finally she slapped the potholder down and said, "I'll kill you if you get a baby and you're not married, understand?"

I said she could be sure I wasn't going to do that.

If I got pregnant without a husband I'd be like Dee Dee's daughter Lou. Then May would have to live in Dee Dee's shoes, and that's one place she didn't want to experience. May didn't pay too much attention to my answer. She was watching me drift away. She saw me getting married and blasting off in the getaway car decorated with tin cans. I could see plainly on her face that she was thinking to herself. She was asking, Who's going to take care of me when I'm over the hill? How am I going to pay the bills with my puny salary? She was watching herself move into the low-income housing apartments in Stillwater. The walls are cardboard, and there's millions of kids chasing up and down the halls. You can smell everyone's cooking and there isn't a back yard for a garden. She was picturing herself without a soul in the world. Her narrow eyes said to me, I don't need you; go ahead, leave. But I knew she wished I'd run to her feet and kiss her slippers that look like dirty carpet you let the dog sleep on. She wished I'd say, I'll never ever leave you, Ma, please be my friend. I had to laugh at her fears. I had about one hundred dollars in my old plastic pig. How was I supposed to pick up and leave? Did she imagine that Ruby was actually a millionaire disguised as a drunk driver? He didn't even have a job.

May was sore over what I said about Elmer, even though she knew I was right, and that she couldn't make an argument. It was a wound that festered for a long time. She didn't forget easily. She put the fight away, for a later date. Her big worry right at the moment was getting old and uglier, and being left alone. She was going to be left to rot away. She'd tell me details at supper out of the blue. She'd push her chair back, and she'd say, "All them piles of dirty diapers that I used to wash." She said having babies made her body change its shape drastically. May had the habit of saying, "Don't have kids, they let you down each time." She had a nick on her nipple where I bit her once. She made it clear that I owed her something. I owed her double, since we both knew Matt wasn't going to come through.

At any rate, Ruby came bowling with us, and I have to admit as a bowler he was a lost cause. He couldn't get that ball to go anywhere except the gutter. He laughed and turned around to find me when he didn't knock one pin down. I felt like part of a big family, though: there was May and Dee Dee and Daisy and Ruby and Artie, even Randall with his Bit O' Honey, sitting around making sure we weren't cheating on the score sheet. Daisy and Ruby talked about their social workers down at the resource center and the different times they got crocked.

In those days I didn't write Aunt Sid too much because I couldn't explain how it was for me, and I was afraid she might not like me any more if she knew I drank alcohol and spent half my life in a bowling alley. I didn't want her to know I thought about Ruby every single minute. Aunt Sid, with her choir and lilies pinned to her chest, might think I'm trash and stop telling me I'm a good person. I couldn't stand to think of that, so I wrote her short letters saying Trim 'N Tidy was perfect, and May hadn't bawled me out too much, telling me to say, "Have a nice day." I mentioned briefly that I kind of liked to bowl and that we all went to Town Lanes occasionally.

Aunt Sid wrote back and asked me, "Have you read a good book lately?"

I knew I disappointed her. The cassette recorder she had given me didn't work any more. I only thought about the blind tapes. They were living inside of me: there were thousands of different characters milling around saying advice, telling their stories to each other. There was Huck Finn, giving Madame Bovary a ride down the Mississippi, telling her not to worry about her dumb husband and all the cash she owed people for silk shawls and other things she couldn't resist. They lay on that raft, smelled the muddy water, and she called the clouds names of men from her village. She wanted to kiss Huck like crazy but she knew it wasn't appropriate. She controlled herself pretty carefully. I didn't tell Aunt Sid that now when I conjured up Mr. Darcy he looked almost exactly like Ruby. I wondered if Mr. Darcy had rotten teeth. Maybe he did because I bet in those days they didn't have dentists. I heard on the radio that people in England eat pounds of sugar and their teeth aren't good like ours over here in the U.S.

Ruby and I went out to various dark places. We drank beer and talked about fishing. We kissed like wild horses in the back of his car. He always said, "Please, baby, come on, come on," and I had to say, like someone's mother, "That's enough now," even though I wanted it all as fiercely as he did. It seemed like there wasn't anything more important on earth except having him near me that way. Buildings could burn right next to us in the car, and if we were in the middle of a kiss we wouldn't notice. I was learning about the perverse streaks within us: for example, I knew Ruby admired me for my strict control. We were experiencing something serious partly because I wasn't like Hazel or Daisy, just letting the man have his way. We were developing a friendship; I can say in perfect truth that that's what it was. Ruby would say to me, "You must be a goddess or somethin'," and I'd smile at him mysteriously. He teased me; he'd say, "Baby, you a nun underneath your clothes?"

Sometimes, maybe it isn't very nice, I felt I had him eating out of my hand, the way he whispered into my face, "Ain't you a goddess?" We had such sweet times in his car, parked up on Andrew's Hill, in the hunting grounds. With the windows open, we sat, watching the night go by us, feeling that we were the only people who had ever breathed the air together and admired the evening.

I had to feel sorry for Ruby because he didn't have an easy life. You could tell it by looking at him. He smiled too much. He was covering up aches he didn't want to speak of. One time, we were down at Mabel's and Ruby was guzzling more than usual. Instead of getting raucous and joyful, he became more somber with each drink. I didn't know what to do so I talked about nothing. Finally he interrupted me; he said, "Baby, what happens when someone dies?"

"Huh?" I said.

"Where do they go?" He was starting to cry.

I thought of all the carcasses of sheep I had seen in my life, sinking into the pasture until all you saw was a rib cage and skull, picked clean.

"They don't go anywhere, Ruby, far as I know." I figured I

might as well tell it like it was. "Their bodies rot in the ground, and all you have left is the memory. It's up to you to remember the person." It was no comfort but I didn't know what else to say except, "That's about it."

He was bawling into his sleeve, and I felt so sorry. I took his hands and held them with all my might. "Don't think about it," I said. "We're here now, and—and I love you so much."

I wasn't planning on saying those words but there they were. Ruby stopped crying instantly. He blinked several times, and wiped his nose on his sleeve.

I leaned across the table and put my hand on his face to make him know better. I whispered again, "I love you, Ruby."

He burst into a grin and then jumped up and started dancing around, as if he were a wind-up bear and my words had activated him. He made me laugh until my side ached. He went up to the bar and told the farmers he didn't even know that I loved him. He went to each one and said, "See that lady? She loves me."

Then he came back and took my hand and kneeled on the floor, like a chivalrous knight. He put his head in my lap. He kept saying, "Sweet baby, sweet baby, baby, baby." He's the silliest person in the world at times, Ruby is. What I wanted him to do was marry me. Then we'd climb into bed and it'd be like a ship. We'd sail away.

I didn't think too hard about what it meant to get married. I figured I wanted to be a wife because I loved Ruby, and I could tell he needed a girl to cook him good food and buy him clean undershirts. I figured with those three ingredients, especially counting true love, a person couldn't go wrong being married. I didn't stop to think because I knew I was plunging headfirst toward happiness. In addition, I was fed up watching the world march by me. I couldn't stand seeing people such as Daisy's little sister Lou have a baby. They named her Midnight Star Sandra Dee.

The baby was called Midnight for short, but maybe when she went to first grade she'd want to be Sandra Dee. "She's got the option," is how Daisy explained it. Lou was sixteen years old and already she was a mother. I knew if I didn't hurry up I was going to be past the prime in no time flat. They brought Midnight over on their way home from the hospital. Lou said when the baby came out her toenails were already long and they had to cut them right away. I couldn't stop looking at the baby, complete with all her parts. I couldn't get over how she started with Lou and one of three possible boys who cornered her one night by the drugstore while she giggled. "In the beginning was that old word," always comes to me. That's a sentence the Rev uses nearly every Sunday. Maybe inside of me all that existed, besides I LOVE RUBY, were letters floating around in my body, the names of my babies. When I saw Midnight Star Sandra Dee, I knew I wanted to be in a family. I knew I wanted to look after a baby, all mine. I could picture Ruby and me, the father and the mother. I conjured up Ruby coming home from work, singing. I'd be feeding our baby something delicious from a jar.

A couple of nights after I told Ruby the news, exactly how I felt about him, he came over and we went outside. I took him to the woods because I couldn't wait to show him some of my favorite places. We were listening to the crickets in the grass. I've always wanted to sneak up on crickets so they keep making their racket even while I'm close. Although they quit singing we could almost feel them breathing. I could imagine myself a cricket with my antennae on alert sensing two pairs of gigantic feet coming closer, and being too terrified to squeak or run. When we moved away they started up again. They were so relieved. We were sitting on a blanket listening, when Ruby said, "Baby, you make my crazy head feel better, you know that. You're so sweet and nice."

I lapped up all the words. I asked him to say that sentence over again.

He didn't say anything for a second. He took a deep breath and then whispered, "How about you and me get married?" I quick told him, "Yes, yes, yes, yes."

He took a ring out of his pocket. He said he bought it with Green Stamps once, and couldn't figure out why he did it, but now he knew he had been saving it for me. It had been for me all along. It had five sparkling diamonds in a row. Ruby put it on my finger and said now we were engaged and I was his girl. I said that was just fine with me. There's times I wish I could have keeled over and died right then and there.

Ten

IT was the end of August when Ruby proposed to me, when we were out in the woods and he slipped diamonds on my finger. He put his head on my lap and I stroked his hair. We talked about our romance, remembering the high points. Ruby told me Daisy gave him advice all the time, in particular after our first date. She told him I was pretty upset and what he should do to make friends with me again. They rehearsed speeches he could say to make me forgive him. She even gave him pointers on proposing. We laughed over Daisy and what a busybody she can be. I was engaged to be married; I couldn't be angry at Daisy for running my life.

When it started to rain, and we were damp and uncomfortable, I figured I better tell May what we were up to, get it over with. Ruby and I kissed leaning against his car. I half wanted to get in, forget the wedding, and drive off with him to the wilds of Indiana.

I came into the kitchen where May was making pickles. She had on her pickle apron, the green one with yellow flowers that stretches across the hill of her middle and ties in a large crisp bow at the back. The whole place smelled like dill and vinegar, so strong I'm sure the stench in there could have cured any disease you had, guaranteed. I sat down and put my hands out on the table, with the five diamonds showing. While she stuffed pickles in the quart jar — she packed them in so there wasn't any air space — I said, "Ma, I'm going to marry Ruby." She didn't even quit stuffing; she laughed as if I'd just told her the joke of the year. She said, "How was a man" — then she stopped because she had to shove a gherkin in so tight, and it took all her concentration — "who don't have no job, going to support a wife and then a whole slew of babies?"

"Ruby'll find himself a job, that's how," I said.

She shook her head and pursed her lips. She didn't know why anyone would hire Ruby with what she called "his disconnected brain." It was starting to thunder but we hardly noticed it.

"Don't say that, Ma," I cried. "There ain't a thing wrong with his brain. Whenever people ain't exactly how you think they should be you call them retarded. It ain't fair. Ruby's good and kind," I shouted. "He's good and kind."

"Turn off the boiling water," she said. "Well, my my my, you can't eat good and kind. You ever had good and kind sandwiches? They're real juicy, all right; they don't stick to your ribs too good though." She was snickering and snorting, shaking her head and slamming the lids on her pickles, screwing on the covers.

"These better seal," she said to me, like it was going to be my fault if they didn't. "You listen for them to click — my ears ain't that accurate. I'm getting so old."

She was always saying words of that sort. I should have told her Ruby had weak ears too. Perhaps it was something they could have talked about, in common. "Ma," I said, "I'm going to marry Ruby. CAN YOU HEAR ME? Should I shout them words into your deaf ears?"

That was the clincher. She turned around to me as fast as an old lady can, and said in a stream, "I suppose you think you're

going to live here. I bet you think I'll make the money and you'll
sit around staring into space and Ruby'll drink morning, noon,
and night. I know what you're planning."

She closed her eyes, and then she chuckled over how we were
going to dupe her. That's how May is sometimes. She thinks
everyone is against her, and she's left with nothing but a scrubby
chicken yard.

I didn't say anything. I got up and walked over and stood in
front of her at the sink. The rain was coming in through the
window, splashing the counter, but I said to myself, So what?
In those days I felt like a strong nun, skinny and tough, who had
the words from God, or someone who knew the answers. It was
Ruby who made me feel absolute.

I said softly, but actually wanting to make a display like the
thunder, "Ma, how can you think we're trying to trick you?" I
could tell by her small eyes that she was scared of certain events
in the future. I said, "I'm going to keep working and Ruby'll do
his best to find a job. I know he will." I had to shiver from my
dripping clothes. For once May didn't make any mention of my
mess. I talked quietly still. I said, "You know we don't have a
single cent. We love each other, ain't that enough? Don't you
remember what it was like when you were in my position? Can't
you be happy for me?"

I had practiced my speech out in the rain before I came in to
tell May the good news. I felt as if a soap opera personality had
fed me the words, they came out so smooth.

"Close the window," she said and then she went to the table.
She put her head in her hands. I followed, saying, "If it's OK,
we'll live here for a while, while we get our bearings. We don't
have a place to go." I said, "We'll help you out, Ma, we'll do
the heavy work." I said it like I was beseeching her, only I knew
those exact words were what she wanted to hear.

The rain pounded at the windows as if it wanted to get in on
the discussion. May squeezed her eyes shut again and bit her

lower lip. I waited. Maybe she was praying. After the longest
time she took a deep breath and said she figured it might be all
right to have some company before her heart gave out and she
died alone.

"You're not going to die for a long time," I said to her in my
cheerful voice. I couldn't imagine anyone as large as May dying.
But she started to cry; she said she hoped Matt would get famous
before she kicked off so she could celebrate.

"Maybe he'll get into *People* magazine," she said. "I hope so,
and they'll have us in there too, only we won't be in Honey
Creek any more. Matt will come get us and buy us one of them
condominiums, and we'll go live in Florida, in all that hot sunshine."

"Sure, Ma," I said.

"Did one of those jars click? Didn't I hear one of them seal?"
she asked.

And I said, "No, Ma, that's rain out there." She mentioned
again how her ears weren't worth a noodle.

She had seen my ring but she didn't make a comment until
about six months later, when she told me she could tell the
diamonds were phony. She murmured that Ruby probably robbed
a dime store.

I picked Daisy for my bridesmaid. Dee Dee and May and Daisy
and I went all the way to Rockford to buy material for Daisy's
dress, and then Dee Dee sewed it. It was blue with white dots
all over it, and it had a ruffle swooping down over her chest. She
was going to look glamorous in it, I could predict that much. I
figured she'd wear gallons of makeup for the ceremony, and I
had to laugh thinking of her prancing down the aisle like she's
a bird we don't even have in Illinois.

When I asked Ruby who we should invite, he said he didn't
have too many friends to speak of, and his family lived so far
away now. They weren't crazy about him anyhow. He's kind of

a loner, Ruby is; that's why we were meant for each other. So I said, "Why don't we have a real small wedding?"

"Baby, I don't care," he whispered in my ear. "I just want to marry you. We could do it in the swamp, I got some of them gators."

We invited May and Dee Dee's family, and the girls and Artie from Trim 'N Tidy, and the Red Bell Bowling League, and the Rev, of course, plus a few of the ladies from the church. May began to get thrilled when she realized she had a perfect excuse to get Matt home. She wrote him a letter and said I was getting married so he'd have to be there to give me away. We never once mentioned contacting Elmer. Matt wrote back and said he could get away for two days. Isn't that an honor? Probably all the experiments in his lab would get ruined if he was gone longer than forty-eight hours. He probably had to get a baby sitter to watch over his moldy petri dishes. May flipped when his postcard came; the five smeared lines almost had her convinced that he was coming home to stay.

I wanted Aunt Sid to come more than anyone, and I wrote her and asked her if she would mind being present even though May still had the grudge. I thought that if I ever got terribly brave I would ask May if she could remember why she was mad at Sid. Aunt Sid wrote back and said she wouldn't miss my wedding for all the world, and that if she wasn't now chairman of the music department she would have visited us at least once a year. She hadn't been to see us in quite a while but I honestly hadn't missed her brief visits. I didn't like the thought of her surprising me at Trim 'N Tidy. I hated the vision of her blond head looming up in the door, and then she'd come to greet me with outstretched arms and I'd have my hands full of Mrs. Portland's red cashmere dress with turkey gravy all down the front. The pads on my fingers were always inky from the carbons in the checks. If she had come I would have had to feel shame at being one dumb finisher, and that was something I could easily do without. My wedding was a different matter altogether. It was supposed to be the greatest day in a girl's life.

"Ma," I said one night at supper, "Aunt Sid is coming to my wedding."

May stopped chewing. She called the air names I wouldn't repeat. I don't know if she was talking about me or Aunt Sid.

"Don't wreck it for me," I said. "You have Matt and I have Aunt Sid. Fair is fair."

Ruby used to come over in the early days and we'd sit at the table eating pie and making plans. Ruby loved baseball. He knew all the teams and he'd tell me facts about the players. "Someday, baby," he said, "you and me are going to go to a Cubs game." He taught me information about sports, sitting there at the kitchen table. He told me what all the yards were for in football. He ran around in the kitchen explaining it to me like he was one whole team himself. Matter of fact, he was both teams. Never mind that I couldn't understand a word he said. He still bought packets of baseball cards with the pink gum inside. I saw his shoeboxes filled with the cards; I saw his face when he blew bubbles that popped and got stuck on his eyes and on every inch of his nose. We laughed hard, scrubbing his cheeks with rubbing alcohol.

We were getting married in October. May said that was pretty hasty, considering I had only met Ruby in July, but we didn't want to wait around until next spring. I couldn't see what was wrong with October. I felt like I was a horse galloping toward October with an urgent message. I could taste how desperately I wanted Ruby; the desire for him was a flavor that rose up my throat and made my whole body thirst. We didn't talk about life plans too much because we were concentrating on holding out until our wedding night. I thought maybe Ruby was worried about coming to live in May's house, but he grinned and kissed my hands when I told him how it was going to be for a while.

I told him, "There ain't any way we can afford our own place,

Ruby." I said, "We'll have to do our best to get along with her. She ain't exactly Little Miss Sunshine every minute."

All Ruby said was, "It's OK, baby."

You should have seen the pigsty Ruby lived in before we got married. It was one small room with a toilet in the hall. Nobody had cleaned it since the Huns invaded Rome. May's house was like a palace, compared.

We had our picture taken for the wedding section of the newspaper. I'm sitting down smiling with my mouth closed and Ruby's standing, his hand on my shoulder. He's staring straight ahead as if he's bracing himself for something. The picture took me by surprise because Ruby looks like Miss Finch. His eyes are red dots.

May said I should register down at Marcie's in town so we could get some new plates and glasses, and then she and I picked out towels, and dishes with rosebuds and violets and daisies around the border. I had my name up on the wedding board at the drugstore in Stillwater. It said my wedding date also. I went in there about every day to look at the bulletin board, to see my name in the white letters. Sometimes you need something like that to make sure you're on the planet.

We received other presents too, because the girls at Trim 'N Tidy gave me a shower at lunch hour. I got a blender and a red nightie with fringe all over it. There wasn't any solid fabric to speak of attached to it. Artie was allowed to attend and he said he thought the garment was snazzy, plus he thought the bride was snazzy also. Actually, I wanted to wear the nightie on a gigantic Harley motorcycle, with no underpants on. I wished Ruby owned a bike. Perhaps May would have liked him instantly if he had owned something large.

She was quiet in the weeks before the wedding. She knew there was nothing she could say to me about my decision, since I was an adult taking charge of my life. Naturally she still had the comments about how I should brush my hair, it looked like a bush; how the chickens were going to starve if I didn't feed them this instant—the usual commands I didn't even hear any more. To myself I said, It's time for me to accomplish something, be part of a family. I was feeling alive, picking out invitations and flowers. I knew how all the animals in spring must feel, building nests and waiting for the male to bring in their catch. May was counting the days until Matt arrived in Honey Creek. I swear I could hear her counting. I knew she wasn't wild about Ruby— it didn't take an advanced degree to appreciate her opinion— but I wanted the arrangement to work out. I knew that when she saw how much we loved each other, it'd catch on, and she'd be glad in herself. I prayed up on the plateau. I prayed to the winter constellations that weren't yet visible. I prayed for their mercy.

Matt came home on Friday afternoon, the day before my wedding. When he walked in the door May rushed to him and nearly knocked him down. He caught himself and backed up to the wall and said, "Hi." She was already crying about how he never wrote, how he had forgotten we were his family—she was dead right on that score. I can't stand looking at May when she breaks down. It's terrifying to see her lose her strength. Matt didn't seem to want to look at her either. He stared at the floor until she came to kiss him and paw him. Then he closed his eyes.

"Hi, Matt," I said from the living room, and he said, "Hi." He was wearing a gray raincoat that came past his knees, and it had pleats in the back. I didn't say anything because I guessed I was the person of honor and for once he could ask me questions if he felt like it. I wasn't going to bow before his large head just because he went to MIT and had his name in *Time* magazine for thinking one thought about comets.

He said, "I hear you're getting married," and I said, "Yep, that's right." I wanted to ask him then and there if he had a girlfriend, but I didn't have the nerve. He looked smaller than I remembered, but handsome, as usual. His face was thinner, his brown eyes larger, and he had a sparse blond mustache. His perfect skin was stretched tight over the small knobs of his cheekbones. I said, "How's your science going?" and he said, "Very well, thanks."

"You like it out there?" I asked.

"Yes, I do." He nodded his head, just in case I didn't understand the words "Yes, I do."

Still, I felt like we were finally grown up, and we could have a conversation.

"That's great, Matt," I said. "You going to stick around for a while?" I asked, after a little. We were both shifting around on our feet while he told me he had to get back because he was running experiments in his lab. He was working on his physics. He knew everything about comets and stars. I wished I had a list of questions to ask him but my mind always dried up in front of smart people. There wasn't one particle of intelligent matter in my head. Then he said he was exhausted from the flight, that he better rest. May led him to his room to show him the new bedspread and the new curtains she had bought. He didn't exactly go wild over them. He mumbled something about how they were nice and she shouldn't have gone to the trouble. That was enough for May. She hummed all afternoon, tiptoeing past his closed door.

We went to church for the rehearsal that night. I had to come down the aisle on Matt's arm. We weren't supposed to say anything to each other since we were practicing being solemn. The Rev gave us the instructions, as if he thought we'd be gabbing, catching up on the last twenty years. It felt queer to touch Matt's arm, to hold it. I wanted to halt, to say, *Wait!* Did you say you were actually my brother? I kept still, as usual. I didn't make one single wave. I didn't even introduce my brother to my future husband. They didn't seem like they were members of the same species.

Afterwards, we went to Johnny's for fish fry — that is, everybody went except Matt. He drove away to see Dr. Heck, to tell him the latest news from the galaxy. Daisy stole the show in her white and black shirt that didn't have shoulders and her sheer white pants. Her earrings were large black metal circles that looked like manhole covers. She kept calling me Pollyanna because of my pink dress with the puffed sleeves that May got at St. Vincent de Paul. Of course Daisy got loaded and told her collection of dirty jokes, her favorites about the nun floating down the river on a turd. We were all screaming our heads off even though we'd heard the jokes before. Then she said she wanted to get Matt in the woods, feel his cute little dick. She was so smashed she didn't care what she said. Ruby and I held hands under the table and avoided looking at each other. I felt like the luckiest person, to be getting my very own husband. All my friends and Aunt Sid were coming in my honor, to watch us take the vows.

When Ruby and I were saying good night outside of Johnny's we kissed quickly, shyly, and Daisy cheered at us. She could whistle with her two fingers in her mouth. Dee Dee tried to get us to kiss a long one, but we were too embarrassed. Everyone had it on their minds that tomorrow night we would be in a bed together, touching each other, and quivering, waiting for Ruby to explode with my gift to him.

I'm getting married, I kept saying to myself. I couldn't sleep all night long. It was the last time in my life I was going to be one person to think of, besides May. In the future it would be We, Ruby and I. We were to be a pair. I stared at the ceiling fondly — it was the last night I was ever going to dream in my bedroom. Tomorrow we would switch with May; we'd move to the front room, to the bigger bed. I felt slowly over my body, my chest, my hair, and my thighs. I was seeing how they were going to feel to Ruby's hands.

We were married at ten o'clock in the morning. I had May's wedding dress on, the one she wore for Willard Jenson. I caught her unpacking the dress and smoothing the satin, and then staring out the church basement window. I wasn't used to seeing her stand absolutely still. Before the ceremony, in the dressing room, I had half an urge to give her a hug, but instead I fooled with the clothes hangers and the cosmetics. She helped me get dressed and then she stood back studying me up and down, examining my hair, the flowers, my white heels.

"Well, you ain't too bad looking," she said faintly.

If I squinted at her she looked like a plastic bag filled with blood, in her crimson-and-orange-checkered dress that was some kind of treated shiny polyester. "Thanks, Ma," I said. "Everybody says I look like you."

She couldn't figure out whether she should laugh or tell me I'm sassy, or break down and howl. Her wedding dress is awfully pretty. It's up in the attic in Honey Creek still. It has a plain white satin skirt and a lacy bodice that fit me quite decently, after Dee Dee altered it. Aunt Sid sent me pearls to wear and to keep. They belonged to my grandmother. I swore I wasn't ever going to lose them. In the bride's room, down in the church basement, I wanted to remember all of my life, with May there, helping me to dress. I wanted to remember with her the time I lost the pin at the spelling bee and she practically turned me in to the police. I still feel sorry about the loss. I wanted to tell her how sorry I was but my hand was stiff and inert. I couldn't stretch it out to May. Possibly somewhere my mind was ticking off the times she smacked me for nothing. I couldn't find my voice to say, Where's the garter? so how was I supposed to talk about our long life together? I was making jerky movements, knocking over the hair spray, trying to remember I was actually the bride. I had a crown of fake flowers on my head. Daisy put lipstick on my mouth, made my upper lip look like it was two red mountain peaks, and rouge on my cheeks. She rubbed it in gently, just as she would have done for a celebrity in the television industry.

Right when it was time to go upstairs I grabbed May's hand

at the door. I was going to say, I know I haven't been an ideal daughter, but she turned to me in alarm and said, "It's too late to back out of it now—everyone is up there waiting."

I mumbled, "I know, Ma," and let go of her hand.

Matt was out of place. He wore a dark suit with nearly invisible white stripes and a matching vest, and he had a gold chain coming out of his pocket. He was clean and pressed and washed and brushed, and he didn't fit our group. Daisy kept trying to catch his eye but he wouldn't face her. Maybe he was promised to a girl in Boston who was helping him figure out why comets zip through the universe. Daisy flirted with him, but it didn't do a bit of good. He turned his back and walked away. I had to feel sorry for her all of a sudden, making such a fool out of herself.

The Rev had twisted his brother's arm to play the trumpet, since Ruby and I wanted music but knew nothing about serious works for church. Ruby wished the Supremes could come and sing something, but those Negro singers aren't appropriate. The trumpet player blasted out a marching song that filled me up and made me feel so holy I thought I was turning into an angel when I came down the aisle. The Rev told me afterwards it was music written by a man named Purcell, and that it was the only wedding music his brother cared to play. Purcell died hundreds of years ago, and I couldn't help thinking it was a handy arrangement— to have people loving your music when you aren't anything but a cloud of dust. The sun streamed through the stained glass, morning light, white and pure, making patches here and there on the green carpet, as if someone had spilled it. Everyone I knew watched me come down the aisle with my hand through Matt's arm. He stared straight ahead, taking his job with utter seriousness. I could see Aunt Sid standing alone, at the end of a pew. I stopped when we came to her, only Matt dragged me along. He didn't have instructions for stopping. She was wearing a perfectly plain silver dress. It was raw silk, without a doubt.

Suddenly the rest of the congregation looked like dandelions gone to seed, compared to the rare silver orchid. Aunt Sid has a heap of hair on her head in this thing Daisy said is called a French twist, and it's blond hair. She's tall and beefy, like May, but she carries herself like a prize cow. And she has a beautiful smile. There isn't any meanness or jeering in it. There were tears in her eyes. I turned my head to stare back down the aisle. I wished I was marrying her.

Ruby was waiting for me up at the altar, of course, looking like a big old tomcat, about to get chow. When Matt left me off Ruby whispered to me, "Whoopie, I got me a bridie." I shot him a stately glance.

My wedding was the first one I had ever been to, not counting TV shows, plus commericals for deodorant. I didn't understand about weddings at first but now I finally have them figured out. Weddings don't have one thing to do with real life. The Rev told us about the joy we were going to find and how God made man and woman with different molds so they could share each other's bodies. He also kept talking about our spirits and our souls. He threw in Jesus Christ every other sentence, although as far as I could see he didn't have much to do with our situation. Ruby likes him for curing all the people, and for the halo he sometimes wears in his picture.

I had trouble paying strict attention at my wedding. I was thinking about how I used to hide in the rhubarb when I was small, when May called me in for supper. Now that I'm slightly smarter, I know that the Rev was telling us how marriage is in an ideal world, where the humans don't have flaws, where they don't have anything but love in their hearts. It's a condition to shoot for. People go to weddings to get purified, as if they're going through a strainer. That's what happened at our wedding: Ruby and I were put through the strainer, and what was left in the wire mesh were the little pieces of gold, our perfect souls. We left them at the altar.

We promised through sickness and health, until death, but the Rev said nothing about other possibilities, such as limbo. The Rev is a large clean man, probably even behind his ears, and we're friends, but I always keep in mind that he does not know everything, despite the fact that he's second in command to the Lord. What he said that I love, after Ruby and I kissed —we made a smacking sound and everyone laughed—was, "The Lord bless you and keep you. May the Lord make his face to shine upon you for all of your days."

I sneak comfort on occasion, imagining someone, I don't care who, blessing and keeping me.

Then the trumpet blasted away and we flew down the aisle, beaming at Daisy's new boyfriend who was taking pictures. The sunshine splattered the carpet and most everyone except May smiled. She looked straight ahead, pretending she was a pillar holding up the church.

At the reception, down the basement, Aunt Sid hugged me and kissed both of my cheeks. I blushed at her beauty. I couldn't say one sentence. It's so different in letters, when you have a piece of paper and you're writing all your thoughts. It's like talking easily with Miss Finch when she doesn't have the eyes to see. Aunt Sid said how lovely I looked and that she hoped we'd be happy. She said she had missed seeing me and that it was silly to have to have a wedding to get together. I wanted to make her sign in blood that she'd keep writing me, even though this day suggested I was launched. I couldn't find the words to tell her that she'd saved my life roughly one million times. The figure is not an exaggeration, either. I wanted to say that there wasn't one single day when she didn't save me in some way. I stood there shaking my head, my lips trembling because I was going to burst into tears. After only a few minutes she said she better let me go for now, that there were other people to see me, and then she said again that I was a lovely bride.

There was something about Aunt Sid, when she saw how Ruby

slurped the cake off of the serving knife and danced the twist and the bump with Daisy in the church kitchen, that made her look as if she thought I was lost forever. It was as if she didn't want to see me getting married, that deep down she didn't find it a happy occasion. She stood in the back speaking with the Rev while Artie made a speech about my fantastic bowling career, past and future. He made jokes about how I was going to teach Ruby my secrets and then the Red Bell team was going to be in even deeper trouble. All the check-out girls had the courtesy to laugh. After Artie's speech Aunt Sid tried to corner May but May was not to be had. She was cutting more cake and pouring drinks for Dee Dee and licking the feet of the church ladies.

Aunt Sid gave up on May and stopped Matt just as he was escaping out the rear exit. He began telling her about some research with meteors and how every few billion years a bunch of them smash into earth and wreck all the life. I didn't like those two talking together. She was nodding and shaping questions with her hands and telling him it was all fascinating. I walked her to her car when she was finished with him. She was the first person to leave. She clasped my hands, looking directly into my eyes, and wished me luck. She didn't say anything about coming to visit her or when we would meet again. I stood on the curb all by myself, waving at her as the car moved down the street, and I knew, standing there, although I was just married, that I was the loneliest girl in the U.S. Aunt Sid was the only person who knew me, and I had the feeling just by looking at the back of her head, and the rear end of her car pulling away, that she didn't want my acquaintance any more.

Eleven

RUBY and I didn't go on a honeymoon because I didn't have vacation time coming, but Artie gave me Monday off, paid. May had to get up and go to work. She was crashing pots and pans around, putting the dishes away, while we stayed in bed, whispering. We now occupied May and Elmer's old room, the master bedroom. It has tall windows, three of them, where all the cold seeps through in winter. She moved back to my room, reminding us, all the while, that it's the worst place in the whole house. It's over the kitchen so you can smell the fumes of cooking onions and hamburger, chicken fat and bacon grease. Our room has a four-poster bed from the home farm. The story is that some old cousin with a harelip made it for the girl he dreamed of marrying. He lived two hundred years ago so the facts probably aren't accurate any more. He probably only had a scratch under his nose. Don't ask me what the future generations are going to say about us — it will take them hours to explain and lie to the little children. The bed has delicate wooden posters and a few rickety boards tacked at either end. Sometimes it seemed too fragile for the two of us — when we were roughhousing. We slept on a cornhusk mattress, just like pioneers who had a whole new land in front of them. There wasn't any other furniture except a beat-up dresser May had used forever, and a braid rug worn thin on the floor. Ruby didn't have too many belongings. He brought a duffel bag with him, containing his underwear and shirts, a few pair of pants, three old snapshots, socks that needed darning like you wouldn't believe. He didn't own much else.

When we heard May leave for work on Monday we got up and I made pancakes and sausages, and we ate them in the living room. We sat watching *Hollywood Squares*. We sat two feet from each other and smiled at the TV. After it was over Ruby took my hand and we walked upstairs, staring straight in front of ourselves, concentrating on each step.

We didn't even shake hands on our wedding night because Ruby was plowed and I was dead tired and sad on account of Aunt Sid. We pulled ourselves up onto the bed, clutched our separate pillows, and fell asleep. Then the next day, Sunday, May was banging around downstairs. She was shampooing the rugs for the second time in two weeks. Sometimes she gets obsessed with her carpet and her dusting. When I dared to roll over and look at my husband I didn't recognize the heap. The pillow was over most of his head. He had parts of his wedding suit on, and a piece of cake stuffed in his breast pocket. His mouth was wide open. I turned back to the wall and tried to think about the sunshine filling the church, and the trumpet proclaiming heaven on earth.

We didn't do anything on Sunday except eat Sunday dinner. May cooked the roast, as usual. We always had our best meal at noon and then at night we got sandwiches for ourselves. Sunday dinner was a custom May couldn't shake, from the days at the home place when there were hired men and her big family. After dinner Ruby disappeared outside and didn't come back until dark.

Finally, on Monday we climbed into bed after our breakfast. Ruby's stomach was puffed out like a device that could save you in the water. He showed me how fat it was; he pressed it and made it honk. We got in our bed with all our clothes on under the covers and he whispered right down into my ear, "Baby, you're gonna like me better this time, I know you will."

I kept saying, "OK, OK." I closed my eyes; I kept them shut while he took my pants off. I knew I was learning a secret from Ruby. I was drowning in the place where he touched me.

It wasn't as bad, the second time. Ruby bit me hard. He was so worked up he couldn't help it. He kept kissing the wound afterwards and saying, "Baby, you make a man wild, you know that?"

I couldn't do a thing but grin, even though I was wondering if I'd have to get rabies shots. When I turned to the wall he leaned over me and kissed me, in many of the areas Daisy told about. He said, "Hey, baby, wake up," but I pretended I was fast asleep.

When we came downstairs it was two in the afternoon. Ruby said, "Time flies, don't it?" I wanted to go to him and hug him with all my might but instead I went into the kitchen to get the food ready. We had wieners and pretzels and Cokes—it was a holiday. Afterwards we walked in the woods, smelled the air full of burning leaves. Ruby raced to trees and tried to climb up them. He clung to their trunks and then slipped down. He tried with just about every tree he saw. I was sniffing the future right there in the air. You can smell winter coming on, and if you close your eyes you can see the snow falling, covering up the forlorn gray fields. Ruby and I held hands while Ruby talked about how he could eat a lion. He said I wore him out.

I had my diamond engagement ring and a slender silver wedding band also, which Daisy had helped me pick out. The small rings were cheap; of course, they aren't actually pure silver. Ruby got a larger ring, because he's the man. He didn't want to wear it on his finger so he strung it through a chain and put it around his neck. He said, "It ain't sissy, baby. I seen hundreds of men with necklaces."

I paid for the rings with the money I stored in the pig. Every time I looked at mine I'd say to myself, I'm married, and I'd whisper a sentence that had the word *husband* in it.

After our walk I said, "How about we cook supper for Ma?" and Ruby said, "Sure." We were planning to make stew. I showed Ruby how to cut up the vegetables and he had a great time — in between slicing he explained how to pitch. He had a tennis ball from Matt's closet. He was throwing curve balls against the kitchen wall like a professional. I had to shriek because he could really wind up and throw the balls hard and fast.

"Look it!" Ruby shouted. "Reggie hit it to first base, baby. I'm running to tag him out." Ruby jumped over the stools, tagged the ironing board in the corner; he slid into it crying, "He's *out*, we got him!"

I chopped carrots and he said, "You and them vegetables are the whole stadium. Come on, you're supposed to cheer."

When May walked in I was hollering with the potatoes because Ruby threw a fast ball at the wall and the player hit it and it went flying past second base and into the outfield. I was laughing hysterically with my face in my hands. Ruby was running all over the house; I could hear him in the living room, shouting, "*Baby*, your number-one team player caught it on the fly! The crowds have lost control!"

May stood in the doorway staring at the place on the wall where the tennis ball hit. She didn't think the game was so humorous. She marched straight into the living room and she said, as if Ruby were eight years old, "When you want to play ball, you do it outside, understand?"

Our smiles stuck on our grim faces for a minute and then they vanished. If there's anything Ruby hates it's getting yelled at. He likes people to say he does a good job. We ate supper, the stew we made for May, without talking about much of anything. May didn't ask us what we did all morning or if by chance I had a bite on my shoulder. When we were finished eating I washed the dishes and Ruby and May watched shows. They flipped through the channels until it was time to go to sleep. Sitting there close to Ruby, holding his hand in front of May, I thought about how I was married now. I planned what I was going to say when people asked, "How is married life?" I figured I'd say, "Real good."

Even though Ruby didn't have a job he got welfare from the government and cash from his sister. He had the hardest time getting a job, because people knew his history. They weren't willing to trust him one hundred percent. Ruby isn't a smart manager with his money. Somehow it trickles through his fingers, even if he makes a conscious effort to hold it tight. He's generous at times—I love that about him. He went out and bought a toaster oven for May after he was playing ball in the house, to make up to her.

When she came home from work he had it on the table. He said, "Hey, Ma, I got a present for you." Her ears perked up, but she pretended she didn't care about a package with a shiny red ribbon around the middle.

"Open it, Ma," Ruby said. She also wasn't sure she liked having him call her Ma. He was moving back and forth, swinging his arms. He wanted her to like the present an awful lot.

She came to the table and untied the ribbon, and when she saw inside, how a person could bake a potato or heat leftovers, she said, "Well, ain't that nice?" We could see her face stretched out wide in the stainless rim of the toaster. She turned the knobs, opened and shut the door, examined the plug. She didn't have to know that it was on sale at Coast to Coast and that Ruby spent half his cash on it. She was friends with him that day. She thought he wasn't so bad to have around after all.

May suggested, since Ruby couldn't find a job right off the bat, that he help Mr. Buddles. He rents our field land and lives across the way. He's old and doesn't have a strong back. May said that Ruby could take care of our chickens too, wipe the eggs and shovel the manure. Ruby said, "Sure," like he always does, but he didn't mean it. He was afraid to stick his hands under the hens, for fear they might bite his fingers down to the bone. There he was wearing his wedding ring on his hairy chest like the men in dirty magazines and he was scared to death of innocent hens. I told him, "Watch me—see the worst they do is give you a little peck, you don't hardly feel it." Still, he stood back from the laying boxes and stretched his arm out slowly, and naturally the hens scolded him. The fine silver hairs on his neck stood up. I started to laugh when he backed up into the post but when he turned to me, crouching and holding his head and crying, I ran to him and cradled him. I didn't tell May that Ruby hated chickens' sharp beaks and their toenails and their bald legs. I told her I would miss the chickens too much if Ruby did the chores.

He worked with Mr. Buddles that fall we were first married. He helped fill the silo and he milked on weekends—that's not counting the times he overslept. Tardiness really got Mr. Buddles heated up. He'd yell into the phone, "WHERE THE HELL IS RUBY?" I had to hold the receiver a mile away so my eardrums didn't get shattered. Mr. Buddles also complained because Ruby played with the kitties when he was supposed to be washing down cows. He didn't understand that Ruby was without the sense of time. Ruby loves to nap for one thing, but he also doesn't go by the earth's rhythm, sleeping by night and getting up with the morning. And it's no deep secret that he drinks more than he should. I wanted to quiet Mr. Buddles down so I could explain my husband, but he always threatened Ruby before he offered him one last chance.

There were mornings when Ruby couldn't possibly get up to milk because he had worked in the basement all night long. He'd forget to go to bed. Of course then he had to sleep on the couch most of the day; that's when May hit the ceiling. She yelled at him while he slept like a baby. She was perfecting her speech for the time when he would be awake and half listening. It wasn't exactly just the rumor of his bad behavior that made people think twice about hiring Ruby. There was the mystery about him; it was something I love in him—wouldn't most girls love a man who didn't have time on his mind? "There ain't anyone else in the world like Ruby," Daisy had said about him months before.

May said to me in the car on the way to work, in one whole breath, "No one's going to hire Ruby because he's lazier than animals in the zoo who don't have to do nothin' because their keeper comes in and throws big huge slabs of red meat at them."

"He ain't lazy," I said, and we left it at that.

I didn't care if Ruby worked or not. I wanted him to have a wonderful time being married, living together so happily. As long as we were getting along, what difference did it make? We were paying the bills pretty much, keeping warm and fed. We had borrowed money from Artie to help cover the wedding, but we were going to keep our promise and pay him back. I wanted Ruby to be so happy he'd never disappear for an afternoon after dinner.

What he loved to do was build birdhouses. He had a few tools and he made a place in the basement at Elmer's old workbench. He was down there all day, all night sometimes, listening to the radio and building the houses. He was proud of them, even though on some houses the walls didn't come together perfectly and the windows were slightly crooked. He sold them at the bookstore in Stillwater. The lady there didn't mind displaying a few on the table. She had posters in her store about saving poor slaughtered animals, such as seals with mopey eyes and whales caught in black nets. The birdhouses were three dollars each. Ruby carved details on the wood and made different rooms: bird kitchens and bird bathrooms and dens and game rooms and a place to make music. There were always four or five stories. He made chimneys by gluing together pieces of gravel he found on the driveway. When I first saw his houses, I was very impressed. I said, "How do you know how to build?"

"It's nothin'," Ruby said, running his hands over his hair. "I watched my Uncle Jake hammer and I learned how like *that*." He snapped his fingers. "You ever seen all the babies one bird has in a batch?" he asked me. "They need space, all them birdies do."

He wished he could put electricity in the bedrooms. He guessed some of the babies were afraid of the dark during the long black nights. Purple martins were his favorite bird because in spring they actually used all the stories in his houses. You could see their beaks sticking out of the windows, upstairs and downstairs, aunts and sisters, cousins and grandparents. They looked like they cooperated pretty well. In the mornings, while I made my sandwich, Ruby sat in the kitchen and stared out to the yard, watching for the birds to come feed at their stations. He didn't like squirrels too much. He always tore outside and flicked his arms in their direction. He made me move the feathers off the walk if a cat had eaten up most of a bird.

I loved coming home and Ruby would be down the basement hammering and singing, or else he'd be in the Lazy Boy chair watching reruns and drinking a beer, maybe dabbing paint onto his houses. He liked to paint them different colors. He usually picked me up and swooped me around, and he always told me he missed me all day long. He'd say, "Baby, I thought you'd never get home." He was always wanting to party, which meant going anywhere, even a drive in the car to park in a ditch. He'd say, "Where should we go tonight, to party?"

There were certain places he didn't show his face. He hated to run into people he wasn't friends with, such as the owner of the gas station where he used to work. There were a few other people too. Some of his friendships didn't have anything to them but storms brewing. I guess there were individuals who didn't care to discover his good points.

Sometimes we went bowling, like the old days, only May didn't come along any more. Maybe she didn't want to be seen with Ruby, even with the toaster oven. Maybe she couldn't stand all the gutter balls and the way he pretended to play his guitar, looking so dumb when the ball rolled down the gutter, same as his last ten turns. I had to be sort of embarrassed for him in those moments, but he didn't notice. He was usually smashed when he bowled. He said the balls looked like marbles to him; they kept shrinking as they rolled on down. He couldn't see how a puny marble could knock down the giant pins, as tall as the water tower. When he was drunk items were slightly distorted for Ruby. Once he called out to me, just when he was about to take his turn; he said, "Baby, aren't you glad my dick ain't as big as those pins?" Daisy spit her drink all over the floor and had to rush to the ladies' room, and I wished, for the ten millionth time in my life, for a small hole to open in the floor directly underneath me.

Other nights we went to dances the firemen put on to raise money for their new trucks and waterproofs, and for children who had cancer. I didn't do very well dancing the twist. I only waltz. Usually I sat and watched and if I felt brave I got up and walked around the building. I watched Ruby dance with Daisy. They were clowns together. I laughed too loudly at their antics. I knew they were probably only horsing around. They weren't actually flirting. Daisy always ended up going off with a bearded fireman, the newest member. They usually wound up in a corner dancing so slowly you could barely stand to watch. If I got loaded I could dance — Ruby stroked my hindquarters to show me how to wiggle my hips.

At other times we went to the theater in Stillwater that's devoted to dirty pictures. People come from all around to watch. Ruby always wanted to try the moves the actors made on the screen. He wanted to see me suck on my own nipples but my breasts weren't big enough for that kind of behavior. He joked and said we would get all our friends together and make a chain but I didn't laugh too hard. After about two or three of those movies they all seemed exactly the same. I made excuses whenever he said he wanted to go and after a while he didn't ask me. If he was gone when I came home I could be pretty sure he and Randall were at the movies.

I wrote Aunt Sid to say how happy we were. It took me hours to compose the letter. I mentioned at the end that it was a little strange living with May also, because I could tell she wasn't crazy about Ruby and his curve balls. I didn't describe how he tracked in the second week we were married. May had just shampooed the carpet. There were black footprints going straight for the television. When she came in the room and saw the muddy path she screamed her damnations. Ruby stood fixed in his spot, staring at her display. He was still, like a bug stunned by the hot light. He didn't like to get yelled at, Ruby didn't. He wanted to please May. He wanted her to say he was good at sitting around all day with his feet up. She hauled out the Hoover and gave him a demonstration while he was still in a staring mood. She slowed down and lowered her voice, and when she pushed the handle in his direction she smiled. She looked like she was coaxing a wild animal to eat poison. She asked him if he wanted her old apron, the black one with the torn white rickrack. She laid it on the chair for him to use if he wanted to. When she left the room he sat on it and passed gas. At that point I quickly turned on the machine and cleaned the mess. After I finished I handed the thing to Ruby so he could at least turn it off. I could hear May on the phone with Dee Dee while he wrapped the cord up. She said she had the worst headache. She said life was going rotten for her. When I heard May describe her life my blood clotted and came up my throat. I didn't know what to do, standing stiff in front of the vacuum and my husband and the traces of his dirty feet. I didn't know how I was going to fix May's rotten life. Ruby went right down the basement and made about fifty birdhouses. He made another purple one for the back yard.

At supper May said, "Birds don't like purple."

Ruby didn't say anything. After a few minutes he looked up

at the salt shaker. There were tears in his eyes when he whispered, "How do you know? You ain't a bird."

While we ate supper we didn't talk much. We worked at getting that food down our throats.

Aunt Sid wrote me right back and said she liked seeing me so much at the wedding. She said I had astonished her, that she wasn't prepared to see a woman marching down the aisle. She said we would meet soon, she was sure we would; we'd have so many things to talk over! Aunt Sid never used exclamation points, and I was suspicious of that one, the first she had ever used on me. It was as if she had to pretend to be cheerful. I had such an odd sensation about Aunt Sid, now that I was married. I guess I didn't feel too much like my old self. I was a new person, only I didn't know myself well enough to say Hi. I didn't know exactly how I was supposed to act in front of people. Actually, we were all stumbling around trying to figure out how to act. May was probably mixed up too. There's a good chance she didn't know if she was still supposed to be the mother, bawling children out if they wrecked up her house, but if she wasn't the mother, who was she then? She didn't have any answers.

There was some good news right after we were married: I got promoted at Trim 'N Tidy. Dry cleaning isn't exactly my life's passion, but Artie was teaching me how fabrics behaved, training me to be skilled and do a fine job. I learned how to be a spotter, the job that takes the most intelligence in dry cleaning. My job comes after the clothes are first inspected, and after they have been thrown in a machine with chemicals. They come out and then I look them over and find problem stains. If there are trick spots I take more chemicals and I do what's called tamping the fabric. You just kind of beat at the cloth with a brush and then you flush it with a special steam air gun. I didn't mind looking at people's stains, trying to figure out what they had for dinner, identifying the puzzling spots. I tried to guess who owned the gigantic sweaters. There's plenty of fat people in Honey Creek and Stillwater, weaned on chips and cola. A spotter has to be smart and pay attention to the fabrics and dyes because you can ruin the clothes easily with chemicals. Customers are not pleased when their goods come back covered with holes. Artie told me I did fantastic work, that I listened carefully and learned quickly. He hiked up my pay. I could tell May didn't like my being a spotter when she was only a finisher. I think she saw me, her daughter, the married spotter, and I think she felt quiet and near death. She imagined that there was nothing left for her.

May and I came home at night and I did the chores with Ruby trailing behind like a good old dog. May always made the meal. We all had tasks we were responsible for in our household. When I came in with the eggs we sat right down to supper and usually we ate in silence, working on chewing and swallowing, getting nourished. May isn't the greatest chef on earth, but I was used to her food because I had eaten it every day of my life. She made three pans of meat loaf stretched with ground soybeans, which lasted for a week, and then the next week we ate macaroni and cheese for as long as possible, and occasionally she butchered a chicken, which meant eating the entire bird: liver, gizzard, necks, heart. Of course we always had something special for Sunday noon, a good day to be alive if eating was something a person enjoyed. We usually had a roast and mashed potatoes and Jell-O or fruit salad, and cake. And then back to Mondays, and May's habit of making enough goulash for two million people, so it would last for eternity. This was her way of being The Cook. She was always so tired at the end of the day. She didn't want to spend each night over the boiling pot. There were TV shows she wanted to watch; there were her sore feet she wanted to elevate.

May and I could tell Ruby didn't savor her menus. He wasn't crazy about onions and watered-down stew. He called out "jackpot" once, when he hit a piece of meat. He was used to eating hamburgers and fish sandwiches at McDonald's. He ate five a day when he was a bachelor. French fries were his idea of food, which is why his complexion was the color of asphalt. If Ruby hit something distasteful in May's casserole, such as a tough piece of eggplant, he spit it out in his napkin, for all to see and hear. I practically wanted to take him aside and scold him, not to mention regurgitate, because I knew how insulted May felt. She's sensitive about her cooking. But May, perhaps because her brand-new life was going downhill, apparently said to herself, Why bother? She started to make the suppers worse and worse. Her favorite slogan was "Give people their money's worth."

When she washed the dishes she'd say to Ruby, "I always save the dishwater for soup stock. It cooks up so wonderful."

He couldn't figure out if she was joking or not. He stood still in the middle of the floor staring at her while she poured the gray dishwater into a half-gallon container. He never blinked, watching the crumbs swirl around in the jar.

The first two weeks in December May served split-pea soup without relief. Seemed like there wasn't any ham in it, if you don't count the gristle. The soup was green and loosey-goosey, and Ruby figured she went out to the chicken shed and scraped up what the sick chickens made. I didn't like to think about such unpleasantness, but I had to agree with him. One night, after what seemed like three years of split-pea soup, Ruby pushed his chair out when May stuck the bowl of chicken loosey-goosey in front of him, and he made a long noise that suggested trouble forthcoming from deep in his gut. May was waiting for it, you could just tell. She stood over him and said so sweetly, "You think you're awful smart, sitting around all day long, waiting for me to serve you — *you* cook, see how it suits you, Mr. Fancy Pants, see if it changes your attitude." She smiled long and nice. He didn't know where to look.

He got up and went out that night, without me. He drove the lemon Daisy dumped in our yard into town and bought a hamburger. Louise from the cleaners said later that she saw him at the Stillwater Cafe, sitting all by himself with two burgers and a pile of fries. She said she could hear the juke box just by looking at the quaking windows. Ruby knows where the switch is to turn it way up.

When he got home at midnight I was in bed. I couldn't figure out what else to do, except try to dream of Mr. Darcy. I saw Mr. Darcy eating french fries, Mr. Darcy whacking on birdhouses, Mr. Darcy rubbing up against tree trunks. I was terrified that Ruby was gone for good. We hadn't been married two months yet. What would I tell everybody? He crawled over me as if I was an irritating stump. When he got comfortable he said, "Baby, here I am. It's Mr. Chef Boy-R-Dee."

I managed to laugh while Ruby talked about how he was going to go out and shoot a deer for May. He talked about wrapping the tail up in banana peel and coating it with chocolate. Sometimes I think my calling is the stage. I could be an actress with convincing fake smiles. I hugged Ruby, because we were still a couple. I was so thankful.

The first night Ruby made frozen pizza. I bought him his favorite — pepperoni — on the way home from work. When he set it on the table he said, "Ladies, you're getting my special tonight." May didn't crack a smile.

The next night we had hot dogs. We had some in the freezer and Ruby boiled them for so long they blew up to the size of sewer pipes. May spat her bites out in her napkin. Ruby loved using the tongs we had to serve the wieners. He got a charge out of handling everything in the kitchen, hot and cold, with them. The whole time we ate he was doing a dance with the tongs and a bag of potato chips. I was dying of laughter but I kept a straight face while May ate her parboiled peas. After supper she marched into the living room, making it clear she wanted to watch her programs alone. Ruby and I spent all night doing the dishes and dancing and grabbing each other with the tongs. We ended up under the table with our pants off. After May went to bed, Ruby insisted I use the tongs to guide him inside.

The third night we had scrambled eggs and dry toast, because I forgot to buy margarine on the way home. When May put her fork into her mouth, she all of a sudden looked like she was tasting the most bitter substance in existence. Her frown stretched down into her neck. She got up and spat her food into the sink so vigorously I thought she might bring up a shrunken heart.

She turned around when she uttered, "That is the most revolting food I ever ate in my life." She probably wasn't counting the time I made scalloped onions out of tulip bulbs. May's gigantic head became enlarged when she was disgusted or angry, and the veins in her neck stood out and throbbed.

Ruby didn't say anything. He ate his eggs. He whispered, "Looks like Ma didn't like my extra-special creation. I put the hen's mash in our eggs just for her." He took another bite. "Cluck cluck, they ain't too bad."

I was too tired and hungry and frightened to laugh. I dropped my fork thinking about what May would do if she ever realized that Ruby was feeding her mash. She might sue for divorce, or put a gun to Ruby's head and make him vacuum forever.

After we ate our gritty eggs Ruby and I went outside to walk in the woods. It was raw and we shivered, but we made no attempt to touch each other and get warm. We sat up in the haymow, only there isn't a single bale of hay, and Ruby tried to make me laugh by doing a concert. I didn't feel like laughing. His fingers were white with the cold, playing his pretend guitar.

The next night no one said anything. Ruby didn't cook and May didn't cook. There we were after a long day at work without one speck to eat. Ruby and May sat in the living room watching TV with all their might. They sat upright. They weren't either one of them going to budge. It looked funny, if you were in a giggling mood, to see their good posture. I stared out into the night, seeing my own reflection, and it seemed to me it was shriveling with every second I stood waiting. I knew I was going to scream. I was opening my mouth when Ruby jumped up. He stood shifting around on his feet, scratching his chin and glancing quickly at the sofa.

May didn't pay attention so he left for the kitchen. I was about to go after him when I heard him say to the refrigerator, "You are one great big field of fart."

"What'd did he say?" May asked, alert all of a sudden.

I didn't know what to tell her. I said, "Nothin'."

"WHAT'D HE SAY?"

"That you remind him of some of them natural processes," I said. Ruby was already out of the house. We could hear the car starting up.

I didn't stay to hear May return his compliment. I was so mad at those two for wrecking our lives over a few eggs. I stalked off without looking to see if she was still glued to the TV. Perhaps she was going to settle down to eat her private stash of sweet rolls.

It was December. The wind was in no way attentive to my sorrows as I went along the road. It slashed right through my body. I had to wish for a planet where the breeze takes you in its arms and rocks you to sleep. I held my hat to my head and walked along the dark highway. Every time car lights blinded me I felt like an animal exposed and in the limelight right before it becomes a road kill. I saw myself lying in a heap, bruised and dead, waiting to be discovered in the morning by the county highway crew.

"Running away already?" Daisy said to me at the door of the Footes' house, and I said, "Nope."

I walked straight past her into their kitchen. Then I sat down and put my head on the table and cried, just like Dee Dee used to for May. I was ashamed of the scorn I used to feel for Dee Dee and all her problems. I was just as needy, and probably always had been. Even though Daisy was a slut, if you're speaking plain English, she's got this big heart. She put her hands on my shoulders and said, "You tell me about it."

Wouldn't you know it, before I could get a word out the phone rang. Dee Dee kept saying into the receiver, "Well! . . . Well! . . . Oh? Dear!"

I raised my head long enough to say to Daisy, "I bet you a dollar it's my ma."

Sure enough, Dee Dee hung up the phone, made a beeline for the freezer, took some food out, turned to Daisy, and said, "Poor May." She drove off to our house instantly, just as good friends should. We all needed people to tell us that we were the ones who had been deeply wronged.

I sat sobbing, telling Daisy that May and Ruby couldn't stand each other, and that sometimes Ruby was scared of her because she let her rattling false teeth swim around in her mouth. I tried to describe May for the first time in my life. I said, "Daisy, the only pleasure she gets is from holding people under her thumb. She's happy when she's let you know how miserable her life is. If you catch her smiling she quick frowns." I stopped because I wanted to get it right. It was all coming out in little pieces and that's not how I intended it. I looked into Daisy's face and said, "I let her down every day."

I don't think Daisy heard me because she said, "If only we could find her a man. She probably just needs a good screw. I bet all her problems would improve after a one-night stand."

I hated advice like that. I said, "How are we going to do anything different, Daisy?"

I explained that May was the banker and we barely made ends meet. She made Ruby fork over cash for his food and the hot baths he loved to take, but we weren't extra rich, especially with deep winter coming and the oil it took to heat the house. I admitted that in October we had three dollars at the end of the month. There were two days when we didn't have groceries and May dug up a chicken in the freezer from 1964. Of course we still had the wedding bills to pay off. May kept complaining about the expensive ceremony, but she was the one who demanded that we have the bakery cake and the flowers.

"Things look bad," Daisy said. "You and me are going to get crocked."

Daisy and I went downtown. She was working at the grocery store so she treated. We drank too much of a certain mixed drink that contained everything in the liquor cabinet. When I was under the influence I told Daisy I'd love to see her on a motorcycle with nothing on, and she cracked up. She picked out all the old men in the room and discussed how they'd suit May as a boyfriend. Mr. Stevens, the one with the wooden leg who's always the Indian in parades, was her favorite choice. "Don't he look sexy in his headdress on the Fourth of July?" she asked me. "Come to think of it, I bet your brother would like him. I bet you a million dollars he's a homo."

We looked at each other and burst out laughing. We had to get up and squat against the wall, and take walks holding our stomachs, and just when we'd get control we'd look at each other and break up all over again.

When I knew it was coming I went out in the cold and got sick on the curb. I cried all the way home while Daisy drove like a maniac. I was half hoping we'd crash into a tree and lose our lights.

After Daisy let me off I stood on the back porch spying in the kitchen window. There's no storms on the windows so I could hear every word. May was standing at the counter cutting up a chicken and Dee Dee worked at the table chopping onions. It looked like they were cooking enough for the next two months. Dee Dee set her knife down, raised her glass high, and said, "Here's another one to you and me." She chugged it and then wiped her mouth on the hem of one of May's gingham aprons that she was wearing. She said, "Nobody knows what we suffer. They drive off and get broken and expect us to lick their wounds when they come back. At least you have Matt. Count your blessings. Did he call you this week?"

I heard May say, "Every Sunday."

"Is he coming for Christmas?" Tears caused by onions were dripping from Dee Dee's eyes. May always gave her the lowest jobs.

May gnawed on her toothpick before she spoke. "He just can't get away from his work for more than two seconds. Them professors have him working night and day. Course he's the top student. There ain't no free lunch though — that's what you have to do when you're on full scholarship."

"Did he send you a picture of his girlfriend yet?" Dee Dee asked.

"Now where did I put it?" May rustled up a bunch of *Pennysavers* that were on the sideboard. "Yeah, he sent one, but just like a boy, you can't hardly see nothin' of her face. If it would have been a good photo I wouldn't have lost it. She's a cheerleader for the football team. Real cute. He said maybe for Easter vacation he'd bring her home."

"Now, May," Dee Dee said, coming over to look through the piles of clipped coupons, "you have such a good son. Count your blessings. I got three lousy kids, not one born with any sense. Randall's a good boy, and I couldn't live without him, but you know as well as I do that he ain't going to amount to anything big like your Matt."

May went to the pot on the stove and stirred. "I have a feeling them two sex fiends ain't ever coming back."

"Still, you count your blessings. You hatched one first-class star and that's more than some get. You have a handsome smart son and pretty soon you'll probably have a real cute daughter-in-law."

May stuck her face into the steam. She was probably wondering how she was going to get Matt to marry the cheerleader of her dreams.

I had had enough by now. I opened the door and stamped my feet. I didn't say one word to either one of them. My nose was runny and my head felt perfectly round. I just stood there staring.

Dee Dee thought I was looking at the empty chicken pot pie tins on the counter and she said, "I know she's used to better but it's all I had in my freezer, what with you two running off without making supper. For shame!"

I didn't stay for the rest of the conversation. My sixth sense told me I should have laughed at Dee Dee, the greatest sucker for May's lies, scolding *me*, but I couldn't quite get into the mood for humor. I lay down in bed with my jacket on and went to sleep. When Ruby got home at two in the morning he smelled like booze and pot. He fell off the bed twice before he made it in. He tried touching me, but I wouldn't let him. I cried out, "Why can't you and Ma be friends?" I asked him the question, although I knew the answer.

"She don't like me," he said. "Let's forget her, baby." He was trying to stroke my neck and arms.

"Don't touch me, Ruby," I said, flicking him away. He was so loaded he fell right asleep. I guess you'd have to say that that was our very first lovers' spat.

Twelve

I T isn't fair that Ruby can't tell everybody what happened in
his life and here I am talking about the kind of person he is,
talking about his wide blue eyes and his gutter balls at Town
Lanes. Even though it isn't fair there doesn't seem to be a way
around it. I can't leave him out. I can't pretend he doesn't exist.
After being stymied for months I realized I would just have to
do my best to explain what happened to us. I would have to look
at him as if I were a judge with jowls and squinty eyes, the type
who can see around all sides of a person. If I were a judge I'd
try to congratulate people for their good points and then I'd tell
them gently how to improve. Except you have to have crystal
clear vision to judge — and that's a quality I don't have perfected
yet.

Afterwards, they brought Ruby's counselor, Sherry, to see me.
I think the idea was to try to make me understand absolutely
everything so I could kiss it goodbye and not have it come nagging
back at me. Sherry always smiled and said, "Hi there," when
she came for her visits, as if we'd been best friends for years. We
weren't best friends. I always had to look twice to see that her
short blond hair wasn't a snug-fitting cap. She came in her profes-

sional clothes and I imagined her putting on her sleek white pants without a thought of Ruby or me or Ma or Justy. She told me quite a bit about Ruby, while I sat hating her unless I got especially interested. She knew so many details about his life because she got him to talk to her through tricks and games. She had a glass bowl full of black licorice twists on her desk, which is probably the only reason he even showed up for his appointments.

Ruby and I didn't talk about his life history all that much because we were creatures of the moment. I like to think of us rolling in the grass and chasing through the woods like we had no more notion of the world than savages. Sherry sat in the recliner chair by the window in its upright position and she said she wondered where she should start; she laughed, ruffling up her hair, saying that I should probably be telling her about Ruby. Then, as if she'd had a novel idea, she said maybe we could help each other understand him, fill in each other's blanks. I knew she probably got her act straight out of a textbook that said, First, make a suggestion hinting at what you want; next, act surprised and laugh at your own thoughts; third, do whatever you need to do to trick the person into giving away all the secrets. I was on to her. She so wanted, she said, to start at the beginning of Ruby's life, and naturally we followed her wishes. I didn't add one speck to her wealth of knowledge, though; I kept the facts I knew of to myself.

I owe Sherry a lot for Ruby's story, but many of the details are mine. I already knew that Ruby and his two sisters grew up in a rambling old house down by the river in Stillwater. The parents rented it from absentee landlords who came to check up on it at a moment's notice. The whole house was available to Ruby's family, except for two rooms upstairs where the landlords stored their heirlooms. The special doors were secured with padlocks. Ruby and his sisters couldn't help feeling curious about the valuables inside. He drove me by the house once when we were first married to see how it was getting along. Sometimes he prowled around there, I know he did, because he liked to remember fragments from the old days.

Sherry had been in touch with Nancy and Sally Jane, Ruby's older sisters, but they hardly knew Ruby. Sherry explained that a professional has to go way back to the family, to the start, to get the answers. I laughed at the thought of her asking me in her innocent soft way, "Do you feel like talking about your mother?" I'd be so clever that she would never figure out that everything I've ever said in my life is in some way a reflection of May. I'd make her believe I was raised by Dinah Shore. At any rate, I've seen Ruby's sisters' senior pictures in Ruby's wallet. They were quite a bit older than their baby brother. Ruby was a mistake — that's what his father called him when he was riled. I never met either one of the girls even though they went to Stillwater High. Sally Jane was in all the plays and Nancy twirled batons in parades without dropping them. They both grew up, got married, moved away, and had children. Bingo, that's their lives in front of me. Sally Jane almost came to our wedding, but she was expecting and they said she couldn't fly on an airplane.

The sisters were half grown by the time Ruby was forced into the world with a pair of tongs at his head. He was awfully sick at first, according to Sherry. His organs couldn't handle food. He spit up constantly, and not simply a dribble here and there. Ruby launched that old vomit so far it wrapped itself around Saturn, which is why weathermen keep finding new rings. Naturally, the parents couldn't take him home right away. I can imagine all the adorable babies in the nursery, and then Ruby, screaming and puking on the soft white hospital blankets. Nobody said he looked precious. His mother cried the minute he was born probably, after she caught a glimpse of him. It didn't take her long to shorten the Reuben to Ruby. She wanted him to know that she could convince herself of his beauty, even if he did look like a mongrel.

Ruby finally had a stomach operation after three weeks of his constant howling. There was a disconnected tube inside him, but they were able to patch it up, good as new. He didn't have screaming fits now that he was put back together. The parents were only to keep observing their baby boy, see if he had strange behavior.

Then, as if the first weeks weren't strain enough, Ruby's mother, one warm summer evening, had a highball in the bathtub, holding her three-month-old baby in her arms. Next thing she knew her husband was slapping her awake and holding the baby upside down to drain water out of his lungs. In a voice as steady and quiet as a car's idle he told her she was not fit to be a mother. When she was asleep Ruby had slipped into the water, maybe thinking it was time to go back where he came from. After a while the rescue squad screeched up to the house and the paramedics jumped out and saved Ruby's life. The incident didn't help the parents' marriage too much. From the moment Mrs. Dahl stepped out of the bathtub, she decided, if her boy survived, that she would devote every inch of her life to him.

Sherry often hesitated before she spoke, as if she was sorting out the information she wanted to give me. She had said at first that she never betrayed confidences, but she had given this case a lot of hard thought and decided that it was important for me to know as much as possible about Ruby. To which I silently replied, "Remind me never to tell you anything." Still, it was her soft voice and the way she tilted her head, looking at me with her expression of understanding and sympathy, which might have eventually won me over. She told me that Ruby's first memory was of his father, in the living room, showing him how to put the toys away. Cleaning up was the last thing Ruby wanted to do. He sat picking his nose and then his father spanked him until his skin was raw and flaking. His father's methods didn't help Ruby learn to follow instructions or be tidy. As far as I can tell, when his parents explained a chore, Ruby's brain danced a jig into the next county. If he didn't respond, his father made him hang from the shower rod or he put him in the closet. Ruby sat still under the coats. He wasn't so afraid of the dark. It wrapped around him warm and close. He could think to himself, be his own best friend. If his mother was watching Ruby she said, "It's OK, sweetie, I'll put the blocks away. It's too hard for you." Ruby had her number down pat — he knew she loved doing any task for him.

I was always dreaming about being a princess when May said I should clean the chicken shed. Ruby and I were taken from the same mold, I'm sure of it. Except that Ruby was born lazier. He was born smiling at the thoughts in his head that no one could imagine, not even doctors with their brain scanners.

Sherry went on in her kind, kind voice to tell me about the time in kindergarten when the teachers had the children put puzzles together so they could tell how smart everyone was going to be in life. Sherry had read Ruby's top-secret school file to learn about his problems. Ruby didn't want to do quizzes for intelligence. He sat and stared and grinned. He refused to look at the games. When he knew all the teachers were watching him he shoved the puzzles off the table and the pieces went flying. He wasn't about to be a guinea pig. Sherry then explained the pattern at home for punishment: the father came in with his big stick and bashed Ruby over the head; the mother tried to rescue him and tell him he hadn't done a single thing; and then the father slapped one or both of them to demonstrate that he knew right from wrong.

I couldn't help blurting out that Ruby had always been a glutton for accidents. "How so?" Sherry asked, cocking her head so that the blond cap that was her hair flopped over to one side.

I told her about the time ten-year-old Ruby stuck a piece of macaroni up his nose and it practically killed him. His nose swelled up and took over his face. It sure was lucky, everyone at the hospital said, that he didn't shove a navy bean up there,

because at least the macaroni let him breathe through the hole.
All of his nasal membranes got infected. They had to knock him
out so they could fish up his nose and get at the noodle. Ruby
wasn't too crazy about doctors and hospitals. He felt like his nose
was one of the seven wonders the way the staff wanted to look
up it. He still breathes loudly — I think the macaroni made his
sinuses get permanently out of whack.

Sherry and I found ourselves laughing over Ruby's macaroni
nose, until we remembered everything else and then we shut up.
I was about to show her the pictures of Ruby's parents but I
decided I'd keep them to myself. Ruby's mother looks forlorn
and nice. She has bleached blond hair floating around her head
like it's cotton candy. You can barely make out the roots. Her
eyes are pale blue as if someone washed them out with bleach,
and they're not as wide as Ruby's. She looks dead tired in the
pictures, but you can tell she's a good person; you can tell she's
so sorry for drowning her boy.

Ruby told me once, when he was loaded and happy, that when
he grew up his mother appreciated him all the time because he
always helped her out. He hated to go to Longfellow elementary
school because he was nothing but a troublemaker and he spent
half his career in the principal's office. Classmates teased him
for reasons that are clear to me. They laughed because Ruby's
eyes were so far apart and dumb-looking, and because they turned
their noses downwind and sniffed something different. Children
have an advanced sense of smell and if your odor is off, they'll
punish you. Ruby wasn't crazy about baths until he moved into
our house and discovered the perfect combination: stewing in a
hot tub and listening to the ball game. Perhaps the children
thought the way he walked along the hall at Longfellow, banging
on each locker, with his pants falling down and his hair sticking
up, was queer, and they couldn't help taunting him. He didn't
have good luck when he tried to behave like other people. Everyone knew that he got expelled from Sunday school for goosing

all the boys and girls repeatedly. The Sunday school teacher said he was a little devil; that's the exact person ministers don't want to have in church. Ruby punched classmates whenever he got a chance, to get back at them for mocking him, and at home his father made him stick his head in a bucket and then he spanked him. It happened over and over, thousands of times. It doesn't seem a mystery to me, that violence won't cure violence. I suspect Mr. Dahl was a bale short of a full load.

But when Ruby came home from Longfellow in the afternoons there was his mother with her soft wide waist. She always had her apron on, and she hugged him so his head hit her middle. He just wanted to go to sleep right there on her small pot belly. After school they did activities together. She baked cookies and he measured the ingredients. He probably ate half the batter, but his mother didn't mind—that's how she was. They went to the grocery store and Ruby fetched items for her, because she walked slowly. She got winded if she went at a normal pace. He brought everything she said back to the cart and she never yelled at him, not once, even when he couldn't see that the pancake syrup was right in front of his face. He didn't have to do anything all that difficult for her to say he was a smart boy, a good boy.

When he was in high school he didn't tear around wrecking things too much. He stayed close by and helped his mother in the back yard. Or he went over to the neighbor, Uncle Jake, and learned how to build birdhouses. Jake wasn't actually his uncle, but that's what the sisters, Nancy and Sally Jane, called him when they were youngsters. Uncle Jake didn't talk a lot but he showed Ruby how to hammer and saw, drive nails into boards. I think Ruby was scared of him because he grumbled at mistakes and made sour comments into his beard. But Ruby liked doing crafts with his hands; he liked to see all the tools hung up neatly on the peg board, and Uncle Jake never yelled at him outright, except the time Ruby hocked his best wrench. Uncle Jake was so old he couldn't help being annoyed with young boys. I didn't find out until much later, until Sherry came to me, that it was Ruby who discovered Uncle Jake shot dead in his tool shed, and that Ruby didn't tell anyone for two weeks. Finally he told his girlfriend Hazel and she came to look at what was left, and then she called the police. Sherry said that years later, when Ruby was in her office telling her about Uncle Jake, he ate the whole bowl of black licorice while he paced.

All through school there were classmates who called Ruby a wimp for grocery shopping and doing laundry with his mother, but he couldn't care less. He continued to show them, by beating them up in private. Ruby was the class bully without one single friend to help him in the battle. It was Ruby, solo, against five or ten boys. I imagine he only had the afternoons to look forward to, when his mother sat on the lawn chair and told Ruby where to rake. She did it gently, plus she always raved about how strong he was. She couldn't believe the strength in his body. She loved looking at his back when he didn't have a shirt on. Sometimes, they went fishing down at the river together. They caught bass and brought them home for supper. He didn't like the skinning part. He let his mother take the guts out and chop off the heads. He didn't like to watch her, but he did mention that he was going to skin some of the boys at school and toss their brains in the garbage. She petted his hair and told him, "Shhh." They were both true sports enthusiasts. They made popcorn and watched baseball because his mother was also a Cubs fan. They liked rooting for the team they knew wasn't going to win.

Don't ask me where Ruby's father was in all this, besides being nearby with the billyclub. Ruby didn't ever talk about him. He didn't speak of his strong points. I have an image of Mr. Dahl in my head, however, from snapshots I've seen and now own. He is short with a belly made from beer and ham. There's a picture of him putting up screens on the back porch. He either just had a losing fight with someone or putting up screens is his idea of the afterlife in hell. He isn't a fat man, if you don't count his pot and his wide flabby cheeks and his lips. Those lips look like an African's lips, where there's so much meat they wear sticks through them for decorations. He's a real charmer, the kind of person you cross the street a block away to avoid.

Sherry tried to explain away Mr. Dahl. She said, "There's a lot of disappointment and anger there. Ruby's the only son and he simply doesn't have the kind of behaviors Mr. Dahl expects and demands."

I stared at the wall and thought of Mr. Dahl in the snapshot I have of him, when he was in the Marines. He's saluting and he has a grin on his face. I wished, while I listened to Sherry's words wash over me, that Mr. Dahl had never left his boat, that he had stayed in his bunk following orders forever. He never gave Ruby enough chances. He's the kind of person you could imagine biting the heads off of game birds.

It is probably worse for a father when he has a son that doesn't amount to much. It doesn't seem as important if the daughter is dumb. Perhaps it did make Mr. Dahl mad after a while, the way Ruby stared and smiled — because sometimes, if you didn't know better, you'd think there was nothing going on inside that brain of Ruby's; it's as if he was a round shiny glass ball. You have to take the time to look beyond his expressions. He's got hundreds of ideas inside him, rushing around in different directions. All the thoughts in his skull are having traffic jams. He had to hide behind his face with his father because he didn't have any wits in that man's presence. Sometimes I can laugh, in a sinister way, when I wonder what would have happened if May and Mr. Dahl had married each other. It would be like a cat fight every night, I wager. Fur flying and the sound of death in the air until one of them is far up a tree licking its wounds, waiting for the next round.

All through high school Ruby's mother dreaded the phone ringing. It was sure to be someone's mother saying that Ruby gave the son a bloody lip, or his teacher calling to say she was going to have to fail him for the fifth time. Ruby simply is not a scholar — that's why he was bored to death by every subject. He fell asleep when the teacher taught him about Hitler. It didn't bother him that two million people were gassed a day in Germany. He never even heard of that country. He liked building wood houses and watching sports; he liked to be sick and watch TV from his bed.

Both Sherry and I knew the story of Ruby scooping ice cream in high school at the Dairy Queen. The job didn't last too long. He couldn't remember how to make banana splits. He told customers Dairy Queen was all out of bananas — the truck didn't bring in a load yet. The boss heard him telling the story about how the bananas went rotten in the back room; there were bugs eating them — you couldn't see any bananas for the black beetles. He grabbed Ruby by the collar and shoved him against the ice cream machine. Mr. Dahl didn't have kind words when Ruby came home without his uniform.

When Ruby finally graduated from Stillwater High, long before I went there, his mother called around to find him a job. She couldn't help doing dirty work for him because she was afraid of what would happen to him. She probably felt like he was a cat who didn't have claws, couldn't defend himself.

First, Ruby worked down at Sears with his father in the shipping room. I didn't have to guess too long to find out how that episode turned out. They had to tell him every step, every other day, and sometimes he got it wrong. His father stood over him with his pitchfork planted firmly on the floor and naturally Ruby's face twitched and his hands went stiff. He knew he was going to make a mistake any minute.

One night in bed when he was in a rare mood for thinking about the past, he said to me, "This is a secret, OK, baby?"

"I won't tell," I whispered.

"I wet my pants down there in the shipping department. My father could tell, he sniffed it out. I was scared because I screwed up an order royal. I sent a whole box of ladies' slips to the bank manager, instead of drapes. I was sure all the men at Sears was going to come in a row to slit my throat."

I told him it didn't matter. I said I would have done worse than wet my pants. He felt my face in the dark, like Miss Finch used to. His hands were saying that I was beautiful and that together we could make a path through a whole state of thorns and poisonous berries.

Sherry told me that Ruby ditched work at Sears, and he messed up the invoices when he was there, and that finally he went to his mother and cried while he banged his head against the kitchen door. He said he wasn't going to work any more. Most certainly his mother stroked his hair and said, "It's OK, Ruby, we'll find you something else." For several months he didn't do anything. I know how he spent his time because although I am not a social worker I know Ruby and his hobbies. I have a clear picture of him sitting around the house, listening to the radio and singing along with rock musicians. Ruby's gift is his sweet high voice, almost as high as a girl's. It sounds awfully pretty, and he can sing any song you say. I wished Aunt Sid had heard him sing. He could figure out songs on the piano down in the church basement and no one ever taught him how. Probably his musical genius is one more reason Ruby's father thought he was cracked — and to top it off Ruby spent whatever money he earned on records. He sang along with his favorite groups, pretending he was the lead singer, bending his knees and making faces into the mike. He danced around in the living room strumming his fake guitar. It was the one without strings that he garbage picked. He was the drummer, the singer, and the guitar player simultaneously. With the music he was set free from all the ideas people had about him; with the records on Ruby sang himself into a dream state where he was number one on the charts.

However, finally Ruby's mother told him, when he was slouching on the sofa doing nothing, "Ruby, I'm not always going to be here to take care of you. You have to get a job. You can't sit home for the rest of your life and dance around the living room."

So Ruby found employment at the Zephyr gas station pumping gas. His neighbor, Mr. Wallace, owned it. He was willing to give Ruby a chance and Ruby came through—he was a pretty good gas pumper. He wiped up the car windows and performed responsible tasks such as making change. The fact about Ruby is that he can do jobs if he wants to, if you can teach him as patiently as possible. He gets so frustrated when he does something wrong; he rips up sheets of paper and grinds his teeth. I bet he could do a lot more capable jobs than people think, if they could only give him chances. Employers don't understand that Ruby is so proud he's afraid to try. He hates it when people laugh at him for messing up—that's not counting bowling. He didn't care about his gutter balls, probably because whenever he bowled he was smashed. If I had once said, "Ruby, here's how you bowl," or said he was a dumb bowler, he would never have set foot in Town Lanes again. He has this big proud scared heart.

Ruby never explained the next chapter in his life. Again, Sherry had to fill me in on the details. She told me that she had asked him to draw pictures, and then they'd talk about his portraits. He never drew his father, if you don't count the one with King Kong devouring a few children. Ruby always came up with the same picture: himself in the foreground nursing his beautiful golden-haired mother. All her life she had asthma, plus she smoked constantly. Maybe when she lit up, the delicious cigarettes took her mind off her Marine husband and how he turned purple with his rages if the storm windows weren't washed properly. The whole neighborhood could hear him if a piece of dust landed on the kitchen table and it didn't get cleaned up instantly. Cigarettes took her mind off the fact that he didn't have one soft spot. She couldn't breathe half the day and night and she wasn't going to go to a doctor because they always told her she had to quit smoking. She tried but she didn't have any will power in that department. Smoking brought her peace of mind for a few seconds at a time.

She hacked so often she wore herself out. She'd get attacks, and all you could do was stand and stare at her twisting and hacking and spitting. Her problem wasn't anything aspirin could solve and she was allergic to drugs doctors wanted to prescribe. And because Ruby thought parents, for example, Mr. Dahl, were permanent, it was a shock for him when she gasped for breath hysterically one morning. She was stuck halfway out of bed. Medics had to rush in with oxygen for her and then they removed her to the hospital.

When the attack occurred they made her quit smoking, no ifs, ands, or buts. She wasn't going to ever take a drag again, period. By the time Ruby was working at the Zephyr gas station she had to stay at home, close to the tanks of oxygen they had for her, in case she felt the urge to go blue. Ruby could not fail to notice her habit of inhaling as if she had twelve tin cans tied together down in her throat. A person could always tell where she was in the house by following the noise of her constricted breaths. She got cross because her nerves were on edge without nicotine, plus she felt absolutely rotten. She didn't have such a nice sweet character any more. Her daughters had moved away, Ruby was at work, her husband drank alcohol at night to settle his fat stomach. She watched TV for ten hours straight. Television doesn't do one thing to make a person happy: first you begin to think you're straight out of a soap opera, where people are either thoroughly wicked or absolutely pure, and then your head turns to Jell-O. Mr. Dahl did the best he could, probably, to take care of Ruby's mother, considering his personality. He worked overtime to pay for the nurse who checked up on his wife twice a week.

Sherry said that finally Nancy, Ruby's sister, came up from

Florida and she convinced her parents that they should move down South with her, to the sunshine that makes old bones feel better, to the air that is free of dust and pollen. They were going to walk along the ocean and breathe the brisk salt air. Mr. Dahl arranged a transfer with Sears and then they packed up the house and moved to Florida. There wasn't extra room at Nancy's place for Ruby, and besides, Mr. Dahl told Ruby he was grown now; it was high time he got out on his own. His mother hardly resembled her old self. She no longer commented on her fine boy, Ruby, who filled Mrs. Carson's brand-new Buick with regular gasoline when her car required lead-free. Mrs. Dahl could hardly walk, let alone breathe. She couldn't make any more nice rules. She told Ruby they'd send him the money to fly down next winter and then she'd find him a job, but he knew there wasn't a place for him there. He could tell it in the way his father stared blankly when she said, "Sweetheart, we'll send you money, I promise." Ruby was no dumbbell. He cried uncontrollably when they loaded her into the car. They had to lift her in and bend her legs for her, as if she were a stiff corpse already. He prayed, for the first time in his life, while they put pillows around her. He wished she'd come walking back to him, singing country and western — she'd have that much extra breath to sing songs.

There wasn't anyone to take care of Ruby now. He was an adult, full-fledged. He found a place that looked just like a pigsty. It cost fifty dollars a month because it wasn't too much bigger than a closet. If Ruby had pizza for supper, say, and didn't finish, there it would be three weeks later still on the counter, only you couldn't tell it was a pizza because it looked like where the ants lived. Now that he was an adult he began wrecking other people's possessions. He walked into the house down by the river and broke the locks on the rooms where the landlords had all the heirlooms stored. He smashed the bureaus; he took a knife and slashed the upholstery that was from the time of George Washington. The landlords weren't thrilled about the ruins.

He got loaded and drove around bashing into people's cars. He didn't even have a license, plus he stole a junker down at the gas station. He shoplifted from stores without trying to act like a burglar. He walked into the drugstore, picked up a couple of watches from the counter, and then swaggered out, holding on to the loot. Anyone could see him. And when they came chasing after him he socked people and kicked them. Sherry said, "He knew he needed help desperately, and this was the way he could count on attention. His deviance was a scream for help."

I said, "Sure," and stared directly at her until she had to avert her eyes.

Ruby went crazy on drugs one night, waited outside the Sears store, and beat up his former boss. The old man had to go to the hospital for concussion. Ruby should have gone to jail but the boss was best friends with Mr. Dahl. They settled it out of court. Ruby had to see a counselor and report to an officer. He never liked to discuss it with me, because he was ashamed. He bragged about it sometimes, if he was with Daisy. They talked about the thousands of times they fooled police. Ruby even boasted to Daisy that he had been in jail: he said there was a huge room filled with chairs and then up in front sat a TV. He said the guard was the one who decided what channel they could watch, so all they got to see was *Outdoor World* and *Wild Kingdom*, while they wolfed down their coffee cake. He was daydreaming about prison—Sherry herself said he had a clear record.

Daisy and Ruby met down at the police station. They clowned around while they were waiting to see their officers. Occasionally they bumped into each other at the resource center, where Ruby had his appointments with God Almighty Sherry. I remember once, before we were married, when we almost ran over Herself at the grocery store. She chatted and laughed with Ruby, asked him how he was doing that day. You could tell he was one of her favorite victims. I walked down the aisle so I wouldn't tip the sacks of flour on her head. I didn't want to be responsible for knocking her out cold.

When I met Ruby he had long since had dates with Hazel, the old bag he learned on, and Hazel's cousin, Isabel. They were both available for several young boys. They liked fresh ones best since they're juicier. Ruby didn't have any friends except the old ladies and his counselor, and Daisy talked to him now and then. They slapped each other five on the street. She'll talk with anything that wears jockey shorts. When I met Ruby he wasn't seeing his officer any more. He had exemplary behavior, if you don't count the alcohol he drank for recreation and the stunts he pulled when he was under the influence. Sherry made him go to night classes to learn skills such as power mechanics. He hated the class; he almost chopped off his thumb on the band saw. Still, Sherry always told him what a marvelous job he did with his fingers. I had to face the fact that she had attractions for him besides the black licorice on her desk; I could tell he worshiped her. He loved her when she said he was making fantastic progress. Sometimes he went to the Catholic Church for mass. He sat in the back and prayed for his mother. He went over her whole body in his mind calling upon the good Lord to come on down with his vacuum and do a job on her lungs.

Ruby still went to see Sherry after we were married. He was addicted to her loving gaze. She gave him suggestions about exactly how to run his life. I know Ruby, more than Sherry does, even if I don't know every single detail of his past life. I know that in the bottom of his soul all he wants to do is be a gentle person, a good boy. He wants friends to tell him what a sensational job he's doing. I know, because I'm married to him.

I liked Ruby to tell me about his mother, only the stories got him choked up. She passed away from pneumonia the year before we were married. The infection seeped into her brain and she died without one memory. She didn't remember that she had a son named Ruby. She stared at her husband with no expression on her face and then died with her eyes open. Ruby and Sherry told me the facts and I figure it's my job to fill in the details as vividly as I can. Even if I've elaborated a little I'd say it gets to the heart of the matter.

When Sherry left me for the last time she said, "We carry Ruby with us, don't we?" I had to look at her, and I realized, for a split second, that she felt the burden of it. I didn't answer her, but I have to admit I felt just a little of my weight lift. If I ever see her again I might just say thank you.

Thirteen

THE times in bed, when Ruby told me scenes from his life, were secret for us. They didn't happen that often because he didn't want to think about the past too much. He didn't crack jokes when he was telling the stories. He was dead serious. There's a place in Ruby that's about as sterling as the heart of the most blessed saint who ever lived on earth. I see the place as a pouch, filled with all the ingredients that could make a person behave perfectly.

Every now and then though, he did do something haywire. Never mind about the time the police found him in the marsh, drunk and covered with mud. They shone their beam on him and he thought it was an angel. Nothing I said to him for weeks afterwards convinced him that the police had brought him home. He insisted on angels.

There were other incidents which made May suggest the loony bin out loud. She knew the exact words to wound me. May and Ruby and I used to go together to the orchard nearby to get our apples. They have hundreds of varieties and May knows every single apple, because she's been going there for forty years. It's the strangest place to visit in the fall. You can smell the windfall apples on the ground, rotting into sweet mush, and up in the trees on ladders are people from the deaf school. It isn't far from Stillwater. You can't hear anything but animal sounds in the orchard — it's the hired deaf people speaking to each other in grunts and groans from the middle of trees. I wondered what they were talking about in their language while their swift hands moved to pick the apples. Maybe they were calling out joyfully without even knowing it. Maybe they had music in their heads, sounds they invented that were as lovely as waves coming to shore, or birds making their way South. Their sounds were trapped inside the small space of their heads, never to reach their own ears.

In the winter, when we went for apples, with only the memory of harvest smells and sounds, May and Ruby had to argue over what variety to get, and they made the man give out samples. That's when I wished I didn't have ears in working order. May spat the skins into her hand and automatically hated the ones Ruby wanted, and then they bickered over who should pay. I remember one time in particular when Ruby said, "I'll take ten pounds of Ida Red apples" — they were his favorites — and May said, "Ida Reds don't cook up good for my pies; I like saucy pies."

So Ruby looked at the ground and told the man, "OK, five pounds Ida Reds, five pounds saucy cooker," and he whispered to me, "Baby, *you're* a saucy cooker."

He elbowed me in the ribs so affectionately. If May hadn't been there I would have giggled into my hands.

"I'm not paying," May said, going into her song and dance. "I'm alone now," she explained. "I'm just one person and you two are two people, see, so you should pay."

May apparently had the idea that Ruby was a heart surgeon or president of the company. But actually she was mocking him, in her own style, on account of the way he could put away a twelve-pack of beer and sit still for so long in front of the TV. She was making him understand how low he was, not being able to pay the food bill for his family. She knew he didn't have any money; she knew she was picking a fight. I looked at the ground the entire time pretending I was a regular person who might well say, "Now ain't they the dumbest people you've ever seen?" May always ended up paying. She was the only one who had the cash and we knew it from the start.

She kept saying that she was alone, but it wasn't so. It was Ruby and May and myself, all together. It was something we had to face up to.

When we came home from the orchard May seemed to be in a particularly bad mood. She talked about how we never got the kind of apples she liked, and Ruby had already eaten half of the cookers, and look who paid for them too, and she was working her life away down at Trim 'N Tidy, and I don't want to remember all the things that irritated her; she could go on and on in an endless stream about how nothing was right for her. I always stared at one object, except sometimes my eyes would land on her red twisted lobster hands and they'd get me in my weak spot. They were hideous. I could see that time did a job on those knuckles of hers.

After we ate supper and May's pies weren't saucy enough, because of the Ida Red apples she had to use, Ruby walked into Honey Creek. I assumed he was going to fetch Randall so they could watch a movie about men pricking animals, their favorite subject. I wished he was down the basement trying to make warped boards fit snugly together but there wasn't anything I could do about it. I didn't know what happened to him until the phone rang.

I remember hearing the sirens but I didn't think anything of it. The rescue squad went roaring into town and I said my usual line to myself, "I'm glad it isn't coming for me; knock on wood."

With Ruby, ideas are born instantly: he's walking along in the dark holding on to the railing, watching for ducks, and the next thing he's over the bridge, screaming down to the water. It's only about three feet deep and a jump of twenty. He didn't plan to leap from the bridge, but something must have whispered to him. The scheme appealed to the crawdad he's had buried in him since before birth. When the rescue squad chased down the road it was to fish Ruby out of the water, for the second time in his life. Jonathan Baker was tampering with the pay phone there on the corner so he saw Ruby jump. Although it was December the river wasn't quite frozen over yet. Still, it was cold enough for the fish to shut down, too stiff to move from the hard mud bottom. Paramedics had to wear special suits to get Ruby, to protect their bodies. They dragged him out, slapped his face, wrapped him up. He was limp and filthy. When the hospital called me I started to cry. I didn't know what they were saying; I heard only that Ruby was there, room 209. It was an accident, they said. They told me he was shivering so fiercely he bumped his head on the bed rail and fainted.

May tried to pat me when I stood up in the living room blabbering about how I had to go to the hospital. I didn't make any sense. I mentioned the words "cold river water" and "Ruby" and then I burst into tears. I guess I cried constantly in those days. She turned the TV down and led me into the kitchen, sat me down and made me drink cocoa, as if I were the one with the chill.

"Ruby is going to be fine," she said. "You'll see."

She didn't even know the story. She made me repeat the doctor's speech as clearly as I could. When she heard the news she said, "Don't cry, angel" — she hadn't called me that in about twenty years. "He'll be OK," she said gently, in the voice she reserved for Dee Dee.

Then she drove me to the hospital. I was sobbing the whole time but she talked a blue streak about nothing special — how we were running out of jelly already, we better put hay around the basement windows, everyone said it was going to be record cold this winter, she couldn't remember how many mice we had caught in the past week, but the cats were cheerful about the

quantity. She kept on talking. She dropped me off before she
parked so I could rush up to his room.

There he was all wrapped up in blankets, his lips purple, his
face cut. He was covered with bruises and was suffering from
shock. He lost hundreds of degrees from his body. It's a miracle
he didn't break his neck off or turn into an ice cube. He managed
to grin; I cried even harder because his lips were the brown color
of a mummy's. He said he didn't know what made him do it.
All he knew was for a few seconds he felt pretty spectacular, like
Clark Kent does in every single emergency, and then *splat* he
hit the water.

"Don't ever do that again," I whimpered, and he grinned at
me even wider, saying, "Baby, I'll listen to you, I'll do whatever
you say."

Every now and then Ruby did something exceptional, as I said,
but he's my husband and there are qualities I love in him. I
didn't tell anyone at work about the river escapade.

When he got out two days later May paid the hospital bill.
Sherry was going to wangle Medical Assistance for us, but still I
hated to see May at the desk paying for Ruby to jump in the
river, on account of I knew in my bones that it was going to be
fuel for her later.

It was a difficult winter, not only because Ruby looked like a
washed-up fish, but because Daisy went way down to Peoria to
the beauty college there. It wasn't any fun to bowl without Daisy,
so I retired from my favorite sport. And she never wrote letters,
so I felt as if I'd lost a friend. I still wrote Aunt Sid on occasion.
I told her it was a new sensation, getting promoted at Trim 'N
Tidy, because I was a spotter now, but May was only a finisher.
I tried to act puny around May when we were at work because
I knew it grated on her nerves, to see me doing such a hotshot
job. I was always excluding small truths from Aunt Sid—for
instance, I didn't say that acting puny probably made me feel

kind of puny too. Being a newlywed and acting small all day long was bound to make my brain feel two quarts low. I didn't know if I could kiss Ruby in front of May when we came home from work. I wanted to, but I felt shy. I always stood in the door smiling at him like a fool.

Aunt Sid was still asking me what books I liked. She didn't seem to get the picture. How was I supposed to read books when I was trying to be a good spotter, and then when I came home I had to feed the chickens and wash the dishes? I had to learn how to be Mrs. Ruby Dahl. I didn't have time or spunk to go outside and sit and stare at the world. The young girl I had been was gone.

My favorite time, that first year of our marriage, was Christmas Eve. Matt didn't come home, of course, but Dee Dee and Daisy came over and we had a celebration. There were the five of us — Randall was along too, but he doesn't count. He sat on the sofa stuffing potato chips in his mouth, watching *Love Boat*. We all got smashed and Ruby began leading us in song. We were singing Christmas carols in the kitchen while Ruby stood on the stool conducting like Aunt Sid. I pinned a fake rose to his shirt and it drooped. Daisy quietly stripped to "Silent Night." We howled at the sight of her taking off her sweater inch by inch. She got as far down as her long underwear but you could see through to her hot pink bikinis. I guess stripping is her idea of heavenly peace. May had her mouth open so wide when she laughed it looked like it might get stuck and never close. She was royally corked. After a while Ruby turned on the radio and we danced around. I thought I was delirious when I saw that Ruby and May were dancing. They were doing the polka and the fox trot, with May as instructor. They were a perfect match for a couple, out there on the kitchen floor. Ruby bent his knees and stuck out his hind end so he'd be the same height, so they could skim along the linoleum. May's lids were at half-mast.

You couldn't see anything but the whites of her eyes. When Ruby stood tall she rested her head on his shoulder; she about fell asleep in his drunk arms. She didn't notice if they bashed into chairs. Finally he dumped her off on the sofa and she curled right up and went out.

The next day, Christmas morning, when we all looked as if we were afflicted with the same terrible disease which made your skin turn gray, your eyes go bloodshot, and your lips dry up, I told her that she had danced with Ruby. She said I was crazy. She didn't remember one minute of it. I wanted to shake her so she'd have the pleasure of remembering her best party self. I wanted her to remember that everyone in the room had been her friend.

It was January when Ruby got a part-time job down at the can truck that sits outside of the grocery store in Stillwater. It's open twice a month for three hours on Saturdays. It's the place for cans and dead batteries and newspapers. Ruby weighed all the recycled stuff and paid the customers. Being the Can Man was the ideal job for Ruby. One of the check-out girls lent him her little tiny TV set and he sat in the truck and watched his favorite shows if no one came. Right after he started I asked May for some of my paycheck money. She said, "What for?"

I mumbled, "I need to buy Ruby something." I didn't care if we ran short at the end of the month.

She waited for me to elaborate. I held out as long as I could and then I spit it out—"A winter suit, for work."

The next day she come home and inside her Goodwill bag was an enormous brown snowmobile suit. She said, "Go get him, see if it fits." I couldn't find him anywhere, but later when he came in and tried it on he said to the mirror, "Hey, it's me, Yogi the Bear." He scratched his head and made his teeth buck and then grinned at himself. He liked the two zippers up and down the front, which he explained were for pissing in the snow without having to take the whole works off. He liked the can truck and his special suit. He'd say to me when he came in the kitchen door, "Baby, it's me, your sugar, the Can Man."

When we were home in the evenings he performed concerts up in our room. He turned on the radio and sang to me, his best girl. I liked the slow songs he sang too, the one called "If You Leave Me Now," which he'd sing mournfully to me.

My devotion to mother nature fails me when the temperature drops below zero. It was ten below for three weeks in a row that year, and our place isn't all that cozy. There's frost on the inside walls on winter mornings and it is almost impossible to step out of the warm spot you've worked so hard to make under the pile of thin wool blankets. We could see our breath in our bedroom; we could feel the wind sweeping across the fields, battering the house. The wind didn't have any mercy for the likes of us. It didn't care that we aren't equipped with fur, and that May never turned the heat up far enough. She refused to waste the oil.

Winter wasn't May's favorite time of year either. She always said that them bones of hers felt petrified. She sat in her chair in the kitchen some days, when it was the terrible cold, and she conducted to me. She told me precisely how much water to put in the hot cereal, how many seconds to stir the orange juice. She had to conduct from her chair on account of her fossilized bones. I sure wished May and Ruby's mother could have met. They would have had a lot to discuss. They could have compared their dying bodies.

Sometimes I felt so mixed up, being a wife and a daughter under the same roof. There was the Saturday when Ruby came in from work; he didn't stop to take off his snowsuit; he said urgently, "Baby, I got to show you something. Come this way with me."

We went up to our room. He shut the door and said, "Close your eyes." I could feel him tying an object around my waist, and when I looked there was a tail, a coon's tail, hanging down behind me. Someone threw it out in the can truck. Ruby found it under a sack of newspapers. He stood grinning at me and he said, "Now you're my jungle kitten." He said I should take my clothes off except for the tail, so I did it, even in the cold. We were prancing around our bedroom, laughing so hard because I bit him, nipped at his flanks. That's what jungle kittens do. I knew their behavior instinctively. I chased him over the bed, jumped down on the floor clawing gently at the backs of his hairy knees. I trapped him in the corner. He let me. He wanted me to purr right on his favorite organ. Did I light the fire! He threw his head back and roared. He was Jungle Tom, beating on his chest and coming after me, growling deep down in his throat. I couldn't help screaming timid screams, so delicately. The noises made Ruby growl even more; finally he pinned me to the bed and forced my legs apart while I giggled and screeched.

We did a repeat performance right away even though I knew May was down scrubbing carrots in the sink for her famous stew. Ruby and I lay in bed and I whispered to him that he was the best man I knew of in the universe, the way he could keep going two million times. Finally, when I cooled off, I went downstairs to give May a hand. She said, without looking up, "Well, well, well, if it ain't the jungle kitten herself."

I stood still. I wished that moment wasn't there. I wanted to rewind and have a miracle take place; I wanted to hear May say, "Hello there, angel. I've never seen you look so happy."

We sat down to supper. No one said one thing. I didn't eat. I stared at my plate. I wanted to do something extreme to pay her for ruining our fun, to pay her for making us feel like slimy creatures who don't have anything on their minds but mating dances. What did she wish for in a daughter—that I had been born without sensation? I wanted to wreck something special of hers, break it into pieces she would not be able to fit back together. Then I'd snip the phone cord so she couldn't call Dee Dee. When I didn't touch my potatoes May barked, "What's wrong?"

"Nothin'," I muttered.

After that it wasn't fun roughhousing with the tail. I hid it way in the back of the closet even though I was a star jungle kitten.

As the winter months wore on, as it got muddier and damper without warming up, our tempers frayed. After a while there wasn't anything left of our restraint. We'd had the cold for so long, and we were just waiting, waiting for our emotions to ignite. We were sitting at supper, silent like always, except for May's griping. It was a rainy March night, and you couldn't see anything but black and the glittering rain catching our lights. It was cold in the house because May was trying to get by without ordering another tank of oil. Our hands and noses were raw.

She got up from the table to get some more soup and she noticed a few spots of red paint on the floor. She stooped down to examine the spots. She said, as if she was surprised, "Ruby, I do believe you spilled some paint from the birdhouses of yours on the floor."

Ruby didn't say anything. It wasn't a big deal to him. He was picking dead skin off his hands very carefully. She came to the table and leaned over. She said, "You listening to me, Mr. Jungle Tomcat?"

We both had to look up into her narrow eyes. She spoke low and distinct. She said, "You clean up that paint right now or I'm kicking you out of here. All you do is build them birdhouses like a moron. That's about the biggest laugh I ever thought of, a grown man building houses for the little birdies, now ain't that sweet?"

He sat for a minute hearing her special tones. After only a minute or two of delayed reaction he sprang from the table, picked up two of his houses in his wide spread hands and threw them expertly, like his curve balls, against the wall. They busted apart. They aren't made to survive a blast. He whacked the others down on the floor. I stood still in the middle of the floor. I couldn't make sense of the wood splinters exploding in the air, May's smirk, saliva and tears making Ruby's face shiny, as if someone went and shellacked it. I thought that if I stood still maybe it all would stop.

After the houses were ruined and there was the near silence, the ringing from past noise, Ruby ran out of the house. I had to follow him. I ran down the porch stairs calling out into the rain, "Ruubeeeee, Ruuuuuubeeeeee, come back."

He didn't answer. I found him close by, in the middle of the yard, standing in the mud. He stooped so he could cry on my shoulder. He was his own rainstorm, and I held him and stroked his wet hair. He loved the houses and he went and wrecked them. No one had ever told him before that they were stupid. Everyone — that's Dee Dee and I — always said they were extremely beautiful. He wept. It was so cold his tears were the consistency of slush.

"Baby," he whimpered, "I just got to take a walk."

I held him up and we started off down the road. We had nothing on but our sweaters and pants, already soaked. It was dark and misty. The cars came slowly out of nowhere and splashed us at the side of the road. I didn't ask where we were going. We must have walked halfway to Stillwater, holding hands, not saying a word.

When we came to the house it was all lit up. I knew, by the sixth sense, when Ruby turned up the drive, that it was where Hazel lived, with her cousin, Isabel, and whoever else happened to be around. Every single light was on. Ruby walked right into the house, without knocking.

Hazel and Isabel were in the kitchen, playing gin rummy. They must have been at it for a while because there were lots of empty bottles around. Their kitchen was spacious but all they had was a small white linoleum table against the wall and two yellow kitchen chairs with the stuffing coming out. There were bottles everywhere and empty shelves, as if they never had the occasion to eat or cook in the room. When Hazel bothered to look up she said, "Well, if it ain't the newlyweds!" Then she looked at us more carefully and said, "Hey, Izzy, do you think it's Halloween? Don't them two look like they're dressed up as drowned rats?" She laughed at her joke and then got serious. "Do we have any candy?"

Isabel was quiet. She was young and blond and had a waist the size of a signpost. She was bored by everything, even jokes.

Ruby pulled up a stool and helped himself to an open beer while I stood, waiting again for the scene to evaporate. I was convinced that if I stood long enough it would just go away.

After a long time listening to the two slap their cards and shuffle and deal, and listening to Ruby guzzle and burp, Hazel looked up again and said, "I bet Mrs. Dahl would love to see the zoo."

"No, she don't," Ruby said, but Hazel had me by the hand. She took me down the basement and turned the light on, and I saw the snake cages on one wall and the mice cages on the other. "We'll get one of the constrictors for you to hold, sweetheart," she said to me, smiling so that her smooth face wrinkled up. While she fiddled with the latch she said, "I bet Ruby's told you all about me, all about our magic times down here."

I whispered, "No."

She laughed and said, "You mean he don't brag about the time he nipped my boob so bad I was a living blood bath?" She had a puckered look come over her for a split second and then she turned to the snake and crooned, "Come on, honey bun."

I took the thing in both my hands, wondering when I was going to wake up. "Take it to Ruby," she said. "He loves my pets."

I carried the python up while it slowly wrapped around my arm. It was four feet long and as big around as Isabel's waist. I didn't mind it so much. It hadn't asked to be Hazel's snake.

When I came up into the light of the kitchen Ruby took one look at me and put the whiskey bottle down. He retched into his sleeve and was gone out the door. If I'd had my wits about me I would have thanked Hazel for making him leave, but as soon as I could unwind the creature from my arm I set him on the table and followed Ruby.

I caught up with him near home. He had his pocket-size pancake syrup jug full of liquor and we drank as we walked along. I had hundreds of questions I wanted to ask him, such as "Why did we go there?" but I was afraid to ask him. I was afraid Ruby would say, "They are my best friends." I knew that a person always got the urge to see their best friend when they found themselves in trouble.

For a while we sat with the hens. Ruby finally said, "I like birds better than people." He took a drink and said, "I bet angels look like doves, white ones."

"Sure," I said.

We sat out there drinking and singing "Sunshine on My Shoulders," and other songs by Ruby's favorite composer, John Denver. Every now and then Ruby would start daydreaming about how he was going to climb mountains with John Denver, the tallest mountains, and all you'd have to do is take one little step off the top and you'd be in heaven.

I didn't correct him; I didn't say if he stepped off years later someone would find a skeleton in the darkest valley, and they'd know it was Ruby by his black front tooth.

It took me a long time to get up my nerve but when I finally got it I blurted, "How come you bit Hazel?"

Ruby laughed one of his genuine laughs, not the big ha-ha's that mean he's nervous. He said, "She took me down to her zoo one day, calls out, 'Who wants to be lunch?' Then she grabs a mousie from a cage and beats it with a ruler in the wastebasket." He looked like he was going to be sick again. "She made me watch the snake eat it up.

"Baby," he whispered, "she deserved to be bit. If she hadn't squirmed so much I would have swallowed her whole."

We didn't say anything more. We slumped down and lay still. Finally, we climbed the back steps clutching each other, stiff and shivering. The whiskey was long gone and the old horse blanket I'd found in the barn was soaked from our wet skins. After May went to work in the morning I called up Artie and told him I was sick as a dead pig. It was not a lie. Ruby and I were both feverish. We lay in bed throwing wads of Kleenex on the floor. We didn't do anything but lie there side by side, throwing off the covers one minute and the next huddling under them, all the while trying to breathe.

When May came home in the evening she was prepared to be huffy and prim. She was probably dying to know where we'd been all night, but she wasn't about to ask. We could hear her walking around downstairs, looking for us so she could show us her aloof personality. Finally she heaved upstairs. She came and stood by our door. She could not figure out what was going on. When she peered in and saw us on our bed I started sneezing and moaning. It was a good show. My head felt like a bowl full of hot applesauce. I couldn't breathe; I felt as if I was going to suffocate from all my clogged byways. Ruby wasn't any better off, plus he had to vomit now and then in a bucket, side effects of the whiskey.

"Don't stand there staring, Ma," I snorted. "Look what you've done to us, chasing us out of the house." I started to cry. I said, "I think you better apologize to my husband Ruby."

Of course May never says she's sorry but she did make us chicken soup. She brought us Cokes. She felt halfway responsible, I know she did, for the fact that we were so miserable. She could hear our sniffles and our whimpering. She must have actually felt guilty because she took the next day off. She waited on us hand and toe. In between some of the shows she watched on TV she put trays of orange juice outside our door. We could come and fetch some whenever we were thirsty. And when I came down for lunch she made me stick the thermometer in my mouth. After she read it she shook it out so vigorously I doubted her advanced age. She could have been a head nurse easily. We never mentioned the scene in our kitchen. We put it away, inside ourselves. But those birdhouses were the last Ruby ever made in his whole life, as far as I know.

It wasn't too long after our sickness that I found out. We were going along, having our silent suppers, but it wasn't like we were at the end of our ropes any more. We were tired and quiet. We were sick to death of winter and our fighting. I was at Trim 'N Tidy one day, watching the stains go by me, the dirt and grease speckling the clothes, and a wave came over me. There wasn't any way my breakfast was going to remain in my stomach. I started staggering around the back room. Artie came to me, grabbed my elbow, and said, "What's the matter, sweetie?"

"I don't know," I said, and then for no reason I sat down and cried, again, for about the billionth time that year. It seemed to me that I was weeping for the race of man, for everyone who had ever lived through adolescence and marriage and then died. I went into the restroom, just in time, and of course after the vomiting I had to cry some more, leaning over the sink. Artie demanded that I call the doctor at the clinic. He stood next to me while I explained over the phone that I couldn't hold anything down in my stomach, and he made me ask if it was food poisoning on account of sharing Louise's old hard-boiled Easter eggs.

The doctor asked me some questions and then he said, "It sounds to me like what you have is a baby, Mrs. Dahl."

"No," I said. "No." I turned away from Artie and whispered into the receiver, "I've only been married six months."

"That's about how long it takes," he said.

For some reason it never occurred to me that it was a baby inside making me sick, because all the time I had been trying to keep track of May and Ruby. That was an enormous job. I didn't think of anything else but our relationships together. Also, expert

Ruby said I wouldn't get pregnant if I washed myself off very carefully.

Artie must have guessed because he slowly backed off from the phone and left me alone.

A few days later I had an appointment at the clinic. Louise had to go to town so she drove me in during lunch. They took blood and wished me luck. I couldn't wait for the nurses to tell me the news—I suspended myself for three days like I was a hung garment in the closet. I didn't think of one single thing except the baby inside me. I knew it was there; I knew absolutely that's why I felt so sad one minute and then the next like I was a rocket going straight up to the sword of Orion, one of my favorite places. I didn't tell anyone about the possibility. Finally they called me at work and said the test was accurate: I was going to have a baby.

Naturally, I instantly sat down and bawled. I was thinking about the night our baby probably came to life, when we were both loaded up to our eyeballs. I wondered if that meant it was going to be born drunk, if it would come out without the capacity to imagine and remember. It was Artie who came to me again, and I couldn't help telling him. He seemed to know everything. He said that most new mothers worried that their babies were going to come out mooing like a cow or squawking like a chicken. I suddenly loved him so much, not only because he was short with a little round head and hair so thin it looked like a cloud traveling over his skull, but because he patted my hand and said, "Don't worry." He looked me in the eye and said, "No more liquor, no more smokes." Then he laughed and said, "Why ain't I in the medical profession?"

I nodded my head and said he could be my doctor any old day.

I swear it had been raining solid through March and now into April. Perhaps it was just my spirit. The fields were so muddy they beckoned me each day to sink in and wait for the day when

I could sprout along with the plants, start a whole new life. But the afternoon I found out and Artie said I shouldn't worry, the sun appeared, there was steam pouring off the fields, and the air was warm. I couldn't believe my luck.

I came home, went straight into the living room and announced, "Ruby, we are going to celebrate," and he said, "Great, baby," without asking what it was for. He didn't care, as long as he could be giddy and party. I told May matter-of-factly that we were taking the car. I didn't give her a chance to come out of shock and say, "No you don't."

We went to Audrey's and when we were seated I said, "Ruby, I'm not supposed to drink beer."

"Really, baby? That don't sound like too much fun."

"Guess why," I said.

He was trying to figure out the menu. He couldn't think of a reason.

I reached over and held his hand; I said, "You and me, Ruby, we're going to have a little baby."

His eyes just about popped out of his sockets while that slow smile spread over his face. He asked me, "What did you say?" and I told him again. I showed him about where it was inside me, way down by my fly.

He got so excited he knocked over his water glass. He whispered, "We're going to have a jungle baby?" He made his fingers dance all over the place mats to his favorite song that goes Do-do-doot-do-doot.

Then he told the waitress his wife was PG. He said he was the father and he asked her what we should name it. I laughed at Ruby, asking the dumb waitress what we're going to name our own baby. When we finished our supper Ruby came over and held my elbow while I stood up. He was already being sweet and careful with me. He kept saying, "Baby, you got a person inside you. I wish I could peek in there and see what it's up to."

We walked in the kitchen at home looking so happy, I know

we did, and May said, "What's going on with you two? You got some big secret?"

And Ruby blurted out, "She's gonna have a baby!" He said so nicely to May, "Hey, Ma, that means you're a grandmother."

She sat down. She didn't know what to make of it. I took out a minuscule T-shirt I'd got at the grocery store and I said, "Look, Ma, look at how small it's going to be."

She didn't say anything for three days. I was so nervous in front of her I didn't know where to look when she was in the room. I tiptoed and knocked over vases. I couldn't tell if she was mad or what. On Sunday, after church, she cut the first tulips. We were all sure winter was truly over. She came in the kitchen with tulips and a gift box. She handed the present to me and said, "Don't just sit there, open it."

I did without saying a word. It was a yellow fuzzy suit that keeps babies toasty.

"See what I got for my grandson?" she said, wiping her nose. She already had it figured out. It was going to be a boy.

Fourteen

B Y the time the month of May came and there were purple
and red tulips and yellow daffodils all over the lawn, and
the grass was so lush and green I half hoped someone would put
me out to pasture, we had a better attitude about living together
on the planet. We weren't burning oil to keep us warm. Everything we needed, it seemed, was right out the back door. May
and Ruby and I now had the habit of sitting at supper with the
kitchen door open, the smells of the steaming ground coming
in, and we talked about what the baby was going to be like. We
couldn't be quiet at the table because we had stories to tell. We
were planning together. We were in the future together. We
bought wallpaper with clowns on it for the nursery — May bargained with the lady at the hardware store and got it cheap. She
repeatedly described how she had had her babies: all of a sudden
giving birth was the biggest drama May had ever lived through.
She talked about her infants as if they were dear and long dead.
She didn't make the connection that I was what sprang out of
her.

She said perhaps the baby would have an enormous intelligent
brain like Matt's, and he would achieve in school — wouldn't we

be surprised? Ruby, sucking up his macaroni from his spoon, said the baby was going to be a baseball star. He'd play on the Cubs team, make them Cubbies win.

I sat back and grinned at them both, the way they were carrying on. I had to ask, "What if it's a girl?"

Ruby took a bite of the peanut butter sandwich he had on the side, and he said with his mouth full, "A girl can play on the Cubs too." May snickered and said, "Don't kid yourself, Buster, they don't let girls do one thing except wash uniforms and clean out the shower stalls."

I felt lousy half the time but I tried to shrug it off. I kept telling myself that I was going to get a baby out of the arrangement. I sat by the window pretending I was on an ocean vessel. I imagined I was on a cruise with fancy food prepared by experts. It didn't matter that I couldn't eat any of it, even though the waiters offered me shrimp from a silver platter. I was thankful to be on the boat, rocking back and forth, looking out to the sparkly blue water. I tried to think those voyage thoughts when I felt seasick, all day long.

I sat in the window and watched Ruby helping May rake up last year's leaves. She gave orders and he did just what she said. He had the humiliation buried away. He was practically enthusiastic. I suppose they had a common purpose. He hardly missed any spots that she said to rake clean. He took care of the chickens too, after I told him the feel of the warm eggs made me gag. He said, "Baby, don't you lift one of them little white fingers of yours, I'm going to take care of the hens."

Ruby and May weren't hugging each other after long absences but they seemed to be making a special effort while I was upstairs in the bathroom waiting to heave. He still did the things that irked May — she hated the way he came down the stairs in the morning with nothing on except a towel wrapped around his waist. His eyes weren't open yet. She looked every which way around him. Possibly Daisy was right: perhaps if May had glanced at near-naked Ruby she would have knocked him down, ripped off his towel, and forced herself. Maybe she was lusty. She didn't really seem in the market for such things but perhaps when I'm an advanced age I'll understand. He left eggshells on the counter and the cereal box out; there was usually a puddle of milk by his glass, and a licked jelly spoon in the puddle. He isn't the tidiest person we ever met. She hated the way he dumped into the chair and turned on the TV. Still, she had something else to occupy her mind now. She didn't have to concentrate on Ruby's mess, and since I was home more I could clean up after him, hide the traces. He wasn't actually what you'd call a slob, that much, he just didn't notice items if they were out of place.

Maybe we were all feeling extra-generous and trying to shape up a little since in the future we were going to have to be examples. It could have been my hormones crisscrossing through my body in massive doses, but I felt a lot sorrier for people than usual. One day in the early summer, I walked into the Footes' house, and I could tell instantly that one of the Foote children had done something seriously wrong. Dee Dee had her head set tight into her neck and her shoulders came up to her ears. She was furiously balling up cookie dough and splatting it on her trays. She had three earthenware bowls filled with dough; she had all the greased trays lined up in a row. I wasn't about to tangle with her so I walked past her into the living room. Daisy was home from Peoria for a week, sewing padding into the top of her swimming suit.

I raised my eyebrows to ask her what was going on.

"You don't want to know," she said, glad for the opportunity to tell me. "Randall's got a girlfriend." She looked straight at me. "She lives over on the Kates' old place."

Naturally I was surprised. Furthermore, I didn't know there was anyone eligible living there. I started to ask who but Daisy said, "Baaaaaaaaa."

I stood staring while Daisy stuck her tongue into her cheek to keep from laughing. It didn't take me long to understand. Ruby had told me the plots of the movies he and Randall loved to drool over. I nodded my head and went out the front door.

I walked for a long time before I saw him. He was in the cemetery, sitting on a large rectangular gravestone. His knees came up to his chin.

"Move over," I said. He did. "Just a little more."

He moved around the corner and we sat back touching back.

"I never thought anyone was going to like me," I said. "I know I ain't pretty." I felt his back sink into mine a little. "But I got taken by surprise, and I bet some time you might be surprised too."

When he started to cry I got up and went around to his side. I kneeled down and kissed him on his fat wet lips. I moved his hair out of his eyes as tenderly as I could and felt along his bristly cheek. Then I kissed him again. He kept his eyes closed. "You sure are a handsome fat man," I said.

"Naw," he said, looking sideways and wiping the tears from his cheeks. "One more," I said, kissing him again. "Now. Go home to your mother. She's got some cookies for you."

I got up and walked away, and when I turned around I saw him lumbering in the other direction. He moved slowly because if he walked quickly his thighs rubbing together probably would have started a fire. He took up so much space cars passing him swerved way over to the other side of the road. For the first time, watching him lug his body home, I felt how lonesome he would always be.

Dee Dee and Randall came every day that summer because May and Dee Dee were making a quilt for the baby. Randall was hanging around a lot more than usual, watching the ladies sew. I could tell that May was looking out for him too. She made sure his plate was always full and she patted him on the back. He had his stool drawn up to the table, and with his change purse in his clutches he pored over his *Mad* magazines. They all sat in the dining room with the fan blowing on them, Dee Dee's behind lapping over the edge of her stool, and she and May talked about babies for hours. They talked without listening to each other, about how it was when they raised theirs up. Even then I knew they had amnesia: they were talking with fondness in their voices. They recalled how a baby's neck smells, and how it gurgles. They laughed at the way toddlers can wreck a house if you let them. I lay on the sofa feeling the glow of pride creep all the way up to my forehead. I was doing something they were awfully excited about and they didn't try to hide it. Dee Dee missed the world of infants because her daughter Lou had given up Midnight Star Sandra Dee when she realized having a baby wasn't a picnic, even if she was the only mother in the sophomore class. She went South, gave it up for adoption, and moved into a house with a lot of girls. She sent word that she was working long night shifts waitressing, but Daisy had a theory about the true nature of her long nights. Dee Dee blew her nose and frowned every time she thought about Lou. Her breasts heaved so that the dress zipper down her front undid itself an inch or two.

The quilt was a light blue pond with green and orange ducks swimming around the reeds. May said there wasn't going to be one spot of pink in it. I didn't do anything but lie on the couch in the living room while they stitched. Randall lent me his reel-to-reel tape recorder and Dee Dee got me blind tapes through the library. I had to call in sick to Trim 'N Tidy half the time because I was so hot and miserable. I lay on the couch listening to my favorite books by Charles Dickens, in particular that one called *Bleak House*. It's about one million years long, and that's hardly exaggerating. It has Esther in it, the heroine in literature I root for the most. I always felt so sorry for her because she had a very pure heart, and all the same there were people who treated her cruelly. I wished I could be some kind of magical wise person who was able to walk into books and change their course. I would slip in and be Esther's long-lost sister, comfort little Jo before he died, tell Ada that loving Richard Carstone was a dead end, and finally, melt the ice out of Lady Dedlock's heart and reunite her with Esther, and me, and then we'd both inherit her fortune.

May was bossy with me but I could laugh behind my pale sick face because I knew she was thinking about the baby. She said so sternly that I had to have vegetables, and she butchered two chickens and fried me their livers. They made my stomach do cartwheels so she fed the organs to Randall with chocolate cake on the side. We were all ready to be happy about something; it almost didn't matter what. If we had had a dog that was going to have puppies May probably would have fried up livers for the bitch and sewed a quilt for the puppies to lie on. She had been waiting for something great in her life for a long time, ever since Matt left home and I met Ruby.

Finally, in September, I started feeling better. I woke up one morning and told Ruby I had to have a cheeseburger without delay. He ran and told May and she made me one lickety-split. She sprinkled olives on top and set me a place with the doily napkins. I had figured out how to be queen quite by accident. Everyone was concerned about me; if I picked up the laundry basket, say, both May and Dee Dee ordered me to put it down. They yelled in unison as if they were trying to sing a duet. I did exactly what they said. Even Ruby took the laundry himself and hung it on the line, never mind that he left it out in the rain and we didn't have any clean underwear.

I love being pregnant, feeling like a big old elephant. Some girls hate the sensation, I know, but if you throw your shoulders back and let your belly lead you down the street, never fails, people smile going by. I love how suddenly everything tiny seems beautiful, the tiniest, thinnest blade of grass. You want to go out and put a fence around it, so no one will step on it. I like thinking about the drama going on in a mother's body—for instance, Artie told me the fluid the baby grows in is the same as the salt water in the sea, exactly. That information gave me goose pimples and I felt glad knowing porpoises are my cousins. I could almost remember jumping up to get the fish out of my keeper's hands. Although I'm a small person, during my first pregnancy Ruby said my stomach was as tremendous as them blown-up hot air balloons. When he walked with me in town he loved to watch people thinking I was a fat girl. He swelled and beamed, knowing that he was the one who did it to me.

The doctor at the clinic told us about classes at the hospital in Humphrey where nurses teach girls how to grin through labor. He said we ought to attend. I got up my nerve and asked May to write a check for twenty-five dollars, so we could go to class. She only scowled for a minute. There were ten other couples learning about babies also. I knew everyone was examining us in great detail. I felt their eyes piercing through the holes in my shoes and the tears in my socks. At the cleaners you don't actually have to talk to the people; you say the same conversation all day long, like "Is it cold enough out there for you?" And then you tell them how much their clean clothes cost, and naturally at the end you say, "Have a nice day." But in the childbirth class the couples were so different from us. We had to go around and say what our occupation was: ninety-nine percent were physical therapists and salesmen. One of the ladies worked on a newspaper writing stories. Ruby said right out that he was the can man in the grocery store parking lot; he sang it out, and I said quietly that I was the spotter at Trim 'N Tidy. Our teacher, Silvia, had to ask, "What did you say? Can you speak up?"

I could tell people were laughing at us, or commenting, "Oh brother," under their breaths. We were right back in grade school again, saying the wrong answer, sounding dumb. The other mothers had blond hair, all of them — I'm not lying — nice and straight, and they dressed in pink maternity sweaters with initials on the front. Their plump soft faces made them all look like identical stuffed animals.

I knew we were poor and strange against the people in our

class. Sometimes I felt so sad for my baby. I didn't want it to see
the world, if it was going to find out about our oddness. I talked
to it down in my stomach. I told it not to worry; we'd hide it
away, we wouldn't let other children taunt it. We'd chase bullies
out of the yard and throw stones after them.

It always relieved me to get home, back with my Ruby, back
up to our room. He played his music on his guitar with the radio
and he'd say, "OK, baby, breathe in, breathe out, let's practice
you having a kid. Look at the speck on the wall and imagine all
them magic nights we've had, breathe in one of them cleansing
breaths, pant blow pant blow."

One night he pretended he was the doctor giving me a Cesarean
section. He strapped a flashlight bulb to his head and outlined
my stomach with his fingernail. He told me, "I'm gonna open
you up and get the kid out in no time flat. I got to fish in real
quick before you wake up." I laughed and squirmed and then
he tore the rest of my clothes off. He whispered that he was going
to keep me pregnant all the time because he liked my boobies
to be the size of a cow's bag.

Artie kept saying that I was the best worker and what was he
to do when I had Oscar. I said, "Artie, you think I'm going to
quit? How do you think I'm supposed to pay for our Oscar's
doctor bills if I'm not working?" Artie was good to me, as always,
because he said when it was born he'd figure out a part-time
schedule for both May and me.

Those nine months were serene. I worked, thinking about the
baby every other minute. My mind wasn't at Trim 'N Tidy; my
mind was inside my stomach, with our child. We were swimming
around together like goldfish circling in a bowl. I felt the world
closing in on me. The space in front of me was getting smaller
and smaller, until all I could see was my family, and the three-
some we were to become. I told Daisy, when she came home
from Peoria for a week, that I was with my baby constantly, and
she looked at me as if I was cracked.

"You think you're swimming inside your own stomach?" she said. "Maybe that baby is growing in your head and it's going to swim down your nose." She smirked at her joke. I didn't tell her further thoughts about being a mother, but when I felt the baby I had to stop whatever I was doing, no matter who was present. I had to put down the steam iron and hold my stomach to feel the kicks. Ruby felt the movement too. We sat in bed and he put his ear against me to listen. "Baby," he whispered, "it's spooky in there, inside of you."

We didn't notice the winter coming on because we were preoccupied with ourselves. We didn't mind how cold it was getting. The night of our anniversary Ruby brought home pizzas, with some coaching on the part of Dee Dee, and all of us sat in the kitchen talking about what we should name the baby. I never said out loud the name I wanted. I was keeping it secret. I went along with Ruby and May very agreeably. May bought a book from the store filled with names and she read them to us — it took her two hours just for the boys. The one she wanted was Josiah, but to me it sounded like those old men in the Bible who are always getting into trouble with God. Ruby liked the name Clover. He said it should be called Clover Reuben Dahl. May said if we named it that it would turn into a homo. I've never seen one that I know of, so I can't tell if it's a bad way to be. I said no way in a million years was our baby going to be called Clover, we might as well call it Wheat Groats or Quack Grass. After Ruby watched a *Bewitched* rerun one night he declared the baby was going to be christened Darren. I smiled at him and whispered, "You're out of your gourd."

I stopped working in December. I couldn't get through the doors. I was waiting — all I could do was wait, staring at nothing, crying all of a sudden for no reason. I felt so large, as if there were a gigantic hen inside me scratching with its feet. I had dreams that our infant chicken burst out of my stomach. I woke up thinking there wasn't anything left of my belly; there was eggshell scattered on the floor, a baby shaking its downy skin beside me.

I couldn't get anything done at home. I was trying to paint the crib Dee Dee loaned us. I'd stand up to start a task and it always looked so tiresome I had to sit back down and stare at the open can of paint. Ruby and I watched TV. We watched the soap operas where people don't have anything to do except fall in love with the wrong person. They wear so much hair spray not one piece of hair gets dislodged, even when they're kissing each other's bruised mouths. We didn't do much else except play cards and get headaches from staring at kings and queens and spades.

On New Year's Eve I didn't celebrate. I was big and tired. I didn't ever get rest because our baby always went on hikes at bedtime. It was training with those clubs that go up that stupid giant Mount Everest. Artie's son climbs mountains—Artie always tells me how many people died on certain peaks, right when they were two inches from the top. At any rate, Ruby and I were asleep when suddenly I woke up. My side of the bed was soaked. I didn't think I could have wet the bed; I hadn't done that since I was nine. I knew that it was my water bag, busted. "Ruby," I said, nudging him. "Wake up. We have to go to the hospital."

He sat bolt upright. He didn't have one piece of clothing on, and he said, "I'm ready."

"You ain't ready either," I said, laughing. "You're a nudey man." He grinned at me in the dark. I could see that dazzling smile of his shining through the murky night.

We woke up May and explained that we were on our way to the hospital and she said, "I'm coming with." She put her clothes on before we could ask if she meant it—her outfit had been folded neatly by her bed just for the occasion. So we three bundled into the car, it's only two in the morning and ten below zero, and May said, "It's colder than a witch's tit in a copper bra." We were all so frozen none of us laughed. What she said was true.

May couldn't come into the labor room no matter how long she swore at the nurse just barely under her breath. She had to wait outside in the fathers' lounge. She smoked about ten packs of cigarettes with Dee Dee, who lied to the nurses, telling them that she was Ruby's mother. The nurses said they didn't usually have both grandmothers there too, and I mumbled something about how I guessed we were different. Nothing much was happening so we played crazy eights. I beat Ruby each time; I could tell his brain wasn't on Function. He was nervous about being in a hospital. He went out of the room each time the nurse came to check on my progress.

When the contractions got closer together they hooked me to a machine that measures the pains. Ruby watched it so he could see how miserable I felt.

"Baby," he said, looking at the screen, "it's a good thing them waves ain't from your brain, they'd put you in the circus."

I had to laugh over that one. Ruby was always cheering me up. He sat down in the chair and got out his carton of food he had brought with him. He was diving into the box of Wheaties when he looked up and said, "Hey, baby, remember to do all the breathing you learned about. You're gonna do real good, I just know it."

The husbands were supposed to say that to the wives. They were supposed to encourage them. He concentrated awfully hard when I said he had to throw ice water on my face. There were frown lines on his forehead. He wanted to do a perfect job. He said, "Ain't I a great coach for you?"

I managed to say, "Yes, Ruby." I was so glad he was my husband. I knew May was impressed that the fathers got to assist at the birth.

As the pains came stronger and closer together I kept asking myself, Is this actually happening to me? Aren't I still the little girl who's getting laughed at for not having a brassiere? Why aren't I at the kitchen table while my daddy's dumping ice cream on top of my head? All of a sudden it seemed that my life had gone so quickly.

I was in labor for sixteen hours. Ruby looked like a car wreck after eight. When I was having the contractions I remembered pulling the little lamb from the mother sheep, so long ago, and how she didn't complain, although her eyeballs were in the back of her head. I thought about her and tried not to moan too loudly. I tried not to call out to God and the devil but their names came soaring from my mouth and then echoed around the room. I told the doctor I didn't want to have a baby any more, that all I wanted was a shot in my thigh which would erase me. He said, "It won't be long now." I was glad I couldn't see myself having a baby. I bet my face looked like a raisin somebody stepped on.

I kept trying to get Ruby's attention so I could ask him if I was going to the ladies' room all over the bed, but he had wandered off to the TV screen. I just knew the doctor was going to bawl me out for messing the sheets. Finally the doctor said again that it wouldn't be long, and Ruby called out, "Come on, baby, let's get this show on the road." I pushed as if I had a Greyhound bus, deluxe coach, inside me, stuck between two snowbanks. The doctor counted to ten, repeatedly, while I screamed and groaned.

"I don't have no energy," I cried after forever, and the doctor said that the head was practically out, a few more good pushes was going to wrap it up.

I tried, I mustered my forces, I revved that bus's engine and at last, *splam*, comes a slippery small package with white film all over it. Dr. Hanson caught it on the fly. Ruby looked over and said, "Hey, Doc, you'd be a great outfielder if you was younger."

"Oh, sweetie," I choked. "Oh, angel."

Ruby sank back into the chair. He probably was crying too. I couldn't see his face while he stared at the wall. The nurse cleaned up our baby, and then they brought it to me. I touched him and he looked at me with the darkest blue eyes; they were so blue, like the mill pond in spring.

"It's our Justin," I whispered, because that was the name I had chosen. He was something I had made from scratch. He was our Justin.

"Come see," I said to Ruby, who was still having a catnap. When I spoke louder he pulled himself up and walked over on his tiptoes. He looked about the way he used to look when I tried to get him to reach under and grab a hen's egg.

I kept saying our baby's name time and time again—we were meeting for the first time in our lives. The nurse came and helped me put him on my nipple. He sucked so knowledgeably I had to boast right away about his appetite and his intelligence. He made little grunting noises, enjoying the very best food he had ever tasted.

I checked our baby, made sure he had ten toes. I couldn't believe that he came out with eyebrows, and he could grimace and cry. He had wrists, thinner than electrician's conduit, and perfect small hands, better than fresh rosy apricots. He looked exactly like Ruby. He was bound to be handsome.

Right away, when they wheeled me to my room, May came in. She wasn't supposed to be there but she bulldozed over the nurses.

"Here's your grandson, Ma," I said. "Meet Justin."

She petted his cheek. She didn't say anything except "Bless you" to him, in a thin wavering voice, one I had never heard her use before. She couldn't believe that here in the flesh was another chance for her; here was a baby coming to live and grow at her house. She was listening, already, to the stories Justy was going to tell about his grandmother, how she leaped up on the roof when the house was burning and pulled him from the fire.

Fifteen

JUSTY was born with absolutely no baby spots. He came out complete and flawless. I'm not even prejudiced. The nurses said he was one of the most beautiful babies they had ever seen, and nurses have been around the block a few times. It was as if Ruby and I weren't poor ugly people but, actually, in our blood and bones and seeds, royal monarchs. May kept saying, "It's a miracle he's so damn pretty."

I was happiest when there was no one else in the hospital room, only Justy and his mother. He looked up at me with his wise blue eyes saying, "It's all right now, I'm here." J.C. was supposed to say those words when he was born, but I knew Jesus wasn't any better than our Justin. He wasn't any more of a holy big deal than our own baby. The three days in the hospital were the closest to heaven I'll probably ever get: I loved filling in the menu chart, circling whatever I wanted to eat, and then they brought it, steaming and fragrant. They propped up my pillows so I could eat in bed. The nurses were always swooping in and out of the room like barn swallows, offering to give me the little baths that heal the wounds.

Ruby and Dee Dee came to visit me in the afternoons, and

Ruby brought me beer because it's supposed to be good for nursing mothers. It lets their milk come down. Dee Dee gave Ruby that information when she was guzzling a twelve-pack for old times' sake. Ruby and I looked at Justy, that's all we did; we couldn't stop looking at him. Ruby flipped through the TV channels with the remote control panel he loved so much. He held Justy awkwardly, with his shoulders all hunched up, since he had never been around a newborn. And when Justy cried Ruby said, "OK, little baby, you want to go back to your ma-ma?" He said mama deliberately, as if he had just learned an exotic word. I beamed hearing him comfort Justin. He'd say, "There, don't you cry now, here's your ma-ma."

And when I held Justy I could give him what he wanted. He usually stopped crying. I admired how I knew what to do without having to go to some school way down in Peoria to learn about it. When you're a mother you know what your baby needs. Also, the nurses gave me, along with some other girls, classes about washing and changing your infant. Ruby thought I was the smartest person on earth, for jiggling Justy and making him quiet down, and talking sweetly in a high voice to him. He looked forlorn in his corner sometimes, when I was speaking to Justy. He'd pipe up and say that he couldn't wait to get me home; he was going to eat me whole.

"It's been a long time, baby," he said. "I can't wait until it ain't like climbing a mountain to get on top of you."

When he brought up that mountain-climbing topic I quick said I had to take a nap. I closed my eyes and prayed for divine interference to freeze Ruby's appetite.

All my life, when we went to church, I didn't listen hard to what the Rev said. I sat in the pew thinking about the dirt on people's collars and the way their hair hit the back of their necks. But every now and then some of the Rev's words blasted through. They sat in my ears for some reason and I had to perk up and think. Right after Justy was born I fidgeted in church until the

Rev said, "Blessed are the meek, for they shall inherit the earth. Blessed are they which do hunger and thirst after righteousness, for they shall be filled. Blessed are the pure of heart, for they shall see God."

The Rev no doubt had said those verses hundreds of times when I wasn't paying attention, but for once I heard the words. I sat still in the pew, biting my lip, filling my head with the phrase "for they shall inherit the earth." I didn't know what that involved, precisely, or where you had to go to put in your claim—but I knew Justy had something to do with the deal, now that he was part of the earth, and I had made him myself. Justy would carry on from where I left off, and it was my body which gave him the life to do it, plus Ruby's. I figured I was going to inherit the earth in a way I didn't yet know about. I was in a special club because I had made a human being to do the work of man.

Ever since I was a little girl I only half believed in the fabrications the Rev preached. After Aunt Sid got me thinking about symbols I knew the baby Jesus never actually was born at Christmas. I figured the Rev was merely telling stories that were designed to make us behave. Still, there were the times when he said poems, like how the meek are blessed, and I fiercely wanted to believe the promises.

May went out and bought Justy a blue dress with smocking across the front for his baptism. It probably cost her a fortune, but money in this case was no object. She said we had to get Justy baptized because then he wouldn't go to hell, guaranteed. There's an old man in our church, Oscar Baily, who rants and raves about Jesus to anyone who will give him the ear. He was forever musing about the savages in the jungles around the world who've never heard of Christ. He couldn't help feeling sorry for them because they don't have anyone to tell them the Gospel. Finally, after several weeks of pondering, he decided there was comfort after all. He figured Jesus could eyeball each savage's heart and say which one would accept him, *if* they knew about him, and that way certain Africans are surely saved. Oscar was telling me this opinion on the day Justy got baptized. He was giving the benefit of the doubt to the poor dumb savages. I forced a sweet smile while I held Justy in my arms so I'd look like the good mother. I wanted to tell Oscar he was full of it, that Jesus wasn't anything more than a figment in his mind, and that savages were much better off without Jesus' mumbo jumbo—for example, they didn't have to fight wars to force their neighbors to go to church. I didn't say boo, however. We had, only ten minutes before, stood up in front of the altar. I had held Justy while the Rev sprinkled water on his head and told us we were supposed to raise our son a Christian. I had nodded. There were only one hundred people watching: how was I going to inform the Rev that I didn't believe in The Man?

The ladies at coffee hour afterwards said how beautiful Justy looked. It was true. He had lush dark hair and a delicate thin mouth and round blue eyes the size of half dollars, and a long nose, fit for the princes they have over in England. He crossed his eyes and then smiled, as if seeing us double was twice the pleasure.

For the first three months I was allowed to stay home with Justy. Artie said I wouldn't lose my job, that it would be there when I was ready. He called to say that Trim 'N Tidy never won bowling games against the Red Bell Market, on account of I wasn't there to score. I have to admit, I kind of missed seeing the team trophy Artie has on display at the cleaners. It's the one we got after I did the miracle shot, the seven and ten split.

If I ever have the chance to go back and live my days over, the first months with Justy are the ones I'd choose. It was like real life, how I always imagined it was supposed to be. May went to work in the morning and then Mr. and Mrs. Dahl were adults keeping house, blasting the roof off with our furious vacuuming and our love songs. I kept asking myself, Am I a real live woman?

Is my body actually making the milk in my breasts? Is this truly my husband who's handing me the talcum powder so I can make our baby clean and dry? I asked questions constantly, to make sure it all wasn't one magic cream puff.

After May was gone to work we cooked ourselves breakfast. Ruby fried the bacon because I always felt as if I could eat something fresh killed. I loved being so hungry and then hearing Justy cry and feeling the sting of the milk let down. Ruby said he wished he could get Coke from my nipples—he said then I could feed the neighborhood and we'd get rich.

When I was eating and Justy bawled, Ruby picked him up from his basket when I said, and handed him to me, and I'd feed him. Justy didn't have any problem with his appetite. He sucked and grunted and smacked his lips. May said that I had it made, that Justy was an angel baby, so well behaved. I don't think Justy's good nature was all luck. Probably his parents had something to do with it. I see so clearly, as if it were an hour ago, Ruby washing up the dishes, just as I'd told him—he didn't complain too long—and singing a tune to himself while our baby nursed. He made up songs for Justy, about how Justy was riding his horse across the range, how he was the biggest, smartest cowboy, killing off Indian tribes.

Then, after Justy ate, I gave him over to Ruby. I showed him patiently how to burp a baby, and he did the job very gently. He sang some more in his soprano voice, songs such as "Colorado Rocky Mountain High" and "Jet Plane." Sometimes, after I healed, when I sat on the couch with our baby smiling up at me, Ruby came over and felt my breasts. He liked them gigantic. He petted my hair and face. He said certain equipment he had was swelling to the size of a fungo bat. He was missing me urgently. I had to laugh at my two babies; I had to glow triumphantly at how they were ravenous for my body. If Justy was sleeping I put him in his basket. Then Ruby and I climbed upstairs to our room and we shut the door.

▼

I had enough company with my family. I didn't have energy to spare. I didn't want to go talk with other mothers in Stillwater. They have a group of people who nurse their babies. They get together twice a month to chew the fat, eat cupcakes, and brag about their children. All the mothers probably wear pink sweaters with their initials on them, made especially for over-size knockers. There was one lady, Donna, who kept calling to invite me to the parties. I always told her I was awfully busy in the home. I didn't want to talk to anyone. I felt happy in my own family.

Ruby and I took Justy on trips to the grocery store, to the Town Lanes, to the police station. We showed the officer our baby, and we couldn't help saying with our whole selves, "Look at what we made, we finally came to some good, don't you see?" And when we bought a few groceries I always liked exactly the things Ruby liked, no matter what. Ruby paid because he was the man of the family. When we came home we danced around with the exercise shows on TV, and if we had it up so loud Justy cried, Ruby took him in his arms and danced with him around the circle of the house.

In the evenings, after May got back, we were ready for a break. Justy always got cranky around five. May cradled him and crooned. She had to tell him about her day in a high squeaky voice while he stared at her and rolled his tongue around. He looked hard at her face, as if he was saying, "I know you're not my parents, I know that much, you look so strange." And Ruby and I some-times said, if we could get a word in edgewise, "Hey, Ma, you want to watch Justy for a minute so we can feed the chickens?" She always said, "Sure I will, you run along."

Here was something she could really be a star at, being an old grandma. It isn't as hard as being a mother because you don't have to be responsible. You simply watch someone else doing most of the work, and you give them suggestions, tell them what they're doing wrong. May was sure Justy smiled at her first, but she didn't know what she was talking about. I know for a fact that he grinned at me about a month before he even gave May the time of day.

So we went out into the winter evenings and collected eggs, and if time allowed we walked in the woods, all the while thinking about our Justin. We held hands, Ruby smoked a joint, and we told each other our thoughts, mainly, what we wanted our son to be like when he got older. Ruby said with them hunky shoulders he'd make a sensational quarterback. I said maybe Ruby could teach Justy to build houses, do work with his hands. Justy has long tapered fingers, like candlesticks, the shape of May's before hers got twisted. They look like hands that could build sculptures or bridges. It burned me up that Ruby stopped making birdhouses. He stopped in his tracks when I mentioned the woodwork. It was still a sore spot with him — the way, all those months before, May had called him a moron for building birdiehouses. We walked along silently, both of us thinking back to that nightmare when we walked into Hazel's house and she gave me the snake.

In the middle of the night, when I was by myself feeding Justin, I had a few new thoughts. My ideas didn't have anything to do with Jesus and savages, I can tell you that much. It came to me that we were nothing more than two human beings, Justin and I — he wasn't so much younger than me, and I was helping him along in life, just as somebody else helped me a while back. We were all supposed to be humans helping each other.

I also realized that we three adults were changing. I couldn't see how right then, but I knew it was happening. For one thing, it seemed as if Ruby must have wanted to have a son all his life, there in his subconscious brain. He finally saw what it was that could make him happy. He was proud of his family; anyone could see by the way he acted in church. He walked straight, he always wanted to be the one to carry Justy, and he sang out clearly, as if with song he could celebrate our lives together. I had to hand Justy over the minute we were in public because he

wanted people to know he was the father. I teased Ruby constantly, about how he was going to spoil his baby rotten. He used
to come in from outside shouting, "Hey, Justy, look at this!"
Justy's only about twelve weeks old and Ruby's showing him a
warty toad or a robin's egg. With a baby you have to look at the
world as if someone has just given you a pair of eyes for the first
time.

When Justy was almost three months old, May said we sure
were running low on cash. She was ready for me to get off my
high horse and get back to work. She reminded me every day
that my time was almost up. I knew we were flat broke. I said,
"I'm going back in two short weeks, Ma, it's in my plan" —
but I didn't ever want to work at Trim 'N Tidy again. I wanted
to stay home for the rest of my life and have about ten babies.
Here was something I was good at, finally. I was never any good
at subjects or sports at school. Besides bowling and dry cleaning,
having handsome babies was the job I could do with the hope
of success.

Artie called me a week earlier than he was supposed to and
said they needed me because they were all getting the flu, not
to mention the fact that I was the best spotter in the city. I didn't
care about being a sensational spotter any more, but there wasn't
anything I could do about it. May said we had a dollar fifty in
the checking account. I also have the habit of being meek and
mild, which is one of the reasons I'm going to inherit the earth,
if the Bible is correct. May sat me down at the table and figured
it out. We decided we were both going to go part time. Since I
made a higher wage than May I worked more than she did. She
would put in about fifteen hours. It didn't bother her to cut back.
Artie felt sorry enough for us to give Ruby a job, and Ruby was
still the can man every other weekend. At Trim 'N Tidy Ruby
waited on people at the counter and wrapped up the clothes in
plastic, like May did. They were both finishers. When Ruby does

jobs he's not just wild about he complains a little. I told him he had to support a family now and that fact shut him up, temporarily. We were on a crazy schedule of either coming or going, like bees running off to the hottest flower and then coming back to agitate in the hive. We didn't ever stay put to catch our breath or gather our wits. But there was always someone at home; if I went to work May and Ruby stayed home, or May, solo; and when May worked it was me, alone or with Ruby. Somehow it came out that Ruby wasn't home by himself with Justy for more than two hours during the week. If I had to point a finger I'd say May figured it that way, deliberately.

The truth is I'd get jealous of May. When I'd come home there she always was in the living room walking around with Justy in her arms, and she never handed him over right away. I had to ask her. I had a stone near my heart, a large jagged black rock. It was crushing my organs while I watched May kissing Justy on his cheeks, saying, "Hush-a-bye, hush-a-bye." I hinted around. I'd say, "I bet it's time to feed Justy," and she'd say, "No, it ain't, I just gave him his formula."

I wanted to shout, I *hate* formula! I've got what Justy needs right here in my own breasts.

I didn't say anything. I stood sulkily, noticing how her pinched-up mouth was smiling for once. The stone would pierce my heart once and then retreat. She was cooing to Justy so tenderly. So I'd say, as quietly and forcefully as I could, "Ma, let me hold him for a little, and then I'll give him back to you, OK?"

Sometimes she said pleasing phrases the way Ruby did, such as "Here's your mama," and then I was satisfied for a while.

We were going along, Ma and Ruby and Justy and me, maintaining life. Ruby didn't like the smell at Trim 'N Tidy much. He said the plastic made him itch; he said Artie gave him a hard time, telling him to shape up every other minute. I prayed that he wouldn't get fired; I actually sat down and prayed to Jesus Christ. There's all those lines in the Bible when Jesus says, "Ask

and it shall be given you." Sometimes a person gets desperate
and they'll try any trick in the book.

Dee Dee came over every day, without fail. She and May sat
in the kitchen drinking gallons of spiked lemonade. Ruby and I
stayed in the living room, within earshot of the gossip. We walked
Justy around when he was fussy, keeping our eye on the TV
shows. Dee Dee always brought me news of Daisy down in Peoria.
People kept coming back to the beauty college asking for Daisy
since she was the best student in the entire school. Never failed,
her wastebasket had the most hair in it at the end of the day. I
guessed she must have given up drinking because you'd probably
cut hair crooked if you were loaded.

I missed her eyes with the Martian-green lids, and her laugh
— she howled at everything. Nothing ever seemed sad to Daisy.
Before the baptism I said to Ruby, "How about making Daisy
Justy's godmother?" and he said, "Sure."

"You tell Daisy she's Justy's godmother, OK, Dee Dee?" I
hollered into the kitchen. She came and collapsed on the sofa.
She said she couldn't imagine Daisy being a god anything, but
maybe she was shaping up now.

"Dee Dee," I said, "you know your Daisy has a heart of pure
gold."

"I guess that's true," Dee Dee said, cracking up, "that's why
all the men are after her." We chuckled to ourselves over Daisy
and what a nice slut she was.

Sometimes, in the night, I woke up, scared that Justy was
dead. Once I sat straight up in my sleep. My heart was broken
loose from its regular spot, making its way along my throat. When
I opened my eyes the darkness was thick like marsh honey. I
pawed through the night to Justy's room to make sure he was
still breathing. When I got to the door and looked I was so
frightened my chilled blood vessels snapped and I felt pins stuck
on my face. I stood in the door staring at the huge unnatural
shape in there. I couldn't move my feet. The ogre was making

his move to bite off Justin's head, crunch up the skull with tiny sharp teeth. I almost fell to my knees in prayer. I had no power to scream; there was nothing left but prayer.

When I realized it was May I swore under my breath at her, for standing by the crib, for scaring me to the point of religious conviction. She didn't pay attention. She was hanging over Justy's crib, looking at him, arranging his covers, and taking his thumb out of his mouth. We didn't say one word to each other as we looked at him. He was sleeping, twitching his lips with dreaming. I wished, with my fists clenched, that May would sleep through the night. I turned around and felt back through the dark, back to our room. I couldn't get comfortable. Something didn't feel right. Perhaps it was the stone traveling through my body, making reservations to stay in my heart, permanently. May was in Justy's room the whole night, for all I know, whispering, "Say Grandma."

Sixteen

W HEN Ruby and I were sitting on the couch with our Justy
I told him about Miss Finch's books and the islands she
went to. They had white sand and calm ocean water untroubled
by dangerous creatures. I only told Ruby about the books where
people were happy in the end, such as *Great Expectations*. In
the last scene, when Pip and his girl walked out into the night,
the evening mist was coming on, and though the two of them
had been busted to pieces, they looked out to the stars and they
were healed by the prospect of the future. I can see us at that
moment, our arms around each other, telling stories, while Justy
drooled on my lap.

There isn't any way around the bad parts, unless I lie. Our
lives haven't been terrible up until now. I occasionally told myself
about how strange I felt, as Justy got older, how I didn't feel as
if there was a person moving around underneath my skin. I had
conversations with myself on the subject of some of the events
that had taken place in my twenty-one years. After a while, all
the monologues ending up nowhere, I stopped my thoughts mid-
course and said, "This must be what life is — so strange you can't
believe it — and a person has to go along with it." I kept saying

to myself, "Are you ready for the ride?" I didn't have a choice in the matter so I held fast, tried to keep my seat.

After we all went back to work, after we had been carefree for those initial months, our routine didn't go so smoothly. Ruby and May were home together for the whole day, twice a week. I don't know what materials scientists put in bombs but it seems as if they wouldn't need anything more than two personalities who don't get along so wonderfully. May wouldn't let Ruby nurture Justy. She had to hold the baby and diaper him and feed him. She didn't let Ruby be the father he dreamed of being. She sent him down to the basement to put the diapers in the washing machine, like it's the glamour job of the century. To her way of thinking there were millions of things in the environment that weren't healthy for a baby, such as the TV blaring for one, and Ruby not putting enough detergent in the washer. According to May, the diapers came out stinking worse than when they went in.

It was true that Ruby didn't have the best method for diapering. If Justy wet his pants, he was wet from his waist down, and May being how she is would not let Ruby forget such a travesty. All of a sudden May was an expert on babies—she had fooled us for years. It's a good thing she's not here to listen to me because she'd use her four-letter words, and then she'd get on the phone with her best friend and with tears in her voice she would say how rotten her whole family was behaving. If it weren't so awful, it'd almost be funny, in a crazy way, like sad clowns dancing at a circus.

In the spring evenings I came in the back door after Artie dropped me off and I stood quietly in the hall, listening to Ruby and May, and watching. I had an adequate view of the living room, more than I wanted to see, as a matter of fact. I could see May feeding the baby, and I could hear Ruby saying it was *his* baby, and he wanted to feed him now, and May, first looking at Justy, pursing her lips to convey her special love, and then taking time out to glare up at Ruby, would say, "You can't do nothin' right, Mr. Can Man—you diaper Justy and he gets a rash up and down his legs. You don't burp him good and his little stomach aches so terrible." She laughed at Ruby standing around, shifting from his right foot to his left.

Justy lay in her arms, in his jammies that were way too big, flapping his arms like the wounded blackbird I tried to save once. He flailed around like those wings of his were always going to be crippled.

Around about now I always said, "I'm home."

Ruby usually came into the kitchen and sat down at the table. He put his head into his hands. I knew May had called him many names throughout the day while they cared for Justy, terms that are more appropriate for barnyard animals and their urges. She couldn't stand to see Ruby tossing Justy up into the air, especially when she said he drank constantly. As we all knew, she never touched a drop. What made her desperate was the sight of Justy laughing at Ruby's antics. She was fearful, fearful of losing what she saw as queen mother status.

I've seen other fathers throwing their boys around. It's something natural they do. Ruby was careful, I know he was. His gymnastics weren't a major problem. May also despised the dirty animals he brought in to show Justy, and she wasn't crazy about Ruby's consuming interest in TV programs. Sitting directly in front of the set he never heard a thing, even if the end of the world was being heralded by sirens. He often didn't hear Justy crying from his crib upstairs. She said it was lucky Ruby wasn't home alone with the baby because Justy would be found floating face down in a crib full of his own tears.

The idea came to me fairly recently that all of May's griping was born from love. But if something so simple as the love for a child could be the source of our trials I'd say it's a cruel joke on Ruby and Justy and me. Call May's predicament love gone haywire, more like it. To confound matters May didn't know certain rules about human beings. I've got some of them figured out and I know for certain that I've more to learn. The key lesson is trust: if you trust a person—someone like Ruby or me— usually we do a good job. As I said before, we're dying to follow directions perfectly, even for the simple tasks, so we can do remarkably well. May's main point was that since Ruby complained about washing the clothes and taking the garbage out, he didn't deserve to care for Justy. She must have thought he was no older than fifteen. She acted as if he weren't a grown man or a father. Perhaps her vision was out of kilter and she couldn't see the stubble on his face.

So most often Ruby sat at the kitchen table, his arms around my waist. I stood and he cried into my slacks.

"I can't do nothin' right," he always said to me. "I'm such a dumb person. I can't even feed my own baby, he gets stomach-aches."

I whispered to him, "You have a fine brain, Ruby; don't call yourself dumb—give yourself some credit."

Sometimes I made him a peanut butter sandwich to make him feel a little better. While he ate I marched into the living room and said to May, "Let me have Justy, it's my turn now," and of course she had to say, "You're not holding him right, watch out for his head there."

Then Ruby and I took Justy outside and played with him in the sand pile Ruby had made for him. We breathed in and out; we kicked dirt and slapped sand. Ruby dug holes in the mountains and watched them collapse. While we were together outdoors May cooked supper. We could smell the food frying; we could hear her clattering around setting the table. Justy's favorite entertainment back in June was grasping toys. He loved holding on to common objects and grunting at them. Everything he saw went into his mouth—May was continually yanking things which she thought were far too filthy from his grip. When Ruby and I were alone with the baby I tried to let Ruby be in charge. Yes, there were a few times when I held my breath, when Ruby tossed Justy high over his head, but there weren't ever any accidents. Ruby knew what he was doing. Justy laughed so hard, so appreciatively. He had a deep belly laugh that sounded like it was coming from an old man who had smoked cigars all his life.

When May and I were home together with Justy it worked out ideally because I was dead tired half the time. I could take a nap if I wanted to, or do the wash. There were buckets filled with dirty diapers, and May was happy to watch her grandson while I dragged the pail down the basement stairs. She was literally happy. About every other day I had to think to myself, How would I manage without May? I always wondered how I would cope when I lay down to sleep in the middle of the afternoon and I could hear her playing with Justy. What would we do if May lived in Texas?

May and I didn't know the thoughts that we stored deep in our hearts; we didn't confess our secrets, but we were familiar with each other. Usually I'd forget that she was so bossy. To me she was only being May. It was when Ruby came home that I had to see her through his eyes, and feel how stingy she could get. She reminded me of the mother coons protecting their young. If you stumble upon a nest the mothers look like they'd be glad to chew your body into bite-size pieces. They don't like anyone tampering with their babies.

Expert May declared that we should start feeding Justy solid food when he was eight weeks old, despite the doctor telling me it was too early and unnecessary. He had current facts about how real food prematurely fouled up babies' digestive systems. But May thought she was Mother Earth herself, and she said doctors with their new theories every five minutes didn't know what they were talking about. She started shoving mashed green beans down Justy's throat, and chicken liver, and canned peaches. She was going to make sure he had the biggest brain in his class. He spat it up, naturally. He knew he wasn't ready for her cooking, that he might not ever be ready. Still, I couldn't figure out how to get May to stop. She was positive Justy needed the extra nutrition. It made me so mad I had to go outside and walk in the woods. I had to observe all the new buds about to burst. The tender young leaves looked like something frail and old, not like something new and vigorous. I had to concentrate on green leaves and flowers to take my mind off certain people and their theories.

Once I asked Dee Dee what she thought about feeding Justy solid food and Dee Dee said May knew the best way, without a doubt.

"My kids ain't Grade A examples," she said, shaking her head.

She didn't help me one single bit. Dee Dee wasn't about to cross her best friend. It didn't matter what I said — when I came in from chores I could see that May had fed Justy something fried and mashed. I could see the diapers he had spit up on in the clothes hamper.

There was one night in June when Ruby didn't come to bed, and finally at two in the morning I went downstairs. He was sitting in front of the TV, staring. His eyes grew so wide and stayed that way, when he watched shows. He was flipping through a book without even looking at the pages.

"What are you up to, Ruby?" My tired voice sounded like there were barbs in my throat, catching the words before they came out.

He didn't take his eyes off the screen. After a minute he said, "You know last Sunday when the Rev was telling about the little boy?"

"What little boy?" I asked, making no effort to disguise my irritation. I didn't usually remember the Rev's topics; there were only certain phrases which remained.

"The boy who had the devil in him," he said. "And his father wanted Jesus to come take it out. None of the disciples could do it but then Jesus arrived, and man, that devil got out fast. Jesus

can get devils out easy. I just got to find that story in the Bible.
I been searching all night but I can't find it, I just can't find it."

I kneeled down and made Ruby look at me. I said, "That's
nothing but a dumb story. Don't think thoughts like that,
Ruby — it ain't the kind of thing to dwell on before bedtime.
Come to sleep with me."

He didn't pay attention. He said, "Baby, I'm watching this
show, see, there's this man, he can't do nothin' right, he's in a
boys' school, you can tell he's letting the devil come in. You
watch, he's gonna do somethin'—"

"It's a trashy movie, Ruby. Turn it off."

I didn't have patience with late-night TV. I was so tired; why
didn't people sleep when they were supposed to? He didn't want
to leave his movie because he had to see how it worked out, who
was going to get murdered.

Ruby's favorite program was the late-night rerun of *Bewitched*.
He liked to see the characters wiggling their noses and then plates
of candy would come over right by their sides. He had knots in
his stomach, I know he did, staying up all night to watch programs
that aren't healthy. I know he wished he was married to someone
like Samantha. He was always saying his belly killed him. I knew
it was May driving him into the television. He didn't ever stand
up to her. He didn't even call her names any more; he didn't
say that she was a thousand miles of fart. He cried into my slacks
and wanted to live in TV land. Sometimes he was in his chair
until the birds started to sing and then when he went to Trim
'N Tidy he wasn't worth a hot dog. You'd see him in the chair
by the register, sound asleep, with his mouth hanging open, drool
slipping over the edge of his pouting lips. All he really wanted
to do was take Justy for walks, teach him a little something about
Honey Creek, and the world.

A few days after Ruby was trying to find the devil story in the
Bible, he came home early from Trim 'N Tidy. Summer is a

slow time of year, because people aren't thinking about getting woolens clean when it's ninety degrees in the shade. Ruby wanted to play with Justy first thing when he walked in the door, because fathers miss their sons desperately when they're out in the work force. He couldn't stand hearing that Justy was still down for his nap. When I told him, his face fell and he kicked the chair. He didn't like the news so he tiptoed up to the baby's room and tickled him gently, trying to wake him up, and of course Justy started to bawl.

Next thing you know May is storming upstairs. She's wearing a hot pink cotton dress from Goodwill, makes her look like a lipstick out of its tube.

"You hear what you just did?" she yelled. "You're making him cry. Don't you ever use that brain of yours?"

They stood at opposite ends of the crib and she hollered, "You woke him up! I bet that's going to put him in a cheerful mood."

She didn't mention that screaming and yelling might turn an infant into a deaf apple picker. She scooped up Justy and crooned at him. "Poor baby, poor little Justin, hush-a-bye, go back to sleep now, that's my boy."

I didn't like Ruby waking Justy too much either, but it wasn't worth rocking the boat. There were going to be other naps in Justy's life. It even made me smile a little at first, that Ruby missed Justy so much he couldn't wait to see him. It's natural for parents to be that way. It doesn't mean that Ruby wasn't using his brain. But May had to be nearby, ready to strike if her master plan was in some way altered. She stayed upstairs, cradling Justin. He was all sweaty as a result of flailing his arms and screaming.

Ruby walked downstairs. He had to stop every three steps because he was thinking to himself. He walked slowly into the kitchen. He stood in the middle of the room for a few minutes, listening to Justy, and then he reached into the dark cupboard. His hands found what they wanted. He held up one of May's quarts of tomato juice—and slammed it against the wall. In our life together there were quite a few objects Ruby pounded into the wall. The jar shattered; the glass went into the darkest corners of the kitchen. All the juice gushed down, as if it were angry and flashing its temper.

May came down with Justy in her arms. She stopped in her tracks when she saw me sweeping the glass away. She was dumbstruck at the mess. I could tell it was going to take her a few seconds to speak so I quickly said, "Be quiet," with warning in my tone.

She patted Justy harder than she should have while she muttered the phrases of hers. I used to think the one about cocks meant rooster until I learned better. The tomato drip marks were there for days. No one bothered to clean them up. Perhaps we were all afraid they were cursed.

When Ruby came in for supper May had her speech prepared but I said, "If anyone says one single thing I'm going to clobber both of you."

I couldn't stand the fighting. While we ate the clanking of our silverware filled the room and covered our silence. We had Justy in his baby seat on the table, so he could watch us and see how adults behaved.

Ruby went to his counselor twice a month and Sherry said time and time again, "Ruby, you have to find a way to move out on your own, with your wife and son." She said he had to get a full-time job that paid better, but he was slow, even down at Trim 'N Tidy. He wasn't the world's greatest employee. She probably told him he should set up a dentist's office. She ignored the fact that he had problems on occasion. He drifted away sometimes: if he was writing up a bill for a customer he might all of a sudden stop and stare at the poinsettias in the window. Artie got them cheap after Christmas about seven years ago and never took them out. Ruby would say later in bed how the plants looked as huge as palm trees and he couldn't stop staring at the leaves. It was the marijuana he smoked, and the pills he popped. Sherry told him he had to quit taking drugs and he always said, "Sure, OK, I will." For a while he tried to get me to smoke a joint; he said, "Baby, it's fun, you got to try it."

I had stopped smoking cigarettes because of Justy. I wasn't about to start another habit. I wished Ruby could have refrained, but he said it helped him get through his day. I knew if it weren't for me, Artie would have fired him first thing.

Ruby said the poinsettias looked gigantic because he was wishing we could live in California. He told me you can have a house with the ocean in your back yard, and they grow pineapples and lemons in the parks—you can grab them off the vines and stuff them in your pockets. Girls, he said, don't wear anything but bikinis and men don't drive Fords, only 12-cylinder cars that shift like melting chocolate.

It didn't take any counselor to figure out that Ruby saw the world on a different scale from other people. Images in his extra-special imagination occurred to him with awful clarity. When he came home from his sessions with Sherry he always told me what she said. I couldn't help being infuriated with the big old smart counselor who lived in a brick mansion with her husband. He was a car salesman. She didn't have any problems. All she had to do was tell everyone else how to act. How were we going to move out on our own, without May to baby-sit? And Ruby—with drugs it's as if his brain was spinning into outer space. Matt, in his observatory, probably thought he was discovering another planet, Planet Matt. It's fine for Sherry to say, "Ruby, move away on your own," but she didn't know the details of the situation. I thought I was an expert on the drama, seeing as I was stuck in the middle of hostilities, just like people all over the world on television news. I felt as if I had to be the anchor. If I could only try to be a good person and take care of my family, it was going to be OK. The Rev's words came to me when I was confused: "Blessed are they that mourn, for they shall be comforted." And of course, "Blessed are the meek, for they shall inherit the earth." Those sentences always made me feel that I could carry on, that someday I was going to get what I deserved.

Ruby said, in the middle of the hottest July night, "Baby, do you think there's devils in the world getting inside of people?"

I was asleep. I said, "I don't know about any of that, Ruby. Don't ask me about devils. I don't like to think about them."

I could hear him tossing the rest of the night. I was so tired I could hardly comfort him, but I knew he was worried about demons and how they take over a human heart.

There were the good times that summer, particularly when Daisy came home after she got her beautician's license. She had a real strange haircut. It was short, as usual, but it was cut to points in front of her ears and then in back it came sharp to the nape of her neck. There was something pointy to the way she looked, as if she were an instrument that could cleave rocks to exact specifications. When she came to our house she had pajamas for Justy with a painting of a basset hound on the shirt. She looked at him, picked him up, and shouted, "Hey, everybody, this is my godson."

Then she said he needed a haircut, which cracked us up because Justy didn't have any hair at that stage. She said to me, "I'm going to do a job on *you* right now, just like I promised all them years ago when I first knew you. I don't break promises, that ain't in my nature."

She took her smart leather scissor case out of her purse and sat me down on the kitchen stool. Everyone stood around and watched her do her craft. It was a free show. Daisy said now that she had a college degree she knew what was best for me and my shape. I have quite a bit of curly hair, which looks like a hedgerow people can't see over. My expert hairdresser thinned it, cut it, and wrapped each strand around an electric stick. Some of the curls unwound a little, so my head became soft and fluffy. Then she put black mud on my face. I loved her firm touch on my cheeks and eyelids, and every now and then her fingers swept across my lips. After she washed the mud off she put colors on my eyelids, "earth tones," she told me, brown and rust, and some shiny red lipgloss on my mouth. She took me upstairs to the mirror we have in our room. I couldn't find myself in the looking glass. I could not believe I was the girl. I resembled marine fish with big puckered lips opening and closing right up close to the window of their tank.

"Finally you look like you belong in this century," Daisy said. "I always knew we could turn you into something."

Ruby stared blankly at me and then he said, "Baby, you and me are gonna start a rock band. You look just like a drummer should."

We sat around that night on the steps and ate pretzels. Daisy told us about Peoria and the girls she worked with. None of them were too crazy about her, because she was the number-one star hair stylist. She explained how she was going to fly out to Los Angeles in a little while, after she got some experience. She held Justy the whole time. He had to stare at her — he was your average hot-blooded male already. He was fascinated by those extraterrestrial eyes of hers, plus her large breasts did not pass unnoticed. He patted them so tenderly.

There were a few times that summer when Ruby and I were on our own, without May. On the weekends we took Justy down to the lake in Stillwater, where I first met Ruby. On hot days we took the baby's clothes off and played with him in the water. I had a hand-me-down bikini from Daisy. It was light blue and it didn't fit me. I always felt as if everyone was looking at my body, the way the bottoms hung on me, like extra skin. We lay on the beach from nine o'clock in the morning until it got cold and dark, and then we came home cooked. We got so tired from all the sunshine. May said how lazy we were, to spend the whole day on our backsides, but we were too sleepy to notice her scolding us. We were too hot, too thirsty, too tired, that summer, to think what a strange family we made, May and Ruby and Justy and me.

Seventeen

O N Justy's first birthday we had a party for him. When he was in bed our big family, Dee Dee, Randall, and Daisy, came over. Everyone except me played poker. I didn't feel like celebrating. I wanted to think about the year gone by. I wanted to get the time back right after Justy was born and I stayed at home with him. By some trick I had yet to invent I would command myself and Ruby to sit still on the couch with our newborn, singing our songs, patting each other's knees. We would turn to stone in that attitude. At the birthday party Randall watched TV. He never tried to brag any more. He didn't seem to be anything more than an enormous husk made from old yellowing paper. To my surprise he wasn't eating anything that night. I wondered if he was about to keel over and die from starvation, or if he had lately discovered that food didn't really make him feel happy at all. I put a bowl of peanuts by him and waited until he gave me a feeble smile and dug in.

Everyone else was concentrating on their poker cards so I went upstairs to look at Justy sleeping. There were so many things I wished for him. I hoped that he would never know that evil groups existed in other countries, sneaking and prowling in the mountains and then killing the poor people. I hoped that he would grow up blind to all our shortcomings and that he would understand and forgive my poisoned thoughts.

It seemed both like seconds ago and one thousand years before that Ruby and I were playing cards in the labor room, and now here was our boy, one year old. The days had melted into each other: twelve months of May and Ruby and me, watching Justy in his baby seat, watching Justy rise up on his haunches—all the gray space I tried not to think about, where we were squabbling with each other. Often one day was no different than the next, except for the outside temperature. I didn't have time to look around and see the seasons, since I was either going to Trim 'N Tidy or washing heaps of soiled diapers. When a girl is a teen and when she first gets married she thinks having a baby is going to be a real treat all the time, but it isn't true. For the first year you're so tired the world spins around in front of your face, you feel dizzy, and the sunshine hurts your eyes. I kept saying to myself, every five minutes, "I guess this is what life is; it makes a person so tired."

The summer Justy was one and a half I had a brainstorm. I said to Ruby, "How about you and me going on a vacation somewhere?" I asked Artie if we could take our week in August and he said, "Sure, no problem." Then I went to May and blurted out that we, meaning Ruby and I, were going to go on a holiday in August, if she could watch Justin. She looked up in disbelief, as if I had just announced that we were moving to Texas to pick grapefruits.

Ruby and I needed time alone desperately. The trip was something Sherry suggested—she's not always full of hot air. It was Sherry who insisted we get away. She told Ruby that we needed privacy, and that we must take the time to get to know each other. I knew Ruby well enough, but what we needed, I said to myself, was a vacation from the bristles of everyday life.

"It's only going to be one short week, Ma," I said quickly, after I wrapped up the agenda. I had the time broken up into half-day units on paper so she would know when to take Justin to Aunt Daisy's and when she had to be at the cleaners. It was Artie who had suggested that I make a chart. There was even a night out for May in my plan. Daisy had promised she would watch Justy so May wouldn't get an overdose.

"When we come back, you can take a trip," I said to May. "It's healthy to get away. It's good for a person."

I didn't have any experience with vacations but Sherry said you return refreshed. She said you realize how wonderful home is if you can get away now and then. I didn't think I could ever call Honey Creek wonderful, after no matter how long an absence, but I was willing to give it a try.

May snorted. She said, "I'll go on a cruise by myself, won't that be dandy? I'll send you the bill from the Love Boat. Can't you picture it, an old lady getting sick into the swimming pool in the middle of the ocean? No thanks, that don't sound like my idea of a party."

"Ma," I pleaded, "at least you and Dee Dee could go to Rockford for a day of shopping, anything, just to get away."

Sometimes she acted as if taking Justy was a burden she didn't deserve so late in life. She said, "Go, leave me alone, see what I care"—and she heaved a sigh.

What surprised me was how May coped now that Justy was in one of his impossible stages. He was all motion but he didn't have any coordination. He moved like a drunkard. He wanted to get into everything and if you weren't watching he demolished the house in no time flat. I went around and moved the breakable knickknacks to the top shelves so there weren't valuable objects he could ruin, but it was May who performed continual miracles: she never once lost her patience with him. He was discovering he had his own will, and if he banged on the table with his spoon, so you couldn't tolerate the noise, to get a rise out of us, May, with perfect calm, would gently lift him down so he wouldn't do it any more. He'd bang on the floor instead where it didn't make such a racket or dent the table. She was a genius sometimes, I swear. I was not prepared for her control, because of the way she used to rant around in my younger days. I had fully expected that she would be an older, meaner version of herself, but all the traces of her former days had vanished.

Justy loved to blow out candles, and he and May used to sit at the kitchen table working at a king-size box of matches. She'd light the candle while Justy stared at the flame, utterly fascinated, and then he'd blow it out. There was a pile of used matchsticks, enough wood to keep us warm all winter, there on the table. May liked to kiss Justy all over and he put up with it; he didn't squirm too energetically. While she cooked she had Justy on the floor playing with pots and pans. Over the fried apples sizzling on the stove she told him the high points of her life story. He licked the floor while she described her favorite doll, but she was in a trance and didn't notice.

She spanked him when he was terribly bad, if he whacked her over the head with the bellows, but even then she wasn't crazy about punishment. She wanted me to be the one to hit him if he was about to stick his head into the hot oven, or run out on the road. Her favorite act was taking Justy into town by herself and strutting down the street as if she were a one-person parade and a baby was a novelty no one had ever seen before.

May said to me, "All right, go ahead on your vacation." She said it as if she was dragging her feet, but actually, as I knew from my lifelong association with her, she had a huge old chorus line in her heart, lifting up their legs, doing the cancan. I knew she was gleeful about getting rid of us for a week.

Up in our room Ruby said, "Hey, baby, where we going on our trip?"

"We're visiting Aunt Sidney in De Kalb," I said, "and then we're going to Chicago to see the Cubs." I had counted the money in my pig and I was going to spend every last cent on my husband.

Ruby acted as if Chicago was the place he'd always wanted to visit most. He got up on the bed and started batting and jumping. He was like Justy, loving everything except chores. When I told Justy he could push the button to start the drier he had a nervous breakdown brought on by excitement. However, if you asked him to put the toys away you had to be careful you didn't get a block aimed directly at your rear end. I wrote Aunt Sid and told her that Ruby had a tremendous urge to see a Cubs game, and I wanted to see for myself how millions of people lived in tall buildings. I told her that we were going to stay in a motel in Chicago. It was bound to be the greatest adventure of my lifetime, so far, and I was going to believe it only after it had actually happened. I asked her if we could stop at her house for one night, on our way. I figured when we ran out of money, after two days, we'd sneak home and camp on the lake. Aunt Sid wrote to say that she didn't have her chorus in the summer. She said any time we wanted to come it would be a pleasure to see us.

The real news from Honey Creek that summer was Daisy's marriage. It knocked us all off our stumps. One minute she's on the loose, the next she's promising forever as if she truly understood the meaning of her words. I guess she knew her mind instantly, and didn't need to dwell on her past or future life. She met the man when she was cutting his girlfriend's hair at her beauty shop, Shear Magic. He was waiting for Dolores to hurry up and get done so they could go on a date. Daisy must have done an impressive job shooting the breeze with him. He told Dolores he had a stomachache and couldn't go to the show. Then he called Daisy's shop and asked her out. He felt bad about the whole episode but he couldn't help it. He had his own business doing upholstery for people's furniture. He was starting to go bald, although he wasn't much older than Daisy. It seemed as if he saw through her; he saw what a fine person she was underneath the paint on her face. He understood that she was kind and true, down in the core, despite the fact that she had used her wiles to land nearly every male west of the Atlantic Ocean. He said, "I'll bet you are prettier without that glop on your eyes, Daisy Mae," and he suggested she take it off. He went wild over how great she looked, so she stopped wearing orange mascara and purple and green eyeshadow. She didn't look like she was suffering from gangrene any more. She switched to a calm pale blue above her eyes. They were a nice couple; you could see they cared for each other. He didn't paw at her or goose her, but on occasion he walked up to her and put his arms around her, and she let him stay there, circling her. His name was Bill. He looked like he'd been standing on his own two feet since the day of his birth. Probably there wasn't anyone who could knock him down without a struggle. That's not counting his ex-girlfriend, who punched him in the eye. He took it without flinching because he said he deserved it.

I guessed Daisy wasn't planning on going to New York City or Los Angeles to work in the television industry after all. For a while her ambition was to stay at home and make casserole recipes. She didn't even want to go to Shear Magic. Bill owned a house outside of Stillwater and she couldn't wait to spend his money to fix it up. She was thinking of going to night classes in interior design. It's as if there's a virus that steals under a girl's skin sometimes, and makes her want to be a good wife, even when she wasn't planning on going that route.

They got married in our church. She didn't have any bridesmaids. I wished I could have been in her wedding party, but I wasn't mad at her. It didn't hurt my feelings too much. I knew she wanted to keep it simple, that it wasn't personal. It wasn't because of my looks. She didn't invite any of her old boyfriends so there weren't many people attending. When I asked her, two weeks after they got back from the Wisconsin Dells, if she could take care of Justy while we went on vacation, she said, "Justy's my godson, and he's going to be my little baby guinea pig. What do you bet I want a kid after chasing the Moose around for a week?"

She took my shoulders and said, "You go and have the greatest time. You deserve a break; no, I take that back, you deserve something fabulous. Don't worry about Justy. He won't miss you one bit." She winked at me. Daisy's so professional at winking. It makes a person feel warm all over.

It was the middle of July, two weeks until our trip, although already my nails were bitten to shreds. I could hardly wait to see Aunt Sid. I was going to do all the things I had wanted to do since I was small: sit at her kitchen table, look in her closets and see the dresses she gives concerts in, smell the lilies she probably presses in books after she's worn them on her chest, to commemorate each choral concert.

On a scorching July day, the type where you feel as if you're pinned under an iron, our plans were changed. Ruby walked across the street in Honey Creek—don't ask me where he was going, maybe to church to pray—and he dreamed himself into one of his dazes where he has to stand still and look at something hard; the thing either looks tremendous or minuscule to him. The gas station once looked shrunk and he thought he saw little tiny ants getting into puny cars. It wasn't a secret that Ruby took artificial stimulants, although he did it on the sly. I couldn't always be sure when he was on something, but his bloodshot eyes were often a dead giveaway. Ruby had contacts through Hazel, people who gave him bargains on drugs. He could handle life when he was high, except for the times when objects looked so queer, and he had to tell me about his sensational eyesight.

On July 18th Ruby started across the street, and all of a sudden he had to stop in mid-step to look at the texture of the road. The small asphalt bumps looked like California foothills, and of course the pickup truck didn't expect him to stop. It rammed into his leg and knocked him over. I stood in the door weeping when the driver delivered Ruby, complete with his freshly mangled leg. I have to tell the truth: I cried not for Ruby, but because I knew our vacation was out of the question.

Ruby didn't have to go to the hospital overnight, even though his leg was banged up and out of commission. He could barely make it to the liquor cabinet. May said under her breath, "Why didn't they just run him over?"

We were stuck in July. All the breezes in the world were hovering over Europe and the Virgin Islands. The heat made us feel like screaming and crying at the temperature, but we were too slow and stupid to open our mouths. Ruby spent his time in the living room on the couch with the fan blowing over him and I brought him iced drinks and lemons. I watched TV with him and his hurt leg. I felt like there wasn't anything left inside of me. I was nothing but eyeballs watching reruns of *Hogan's Heroes* and *Bewitched*, *F Troop* and *Gilligan's Island*. Justy was hot and cranky. I yelled at him for the dumbest reasons. I spanked him for ripping the cover off the TV guide. I told him to shut up, repeatedly, when he whined. Good mothers aren't supposed to say words of that sort, but I said all of the worst profanities, trying to vent my spleen so I wouldn't throw Justy out the window. I was so glad when May came home from work. I was at the end of my rope.

After a week Ruby hobbled around but the slightest movement wore him out and he groaned from the living room, from his couch. He didn't want anyone to bother him, except people who were in the mood to serve. He hollered at Justy when Justy got on his nerves — that was about every three minutes. One night, I couldn't bear it any more. I called up Daisy to come over and get me. We went out to the Town Lanes like old times and we played a few games. I let her win a couple; I didn't care about anything. She sat there telling me about her Bill and how great they were getting along, and how she never had met a man before him, who she liked as a person, to talk to. She said it was fabulous, their relationship. All of a sudden she felt mature, she explained. She knew she was a grown woman, not one of them wild girls so crazy for a hunk of flesh. "Not," she added, "that he ain't sensational on the horizontal.

"Bill sure saved me from wrecking my life," she said. "I bet I would have turned into an old broad like Hazel. She practically pays boys to do it to her."

I turned away. I didn't want to hear a word about Hazel, Ruby's former girlfriend.

"Bill knows about all kinds of information." Daisy was still talking. "He teaches me things I never knew about. He's going to teach me how to hunt deer. I mean, how'd I get so lucky?" She looked up to the ceiling as if the crumbling plaster was going to answer her, tell her that she deserved heaven on earth.

The minute she mentioned the word *lucky* I sat down on one of the yellow vinyl chairs they have and I burst into tears. I put my head on the score table and cried the way I always cry with Daisy: flat-out hysterics. I told her how terribly I wanted to visit Aunt Sid, and go to the city, and now I couldn't because Ruby was in bed all day long with his bum leg. It's a miracle she could understand my choking and stuttering. I said I didn't feel like a person any more. I said that Aunt Sid always made me think there was something good about me through the mail, and imagine how seeing her in real life would make it one million times better.

Daisy picked up my sweaty hand, looked me in the eye, and said, "Too bad if Ruby can't go along. You take off anyway. You don't need to go all the way to Chicago, but you could visit your aunt for a few days."

"What do you mean?" I asked. Sometimes her thoughts were so unusual. I stopped crying instantly. I never went anywhere by myself—I told her that.

"Go alone, you big sissy. What are you scared of, muggers and knifers on the bus?"

"No," I lied. My fingers were shaky and wet, even though I got up and put them over the drier they have for your hands, so you won't sweat into your bowling ball and lose your grip.

Daisy kept telling me I should do something for myself, that I had earned a trip. "Besides," she said, "your Aunt Sid don't know Ruby. You wouldn't be able to have no heart-to-hearts with a man hanging around. I never said nothin' but I thought it was a stupid idea to take Ruby along in the first place." We weren't bowling any more. We were standing at the line. We didn't hear any other conversations; we didn't notice pins crashing to the floor. "But Daisy," I said, "it's supposed to be our honeymoon."

"Jeeeeeesus," she whispered, smacking her palm to her forehead. "You don't need a honeymoon. You need a break from your kid and your ma and your husband. Everyone needs time off—it don't mean you ain't a prize-winning wife and mother." She said I should go for it. She kept saying, "Go for it," whenever she got the opportunity.

When we got home I banged the screen door for dramatic effect and stood under the light in the kitchen. May was playing solitaire. She had all her aces up. She was having terrific luck, so I said quickly, "Ma, I'm visiting Aunt Sid next week for a few days without Ruby, for a vacation."

"No you ain't," she said, slapping down the king of hearts. "I'm not going to care for your husband."

Daisy stepped out from the shadows and said, "Now look here, May, you'll be at work half the time and I'll take care of Justy, and Ruby's a grown man. Even though he don't walk like a ballerina, he can take care of himself. I'll get him the things he needs."

May had her card in midair. There wasn't anything she could say after the speech, because Daisy is so tall and gorgeous and well married. She always makes a mess sound easy. There aren't ever any problems for Dais. If she doesn't like someone she says, "Go to hell." Then she wipes her hands and walks away. It was the funniest sight when she came down the aisle for her wedding. She looked like a dewdrop with her lowered eyelids and her blush. It seemed as if she couldn't ever have uttered a filthy word — or experienced the meaning of one of those words — in her life.

Ruby was lying on the couch like a recently decorated and blasted-apart war hero when I told him my plans. His bum leg hung off the side as if it was just barely connected to his body. "Baby," he said with tears in his voice, "don't leave me."

I talked cocky although it was a charade. There were swarms of moths giving birth right inside my stomach. I said, "Don't be silly, Ruby, it's only for two days. You won't even miss me."

"My leg hurts me so bad, baby. It's killing me."

I stood up. I said, "Well, my staying around ain't going to make it feel better. It'll have to heal on its own. You have to be patient, that's all."

I walked out of the room exactly like Daisy does, tossing her head. She wouldn't look back if you paid her fifty dollars.

That's how I found myself packing one bag for a trip, my first voyage away from home. I caught the Greyhound in Stillwater. Daisy calls those buses "metal dogs" and has a whole series of "metal dog" jokes. I was a wreck at first, especially my digestive system. I needed to use the squat box, as Daisy says, every five seconds, but I didn't have the courage to walk to the back of the bus. I sat right up front so I could look out the window and observe my movement through the world. Sitting high you can see the land stretched out flat, as if there's four people at each corner, holding a blanket. And all the rows of corn, whizzing by, row upon row. It gets going so fast it makes you dizzy, all those rows like bristles on a toothbrush, flashing by a person. I got hypnotized thinking about the king-size teeth that corn rows could brush.

De Kalb is forty miles from Honey Creek so it didn't take more than an hour to get there. Suddenly the driver was saying into his microphone that he was glad we'd traveled Greyhound, and he hoped we'd come aboard again soon. I said I would, almost out loud. I felt like telling him that my husband was laid up at home with my mother, because he seemed like such a nice man, with a picture of his daughters on the dashboard, along with his bag of peppermints.

There was Aunt Sid, waving to me as I climbed down the stairs. When I got to her I dropped my bag, thinking to hug her with all my might. I didn't want to be shy. I had planned to tell her what I thought about her. I imagine there's probably so much quiet where you are when you're cold and dead, you might as well say how crazy you are about people while you have a mouth and teeth and tongue. Before I could get it out she grabbed my shoulders and stood looking at me from head to toe. She said that I looked lovely — and I should have, because Daisy lent me her wardrobe. I had on a blue-and-orange-and-yellow-striped cotton skirt, very full it was, and past my knees. My top was a dark blue silky shirt. Not actual silk, spun from worms. Still, I felt like an advertisement for extra-strength brighteners people put in their wash. Daisy did up my hair too. She said I looked like a million dollars but she was probably exaggerating.

Then I did it: I threw my arms around Aunt Sid, and after the two-second contact, while I looked at the sidewalk glinting with sunshine, I told her I had waited for this moment ever since I was five, when I first met her and her coral lipstick. I said I had had the feeling, so long ago, that I was destined to visit her in De Kalb. She has a laugh like water coming over a waterfall, sparkling and frothing.

I wish I could hire Charles Dickens to describe Aunt Sid. I don't have a chance in the world to do her justice. She wore beige slacks and a sleeveless blouse with brown horses galloping in rows across green turf. Her hair was piled on her head, as usual, and her smile came directly from the heart. If I were a

Catholic I'd believe that the Blessed Virgin Mary came to look like Aunt Sid, when she got older, after her son died and her life got on track. When I mentioned that very thought to Daisy, at home, she, an unbeliever, said I could get struck down for thinking such a thing. She also told me I was creating a goddess out of an ordinary person, which, I admitted to myself only for a moment, was exactly the beauty of Aunt Sid. Daisy said, "You'll probably find out one of these days that she picks her nose with a tuning fork."

When Daisy made that remark I stepped in a whole bed of marigolds and ground my heels into the earth. If Ruby and May and Dee Dee, and just about everyone I knew, could have comfort in their alcohol I saw no reason why I couldn't have the fantasy of Aunt Sid. Some day I was bound to find out that she had a terrible quirk, but until then there was no harm in believing she was a good witch.

Aunt Sid drove me all over De Kalb. She showed me the state university. We saw a tour bus full of Chinese people jabbering at each other in their language, which surely requires gymnastic classes for the tongue and voice. I giggled at how crazy they were speaking while Aunt Sid pointed out all the buildings and what kinds of learning took place in them. I kept looking around to see if there were any criminals, fresh from Chicago, waiting to rape the college coeds, but no one looked like a knifer. Summer school was in session and people were scurrying along the paths with their notebooks tucked under their arms.

Finally Aunt Sid took me to her blue wooden house. There is an arch of oak trees over her street so the sunshine can't blast through and make the cement boil. She has a front porch, screened in, and a yard with the wildest display of flowers and colors: crimson and indigo, vermilion and plain yellow, lush green and an entire bed of blinding white petunias. There is a special rubber door with a slit in it so her collie dog, Elizabeth, can go in and out whenever she pleases. She looks at you with moony eyes, hoping for food. I knew I should be sad to think of Ruby back in Honey Creek with his wobbly leg, lying in the heat of the house, but my body, my mind, couldn't conjure up unhappiness for anything just then.

We sat at lunch, on the porch, in elegant white wire lawn furniture, sipping our lemonade politely. Aunt Sid told me about her neighborhood and the children who lived on the block, and gradually she started remembering how she used to play back at the home farm, in the hay fields and pastures, in the creek. I couldn't keep my mind on her words, because I was concentrating on eating daintily, until she started talking about May's Willard Jenson, and the ingenious methods she had for spying on the smooching couple from the closet in the basement. I had had no idea how May felt about Willard. I had only seen pictures of him once, and May got irritated with me for asking about the people. She snatched the photos away and I never saw them again.

After we finished eating our egg salad sandwiches, cut in wedges with green olives and lettuce, and emptying our little bowls filled with melon balls, Aunt Sid brought out her three photo albums, each one filled with old pictures. She sat on the arm of my chair and told me about every picture. I couldn't look at them hard enough. I couldn't stop staring at the snapshots of May when she was a girl, squinting into the sunshine with her hand over her forehead. She was young and thin, with the entire world before her, or so she thought. Aunt Sid told me about how Willard Jenson and May danced in the basement and the dirty clothes went scooting around the floor. There was a picture of the two of them, with their arms around each other, smiling into the great unknown. The photos, the stories, put May in a new light. I almost said out loud that I wished May herself had wanted me to know her as a young girl with heartaches.

After lunch Aunt Sid took me up to my room. She said she often napped in the heat of the day. She disappeared around the corner to her room, which was filled with heavy golden sunlight, and white curtains billowing and snapping in the open windows. When she was gone I took off my skirt and my blouse and climbed under the cool perfumed sheets. I didn't sleep of course, but I lay there, not daring to move, staring around myself. The room was white with paintings in gilded frames on the walls, paintings of haystacks and ponds, blue and yellow, shimmering. My room had a desk in it, and shelves with books, some of which I had read on the blind tapes. I knew the authors. I was half afraid I had taken some of Ruby's drugs and when I came to I would be sitting on the sofa at home absently stirring the ice cubes in his rum and Coke and staring into the gray space. I kept my eyes open so I wouldn't drift off and dream I was in Honey Creek.

Later in the afternoon we went to Aunt Sid's school and I saw the empty room where her choir rehearses. She sat at the piano playing and singing a song by Brahms. She hissed and gurgled softly in the German language. Her lips quivered with the notes while she closed her eyes to listen to herself. If you want to see a sight to make you get lumps in your throat, watch Aunt Sid singing. It will slay you each time.

When we got home Aunt Sid cooked steaks on her small outdoor grill, and I sat on the patio drinking a gin and tonic she had made for me. In the next house someone was playing the piano and it seemed as if everything in the yard, the flowers, the green grass, the still evening itself, heard the music and became part of the melody. Children down the alley were playing kick the can, calling out and laughing. We didn't speak as Aunt Sid prepared the food, and I wasn't really too nervous while I sat waiting.

After a drink we got to talking. I answered her questions about spotting and how to remove tough stains. She wanted to know every single person who worked at Trim 'N Tidy, and I told her about Artie, and how he was always giving me good advice. I mentioned his prize possession: the Trim 'N Tidy bowling trophy.

After my second drink I had enough courage and I said, "Aunt Sid, do you remember when you sent me money to buy May perfume for her birthday?"

Aunt Sid nodded yes. She had a piece of lettuce that she was trying to get into her mouth.

"I didn't get perfume for May. I bought myself some brassieres."

I went scarlet recalling it, but it was funny, I knew it was. Still, it was something that I'd always wanted to confess. Aunt Sid groaned in sympathy with me, and then she said that growing up was so difficult. I banged my hand on the table in agreement. She reached over and petted my arm. She murmured, "You poor thing." I shrugged it off. I wasn't in the mood for crying into a five-gallon drum, plus I didn't want her to think I was a ninny. I said I was a dumb kid back then, I didn't travel places by myself.

Somehow her saying I was a poor thing cast a pall over the rest of the dinner and we quietly ate our steaks and the baked potatoes and the green beans with slivered almonds on them. For coffee she suggested moving to the screened-in porch, and when she brought out the mugs she also had a box, containing all my letters, tied up by the year in green ribbon. She had saved my letters because they were precious to her. I sat in my chair long past dark, reading my life over by candlelight while Sid moved in and out, doing her chores, washing the dishes, reading her paper. Most of the details and events I had written about were exaggerated or had never taken place. The crickets, the moon, the dark cool air moved in through the porch screens but I was unable to budge. I was meeting a strange and familiar person through her words. I couldn't believe I had written the letters; I was actually a little bit impressed, and very horrified, by my imagination.

I found a letter that described my promotion to the superior English class—I hadn't admitted that I was in the lowest of the low, and that I was merely moving one step up into the regular class. I talked about how Mr. Davidson said I was improving miraculously, and that I had such a good grasp of the books we were reading. All lies. I never once mentioned the fact that after a month I was demoted.

"Aunt Sid," I said to her, while she sipped her coffee, "I told so many lies in my letters to you. Half of the things I described didn't even happen."

She chuckled. She said that was what pen pals were for, to share fantasies with.

She rubbed her eyes with her fists; she looked up, serious all of a sudden, and said, "You, all of you, should have visited me years ago—I should have demanded it. I don't know," she said, "I wanted to help May and be friends in some way but we have always lived such different lives. We're practically a different generation, and I had so many more opportunities than she did. Mother and Father had more money by the time I came along, and Marion encouraged me to go to college, and the teachers in Stillwater urged me to pursue voice training. I grew up in a different era." She stirred her coffee and then cupped her hands around the mug, gathering its warmth. "Maybe she just couldn't forgive me." She looked up after a minute, trying to smile cheerfully. "I shouldn't be saying these things to you," she said, "but I want you to know that you're dear to me."

I almost tipped the chair over so I could lie still in the state of grace. I wanted her to stop talking before she said something like "If I'd seen you sooner maybe you wouldn't be retarded." I couldn't stand it when she was solemn. I petted the dog and stared at its limp tongue.

Then Aunt Sid asked me a lot of questions about my life, and wouldn't you know it, I was feeling so lively I didn't tell her every detail. I couldn't bring myself to tell her the truth, for the millionth time. I said that Ruby and Justy and May and I were in the house together still, of course, and that it worked out pretty well, because May baby-sat, and she loved Justy even better than

Rock Hudson. I mentioned that May had had some rough times over the years, when we were growing up and she had to raise us single-handedly. Now that I was a parent, I said, trying to sound knowledgeable, I could imagine how miserable being alone with small children could make a person. I didn't elaborate on how noise and dirt and whining rile you to the point of wanting to strangle everything within reach. Aunt Sid and I agreed that May didn't have anything handed to her on a silver platter. She had had to fight for every gain, what there was of them.

But with Justy here now, I told Aunt Sid, it was an entirely new life for all of us. I mentioned that Matt didn't ever write or come home; he was a missing person, abducted by the world. May had to learn about Matt from Dr. Heck, the school principal. She had to pretend Matt wrote her and told her trivial things, such as what his apartment looked like, when actually she was longing to hear substance. She would ask Dr. Heck, "Did Matt say where he was working?" Dr. Heck probably had it all figured out because he told May in his gentle voice everything she wanted to know about Matt.

"It's the limit," I said to Aunt Sid, not feeling a bit guilty for bad-mouthing Matt. Aunt Sid shook her head and said it was a shame.

I explained that Ruby wasn't the most notorious genius on earth, not like Matt, but I knew his capacities before I married him. I said he wasn't going to solve any riddles of the universe, and he had a little trouble holding down a job but it didn't matter a bit, he had so many good points. I told her about the times he was kind to people, buying May a toaster oven, and what a playful father he was for Justy. I bragged about his high sweet voice, wishing that she could hear him sing. Briefly I mentioned that he drank sometimes, and that it worried us, the way he could guzzle serious quantities. I quickly added that he knew how to handle it, that he didn't trip around or bully people. I mumbled that it scared me, that I knew it wasn't healthy, and that we weren't rich enough to support a drunk. Or a drug addict, I said to myself. I said that Ruby's counselor Sherry was helping him out. He was improving little by little.

I explained my life to Aunt Sid, and how I spent my days, but I skipped over the bad parts. I told her about the qualities I admired in May and Ruby: there was only half a person pictured in my mind, when I got done describing each one. I couldn't bring into my line of vision their heads, or their chests, where their hearts should have been.

Aunt Sid said it was astonishing that we could all live together and get along. She said it was remarkable, that I was a wonder. She thought it must mean so much to May, to have her young people and the baby.

When Aunt Sid said that I was a holy wonder I felt like what I did in my life was worthwhile, helping my family, seeing May into her old age, and having a husband with a singing voice, even though houses shrank in front of him sometimes, and it looked like a midget could live in them.

But finally, as we were standing by the kitchen door, saying goodnight, I told her to her face; I said if she hadn't written the letters to me I wouldn't be able to hold my head up walking down the street. Naturally I didn't have the right words to tell her that she had made me strong, that if it weren't for her telling me time and time again that I was a good person, with novel ideas, I might have shriveled into a warty frog croaking in single syllables from the marsh. I always got the feeling, even when I wasn't telling the whole truth to Aunt Sid, that she took my lies with a grain of salt. When I whispered that she had saved my life she gave me a big hug. I had to clamp my teeth together to keep from crying my entire head off and destroying her real silk shirt.

Eighteen

THE strange thing, when I got off the bus in Stillwater, was
how I didn't recognize the town. It didn't look like where I
wanted to be. My clenched hands were cold and sweaty and there
was nothing left of my fingernails or cuticles. I wished the bus
had gone straight through Stillwater, not stopped for a single
person. Even though I had the front seat I waited to be the last
one off.

It was twilight, only the air was thick and the sky had turned
yellow, as if it were burning up from the heat of the day. Maybe
night had decided not to come. Perhaps we were going to have
afternoon for the rest of our lives. Daisy was on the sidewalk
trying to make Justy wave to me. He had a sucker in his mouth
so he wasn't about to obey. He looked at me with accusing eyes
for the longest time. After a while he whispered, "Ma-ma." When
Daisy gave him to me he buried his head in my neck.

"When are you going to have a baby?" I said, first thing.

"Give me ten years, maybe twenty." Daisy winked at me. She
had to be joking because in twenty years her eggs would be used
up. On the way home in the car she kept asking so cheerfully
how I enjoyed my trip. I told her that yesterday we went to Aunt

⌐id's school, and ate dinner, and today she took me downtown and we ate lunch in a café. I didn't feel like going into much detail. My time with Aunt Sid was a secret I had already stashed away. If I explained to Daisy, out loud, our morning on the porch eating English muffins, my memory of it would become fixed. I wanted the whole experience to remain fluid and new. And there was the danger that Daisy might make a joke, as she later did about the tuning fork, and I'd have to stamp out marigolds and make excuses for myself believing in magic.

I didn't want to know, but finally I had to ask; I said, "How are Ma and Ruby?"

She coughed, saying, "It was sort of a rough two days for them while you was gone."

"That don't surprise me a whole lot," I said, and then we rode quietly the rest of the way home.

May had a pan of chicken frying on the stove. She looked like she didn't have the strength to poke the pieces. Her curls were greasy and slack, and her eyelids hung low.

"I don't want to hear nothin' about Sidney," she said, right when I walked in. "I don't want to know about the great time you had."

"That's fine with me," I said, breezing through the kitchen.

Ruby was lying on the couch with a beer between his legs, in the position I left him. He acted like a real big baby when I touched him.

"Ouch, you're hurting me," he whined.

I hardly put any pressure on his thigh. He squinched up his face so that he looked exactly like the Chinese tourists in De Kalb, focusing their cameras.

"You look like a Jap," I said, and then I gave him a quick peck on the cheek, and told him that I'd thought about him while was gone.

He turned all blubbery and said, "Oh, baby, I missed you too."

I hadn't meant that I'd missed him, but I didn't correct his impression. He told me he didn't like to live without me—he meant, without me serving him.

Daisy went home and then May and Ruby and Justy and I sat down for chicken dinner. The minute her fanny hit the seat May said, "My, what a juicy chicken this is, Ruby, how good of you to get it for us. Don't it smell delicious? Thank you for making it possible." She licked her chops and smiled at Ruby, thanking him.

He didn't look at her, not once. He slurped his milk like a hound dog. I couldn't figure out what was going on with those two so I paid attention to Justy, told him about the oak trees in De Kalb making a bridge over the street. He had an expression on his face that said, "I love how nice you're talking to me, Mama."

"Justy," I said, "I heard Aunt Sid sing. Her voice sets your whole spine shivering, and she sings a language we don't know."

"He don't know a word you're saying," May chimed. "My, ain't this chicken tender?" She tore the skin off a drumstick and sank her teeth into the meat.

"Aunt Sid's house is filled with light and color, Justy. Someday you can see it for yourself. I know you and me will get there, to De Kalb, for another visit."

Ruby suctioned up his Jell-O, face down to his plate. He made one long noisy sucking sound.

"Ruby, you was such a sweetheart to get this scrumptious meal for us. I can't tell you how much I appreciate your thoughts, especially when that leg of yours is good for nothin'." May talked straight to Ruby even though he was looking over his shoulder at the back door.

"Justy," I said, "did you have fun at Aunt Daisy's this afternoon? Were you a good boy?" He nodded his head and said, "Do." "Do" was the only word he spoke clearly, except for "no, no, no, no, no." He could say "no" with perfect diction.

"You know what?" May said, taking a huge ferocious bite of bread, "I don't think I've tasted better chicken in my whole life. Ruby, this one tastes as good as Grandma's devil's-food cake. I think they're improved when they"—she leaned over the table and spit the words out—"hang from their necks."

He was looking clear out the back door. She wanted to catch his eye, tack it up for a trophy.

"What's going on, Ma?" I shouted, banging my hand on the table. "How come you're talking about this chicken like it's Jesus H. Christ?"

She stood up with all her theatrical flair. She had been dying for me to ask. She pointed at Ruby like she was the victim finally pointing out her assailant in the line-up.

"Ruby can't control his emotions too great, oh no he can't." She spoke in her hushed tone; she spit out her *t*'s and her *c*'s. "Don't they have places for people who can't control theirselves? Maybe we better call the funny farm, I'd say it's about time."

If I didn't know there was blood and guts inside a person I'd say what's down in May's belly is a furnace making her words come out to sizzle people, to char them until there's nothing left but smoldering ashes. Daisy always said I went to extremes when I exaggerated, but I have to say my impressions even if they aren't true to science.

May went on to tell the story of how Ruby strangled a chicken and then hung it out on the porch by the macramé plant holder he made down at the resource center in Stillwater, where Sherry works.

Of course, he had to go strangle May's favorite hen, the one which lays the best. She milked that part for all it was worth. She said "My Favorite Hen" about five times in a row. She stood ripping the skin off her second piece of chicken and then she said, "I went to look out the window and there was My Favorite Hen hanging by the neck on the porch."

She wasn't having too much trouble consuming her favorite

creature. Taking a bite for the road she marched to the sink to find her cigarettes. She put one between her lips and it dangled there like a wire hanging from a busted fixture.

I stared at May and at Ruby, back and forth. I knew they expected me to say something. Ruby was watching the kitchen door with his mouth drooping open. All I did was pick up Justy, wipe his mustache, and take him into the living room. We played, seeing as I'm his mother. I made a fort out of chairs and blankets and then we went inside and sat. I escaped to Justy's play world where the blankets caving in on your head is the worst thing that can happen. When I tucked him into bed I sang him a song I made up about a mother and son who drive away to Texas and pick fruit for the rest of their lives. I watched his eyelids get heavy, opening and closing. Every time they opened he looked into my face. He was learning it by heart, for future reference.

When I came downstairs Ruby was watching TV. I stood in front of him and said, "How come you strangled the chicken, Ruby?"

He clamped his jaw shut and stared without blinking, around my form, at a show with cops chasing down alleys. "She gets me riled up," he finally whispered, avoiding my face. I sat down and waited. During the commercial he blurted that he had only wanted to take Justy out in the car to the store, but she wouldn't let him. She said it wasn't safe to drive with that leg of his. She said it wasn't safe to drive with that brain of his, for that matter, and then she went down and threw the keys to both cars into the marsh.

He closed his eyes and said, "I couldn't help it, bab' I had to wreck somethin'."

"Don't pay any attention to her," I whispered, pet his hair. "She don't know everything."

I said the first thing that came into my head se I had to think about the situation. Telling him not attention to May is like saying, Pretend that wasp in yo' dn't just bite you forty times. I was also confused because I secretly had to admit that May was probably right. It's quite possible it wasn't safe for Ruby to drive the way his vision wavers on occasion. Still, a person has got to know himself and figure out what's right without someone else saying, Don't breathe! Don't eat! Wake up! Ruby said May should be the weed commissioner because she'd be a natural at getting people to hack out their thistles. She'd stab people with thorns if they let their wildflowers go to seed.

I went into the kitchen and said to May, "How are we going to go anywhere if you threw the keys into the marsh?"

"I've got spare sets," she said, smirking at me.

I had a fervent need to nip her flanks. We didn't say anything more on the subject of car keys and strangled chickens.

After that episode we settled back down to normal. I knew I had merely dreamed of going to Aunt Sid's, or maybe seen a late-night movie about an aunt and her niece, lounging in chairs, eating orange marmalade and English muffins.

When I think back to that fall of 1977, it seems as if our life went in slow motion. We were taking each step so carefully. It was one of those long autumns; it lasted for years. We woke up to the pale sun coming in over the blankets and we knew it was warm outside. We were being fooled. The ground we walked on was golden and dry, all the grasses dead. Nothing anywhere seemed to have juice.

Artie always came to pick me up for work and we drove past the cemetery in Honey Creek where all the maples turned rust-colored for one minute, and the next thing the smart trees did was le and there were thousands of leaves to rake. Sometimes I took to the cemetery after work. We shuffled through the leaves; ew piles in the air and watched them float down to earth. I I could talk to trees, seems as if they know so much. I myself, jus could turn a beautiful color and then let go of
o.

When I look back on it, I realize that we were all quiet that fall. We were looking into ourselves and kindling our flames. We were tending our fires.

Then, all of a sudden, in the space of Halloween morning, the sky turned cloudy, and the air changed from warm to bitter cold so that when we went outside our nostrils stung and tears dripped from our eyes. The harsh winds were here. We sniffed the air with the knowledge of the woodchuck there in our noses, giving us faith in a cold dark winter. I wished I had a hole in the ground that I could crawl into without leaving any trace.

Ruby didn't go to work because his leg was still giving him trouble. He was getting a tire around his middle from watching TV and drinking beer. He didn't shave. He no longer looked like a cute jungle tom. He did some work around the house now and then. He oiled the doors so they wouldn't squeak at night and scare him, and he took care of the hens when he felt like it— they didn't spook him any more. He went into the henhouse and screamed and clapped his hands and the hens all flew into a corner. When May wondered why egg production was down I shrugged my shoulders. Ruby was also working on a needlepoint rug. Dee Dee bought him a kit because she knows how much he likes to use his hands, and how capable he is. It was a picture of a sailboat against a deep blue background. He was loaded when he sewed the sail so it didn't match up with the rest of the boat. Dee Dee ripped it out in her spare time. It was going to be a bath mat. Ruby sat and watched TV, making his rug. We were all hoping his leg would feel better fairly soon, before we went bankrupt.

Often he played with Justy on the floor and they turned into two rambunctious house pets. I grinned, watching my boys. They wrestled and rolled around, both of them howling, and then Ruby chased Justy up and down the stairs. Justy squealed, running on his fat legs out the kitchen door, covering his face, thinking we couldn't see him. Ruby would growl, "Where'd that midget go?" He'd bang open the door and sniff and roar and then Justy had to shriek with the pleasure and terror of it. May disapproved of roughhouse. She said Justy was going to be traumatized. She said the screams hurt her ears, not that she should be considered, but she didn't like to see Justy so upset. Ruby and Justy learned to play while she was at work. They had some good laughs. They were the men of the family, sharing the joke. It was May and I who disciplined Justy. Ruby left the room whenever Justy started to act up or require a firm hand. Ruby liked only to roll around on the floor and make Justy tremble.

I still went to Trim 'N Tidy half time — could have fooled me; it seemed as if I was there night and day, looking at soiled garments. Artie had to bring sweaters back to me, showing me that I'd missed an enormous stain. He'd say, "You all right?" and I always said, "I'm sorry, I can't figure out what's the matter with me." I laughed a good hearty fake laugh and added, "I need a new brain or something. I can feel mine giving out."

And Artie always said, "You take it easy."

"Sure, Artie, I'll take it easy."

I kept hearing the words "Take it easy" and tried to figure out how a person did it.

I probably wasn't paying enough attention to spotting because I was dreaming about taking Justy away with me in a car. I don't even know how to drive. I couldn't help picturing Justy and me alone: I'm carrying a suitcase full of the money I stole, heading for a place where you can wear T-shirts night and day, winter and summer.

I wrote Aunt Sid to tell her the morning on her porch was fuel to me — I dreamed with my eyes open about eating English muffins and telling true stories to each other.

Now that Justy was going on two years old, getting his nose into every drawer and cabinet, walking and talking, there were a lot more decisions to make about what was best for him. When he was an infant it had been diapers and food, but now he had

thoughts of his own. He was a person, full-fledged, not only a
sweet baby you wanted to kiss and admire. We squabbled about
what was best for him twenty-four hours a day, Ruby and May
and me.

"He's not warm enough in that sweater!" "It's his nap time."
"Don't let him suck on his finger!" "Get him off that stool, he's
going to kill himself!"—it didn't matter what it was because we
all had different ideas. May and I did not want him to have sugar.
We didn't want his teeth to be rotten like Ruby's. But Ruby didn't
care. He wanted to make Justy happy and a piece of gum could
do it. Justy was like a pesty cat, rubbing against your legs, always
begging for something to eat. He knew Ruby carried sticks of
gum in his pockets, that he was always very available. Justy would
eat Double Bubble, chewing it with his front teeth, and then
he'd swallow it. I couldn't bear to think of the gum sticking to
the inside of my boy, but Ruby wouldn't listen to me because
May was always yelling at him about the sweets. Ruby thought
I was on May's side. He saw it as a team sport: May and me
against Ruby and Justy. To Ruby's way of thinking May and I
were the strongest team, beating up the unshaven and the young.
He probably figured, in his dream state, that he was going to
show us a sensational upset one of these days. Then he could
sneak gum to Justy any old time.

The first day it snowed in early December the weatherman didn't
spare us. We woke up to a foot of snow doing nothing but sitting
on the ground, here to stay. I asked myself three things when I
saw the bitter scene out my window: How am I going to get out
of here with Justy? How am I going to get away from this chill?
Where can I steal some money from?

We could all feel how cold it was to be—already there were
icicles poised like daggers from the roof. The winds blew across
the field freezing the inside of your nostrils only minutes after
you stepped outside. It was dangerous to venture two feet from
the kitchen door.

I remember nothing about Christmas, except that Ruby bought Justy a sled and May said Justy was going to kill himself on it. She hated hazardous toys; she said, Didn't Ruby know better?

I had to ask myself, Wait a minute, isn't that kind of regular for a father to buy his boy a sled? I was mixed up; I couldn't begin to answer the question.

There were weeks when Justy couldn't go outside. He went for almost the entire month of January without feeling fresh air. Ruby wouldn't go out either and being cooped up made both of them squirrelly. They were restless: you could hear it in Justy's whine; you could see it in the furious way Ruby tossed things around the house. He stood at the window tapping his foot, not hearing a word I said. The one time we tried going outside, as a family, was a failure. I bundled Justy up and he ran out into the bright day so eagerly, as if he were greeting the cold, making it feel welcome. He ran straight for something brown lying in the snow. When I got to him I saw that it was a golden dog, frozen up. Its fur shimmered in the sunshine and flapped in the wind. It was frozen in a running position.

Justy touched it. He didn't understand about dying yet. He wanted it to get up and play with him. He was crazy about puppies. I said, "Let's leave it, OK?"

It had starved. Its eyes were wide open, staring at the tongue glued to the snow.

"Get in here!" May yelled from the porch. "You're all going to get frost bit. Don't touch that mangy dog, Justin," she commanded, like it was going to come to life and bite his cold fingers off and then lie back down dead.

"Come on, Justy, let's skate on the marsh," is what Ruby said, and they headed for the ice.

I stood in the middle, stuck, growing quieter and quieter, saying to myself, When is the big event going to happen that will get me out of here?

During the winter, when we were shivering and coughing in our bed all night, Ruby treated me as his own thing, if he felt like it. I didn't want to get so close but he said he, Mr. Magic Fingers, could make a dried-up creek bed gush. Besides, he said, I was his wife and there were certain things I had to do. He said that it was the law, that the police were going to catch up with me if I didn't behave right. I'd leave my body behind and with my mind and my heart I'd go sit on the porch at Aunt Sid's, with the warm buns and your choice of three jams.

There were other times when out of the cold night I had terrible dreams. I dreamed I got caught in a tremendous mousetrap, as large as a car. It didn't kill me so I flailed around. There was no one willing to let me out. Even Aunt Sid stood up so she could see me from her porch. She watched my neck breaking, and clapped as I got closer to death. I must have been crying because Ruby rolled over and started singing that old song, "Hush, Little Baby." That's how he could be.

One night, toward the end of January, we were eating supper. Our bodies were covered with goose flesh, even underneath our jackets, because May was still skimping on the oil. We watched our breath coming out of our mouths. The adults sat in silence. May had the oven door open, but it didn't do any good. Justy cried hysterically, at a pitch that pierced the eardrums. May tried to get him to shut up but she didn't have the magic touch. I didn't say anything because all I could do was huddle in my chair, rub my shoulders, and blow on my hands.

"Don't look so damn froze up!" May shouted at me out of the blue. "You always look like you got ten thousand miseries. *Stop* looking so cold."

I laughed under my breath. I laughed louder and louder. I couldn't quit. I howled until tears rolled down my cheeks. Ruby and May stared at me. They thought they might as well roll me down the basement stairs and put me in the pickle barrel, add some salt, and close the lid. I laughed all night long. Don't ask me what Ruby and May did downstairs. Perhaps they had an ice carnival. I ran to our bedroom and laughed face down on my bed, heaving and snorting, and then I cried out loud. I guess I cried myself to sleep. Ruby and I both had our ways of retreating, leaving our bodies in the house. In both our minds we walked out the door going separate routes. We were heading for the place where the climate never changes, it's always warm and still, flooded with light.

Nineteen

O N the first warm day in April Daisy had us over for a bar-
becue. Don't imagine that we were prancing around in tube
tops and hotpants. We were all wearing coats and mittens, in
addition to long underwear, I'd wager. Still, we could party outside at least, listen to the robins chirping halfheartedly. We ate
a pile of chicken at the picnic table, and potato chips. There was
no limit to our salt consumption. We gobbled chips and pickles
and then washed the food down with beer. As it got dark Daisy
and her good Bill started building a bonfire. They fed the flames
with twigs and branches. We gathered around it, staring into the
heat while Dee Dee and Daisy told stories about derelicts, and
about customers who get their hair cut. Daisy explained how you
can tell where every person in Stillwater gets their hair done.
Stella's gives all the girls bowl cuts, but at Hair Village they come
out looking like Olympic skaters. Daisy bet money she could
stand on the street and say where each passing person got their
hair cut; she was that positive. I didn't listen carefully. I held
Justy close, smelled his skin, felt him leaning into me, and it
seemed that all the evil stored up in me from the winter seeped
into the fire and burned. I saw my sins turning into red-hot

embers. My sins were all the occasions I said to myself, I have to get out of here, I'm going to steal a suitcase of cash — and other thoughts too wicked to mention. I looked across the fire to my husband Ruby and clearly saw his strengths again. I couldn't help loving his blue eyes staring back at me, saying I'm such a perfect mother, holding our boy. I thought for sure I'd never have another unkind idea again — I was feeling awfully pure and stupid. When Justy fell asleep I put him inside on Daisy's bed. We all drank buckets of alcohol and got wasted. If you consume intoxicants every now and then it cleans out your spirit, guaranteed. I ran around the yard shouting and jumping, prancing and falling to the ground, a complete stranger to myself.

At about three in the morning, when I was standing over the toilet, sorry for every drop I had swallowed, I heard May in the kitchen talking with Dee Dee. They were both looped out of their skulls. I wasn't trying to hear but the voices came to me anyhow.

"Dee Dee?" May said. "You ever hate yourself so much you could slit your own throat?"

Dee Dee cracked up. She thought May was telling jokes. "Millions of times, every day," she answered. She got up to do a little dance of death. I could hear her wide feet smacking the floor.

"Serious, though," May said. "Sometimes I pray to God to let me be born again, give me another chance to do good. Sometimes I think he's given me the chance, and I've changed, and other times I just ain't sure. I pray that he won't take me before I've healed something." She started to cry, I swear. She sputtered, "I've screwed up so much around me. I figure Justy is my last stab at making a child turn out halfway decent."

Dee Dee was still twirling slowly. She said in a sleepy voice, "What about that smart-ass son of yours — *Time* magazine — ain't that famous enough for you?"

May didn't like to bring up Matt, even when she was loaded. The mere sound of his name hurt her feelings.

She didn't talk any more. She slurped her joyjuice out of a bottle. I wasn't sure I dreamed it or not, if the conversation was a hallucination from throwing up everything inside me, but I couldn't forget the picture of May hating herself. I imagined her sticking her tongue out at herself in a mirror, and the mirror responding.

I had a week off in July, and Ruby and I spent the seven days out on the beach in Stillwater. We took Justy and played in the sand, ate hot dogs and Cokes, stretched out on towels, ran in for swims. We rented an orange boat and rowed out to the middle of the lake. We hooked buckets of fish, but they were mostly bluegills flapping around. I told Ruby to throw them back. I felt so sorry for caught fish. I couldn't help thinking that we were such different people compared to all those years ago when I saw Ruby out on this same lake, basking in the big old full moon. I couldn't remember how we had traveled so far, to be together like we were, with a little boy named Justy.

We were crazy about being out in the lake; we imagined that there wasn't any such thing as land to keep us tied down. Ruby had his radio going and the sun beat down on us with every inch of its fierceness. I lay back and slept in the flames. I wanted that ball of fire to lick me up, blue bikini and all. Ruby sang along to the radio; Justy watched the water, holding on to his baby fishing pole Ruby bought him at Coast to Coast. He was a patient little fisherman, considering he never got a single bite. All we could hear was the water knocking the boat and the rock songs. All we felt was the heat piercing down through our skin, roasting away our thoughts until we lay there empty.

When it got dark we roamed around town. We couldn't imagine ever being cold again—we were almost feverish with our sunburns. We sat in the park by the river and Ruby sang slow songs to put Justy to sleep. He sang, in his moony voice, "Oh, Mandy, you came and you gave without taking, and I need you today, Oh, Mandy . . ." We got ice cream cones and ate them one lick per minute. Sometimes we went over to Daisy's and lay around in her yard, swatting at bugs. If the happily married couple was in bed we sat in the yard anyhow, not talking, watching the unlit house like we thought it might possibly burst into flames for our entertainment. We pretended we didn't have an address, that we were gypsies and we spent our lives going from lake to lake catching fish, cooking them over a fire, and eating them with our own greasy hands. Even though we didn't say a word on the subject, both Ruby and I knew we weren't going to go home if we could help it. But there'd come a time when finally there wasn't anything else to do; we'd have to drag into the kitchen, Ruby carrying Justy in his arms.

May would be at the kitchen table shelling peas, not looking up at us. The kettle was always on the stove for blanching vegetables. The steam floated to the ceiling, right to where the plaster fell out about two years before, when May was canning pears. All the steam must loosen the ceiling bit by bit until it can't help letting go and caving in. The room was filled with the smell of steam and dust and thousands of partially cooked peas. I wished they were jade beads because then we'd be rich and could move to Florida condominiums. Ruby always walked fast through the kitchen. You couldn't see a body; it was a streak. I had never seen a person move so quickly. He must have forgotten that his leg hurt him. Of course May had to follow him into the living room so she could inspect Justin. She'd see his sunburn, the sight of which instantly transformed her from pea canner to best actress in a melodramatic role. She stood and gave us her oration on how you can get skin cancer from the sun. "Why do you do it?" she beseeched. "Why do you let him get exposed?" She stroked her front repeatedly, saying, "In a few years' time moles will appear, and they'll get scabby and pretty soon with that disease your whole body is covered with brownish scabby sores." She itched her face. "It pretty well eats you up." She carried on as

if Justy had three weeks to live. I was tired from the heat and the
hot dogs. All I could say was, "Please, Ma, we're going to bed
now. Don't say anything more now, OK?"

But she had to discuss her age and her poor stiff fingers, and
here she was doing all the canning while her daughter sat on the
beach and got herself fried. Her apron was soaked down the front,
with pea hulls stuck here and there like dewdrops gone moldy.

"It's my vacation, Ma"—I tried to sound firm like Daisy, but
I knew I was whining. May put her red sore hands to her face;
they were wet also, and crooked. There wasn't anything in medicine that could ever straighten them out. Perhaps each time I
looked at those hands I was having a little vision like Ruby has
when he's drunk. Perhaps in real life her hands were lily white
and smooth, the way girls' bodies are in fairy tales. Her hands
didn't do anything but make me feel wretched for the race of
man, plus May on top of it. Sometimes it seemed as if they were
wrecked up for that purpose. So I stayed with her, shelling peas
until two in the morning, listening to the sound of jars clicking
and water boiling, smelling peas, platters of peas both raw and
blanched. It's not an odor I like to call up. May and I didn't
speak for hours. We concentrated on getting the job done while
we listened to all-night radio call-in programs, where people chew
each other out for their strange opinions.

After my vacation I hated to go back to work. At Trim 'N Tidy
I was in a prison where they don't ever let a person see the
sunshine, and with the chemicals stealing down into my body,
contaminating the red blood cells I felt as if I were being slowly
murdered in secret.

There were a few ideas I kept hashing over that summer, looking
at the stained clothes, trying to keep my brain from going on the
blink. I was hardly paying attention to spotting. I often thought
about the words from the Rev's own mouth. It had been back in
the spring, after we all thawed out, that we started going to services

regularly again, because May said it was important for Justy to go to church.

It seemed to me that May was growing more and more concerned about religion as the months went by. I had never realized before that she had a religious streak. Perhaps her age made her think a little; perhaps she couldn't help being slightly anxious about where she was going to end up when she passed. She probably hoped she might have a stab at heaven. She had the idea that the Congregationalists could give her a chance, and if she did good deeds, such as go to church every Sunday, even in summer, and make confections at Christmas time for the church needy basket, her chances would double.

There were things the Rev said that made me feel better on occasion also. When I went to the service, I couldn't help it, I came out feeling holy, as if something had rinsed over me, made me clean again. Even if I didn't pay attention I glistened, putting in my time. Sometimes I had to think over the Rev's words because he looked me right in the eye and spoke. Around Easter he kept shouting out, daring me to meet his gaze: "*Yours is the body of Christ.*" He lowered his voice and said, "We will actually feel the nails coming into our flesh as we approach Good Friday."

I never felt anything like that. I didn't feel nails. I wanted to say, "Hey, Rev, I don't have nails! Give me a break." I couldn't feel very sorry for Jesus and his poor bloody hands, because he lived one trillion years ago. He always made commands, like "Honor thy mother." He sure could dish out advice easily: his mother was a saint.

It wasn't until I was at Trim 'N Tidy trying to get grape juice out of a white linen skirt that it came to me what the Rev meant when he talked about feeling the nails in our hands. He was actually trying to say, despite all the talk of God and Jesus, that there's no one looking after us, that we are alone, and each of us singular. And still, all of us are miraculously the same in our aloneness, with our red blood cells streaming through our veins.

May can list all the diseases that destroy the blood cells, but she wouldn't go on to say that even Polish people and her colored egg customers and the Japs are subject to disease. The only blessed way there is, I realized, is for all of us to feel deeply with a wounded, or sick, or even dead person. What the Rev meant to say, if he could ever have spoken plainly, without all the paraphernalia of the Gospel, was, "*Each man's struggle is mine.*"

If I were a minister I'd shout from the pulpit, "You, you puddle of humans down there, we are all in the same mess." I suppose I'd throw in a meek "Rejoice." I'd say, "Here's my theory: isn't it nice even if I can't always behave like I believe it?" The Rev was always trying to get us to be compassionate by telling us about the life of Jesus. I know if the Rev scrapped Jesus altogether I'd get the same point, how you have to feel with all your might for other people, how you have to go outside of yourself and take part in the world's community. Even though Christians kill each other I finally understood that compassion was the main idea. I knew that salvation was only a carrot, and that in the end there was no such thing.

Still, there were the times when I loved hearing the words from the Bible, for instance, the phrase about light: "For ye were sometimes darkness, but now are ye light in the Lord. Walk as children of light." I thought to myself, I'm going to walk as a child of light, as if I don't have bones and night doesn't ever come. The words always soothed me, even if I knew there was no truth to them.

And even though I didn't believe in the Jesus stories I liked to entertain the notion that a large bearded man up in the sky pointed at objects and then poof, they disappeared, or where there was nothing he put a plant with fully ripe red berries growing in clusters.

When May and Ruby and Justy and I went to church, people smiled at us and it made me feel like we belonged to something good, together. May was on the committee that arranged for refreshments after church, and I signed up for the Human Concerns committee. Their mission was to find stoves and pots and pans for poor people, and when women got divorced — say, if their husbands were beating them — the committee helped them through the hard time and made sure they had a place to live. I didn't do much to serve. Once I brought some canned tomatoes May and I did up, for a person who didn't have any food.

It must have been the church routines, the songs, the committees, the people smiling at us, that kept us rooted to the ground. Justy kept us anchored too, since he needed us all the time. Still, it was lucky our heads didn't float away. Mine was so full of thoughts, trying to be a child of light, and Ruby's and May's were not exactly at sea level, with the pills they consumed. Our kitchen counter could have been mistaken for a pharmacy. May gobbled pills to help her sleep, pills for her arthritis, pills for her headaches, and Ruby took medicine to stop his leg hurting, and aspirin for his sinuses. He could think of thousands of defects in his body that could be comforted by medication. If a person wanted to die all you'd have to do is walk into our kitchen, swallow one capsule from each bottle, and bingo, you'd be dead. There were nights when I dreamed that I was just about to take advantage of that opportunity.

I always hate the month of August. Stars shoot through the sky down to the horizon, dead, and weeds demand every inch of the garden. Even if you try to wipe out the quack grass, the velvet leaf, the pigweed, they go berserk anyway and take over. There isn't one thing you can do to stop the growth — it's their last chance for life. I always have bad dreams in August. The youngsters from town are prowling in empty barns, making love and stealing. There are thunderstorms, lightning cracking right outside the window, and Justy's crying, he's so scared. I used to get up in the night and walk through the house, closing all the windows so the water wouldn't come in and wreck the carpet, and then I'd go out on the front porch to watch the rain pelting the green grasses. There were times when I didn't care about the fierceness of the storms. I stood in my bare feet and my night-gown, feeling the rain and the wind lashing me, feeling how death comes to every single thing.

Then September came and nature dried out, as usual. The tomato vines lost the juice in them and all you could see in the garden was the red rotten tomatoes, sitting there like electronic eyes. That was last fall, about three million years ago, to be exact. Except sometimes I wake up and I think I'm right back there, in September. I imagine we're all asleep upstairs and there's one cricket in the floorboard, trying to keep the song going.

Last fall it was cold and still through October. It rained at night and the world shone by morning. The colors lasted forever; the trees didn't want to let go. But the leaves weren't brilliant like sometimes — they hung dank and dull until a final wind took them. We all sensed the dangerous weather coming on, another winter caged inside, the car not starting. We could hear May bawling me out for acting cold. We remembered how we found the dog in the snow, its golden fur shimmering around its bony rib cage. Most of all we remembered Ruby and May and Justy inside together, for a whole season of storms that never let up.

Twenty

I WROTE to Aunt Sid at the end of October. I mentioned that I didn't like the thought of winter coming. I said I guessed I wasn't a kid any more, because cold didn't mean fun; cold suggested a ferocious, merciless nature. I told her that we stayed inside for months last year, and Justy couldn't help being naughty.

Sometimes, everything we stumble upon or see can be taken for a warning, when actually there is nothing to it. Artie and I had a stone come flying through our windshield once on the way to work. I thought to myself, This isn't a positive omen, and I braced myself for disaster. Nothing happened, not one single thing, although I did get a sliver at lunch. It came out easily. Then there's the other occasions when a warning comes in loud and clear, and we don't hear it.

In the autumn mornings before work I let Justy help me with the dishes. It drove May crazy because he got water on the floor and it took me longer to get the job done and then we had to scramble to get to the cleaners. I had a chair for him to stand on so he could play in the rinse water. He had plastic boats he could sink while I washed the oatmeal pot. He was fascinated by water. He watched the drops flow through his fingers and he splashed me. One morning he had a cup he was dipping into the basin and then spilling out, and he got the idea to be a clown. He said, "Look, Mommy," and then he dumped the water out on his head. There he was standing with water dripping down his face, down his neck, onto the new shirt May had bought for him. He hadn't bargained for that swamped feeling in his ears.

"That surprised you, didn't it?" I said, trying not to laugh at him. He was speechless.

May came in right then; of course I held my breath. I knew she was going to be furious. Usually when her one and only grandson is wet and cold she gets agitated. She moves like a pigeon that's trapped in the attic. I stood frozen, waiting for her to yell at me, but wouldn't you know it, she started to laugh. She covered her mouth, the way a schoolgirl might. She giggled at Justy as he spluttered, registering shock in slow motion. He did look awfully confused and cute. She kneeled down and gave him a big hug and when he broke into a howl she grabbed her dish towel and rubbed his head vigorously, as if she were performing a life-saving technique on a person who can't catch his breath.

It was my turn to stare goggle-eyed. Last time I had Justy at the sink with me, and he was all wet, only two days before, she told me I wasn't fit to take care of a child. She was so mad I thought I saw her little gray curls starting to smoke. She spoke of pneumonia and strep throat resulting from babies playing in dishwater.

"Let's you and me go upstairs and get some dry clothes on, sweetie face," May said, and then they were gone.

I walked over to the cemetery in a daze, trying to think about how to predict certain events. There wasn't any formula, not with May. There is a section in the cemetery under the blue spruce trees that's devoted to May's family. I stood by her parents' stones, and the marker for her little brother who died so young. I tried to imagine the dead people under the earth. There wasn't a living trace of my ancestors, if you don't count my own flesh, and the dried grass nourished by their bones. I didn't hear a thing as I watched the still gravestones, the printing washed away, the dates faded.

Without thinking about it, Ruby and I took care. We were fairly relaxed when May was at work, two days out of the week. The rest of the time we were stick people, moving stiffly and quietly, trying not to get May riled. However, when we went to church we were a family. We put on our best manners. All the neighbors thought we were a miracle of happiness.

In October Ruby and I didn't celebrate our fourth anniversary, because he was acting sick again with his leg. It was over a year since the pickup had bumped him, but he liked to lie on the couch and have people bring him drinks on a silver tray. When he didn't want to work, when he wanted me to feel sorry for him, his leg hurt him desperately. I was dead tired of the game.

The day before Halloween Ruby's Sherry called him up and said that there was an apartment she knew about, cheap. The first floor of a house in Stillwater would be free to rent in December. An old couple lived upstairs with a little gray poodle named Smoky. The price was seventy-five dollars a month, and we would be responsible for mowing the lawn, shoveling the snow, and checking to see that the elderly people hadn't kicked the bucket in the night. Sherry said they were nice people who didn't have the strength to keep up the rickety house. She was probably thinking the situation would give Ruby some focus, that shoveling would make him feel like Superman.

I knew right then, when she mentioned the apartment, that I couldn't take another winter in the same house as May; that fact came clear to me. There was no logic to our fights any more. We were squabbling out of habit. Sherry's call was perfect timing. I had to think that perhaps somebody was watching out for us after all.

Still, it isn't easy to make changes, even for the better. There's something stubborn in me that doesn't want to budge. If I thought too hard about moving, my skin went prickly. I had never lived in the city before. I had to wonder what it would be like, not to be able to walk out and see the constellations so clearly, or smell the fresh-mown hay, or see nothing but darkness on the horizon. I wasn't positive I was going to like living next to hundreds of people on the same street. And I wondered how Ruby and I would be, just ourselves — we hadn't ever been on our own and I couldn't predict if our personalities would change, if I'd become a carbon copy of May, hounding him for spilling his milk and tossing Justy. I had lived in the same place my entire life. I didn't know if I could wash in a bathroom where you didn't need a hammer to turn on the hot water.

We were up in our bedroom after we found out about the apartment, lying on our bed with a candle burning beside us. Ruby lit candles sometimes, so he could pretend we were glamorous lovers straight from television. He had his radio playing softly so he could hum along.

"Let's you and me get that apartment," I said right out to Ruby. "We are going to go nuts living in this house one more minute, you know that?"

He grinned at me and picked his nose. "Baby," he said, "maybe them old people have a lawn mower, you know, the kind that looks like a puny tractor?" Ruby made a sound like he was a car revving up. He got out of bed and started putt-putting around the room.

"We'll have to be so careful with our money," I said — I called out louder so he could hear me. "You'll have to work at Trim 'N Tidy regularly." I didn't mention that he was going to have to quit spending money on dope. "But picture you and me and Justy, I could cook you suppers . . ."

I thought to myself, Finally we'll be like other people. All the cute couples we had seen at our childbirth classes came to mind. I couldn't stand the time we'd wasted bickering with May. Our mistakes seemed obvious all of a sudden, the solution clear.

Ruby came to me on his pretend mower. He came up to the edge of the bed, and he said what I was thinking. He said, "She's gonna croak when she finds out"—he stuck his tongue out like he was a goner.

"She ain't gonna croak, Ruby. She might act like it, but we can see her every day. Stillwater isn't far."

It was the first time we had mentioned May in months. She wasn't our favorite topic. He parked the mower by the closet and climbed into bed. He had to laugh as he wrestled my shirt off and then kissed my chest and neck. I let him do what he wanted. I was imagining our new kitchen with cereal bowls stacked neatly in the cupboards and teacups set on the table, in case company dropped by.

When I told Daisy our plans on the phone the next day she said, "It's about time. If I was you I'd be on the mental ward by now. I can't imagine me and Bill living with my old ma."

I didn't say anything.

"I hope you send Justy to me and lock yourselves in that apartment for a week, not see one single soul. That's what me and Bill did up at the Dells for our honeymoon. We didn't hardly leave our motel."

"We ain't exactly millionaires, Daisy," I sassed at her. "We're going to have to work, you know."

That night, when we were sitting at the table eating supper I looked at Ruby to get my courage up. I stared solemnly into his eyes and at his chewing mouth. Then I put my spoon down and cleared my throat. "Well, Ma," I said, "looks like at the end of December Ruby and me have a chance to move to our own apartment."

She said I should wipe Justy's mouth, that there was applesauce on his cheeks. I knew every word she was and wasn't going to say to me in this situation. She didn't have any new tricks stashed away for surprises this time.

"Ma. Did you hear what I said?"

She looked over at me, as if she had just come out of a dream, and she said, "You ain't going nowhere." She got up and cleared the plates. I wasn't even finished with my meat loaf yet.

"December thirty-first," Ruby said, and then he went into the living room and turned up the television.

I sat following the scratches on the table, examining them thoroughly with my fingertips. I didn't notice May until she stuck the rag in front of me, meaning, Wipe the table. When I tuned into her she was saying, "How am I going to take care of the chickens and the house? Look at these hands."

I had only seen those hands half a million times. I didn't have to look at them to know their shape.

"I'll have to sell the house," she said. "I'm telling you, you ain't gonna get a single cent from the sale."

I surprised myself by the sound of my voice mumbling, "The whole world is not set on doing you wrong, Ma. You're doing battle with yourself." I didn't look up to see where the thought had come from, or if she was stunned. I said, louder now, "We're moving at the end of December, so don't be startled when we're gone."

I walked out. I didn't want to hear her popping the lids off of all her pill bottles. Naturally we never said another word about the move after that.

A few days after we broke the news to May, when Ruby and I were getting up in the morning, Ruby said, "Baby, I'm feeling so sensational lately. I know I got perfect health, if you don't count my leg."

I sure had the notion we were turning over a new leaf.

Sometimes I have to pity May a little, because her Matt went off and she's got nothing, only Justy and her job at Trim 'N Tidy and me. Plus God and her trip to heaven. All that doesn't stack up to much. There is no one who loves her except Justy, and he doesn't actually love her. He's only used to her.

▼

The day I'm working toward wasn't so very long ago. I'm about
to tell how it went so everyone will know. I'd like to think it
won't happen again. Once is enough for the whole earth. It
shouldn't recur and if I tell about the day, step by step, people
can understand certain warning signs. Then nothing like it will
take place again, not ever. I imagine, when I'm sitting here, that
I'm ringing a bell, and someone will hear, but to tell the truth,
I also know that it isn't very often that people change their ways.
Still, I have to ring the bell, keep it sounding.

I figured that we could hold out until Christmas. It was a mis-
calculation, the largest I ever made. I was going to work so hard
at being friendly. I figured we'd stay until Christmas because
I felt sorry for May, decorating a scruffy tree she hauled in from
the woods, with the balls she has in the attic—the ones with
half the paint worn off. The picture of her hanging the angel,
all by herself, made that old lump come into my throat. It was
a task we always did together. I'd hand the floss doll up to May
while she kneeled on the highest rung of the stepladder. Sometimes life gets so pitiful it's tempting to lie down and play dead.
But I knew if we tried we'd have a nice Christmas together. I'd
make a special effort; I'd tell Ruby not to buy Justy any dangerous toys, and then after the celebration my boys and I would
start the new year out in our own home. There was a part of
me that didn't know if I could make the move. It was a high
squeaky voice that mocked me. I always put my hands to my
ears; I didn't want to hear the voice that said, "You've never
lived on your own, you aren't smart enough." I talked back. I
said, "I've got enough intelligence, and May will only be ten
minutes away. It's not like we're going to China. If I need to
walk up to the plateau, Ruby can drive me over. We won't
be so far from nature." And there that voice was saying, "You
can't do anything right. You make scalloped onions out of tulip
bulbs."

I told myself that with Justy May was bound to be over at our place every day. We'd still need her to baby-sit. I had the feeling we could be like girlfriends. I'd cook her supper while Ruby mowed her lawn. I pictured May and me trading recipes over the phone.

The third Sunday in November, right around the time shaggy-haired Charles Manson came up for parole and Prince Charles celebrated his thirtieth birthday with his 350 favorite dates—May loved that man, even though he was unemployed, because he still lived with his mother—we woke up to the sun streaming in our windows, the kind of winter sunlight that doesn't have one speck of gold in it. I had a secret for Ruby, a secret I had been waiting for the right moment to tell him.

"Hey, Ruby," I said. "Guess what?" I petted his sleepy head on the pillow. He opened his eyes, stared at the sunshine as if he was about to say, What the hell is that glittery stuff on the floor? Sometimes his expressions made him look like he didn't know there was a world outside of the riddles in his head. He stretched; he didn't have anything on, and his chest hair stuck out from the covers.

"You and me have a present for Justy," I whispered to him.

"Oh, yeah?" he said, yawning.

I turned over to him and kissed him. "You think Justy's going to like being a big brother?"

Ruby's eyes flared up to an enormous size for a second. He didn't say a word because the news was so serious. He was glad though, I could tell. He stared at the ceiling without moving while I started talking about our times together when Justy was small and we sat on the couch counting his ten toes. I nudged him, reminding him how we thought it was such a miracle that he came with all ten. My breasts were so tender and heavy I figured I was already almost three months pregnant. It was Ruby's fault for not using the balloons to cover himself up. I felt sleepy and slow half the time, as if I didn't have a brain, and some foods, fried eggs for example, made my stomach take nose dives.

I tried to ignore the fact that my body was changing, see if it might snap back to its former shape. I didn't feel anything about having a baby until I told Ruby. But when I recounted Justy's first months I remembered again exactly how happy we used to be. I knew we were lucky to have a second chance.

Ruby got sweet and careful with me, lying in bed. His fingers began following the brown stripe I had running down my belly from having the first baby. His fingers were moving along my swelling body—and then one thing and another. I imagined little goat kids chasing down the hall, butting each other, bleating so gaily. Strange visions flashed before me, of Japanese people sitting cross-legged on the floor, and then the goats charging into their tea party. Sometimes it's impossible to know if your brain really is functioning as it should. The sun streamed into the room, right on top of us, rocking along with us, as if it came to say, "This is the day the Lord has made, rejoice and be glad in it." All the sunshine made the room seem noisy, along with the sound of Ruby's oaths and groans.

When we went downstairs May was feeding Justy breakfast. Of course she said, "Where have you two been? Justy's starved."

She slammed the dishes down on the table—fortunately they were plastic so they didn't usually break—and she muttered, "I can't imagine what you was doing up there for so long."

"Please, Ma," I said. I felt like getting down on my knees and begging her to have a personality transformation. I might believe in our Maker pretty quickly if presto, May turned into Phyllis Diller.

Then we sat at the table and ate breakfast together, the church-going family. May made us pancakes and I fried up sausage and cooked some brown sugar syrup. It tasted so good I couldn't stop eating. We ate, feeling the pleasure in the delicious food. We licked our chops and begged for more. We couldn't wait for May to flip the pancakes and toss them on the platter. Justy kept saying, "Hi, Mommy," and wanting my attention. His words warmed me, made me feel as if the sun had come from under a cloud and was shining on my face.

May was hardly finished when she jumped up and went to look at the clock in the living room. She yelled from right in front of the television that we better hurry, because it was about time for church. I got Justy dressed in his corduroy pants and his plaid vest and tie, so he looked like a little man. He had eyelashes from somewhere, who knows where, because none of us have eyelashes to speak of. Ruby's are blond and invisible, and I got mine burned off one time when I lit the pilot light. I loved dressing Justy and watching his blue eyes and the fluttering lashes.

I put on a dress Daisy gave me. I get the clothes she doesn't want any more. They make me feel like it's Halloween and I'm dressing up to be the farthest thing from myself. Her dress had a white background, decorated with gigantic green shamrocks. It was jersey fabric, not actually intended for winter use. I had to wear a turtleneck underneath for warmth and because the dress had such a low-cut neck. I put on nylon stockings and my new winter church shoes. Ruby didn't get dressed fancy for church. He didn't own a suit coat. He put on a clean sweater and his shiny beige slacks. They hug his rear end so you can see its exact shape. May was the one who always got dolled up. She had a few dresses from right after World War II. There was a rose-colored suit with a tight skirt, in particular. It had little slits up the sides. She wore a fox head at her neck that some great-aunt had given her. It had paws too; Justy loved to pet that poor old fox.

I could hear May and Ruby down in the kitchen while I dressed, having a spat. What else would it be? She asked him why the whiskey bottle wasn't full. Ruby said he didn't know, maybe she drank some of it in her sleep; maybe Dee Dee got trashed on it. May said she didn't think so, she thought Ruby

drank it up. I could hear him saying, "Ma, I'm a new man"—
that about made her have a cerebral hemorrhage the way she
laughed in her forced hoarse laugh, and then had to cough. But
I could see how Ruby might feel new. It made me proud, moving
to our own house with a baby on the back burner. He wanted
people to know he was starting over, that life was going his way
for a change.

We were the last ones in the church, which isn't anything
novel. The choir was already singing their opening number when
we sneaked into the pew. Justy went down to the children's school
where they cut out and glue pictures of Jesus. Ruby and I stood
close together, touching all down our bodies because of the baby
coming, and because we were remembering the morning in our
bed. We had been tender with each other. I smiled shyly at him,
thinking about the frisky goats eating out of rice bowls when his
fingers stroked me as they sometimes do. His face, in church,
was pink, like cooked ham, perhaps from the cold winds and the
effort it took to sing out with his strong sweet voice.

The Rev was on the subject of eternal life—that was a big
one with him. I took in everyone's wardrobe while he droned
on. Mrs. Crawford showed off her green wool suit, the one she
bought in Austria. She travels to Europe every summer. She no
doubt has a bundle in her bank account. I was imagining myself
in a suit like that, with the velvet collar and cuffs, when I heard
the Rev say, "We shall not die but live." He said the phrase
several times, to let it sink in, in case people weren't listening.
It echoed in the church, bouncing off the wooden ceiling fans.
"We shall not die but live." It echoed on when Ruby sang "For
the Beauty of the Earth," praising the Lord like what he had was
all the bounty, like he loved not only me, but everyone. He
looked like he had the power to make nations peaceful. He was
flushed and his eyes sparkled. It was a sight to see Ruby singing,
clutching my hand because we're married and our boy is down
in the basement wearing his best clothes with the other little
children. I bit on my offering envelope to keep from crying.

At the end of the service we sang "Praise God from Whom All Blessings Flow." I like to think of a river full of blessings, gushing along, it's spring and the water is high and fast. I loved the words "from whom all blessings flow." Then we shook hands and said, "Peace," to our neighbors.

Afterwards we trooped downstairs, as usual. It was Mrs. Brierly's turn to make the refreshments. The entire congregation was waiting, smacking their lips, while she unpacked her coffee cakes. Everyone says they're the best in the town. They weren't your ordinary Sunday morning treat; it's as if Betty Crocker made them herself, with our congregation in mind. I told Mrs. Baker some of the cute things Justy'd been up to, because she came to me and asked about him. He was with us, playing with the children, chasing around and screaming, but that's what toddlers do and everyone thinks it's all right. Until, of course, one of them trips and scrapes his knees, starts to howl. Then they're supposed to settle down and find their parents. Ruby watched Justy running; he saw every move, heard every shriek. He wolfed coffee cake. The look on Ruby's face was as if he had already entered the kingdom of heaven, and it was beyond his wildest expectation.

May said to Ruby, "Get Justy from them pack of kids." She signaled for me. It was time to be home so she could check the roast. On the way back Ruby sang the Doxology over and over, trying to get Justy to repeat the words. May told him to sing another tune, she was sick of that song.

I looked up, something made me do it, and along the road, high on the telephone wires, was a row of blackbirds, hanging upside down, burned and dead. Their feet were still gripping the murdering wire. I gasped once, but no one heard me. Isn't that a miserable sight? I asked myself, and I tried to think of the words "from whom all blessings flow."

When we got home I made boiled potatoes, first peeling them, and saving Justy the little raw pieces with salt on top, and May cut up apples and bananas for fruit salad. We were cordial with each other, working together on Sunday dinner. I went to find what Ruby was up to after I finished my duties. He was in the living room pacing back and forth, something I had never seen him do before, as if he had to walk all the ecstasy brought on by church out of him. The minister was on TV talking to Ruby, although the sound was turned down too low to hear. What we saw were his large fleshy lips and his outstretched arms. Still, we understood that his gesticulations were all about Jesus and salvation—certain people's salvation, that is. I asked Ruby, "Do you feel all right?" and he whispered, "Sure." He seemed to be praying as he walked, with the TV pastor.

"Did you eat too much coffee cake?" I asked.

He didn't answer me so I said, "Well, come and have dinner. You'll feel better. Go get Justy from the yard, because it's time." But May went and got him instead. She was beating Ruby to it. Then we sat down and ate like all families on a Sunday afternoon. "Pass the beans, pass the margarine, wasn't Mrs. Brierly's dessert good? I wonder what her secret is, real butter probably—with all them hogs they can afford it."

Ruby's cheeks were still pink. He helped Justy by ripping his meat into tiny pieces. I had to heave a sigh to celebrate arriving at this comfortable resting place, May and Ruby and me. I wanted to lean back and declare, "This is perfect." Ruby was saying, "Pass them spuds," while May told about her favorite subject— how one of the girls in choir had a baby without a husband. Sunday was always our best meal, because as I said, church makes you feel as if you've done something for your spirit. It makes you feel like you're a brand-new person, your past history erased, except good deeds. We were doing everything by the book, being miniature disciples, eating politely, and sharing the news. May finished her meal first and lit a cigarette, and we all patted our stomachs. I laughed about how chubby I was going to get, eating pancakes and now Sunday dinner. Ruby looked up at me suddenly, remembering. He understood that I was speaking only to him, about how enormous I was going to be in a few months' time. We didn't feel like breaking the news about our baby to May yet. We wanted to keep it a secret, only for ourselves.

We were sitting still, breathing deeply, savoring the smells and taste of the roast when Justy said, "I want one of them cookies down the basement."

He knew they were down there because Ruby showed him the stack in the freezer. May makes about thirty different kinds of cookies and gives them to the church needy basket each Christmas, as if we can afford pecans and candied cherries and twenty-pound sacks of sugar. She starts in October and practically every day she's punching out candy canes and angels, or gingerbread boys with raisin eyes, Santas with frosting beards. If she feels like going overboard she'll make peanut brittle and white chocolate candies. None of the goodies ever see the light of day in our house. If we're lucky on Christmas Eve she'll dole out any broken pieces. She says she doesn't see why we can't make a sacrifice, but I think she does it so the church won't think we're the poor.

May said to Justy, "You can't have any, sweetheart, they're not good for you."

I wiped Justy's mouth, told him to blow his nose on the tissue. "There's too much sugar in them, Justin," I said. "They ain't going to make your muscles grow big and strong. You can have some more fruit salad, how about that? Would you like fruit salad?"

"I want *cookies*," he whined at me. "I want a candy-cane *cookie*. My daddy showed me where they're at."

May laughed, leaning over to Justy. "Look at your daddy's teeth, baby pie. You want teeth like that? All rotten? Look at how some of them ain't even there no more. They got so rotten they just plain fell out."

Ruby stood up and untied Justy's bib. "Sure, Justy," he said, like he had all the time in the world. "You can have a cookie. One little cookie ain't going to hurt you. If your stingy old grandma can stand to give up one for her grandson, you can have a cookie."

"Am I a stingy old grandma, Justy?" May asked. Justy whimpered; he didn't have the right answer. She pushed her chair back and stood up. She said, right in Ruby's face, "No, Justy, I paid for your daddy when he was in the hospital. He jumped in the river in December. He thought it was July. His brain was flipping around in his head, sweetie. Grandma paid his bill. I ain't going to feed you sugar—it ain't good for you. Your poor daddy don't know better. He'd feed you trash all day long if I wasn't here, and we'd have to go to the doctor."

"Stop it, you two," I yelled. My voice came out so shrill they stopped in their quarrelsome tracks. "Ruby," I said, "Ma's saving the cookies for the church, you know that. Justy can have salad or a banana but he's not going to have cookies."

"I WANT COOKIES," Justy cried, banging his spoon on the table.

May started gathering up the plates. She said, "You want Justy to have black holes in his mouth like you, Ruby? You're not moving away, Justy, because your daddy wouldn't take care of you for a second. He'd let you starve in the mornings while he banged up—"

"Sure, Justy," Ruby said. "You run down to the basement and get us, you and me, your own daddy, some cookies. You just pull the chair over and open the freezer like I showed you how and take a bag out. We'll have all we want." To me, through his clenched mouth he spit, "I'm the master of the house."

May snickered, slapped her thigh, and said her usual line. "That's a good one, that's about the best joke I heard this year. All your brains are in your ass, Ruby," she added, in addition to other words too low to repeat, and the whole time she wrung the dish towel in her hands with the bulk of her strength. Her red knuckles turned white. The skin was so dry and taut I had the urge to say, "Be careful, Ma, your skin is going to tear."

Ruby whispered something to her that made her stop and screw up her face before he went into the living room to pace. We could feel the vibrations, back and forth, back and forth. I smacked the salt shaker so all the salt poured out on the table. It piled up white and clean.

Justy came through the door, looking like a fat angel, so glad to have sweets, clutching two plastic bags in his chubby hands, one filled with pecan balls and the other with peanut brittle. He ran into the living room to give one to Ruby, as if a person could eat a whole bag of the treats himself in one sitting. He started gobbling up his own, in the corner, afraid that we were going to snatch it away. May yelled at me—I didn't hear the words distinctly; they were hysterical and ran together. I heard the sharp sounds of *t*'s and *k*'s when she grabbed my arm, when she yanked me up from my chair and carried me by my dress sleeve into the living room. The fabric ripped. I heard it go, right in my ear. It was Daisy's dress, ripped beyond repair by May's fingernails. I couldn't get it straight. I couldn't see anything through my tears. I couldn't recall who I was hating. I heard the rip of the dress, or was it skin coming apart, ancient knuckles tearing?

"It's hurting," I wailed. "It's hurting, hurting." I tore at space with my fingers, wanting to wreck something. I wanted to gouge out eyes because we were having such a nice, nice day and suddenly it was a regular nightmare, May dragging me by the sleeve. We came at Ruby like wildcats, screaming and clawing.

He was ready. He stood in the middle of the room waiting for us. I yelled at Ruby, I pulled out May's hair, I screamed, "WE WAS HAVING SUCH A NICE DAY"—over and over I yelled, and I got some of his hair too. It didn't matter to me which head I grabbed for. Justy stared at us from the couch. His cookies tumbled to the floor.

I swear when I looked into Ruby's eyes they were the yellow of a sky right before a fierce summer storm. He looked at me without seeing my face. He saw absolutely nothing but the blazing fire in his own mind. Perhaps I have it wrong and in Ruby's eyes there was only the reflection of my blind stare. We clawed at him; we clawed and snarled until Ruby grabbed the broom, the broom that was May's dancing partner sometimes. I had always thought it was a friendly object. He started to whack me with the handle. He whacked my face and my arms, coming down on me so that I put my hands on top of my head. After a few clumsy strokes I could see him looking around for something better. He stuck the handle at my neck to pin me to the wall, and while he was still holding on he grabbed the poker from the fireplace. It's short and thin and comes to a sharp point. Then he tossed the broom aside and came at me fresh. The power in that old poker was marvelous. I wondered in slow motion how a skull could tolerate the blows. Was my poor head going to topple off my shoulders and go spinning down the hall to the kitchen, look for some dog food? Ruby pushed me to the sofa and beat at my fingers and my wrists as if he'd been wielding a stick all his life — I leaned down, over my lap, to hide and he struck the back of my neck and my shoulders. He jabbed at my ear, tried to spear straight through the brains. I couldn't do anything but sit cowering and screeching. Every time I looked out, tried to speak, he punished me. The poker came flying across my face, back and forth, the sharp end making its cuts, engraving my cheeks and lips. It was moving so fast, like the wind, that I couldn't see it going back and forth. Ruby was conducting wild music in his head. He had to snort to accompany himself, dance on his toes, and smile at the beauty.

"STOP," I shrieked into my lap. I thought I saw May reach for the telephone, but Ruby knocked it out of her hands before she even dialed. He came back to hit me some more, before I could get away. He beat me like I was struggling, when in fact I sat still and limp, waiting for each stroke. I knew he was going to split me in half, down my back, and my brains would spill out onto the floor, spill out and slither into corners like mercury. With my face down on my thighs I sank my teeth into my own leg when my ear felt like it was cut off.

May cried out, desperate cries. I couldn't hear the words be-

cause there was warm blood, thick, oozing in the crawl spaces
of my head. She threw platters and urns at Ruby. They went
hurtling through the air, bouncing off his rear end, like in com-
edies. One bowl hit me in the head; her aim is not perfect. I saw
silver stars rise up from nowhere and spin in circles and then
disappear. Ruby didn't like the feel of saucepans one bit. He went
after her into the kitchen, waving the poker around and around
his head as if he were about to make a perfect lasso throw. She
didn't know what she had set in motion. She didn't realize what
was left when she made for the kitchen.

I ran, my broken hands trailing behind me like caught fish. I
knew my hair was plastered to my bloody skull. I ran out the
front door and I stood panting, leaning against the house, tasting
the blood in my mouth, thinking the words, "You shall not die
but live. The dung heap shall smile." It occurred to me, I'm the
dung heap, and someday I'm going to laugh my head off. I heard
the future metallic laugh while I stood there, one huge fresh
wound, my brain and heart thudding, those organs so close to
the surface of my body I was sure I could just reach in, take my
heart out, pat it a little, make it feel better. I didn't think anything
but the dung-heap words, plus the sentences clattering around
in my head, phrases the Rev says: "His eyes were as a flame of
fire, and on his head were many crowns. His eyes were as a flame
of fire. We shall not die but live."

I'm not sure how long I stood on the porch. I was merely
trying to breathe the air and watch the grass come into focus.
Perhaps it was one thousand years of standing. Perhaps I was
Queen Nefertiti seeing her kingdom fall. I kept hearing, "His
eyes were as a flame of fire," until suddenly it came to me, not
the words, but the thought: it's such an easy thing to do, to kill.
Killing is the easiest thing in the world.

I walked back into the house. The rugs were messed up and
the phone was on the floor and there was no noise. Then I heard
the operator saying so politely, "Please hang up your telephone.

This is a recording from Stillwater, Illinois." She probably said, "Have a nice day." The TV minister talked to me, his great lips making long ovals and hideous smiles. He was probably on a new subject, like how wonderful corn chips taste. I stood looking at him and a chill came into my heart, thinking of Ruby pounding at every living thing he saw. I thought of Justy cut into three pieces. My feet started to move me all over the house in search of my boy. I didn't feel my hands any more. I couldn't see anything on account of tears again, blinding my damn eyes.

Justy was halfway down the basement stairs, sitting, pitching the potatoes one by one down the stairs. Then I heard Ruby below; I heard him laugh and say, "Who wants to be lunch?"

I kept on going down the stairs. It was dark and cold. Way over by the washer in the red glow of the light that means the drier is on, I saw Ruby. I saw Ruby banging at May like he was waiting so patiently for her eyes to pop out and roll around the floor. He growled softly at her, saying, "Don't call my birdie-houses dumb. Don't say I'm a moron for building them birdie-houses." He whacked her one blow for every sentence, coming down on her head and then across her face. "Don't say my teeth are rotten. Don't say I ain't good for nothin'." He hit her in quiet for a while, concentrating on his blows, and then he said, "We'll feed you to the snakes. I've been praying for you for so long, praying for the evil spirit in you to get washed out. I prayed long enough, baby pie. I can't pray one minute longer, it just don't do a bit of good."

With her neck breaking she couldn't say a thing. Her narrow eyes were wider than they had ever been in her life.

I stood by watching. My feet couldn't pick themselves up to move. It seemed as if we had always been there, in the basement, me standing and Ruby with May. We had always been there, standing still. Ruby lifted his poker way over his head and then he came down on May with all his strength. She's tall but he was filled with special strength and speed. He seemed to be the ideal height to smash her with a stick. Plus he had a kitchen knife he used now and again, when he remembered it in his hand, for detail work. She couldn't move an inch since her head was on crooked. Her body was striped with flesh and blood; there was a patch of skin stuck to her skirt. He had her up against the wall where she waited, useless, for each of his blows. She tried to say words but her tongue hung out of her mouth. It must have gotten disconnected. She couldn't pull it in. She was trying awfully hard to make sounds; they were coming out low and terrible. Her noises said, "Now I'm nothing. I am nothing."

He came at her even after she collapsed to the floor. When I heard her head thump on the cement I ran to her.

"Get lost," Ruby hissed. He poked me off in the belly with the flat end of the poker. He poked me back into the corner. He wasn't finished with his task. He went after her neck. There was still throbbing in the blood vessels. He strangled the breathing out of her with his hands. We heard the choking come up from way down inside her. We heard the rattle. It didn't take more than a minute or two — it isn't hard to do, if you can stand the retching. Her eyes were wide, seeing everything and understanding nothing. The Rev's words echoed all over the basement. "We shall not die but live." The words came screaming out of the walls, even the dark light bulbs were talking. There was dead May on the floor in her church clothes and her apron. There were no more vital signs to her, except the fresh blood drying. "WE SHALL NOT DIE BUT LIVE" blinked like beer signs all over the ceiling and Ruby laughed, wheezing, like it was hilarious and he thought of it himself. He kicked her gently, and chuckled and burped, until he remembered me.

I was saying to Justy, "Shoo upstairs, Justin." He had this look on his face like the time he saw Santa in Coast to Coast buying nails. I wanted to take Ruby in my arms but I felt the stick coming down on my head. I screamed for Justy to go upstairs. I was too confused: here I have pity for Ruby and he's clobbering me. My head was knocking so hard I felt like it was a basketball and someone was dribbling it down the court. Ruby probably had it in mind to undo my tongue too, stop my language permanently.

"*Please*, Ruby, quit it, we'll run away, me and you, we'll take Justy, we'll escape down to Florida," but he didn't hear one word I said. He beat at the air trying to get me. Up the basement stairs and out the back door and around the chicken shed — we didn't notice the cold. I couldn't run too well because my head was on the verge of falling off. When Ruby caught me he pinned me to the fence, and with one arm holding my hand and the other working the poker, he stabbed at me, and slashed. He thought I was clods of dirt in the garden he had to loosen up. What woke him was Justin, on the porch, screaming, "DADDY!" and when Ruby grabbed my breast to squeeze it dead he remembered the baby in me and he stopped. He squinted into the sunshine with his yellow eyes, and then looked at me, at the breath coming out of my mouth. He remembered the days when we had Justy on the couch and the way he sang so sweetly to him. He lost interest in killing, seeing it's such an easy thing to do. He dropped his poker and walked inside. I leaned on the fence crying, not with tears, but with my voice.

Twenty-one

ALTHOUGH the police tried to get me to say precisely, I don't know how long I stood there. Finally I walked over to Miss Finch's house. A family by the name of Peterson lives there now. I walked into the Petersons' house and Mrs. Peterson, a dyed red beehive on her head and a lavender dotted swiss apron around her waist, looked at me once, grabbed my arm, and made me speak of my affliction: the Christmas cookies and the poker. I continued to feel the poker making dents in a person's flesh, slashes, portholes for blood, torrents of blood. I described what the poker did, beating brains to pulp so they looked like rotten watermelon, nothing left to salvage. She called the sheriff and the deputies came, as they always do, slowly, but with a great deal of agitation. They have stars pinned to their chests and huge thick waists with belts full of bullets. I recognized one of them from Trim 'N Tidy, Walt, who always talked about how he loved to eat baby beef ribs. Policemen look like they'd never die.

I see myself with perfect clarity, walking into the house after the policemen. I almost put my hands over my head, automatically, like the caught people do on *Hawaii Five-O*. Then I remember we aren't on television. Ruby sits in the armchair, watching a show and drinking milk from the carton, and when he notices the police he points to the basement door. He's watching a Laurel and Hardy movie; the big fat man is making the thin one cry uncontrollably. I have the feeling I'm at a museum, in a display full of dummies doing their prehistoric tasks. I'm blissfully constructed of papier-mâché, with thick smiling lips molded onto my face.

Justy is in the back yard, by some holy miracle. Mrs. Peterson finds him covering his face in the cold grass, trying to make his eyes useless. I go out and take him from her, by another miracle. My body must be operating on automatic pilot. I hold him with the power of my biceps—my flapping hands aren't doing anything for support—and then I kiss him gingerly, only my lips don't realize they're touching flesh. Justy stares into my face. His mouth stays wide open. "Take him," I try to say to Mrs. Peterson, right before my arms give out. I'm having trouble forming the words. I ask her to call up this friend of mine, Daisy. I can't think what her last name is. I keep choking, "Daisy," and "Aunt Sid, get Aunt Sid."

And they take Ruby away. He's as calm and quiet as the starfish we saw at the zoo, sleeping on the bottom of their watery cage, drowned for all I know.

The next episode is murky. I can't focus on the place or time, right after Ruby disappeared. Once he was gone, out of the house, I wondered why they didn't set a match to it. The police stuffed me into their rescue car and we went roaring through town, past Trim 'N Tidy, past Town Lanes, the high school, the funeral parlor. I thought perhaps I was loaded; I felt like shouting to the cleaners; I wanted to wake up laughing but I couldn't find my mouth to crack a smile. Then, when I came to, I was in the hospital in Humphrey. I could tell by the odor. The entire place smells like they're trying to cover up the scent of bedpans and they aren't doing such a successful job. I got the faint whiff of gravy, the kind they make out of dog chow, probably. The first thing I see is my Aunt Sid's huge blond head looming over my face. When I see her, I think I say, "Hey, Aunt Sid, don't cry." My mouth isn't moving so maybe she can't understand me. I reach out to touch her face, but my hands don't work either. "Don't cry, Aunt Sid," I keep whispering. "Tell me what's the matter."

I hate watching people cry; you know how their lips get all quivery? She dabbed her pink eyelids. She couldn't say anything so she patted my arm until I fell asleep again. I didn't feel the pain. I figured I was in a tank of water, swimming around watching humans mope and cry because a cherry fell off the top of their pie.

In those days I floated in and out of sleep, only I couldn't tell which was sleep and which was waking. I dreamed of the smell of the hospital and when I woke up there that smell was, fresh as a daisy. They hooked me up to bottles of juice, a direct connection to Honey Creek, I thought, so I'd know the path home. They didn't let anyone see me, except Aunt Sid. She was by my side constantly. I found out later that she missed her Christmas concert at the high school. She had to get a substitute to direct all her singing students.

In daylight, each time I woke up, there was Aunt Sid. She read books to me. For the longest time I couldn't understand any words, but I loved hearing her voice. I couldn't concentrate on the story she was telling since her words gushed out in streams and then stopped dead at punctuation marks. Often she sang songs; she closed her eyes and sang all the songs she could think of, one after the next. I used to wake in the night, and when I saw she wasn't with me I whined for the touch of her hand. The room was never pitch dark, because they always left the door wide open. In the night, through my sleep, sometimes I heard people running down the corridor. The footsteps were muffled, but I could hear the urgency in them; I sensed that someone had been stabbed or beaten or blinded. I could picture the whole story and I half felt like climbing out of bed and rushing down the hall with the party. In my sleep I was an extra-large nurse to the hurt people, with a plush bosom, and I sang lullabies softly, beautifully.

I had concussions and fractures, wounds to my head. My neck was sprained and my hands and wrists were both broken, and then there was the shock. That's where you feel as if someone's taken a cudgel and delivered a stunning blow to your mind. My spleen was not terribly active — on the blink, I gathered from conversation. Aunt Sid and the doctors debated, in the hall, whether or not to take it out for good.

When the fog lifted and our house came into focus, I'd quick stop and let my thoughts drift away from the scenery. I'd float away out the window and perch on a cloud. My body said to me, "Lie quietly and concentrate on food. Dream of steaks, cooked on a grill, and melon balls." Sometimes my body had the intelligence of a high priestess, and sometimes it was awfully dumb — such as the time, back at the house, when I was beaten up, and I didn't have Justin on my mind. I must have been a rotten mother, not to whisk him away so he wouldn't witness our life. But for now, in my smart phase, I drank the milk shakes Aunt Sid brought me each day from the ice creamery. For a while I couldn't open my mouth wider than the space of a straw. She didn't tell me anything I didn't want to hear. She pressed my arm and petted my cheek; she told me she loved me about every other minute. She said it wouldn't be long now, I was resting so well.

Naturally, after the first week they allowed the Rev in. He always looks big and sad. He isn't a whole lot of consolation, to put it mildly. He couldn't hold my hand and it stumped him for a minute. Finally he took my elbow and cradled it. All I heard was, "We shall not die but live." I stared out the window when he talked to me. I didn't want to hear the words. I didn't want dead people looking down on me. I didn't want to hear one thing about our heavenly father. I said to the Rev, *"Beat it."* He left, just like that. I started saying "Beat it" to the nurses. It amused me, making people move away. If they weren't in the middle of sticking needles in me they usually skittered down the hall soon after I said the magic words.

There wasn't anything to distinguish the days, the weeks, except sometimes we had mashed potatoes and fruit cocktail, and sometimes we didn't. The fried chicken tasted worse than May's, like it had been buried in the sand by a dog. The nurses carted me around part of each day, taking pictures of my body and stabbing me. I felt slightly closer to Jesus now, with my bloody hands. The doctors were either starving me or stuffing me, plus I had to contribute my specimens to the technicians so they could have the time of their life. I'm glad lab work isn't my career. Dry cleaning is about three thousands steps up from lab work, in my estimation.

When they weren't carting me around I lay in bed and slept. I couldn't stand to watch soap operas all day long. People got chased and killed, or they fell in love and then found out that their boyfriend was a criminal. For entertainment I stared at the ceiling planning some of the phrases I was going to say to the nurses when they got on my nerves. I died laughing when I was exceptionally creative. I thought of how to get the Rev angry. I was waiting to have a fight with him, after all the years of swallowing his lies. I could think of hundreds of lies he told me, not counting the time we got married and he blithely announced that we had achieved a glorious state.

The nurses were directly outside my door at their station. I watched them gossiping about the boys they liked and the cranky old bags who buzzed them every five seconds. I glared at them. I didn't have anything to look forward to except Aunt Sid's daily visit. She told me how Justy was doing and she brought me selected news, such as the fact that Laverna's black dog kicked off and the old men wanted to have the post office flag at half-mast. She brought little gifts of shampoo, soap, and perfume from Daisy, who had recently become a Mary Kay distributor. The Foote house was probably filled with boxes of free samples. Daisy and I are friends, but I wasn't in the mood for her wisdom. I needed about fifty years to recover before I could stand the premier hairdresser of Stillwater. I kept watching for Ruby. I couldn't figure out why he wasn't at my bed, but I didn't let myself wonder too hard. In the back of my cracked head I remembered it was something I didn't want to know about. My orders were to keep perfectly still. The doctor was waiting for my internal organs to heal and it wouldn't happen if they jiggled around.

It was the week before Christmas and the Rev came to see me, as usual. I was on his circuit. He gets paid one thousand dollars to see all the invalids. He told me the people in church were praying for me. I said, "You know all them folks in your congregation calling each other to make their precious prayer circle?"

He said, "Yes."

"Well," I said, "they suck on dead goats. That prayer circle is only an excuse for gossip and don't pretend you don't know it." I acted like I was Mrs. Crawford talking into the phone in her singsong voice. " 'Hello, Mrs. Baker? Did you know that Cassandra lost her ovary in the toilet and the highway crew found it floating down the river? Let's get on the line to everyone and tell them all the details. And don't forget to pray for her!' " I took my hand from my ear and said, "I don't want their prayers. They stink to high heaven."

He said some prayer to me right then and there with his lids only half closed and fluttering, probably so he could check up on me. The prayer ended, "Whoever believes and lives in Jesus shall never die." I said, right in his face, "Sure, yeah, leave me alone, go to hell, you big old fart."

When he left me, dazzled by my words, flapping fish rose before me, and I recognized them as my hands, and up from the floor sailed a bag of pecan balls, each one the size of an orange, and then a pair of yellow cat eyes, blind, and I cried out and thrashed. I was being murdered again. I saw May with her head on crooked, her disconnected veins hanging out of her neck. I saw us calmly eating at the table, Ruby saying "Pass them spuds," and Justy asking for a cookie. Our conversation was so loud the phrases banged around knocking over the flower vases I had on the night stand. When I looked at the TV there were happy faces chewing on ears.

I screamed when I saw my neck cut off. I threw up at the sight of the stiff arteries sticking out of my body like telephone wires. Yellow ooze came trickling from May's mouth; I screamed, screamed so that the nurses, three of them, carried me to the bathtub and sprayed cold water on me. I tried to claw them; I tried to kill them with my imaginary poker, but they pinned me down to locate my bulging veins. They rammed something into my mouth and stabbed me with a needle and then the room spun and I fell back, fully dead.

Right after the Rev triggered my memory I got transferred to the hospital near Chicago. They have experts who can deliver babies even when the mothers are dead. Aunt Sid was responsible. They took me in an ambulance, although they didn't bother to fire up the siren. It wasn't an emergency. If I died on the way they probably figured it was no loss.

Something very strange happened on Christmas Day, in the Chicago hospital. I woke up from tangled dreams, people shouting at me and I'm telling them, while I laugh uproariously, where to get off—and a tall blond man without a single blemish on his face was standing at the door. I knew I'd seen him before. He was wondering whether to come in. He was peering over at my roommate, who was always moaning. She wasn't in the greatest health because of her soused liver, plus she was expecting.

"Just like you, Matt," I said to the bed rail. "You get here in the nick of time."

Matt wasn't doing anything about peace on earth. He was

studying meteors and comets until he was blue in the face. He was trying to figure out how often rocks crash into the planet and wipe out animals and people. I had only wondered once if Matt liked stars better than me, since he knew what was inside of them. The answer was perfectly clear.

"How are all them numerals and digits in your big smart brain, Matt?" I asked. "You figured out how to make peace yet?"

He didn't say anything so I looked over to him. He was afraid of me; I saw that plainly in his eyes. I burst out laughing. He made me feel mighty, the way I scared him. He gave me the impression I could gore him with my sharp horns.

Matt said quietly, decorously, having learned well from the Boston school of life, "I have some flowers for you." He placed a vase of yellow daffodils on the table.

"It ain't the season for daffodils, Matt. But then you wouldn't notice that. You've never seen flowers in the spring. You never noticed you were living in the world — you and Dr. Heck were always goosing each other in his office. I bet those daffodils cost you a bundle. Too bad you never sent us money. I know, I know, you were too busy figuring when meteors were going to wipe us out. That sure is a big job."

Matt didn't comment. He looked helpless, staring at me, while sweat gathered above his upper lip to celebrate our reunion.

"Take a picture, it'll last longer," I said. "I ain't a beauty queen like before. I ain't quite so gorgeous."

He was standing still. If I had had a gun I could have hit him easily, shot him right through the eyeballs. "Just go away," I said. "I don't want to see you."

I didn't listen to him saying how sorry he was. I don't know if it was an apology for his whole life or for the last ten minutes. I imagined he was on TV and I had nothing more than to turn the dial and he would be gone.

He came back to see me despite my wizardry. I knew Aunt Sid made him. I never looked him in the face. He read books to me, but I didn't listen to the words. I stared at one handle of the drawer, or the bathroom doorknob, or the rim of the barely visible toilet. I never said anything to Matt except how much I hated him, more than anyone I had ever known, or would know. I always spoke to him while I had my head in the pillow.

I lay there day after day while he droned on. Right when it looked like I was well enough to be moved I'd catch an infection, or my blood pressure would soar to the top of the bulb. I must have been on the germ ward. I called the doctors names under my breath; too bad if they heard me. I lay in bed thinking seriously about all the ways there are to croak. There was always someone watching over me, or my roommate would start blabbing about scotch, and furthermore, I didn't have one sharp razor blade, or even a tack. The only clear path to death was out the window. We were on the fifteenth floor and it was straight down to the sidewalk. Bingo, smashed on the sidewalk, bright and flat like a penny after the train.

I reached the low point on New Year's Day. It was Justin's birthday. I hadn't seen him since I handed him over to Mrs. Peterson. I didn't have anything but cuss words streaming through my brains. Everyone probably thought I was an unsuitable mother and that I'd tear into my son if they brought him up. I didn't tell anyone what I had discovered about foul language, that cuss words are unbearably boring after a while, that they wear you out for good. Everyone I saw, except for Aunt Sid, I told off without a bit of pleasure. I couldn't stand being in the hospital because someone had tried to murder me. Why had it taken me so long to learn that there isn't such a thing as justice? Or perhaps I had somehow committed a crime and I deserved what had happened. Whenever I thought about such questions there was a banging in my head, as if someone were inside with a large stone knocking at my skull. The nurses watched me because they thought I was the number-one criminal of the year. I told them to bring me sharp objects so I could stab my heart to death. I figured when they had their heads turned at the nurses' station down the hall I could fly out of bed and crash through the window. It wouldn't take long. I told them all about how I was going to bleed on the sidewalk and people would have to step over me on their way to work. There'd be bloodstains on their crocodile shoes.

Some of the nurses said so innocently, "Now why would you want to do that?"

I didn't want to go into the details. It was such a long story. I always said, "None of your business, Patsy." I called every nurse Patsy. I got too tired learning their names.

Other nurses mocked me. They said, "Just let us know when you're going to leap, we'll come and watch."

There wasn't anything I could say to people like that, except a string of dirty words. I always figured I'd better wait for lunch though, before I jumped. My stomach was grumbling. I was starved.

In January the Rev came to see me all the way from Honey Creek. I was so lonesome and stiff. I couldn't stand books any more, or television. I hated the nurses, and the way they breezed into the room cheerfully. I hated the physical therapist who made me do exercises with my hands. They were still in partial casts. I was in such a bad mood that I'm sure it wasn't exactly a treat for Aunt Sid to visit me, but somehow she spoke to me as if I was a pleasant person. I was sick to death of my own rotten company, but I didn't know how to suddenly start smiling and gesturing. I would have broken the scale if they could measure hate. I hated me more than I hated any of the nurses; I hated myself almost more than I hated Matt. I was so bored with hate—the word hurts your mouth if you say it ten times in a row.

When the Rev came in January he took my gauze-covered hand and he said his prayers. I stared at the grease he puts in his hair to smush it down. His hair is yellowy in the few places that aren't gray. He said, "My dear, our kingdom on earth is not complete."

It was the only sentence that hit me, out of the whole long jumbled prayer: "Our kingdom on earth is not complete." He squinched up his eyes while he was saying we get our reward in heaven, his favorite place. I couldn't stand his voice so I said, "Listen here, Rev, I don't know what the hell you're talking about, our kingdom not being complete. Don't you have one marble knocking around in your theological head? Do they have plaster casts up in heaven? I never heard them mentioned in your big black book there. My hands are going to be cured in no time and don't tell me Jesus could do it. For your information, Jesus is a crackpot."

The Rev stared. I loved every minute of his dumb gaze. I said, "You ever heard them little frogs screwing their heads off down in the marsh in spring?"

He didn't say anything; he looked without blinking his eyes, a mannerism that was familiar. "Huh?" I said. "You ever heard the racket? Don't tell me anything about the resurrection. Go down to the stinky marsh in spring and listen, and you'll hear what's come to life, what's reborn. They aren't any bigger than a quarter. They was dead before, them frogs was, all winter, and there they are come to get some satisfaction. They call out the words *Urgent, Urgent.*"

"Well, yes," he said, like an idiot.

"Don't tell me our kingdom ain't complete. Don't be one of them big fat greedy assholes, Rev. If those chubby knees of yours can hold your weight, kneel down sometime in early spring and sniff a bloodroot. Just because you can't take it all in with your senses doesn't mean the earth is half-baked. It's ideal, if you don't count the humans."

He said he was glad to see I felt better and that everyone had me in their thoughts at home. He beamed up a few words to our merciful father. When the nurse announced that it was time for my checkup he kissed my cheek. I couldn't help sneering when his lips touched. He might have heard me say "Yuck." Probably at the moment he was thanking God for making mouths. No doubt he was making plans to go to the men's room, clean out his flabby ears, see if he heard all my words correctly.

The doctor came into the room right after the Rev's departure.

He was as thin as a pencil. You could see the knob in his throat go up and down when he swallowed. He was so thin you could understand how his body worked, if you squinted at his transparent flesh. He said, "I have good news for you, little lady." He always called me that. This time I said, "What, little man with the pencil neck?"

He looked startled. I didn't care. I was sick of people calling me names that weren't mine.

"Your baby is going to be just fine if you take it easy for the next few months, ah"—he looked on my chart—"Mrs. Dahl. Your blood pressure is down, the placenta is functioning normally, your infections are cleared up."

They thought the baby was hurt. They thought they were going to have to fish it out, but he isn't hurt at all, far as they can tell. It's a boy, he told me.

I kept saying to myself, "It's a boy. I get another chance." I knew right then that I had to calmly figure out what had happened. I had an enormous task before me. I had to learn about myself before my baby boy was born so I could start fresh, so I could teach him how a person can have a strong mind, a kind heart. Somehow, I knew, I was going to have to come up with strength and kindness in myself. So much of me was set on bearing poison as my offering to every spot on earth. There was a terrible black cloud in my soul, directly under the heart. Somehow I had to fill that terrible dark space with gold. How was I to start when the only thoughts I had were about people thrusting sharp objects of all kinds into each other? I hoped against all hope that the Rev would bring a wand on one of his visits, wave it around while he chanted, do some real magic.

The only fact I knew for sure was that someday it would be up to me to tell a long story to both my boys. Unfortunately, I didn't have a personality transformation simply because I knew about the baby. I didn't presto turn into Esther bringing baskets of food from Bleak House to all the sick dirty people. I told Matt

I hoped a meteor shower landed on his doorstep first thing when he got back to Boston. He was awfully tired of the insults I kept dishing out. I bet he was glad to leave my bedside. The worst I used on a person was the F-word. I told the physical therapist, Sandra, to keep her fucking mitts off my wrists. She told me I had serious problems, which was no news to me. When Dr. Pencil Neck was doing one of his internal exams on me, sticking rubber gloves places that aren't usually for public inspection, I almost asked him if he used a dildo on his wife. I didn't though; I had brakes working somewhere.

The morning after Matt left — right when the nurse came in smiling and I wanted to bash her teeth in for being happy — I had to stop eating my cereal. I was remembering something. I felt the kick. I felt my boy. He was saying, "I know you. I know all your secrets." His body alive in me kept saying, "You can't hide a thing from me. I know who you really are."

I had to stop and feel my stomach. The nurse was so surprised that I didn't have abuse for her. I lay there staring, my hands moving over the bulge of my belly. My boy was part of me, feeding on my sadnesses, remembering back to the old joys. He knew what it was like to have made love and to lie in bed afterwards, like a beautiful stricken deer. And what came to me were words from the Bible: "As the hart panteth after the water brooks, so panteth my soul after thee, O God. My tears have been my meat day and night, while they continually say unto me, Where is thy God?"

I heard the phrases and I wanted all of me to call out in a song, a song that doesn't have words, a song that almost doesn't have noise. A lot of people take a short cut and call that feeling of song love. They just call it that because there isn't a way to describe it. But the word *love* doesn't describe the half of it. It doesn't do anything to bring to mind the song we all want so desperately to sing.

Twenty-two

I GOT out of the hospital in the middle of January. There wasn't anything but filthy snow piled on the sidewalks. They say I have to stay in bed and be quiet, because of the baby. I have toxemia, which the doctor said could kill both of us, if I'm not careful. I looked up the word *toxemia* and found it used to mean arrow poison, which made perfect sense. I knew I'd been hit by something large and quiet. I have to hold out until the month of May, when he's due. I'm supposed to lie on my left side and take it all slow and easy. Slow and easy; I can't even remember how to walk straight.

I stay in Aunt Sid's living room. She has the green carpet that looks, with poor vision, like a field of spring wheat, incandescent and fluid. The place would be living hell for a cow. She rented a hospital bed for me that moves up and down, dances the jig. And she has stocked the room with blind tapes and books and records. She has to be at school all day so she can't perform the great operas for my benefit. I'm by myself in a sea of green grass and spoken words.

At night Aunt Sid teaches me how to type. I have a table that fits over the bed and she sits at my side. It probably isn't all that different from teaching someone to play the piano. I get into trouble if I don't practice. Aunt Sid can tell when I slough off. I can't type too long since my wrists aren't very strong — my stiff fingers punch the keys as if they'd never curled themselves into a bowling ball's three holes. I'm also working at knitting a baby sweater and booties, from a pattern and blue yarn Dee Dee sent me. I feel like Miss Finch must have, sitting up primly in bed, looking down upon the room. I pretend that I'm not helpless, and that I have pride. If I crane my neck I can see the house, across the street, where Justy goes during the day. There are other children to play with, a sandbox in the yard, and the woman who teaches them to count and put their jackets on.

Matt calls up every week. I'm nice to him over the phone, with my fingers crossed for the lies. He always asks, "So how are you feeling?" And I say exuberantly, "*Great!*" Then we don't either of us say a thing.

When Aunt Sid heard me finish off a conversation, when I was saying, "Don't bother calling me again," she came in and sat on the side of the bed. She picked up my stupid hands and said, "You can't blame him forever."

I was still in awe of her, so I wasn't about to tell her I could blame anyone I wanted to.

"Matt is your family," she said. "He's trying so hard."

I thought to myself, Since when is family an asset? I'm better off without.

"Let him help you," she said, brushing the stray blond hairs out of her eyes.

I nodded and thought of the sound of his voice, a voice so soft you imagine you're breathing in cheap perfume. I mumbled something to Aunt Sid, about how I'd just love to hear his story, when he comes to kneel at my bedside once again.

The first time I saw Justy I was in bed in Aunt Sid's living room. He came through the door holding her hand. She had prepared me by saying he hadn't had an easy couple of months.

Why not simply say his life had been ruined irrevocably? While I was in the hospital in Humprey he was shuttled between Dee Dee's and Daisy's. I heard that Matt had tried to befriend him, without success. Justin's mind was probably on one area: a dim basement, a red light, flesh spattering the wall. Everything looked to him like a dark maze, all probable outlets ending in a corner with his favorite character vomiting blood. His third birthday was January first. No one remembered to celebrate.

Aunt Sid and Justin were standing in the light of the hall, the French doors thrown open, without moving. Justy looked down at the blinding green rug; of course I could see his stunning eyelashes veiling his eyes. I held out my arms to him, unable to utter a sound. I had dreamed that at our first meeting we spoke in television language, caressing each other, saying simple sentences, and healing each other within five minutes. But when I woke I knew I was going to have to rely on my own invention. This one time I wasn't going to borrow from daytime TV, or May, or Sid. I wasn't even going to try to steal from Charles Dickens. If that old true word, father of us all, was out there in creation in the beginning, surely it will be there at the end, and all the while in between.

Justin would not look up until I finally whispered his name. "Justy," I whispered again, and he turned into Aunt Sid's skirt. All I could do was stretch my arms his way and try to call his name across the months of separation.

Aunt Sid kneeled down and picked him up. It was then that I remembered the stuffed lamb she had bought for me to give him. I held it out while Aunt Sid walked over. He kept his eye on the soft wool and the curly horns. He took it from me and then Aunt Sid set him down. He stood by the bed and I petted him, his thin brown hair.

He didn't say anything to me for a couple of days. He didn't talk to anyone. He sat quietly in a little rocking chair, rocking back and forth. When he tired of that he lay on the floor pushing

a truck back and forth, noiselessly. At night he screamed in bed.
I'd hear Aunt Sid's bare feet slapping down the hall to his room,
and her song about clay and wattles. She sang, "I will arise and
go now, and go to Innisfree . . ." I could hear him describing
the big turtle that was eating him in his dream. I lay in my bed,
in the dim living room, a pink glow coming through the curtains
from the street light, and I could see Justy's turtle down to the
orange markings on the shell and the yellow eyes that never blink.

Now and then he stands by the window in the late afternoon,
staring at the street, with no expression on his face, but I imagine
I know what is passing through his mind. I know in those moments that there is a huge dark place in his soul too, and maybe
I can't ever heal it, or make him see any possible joy around us,
but I'm beginning to understand my task. Like the Rev says, "We
have to hold fast to that which is good." I know I have to do that
as hard as I can for Justy, when I myself come to the place where
I can choose the good and refuse the evil.

Aunt Sid has a small children's book of proverbs, and I was
reading them one day. I turned to the page where it says, "Come
riddle me, riddle me, riddle me. None are so blind as they who
won't see." I couldn't get past the page. Even after I closed the
book I heard the words, "Come riddle me. Even the blind will
see." Is it possible that even I could see and understand? I thought
to myself. The words leaped up to me, a challenge. I began, in
the damned black mood I was in, to dare everyone, Ruby and
May, the dead and the living, to continue spinning their riddles,
and then watch me make sense of the tangles. "Just don't put no
time limit on me," I whispered. And then I said out loud, "Come
riddle me some more, all of you."

Of course the Rev is continually yanking me by his short rope.
He gives me his advice over the phone: "Trust in the Lord with
all thine heart, and lean not into thine own understanding."

I smile and let him rattle on, because he doesn't know the
riddles are before him. They are the riddles of human nature,

and not the simple ways of God. The Rev merely closes his eyes and trusts when he runs smack into a thorn bush. I have given up on speech with the Rev; there is no use explaining that you have to learn where your pain is. You have to burrow down and find the wound, and if the burden of it is too terrible to shoulder you have to shout it out; you have to shout for help. My trust, even down in that dark place I carry, is that some person will come running. And then finally the way through grief is grieving. There is nothing like lying down to bawl and choke, and then rolling over so the tears can drip out of your ears and settling in for a long sleep. Although I like some of the words in the Bible, I'm not ready for religion yet. Who knows, perhaps when I'm older it will come to me in a white flash. Nothing is impossible. I'm sure Jesus has good points too, and I wouldn't rule out the fact that my vision just isn't broad enough to recognize them.

I assume they wrote about the murder all over Illinois. They did for weeks after in the Stillwater paper. The old men down at the P.O. in Honey Creek are still hashing out the details while Laverna tries to sort the mail. Journalists are no doubt writing about it across the U.S., but the only thing they say in the papers is our names, that May was my mother, and Ruby killed her. They don't say the real reasons, or any of the pity in it. To make it sound normal they probably say Ruby shot her in the head with a pistol. Once, while I was still in the hospital, I was feeling ready. I had been thinking about the question for a while, and finally I spoke out. I said, "Aunt Sid, tell me what happened to Ma. Don't spare me."

She sat down and took a breath, as if she had been waiting for me to ask and had her speech prepared. She told me that May was dead in the basement when the police found her. I could have told her that, because we heard the rattle. What I wanted to know was whether they burned her, or buried her, and if she sat up and complained when they were embalming her. Aunt

Sid said Mrs. Peterson had called her up and she drove to Honey Creek at breakneck speed. She described the funeral service for May. They had purple irises up front in our church and somber organ music droning throughout. The place was packed with people who wanted to pray for dead souls and watch the end of a drama. Matt flew in. That sure was considerate of him. Too bad May couldn't know that he came especially to pay his first and final respects. The Rev talked about her good works and the valley of death, the usual speech. He said she was smiling at the Lord, she was at his feet. That doesn't sound to me like a particular vacation spot. Then they wheeled the gray metal casket with peach satin inside down the aisle. They buried her next to Willard Jenson's stone. Because the ground wasn't frozen yet they tucked her in without any complications. I found it hard to believe May didn't beg the angels to freeze the world, at least give the gravediggers some trouble, and the family extra expense.

I didn't go to May's funeral but I know what they did to her face. Undertakers are masterful with dead people; they're able to unpinch a face for the ceremony in her honor. Under the lid of the closed casket she probably did look halfway joyful, like she wanted to send a postcard to her family saying, "Having a great time, too bad you can't be here with me."

I nodded at all of Aunt Sid's descriptions. Even if you want to you can't go on forever talking about someone who's dead, who has no earthly future. There just is not that much to say. I told her I was ready to change the subject so she left me by myself. I tried to think of May under the ground. Perhaps it's all the bodies in the cemetery that make the maples along the road turn brilliant colors in the fall. I can see May making some old tree turn bright red. That's a perfect job for her dead body.

In the night I wake up, my heart's racing, and I'm convinced I'm May getting shattered. After I calm myself, take deep breaths, wipe my face off, bite my hand, I have to wonder what her thoughts are, in those minutes when her life is giving out. She knows it's the end; there isn't a doubt in her mind. What are her thoughts in the last moment? Is she thinking she's going to meet up with Willard Jenson, that they'll have a night of dancing through piles of laundry? Are her numerous days flashing by, like half-dead people say happens? Is she watching for the Lord's bare feet to peep from under his robe? I feel her flesh and blood beaten to the quick and I know then that there are no thoughts. She is crushed and finished, nothing left but terror.

One day, when I was bored to the point of near-death, I went into Aunt Sid's office. I didn't mean any harm. I was rummaging around, looking for my letters to her. Instead, in a drawer, I found an envelope with handwriting I'd only ever seen on discarded paper covered with formulas, and the occasional postcard. The letter lay in my hand, jeering at me. "Matthew Grey," it said on the return address. I couldn't believe Aunt Sid and Matt were correspondents. I socked the desk with my hand and nearly reopened my wounds.

There wasn't anything to do but open the letter. It was dated right after my wedding, October 1974.

Dear Aunt Sidney,

Thank you for your letter. I also enjoyed talking with you at Ruth's wedding. You ask me questions about the family which I'm afraid I can't answer. I don't know much about them and their situation. It is always strange, going home, facing people and a place with which I have nothing in common. I won't bore you with the difficulties of my childhood, but to be honest my main preoccupation was trying to figure out who was worse, my mother or my sister. Which one to avoid more strenuously. I must have realized early on that my inquiring mind differentiated me from them, and would lead me away from their household. Ruth tormented me continually in the form of physical abuse and my mother seemed to adore me in a sickening, clutching fashion.

I don't think of them much now; I'm thankful I've been able to make family out here.

I agree with you about Ruth's marriage. To me it seems catastrophic. Maybe that's too strong a word, but it seems to me that it can lead to nothing but unhappiness, at the very least. I also can't imagine how it will be with them, living with my mother. Slow death, for all of them, I would think. You ask me what we can do to make life easier, better for Ruth. I honestly can think of nothing, from my distance. That she missed out on a way of life which I was lucky enough to come by is unfortunate, but I don't know how to make amends now. I don't think she was forced to marry the man; she seems to feel something for him. Although I didn't speak with him much, he certainly didn't inspire confidence. I don't know Ruth either, so maybe I'm wrong and they'll be perfectly happy. Don't worry about my thinking you're meddling — you are probably concerned about them with good reason. Still, I know of nothing we can do, short of kidnapping Ruth and finding a Henry Higgins to educate her.

My work goes well. I'm temporarily sidetracked for the moment, helping some people work on simulating a comet. My close friend, Will, is planning a trip to Chicago in January and I hope to come with him. I'd enjoy talking with you again very much, and will at least give you a call.

> All best,
> Matthew

I went into the living room and bashed the typewriter off the table for starters. It fell with a dull thud but I couldn't see if it was broken because of the tears stinging my eyes. I couldn't believe that Matt and Aunt Sid were in cahoots. I had been betrayed and shamed, exposed and humiliated. To celebrate I picked up an indigo glass vase, a prize possession I hoped, and threw it at Aunt Sid's baby grand. The flowers and shattered glass stayed on top and the water dripped down on the keyboard. Then I paced back and forth, making my plans. First I would pack my bags, march to Sid's school, waltz into her choir room and in front of everyone shout, "Shove hair up your ass!" I shouted the words louder and louder, practicing, and then I opened the front door and yelled to the street. For a moment the plan gave me a great deal of satisfaction.

Everyone who knew me realized my life was going to end in catastrophe—they called it the very name—and they didn't do anything to warn me. They stood by watching me choose the wrong way. They watched me parade naked, humiliated, without so much as tapping my shoulder. I rehearsed the choir room scene countless times, bringing up all of May's favorite one-line insults. I knew the student singers would rise to their feet and cheer me on, and then they would scramble down from the risers and help me claw at their conductor. And then suddenly the vision rose before me of my giving birth right in the gutter, with Justy sitting several yards away, staring into the traffic.

After I cried on the sofa and beat on stiff pillows I told myself to get control. I tried to think of places to go. I racked my brain but all I could come up with was the Footes' small house where I'd have to share a room with Randall. I ruled out Artie and the Rev. I tried to imagine sitting down to supper with Mr. and Mrs. Rev, and living through a half-hour sermon while the steaming food got cold. I tried to reasonably tell myself that it is a free country and Sid can like any idiot she wants to. Of course I didn't have the sense to remember my faith in good people, like Aunt Sid, helping the desperate, or in my resolve to calmly solve the riddles.

I spent all day alternately crying and cursing—and I spent a fair amount of time cleaning up the mess on the piano—until I finally fell asleep on the carpet. I dreamed of myself ducking out from the mushroom cloud over Illinois and running a long way in search of clean air.

When Aunt Sid got home from school I didn't act too aloof. She went into her office to write her lesson plan when I didn't answer her greeting. I could hear her humming a song her students were to sing. Before my nerve failed I shouted, "Hey, Aunt Sid, could you come in here for a minute?" I could feel the beads of sweat trickling down my chest and I had to close my eyes because everything looked scarlet. I found myself panting like Sid's collie.

"First of all," I said as businesslike as I could, when she stuck her head into the room, "who is Henry Higgins?"

Aunt Sid cocked her head and furrowed her brow. She looked at me like she knew my dander was up about a million feet. She explained how he took Eliza Doolittle and made her into a princess.

"Fine," I whispered, taking a deep breath. "I'm ready to hear about Ruby now," I said, looking straight into her eyes.

For such a long time I didn't want to know. I imagined him in certain places, such as California, where there are palm trees, olive trees, the ocean waves bringing in glittering rocks. I imagined him cruising along the coast in a new blue hot rod. I knew he would have such a great time. But I couldn't carry on with the delusions forever. It was time to hear the real story.

Aunt Sid stroked my wet cheek with her hand and then she said, "He's in prison, waiting for his trial. It's coming up this week."

"So what's he up to?" I asked. "You seen him lately?"

She looked into my eyes with such kindness. I didn't want to watch her gazing at me like that. She talked about how he had punched someone in the nose and taken swats at the guards. In prison, managers aren't terribly tolerant of roughhousing.

I shoved my knitting project aside so she could sit on the bed. She showed me some of the articles about him. I demanded to see the newspapers. The reporters wrote that Ruby had confessed right away. He said to the police right out, "I killed her." They said that Ruby believed the demon was in May and that she was trying to put it in Justy. Ruby told the police he was set on beating that old devil out of May, so it wouldn't spread. He talked about the devil obsessively in jail, how it can get into people and make them wicked. He strummed his imaginary guitar and sang songs to ward off unwelcome powers.

All the psychiatrists were having a field day with Ruby. He

wasn't schizo like the madmen in the movies who think they're three hundred different people rolled into one. The paper said he had "paranoid personality tendencies," that he perhaps had a "disassociative reaction at the time of the slaying." I crumpled up the paper when I read that part — so many words without saying a thing. I don't think there was anything seriously wrong with Ruby's brain. I have my opinion; I only lived with him for four years. Naturally he behaved in a haywire fashion at times. He got ideas into his head and was damned before he got rid of them. He took drugs which made him see all kinds of exaggerations. But I know reporters mainly want to find a juicy story. They don't care about Ruby's strong points. They don't know the details that could drive a person to grab a hatchet, shoot a pistol.

Aunt Sid said that at the trial the lawyer would try to get Ruby off without too much punishment. She reiterated that he was a very sick person. The lawyer was going to convince the jury that he was out of his mind when he got going with the poker. She said that even if the lawyer won, Ruby would have to go to a hospital for mental cases. She said, "Whatever happens, he won't be free to walk down the street. He won't go free."

She thought she was giving me comfort. For once in her life she didn't have me completely figured out. I could see the rest of Ruby's life before me. They'd stuff him in a hospital where he'd have to do jigsaw puzzles all day long, and walk on burned-out lawns with high fences caging him in. I kept hearing Aunt Sid's words: "He won't be free. They won't let him free."

I told her I needed rest. She kissed my forehead and said, "Call if you want me."

I nodded with closed eyes until I heard the door shut.

I had to say his name over and over. The jewel. Ruby. My Ruby. I saw us playing jungle kitten and jungle tom; I saw him flipping a pancake so exuberantly, and then I saw his whole body turning black, limb by limb, in the dank prison cell. Only his eyes were blue, staring at me. I hid under the covers from the image. I cowered and shivered.

I hear his songs in the night, coming through the window. I wake up suddenly to the tune "You're Sixteen, You're Beautiful, and You're Mine," and I have to look to see if he's out on the lawn, calling for me to come join him. It's where I belong. I never see anyone on the street, but the singing keeps on.

After Aunt Sid broke the news to me I lay still. I moaned softly for a few hours. I wept for days, in private, stopping only to shiver now and again, and cover my head with the blanket. There wasn't one thing I could see or hear that cheered me. Everywhere I looked I saw Ruby huddling against an unpainted wall. Sometimes he didn't have anything in his hands and he was whimpering pitifully without wiping his face; other times he skulked in the corner polishing a knife, watching it catch in the bare light bulb. Sometimes I think I made all the tears there are to make and I don't cry any more for what he had to do, but then a whole new batch comes in. There are mornings when I sit in bed, alone in the house, and I sink under the covers in peace. There is no end to the stream. I want only to escape from the living room and the suffocating heat and the green carpet I swear is growing and is some morning going to be over my head, each blade brutally sharp. I want to find him, stick my head through the bars and say, "I'll trade places with you, Ruby. You go free."

I'm in the prison with him; I'm not scared this time. There isn't a thing but a toilet in the corner and a cot covered with a brown blanket that needs darning. I'm telling him I'm sorry, repeatedly. He's sitting on his cot saying, "Hey, baby, listen to this concert I composed for you, my sweet jungle kitten." He turns on his radio and fetches his broken guitar and sings the song that goes, "If you leave me now, you'll take away the biggest part of me, oh oh oh oh oh baby please don't go." And he sings, "I've just GOT to have your love."

I didn't say goodbye to Ruby when the policemen hauled us away. I didn't say one word of farewell. Aunt Sid told me I wouldn't see Ruby again and I wouldn't go to the trial. She said,

"It won't do a bit of good, not for either one of you." She gave me her earnest fairy godmother gaze I had begun to dislike and said, "You both need to start over fresh." I almost laughed. How is Ruby supposed to start fresh when he's looking at prison for life straight in the eye?

Ruby isn't dead but I won't see him again. It doesn't make sense. I wonder, if I saw him on the street, would my knees lock, would I keel over? Or would I rush to him with those loving arms of mine? I can't say. At times I feel sure one way, and then the next minute my body is shaking under the quilt. I sometimes think May was the lucky one, to have her Willard Jenson blown up into four million pieces. Ruby is living in the same state as I am, but there is no way for us to reach each other. There is no hope for our future. I ask myself how I'm supposed to think of a dead man who's alive. And then I say to myself, It's easy to kill. It's easy to throw it all away. Pretend you're on television, hauling out the trash in an extra-heavy-duty plastic trash bag. If Ruby keeps beating people up, his lawyer and the prison guards, he isn't ever going to see the light of day. I tell myself all this so rationally. I know I can't think he's in the world at all. I can't hope, as I do on occasion, that he'll come and find us, and that we'll sit on the couch with our new son, admiring every inch of his flesh — that we'll forget the old times because we're all each other has, because we don't have the courage to go on alone.

But the truth is, if Ruby ever gets out into the world he won't find us. We'll hide from him. It will be too late. We will be strangers, perhaps hateful strangers. I have to tell myself the words, although I'm not always positive of the meaning. I have to say the words so I learn what they mean. I don't understand my heart; it's confused with fear and pity, and maybe what they call love.

I heard Aunt Sid calling my name from upstairs yesterday. I heard my name when she sang it out so beautifully. It seemed brand-new. I got the urge to look it up in the dictionary she bought me. It's black and enormous and filled with the presence of some sort of God. Ruth. Ruth. To say my name I have to shape my lips as if I'm going to kiss someone. *Ruth* means pity and compassion, so that figures. Half the time I can't stop crying for Ruby, even though I know that what I'm supposed to do is throw him away, let him go. I believe the day will come when I'll go out in the yard and toss up my hands and he'll sail away. The winds will take him. Then I'll tell Justin his father is dead and in heaven, that he's happy for all time. I'll tell him, if I can stomach the deceit.

We have our new counselor, Sue. Sherry came a few times and then handed over her file to Sue. De Kalb is too far for Sherry to drive once a week. Her devotion is limited to a ten-mile radius. She said she hoped she'd hear from me and I said, "Sure."

Sue has long dark hair and bad skin and is so tall she has to duck coming in the door. She looks tense, probably stemming all the way back from her crazy childhood. I'm thinking about going into social work because all you have to do is say, "Tell me about your parents . . . *Oh!* That explains why you're a wreck." Then you look mournful and say, "Sorry, there's no hope for you."

Sue tells me Justy and I should never go back to the house in Honey Creek. And I nod at her and say, "OK," but I don't tell her that before I can throw it all away I have to go back once so I can see my life and say, "There it was. That was me." I have to say goodbye to Honey Creek Ruth. I don't think I'll miss her too much — just a few parts, my favorite episodes, like that one night I did the seven and ten split down at Town Lanes and everyone went wild. They hugged me and yanked on my clothes.

Sue works on me with a plan in mind. She tries to get me to say that I wasn't seeing clearly, that I took abuse greedily, that I have to change so I can protect myself, and that Ruby was a disturbed person all along. She goes about her work nervously, but gently. She makes me tell the story of our life together. She asks, while she pulls at a whisker on her chin, "Did you think it was strange the time Ruby threw the tomato juice against the wall, when he was irritated with your mother?"

And I say, "No, not real strange, all things considered."

She says, "Did you ever think you should move away from your mother?" She actually wants to say, "Aren't you an odd bird, full grown and still attached to the apron strings?"

I don't know how to answer the question. I didn't know how to tell her that May and I were the same: ugly and mean and down with our luck. I stare at the ground and then she knows to change the subject.

Perhaps Ruby was sick. I'm sure I wasn't a perfect specimen either. I know we had some great times together; I'm positive about that fact. But I'm working on truly seeing, I really am. It's about the only thing a person can promise.

I know, certainly, that there's nothing to the Rev's guarantee that the meek are going to inherit the earth. No one inherits one single thing. It's something I've thought a lot about. We're only passers-by, and all you can do is love what you have in your life. A person has to fight the meanness that sometimes comes with you when you're born, sometimes grows if you aren't in lucky surroundings. It's our challenge to fend it off, leave it behind us choking and gasping for breath in the mud. It's our task to seek out something with truth for us, no matter if there is a hundred-mile obstacle course in the way, or a ramshackle old farmhouse that binds and binds. The Bible is right on one score: it doesn't do one bit of good to render evil for evil. I don't mention these ideas of mine to Sue. I keep the thoughts to myself.

I looked up *truth* the other day also. The word has a lot to do with seeing clearly, and with things that are honest and beautiful. Perhaps I should change my name to Ruth Truth. The combination of pity and compassion with honesty and beauty would be a real knockout. People might not see me come into a room but they'd feel like there was something unusual in the air—I have a lot of fantasy dreams, I guess, because I'm by myself so much. I'm not bored too often, though. I have my entire life to think about. I have the ghosts to order away from my room. Ruth Truth. It has a nice ring to it.

I got a letter from Daisy and she said she's running for Mrs. Illinois. She looks so great in a bathing suit; I just know she's going to win. I laughed my head off when I read about it, our Daisy. She'll probably win the Mrs. America contest, which follows after the state pageant. Dee Dee wrote to tell me that Randall came in fourth in the pie-eating race at the church's winter carnival, proof that he's not as big a glutton as was supposed. I also got a letter from Diane Crawford. She must have heard about the trouble. She's married to an aluminum siding salesman who belongs to the Mafia. She sent a small box along with the letter. Inside the parcel was the heirloom pin that I lost years ago at the spelling bee. She said she had seen where it fell on the floor during the fire alarm, and she picked it up and kept it. She said it was a terribly mean thing to do, and she apologized. She hoped I'd forgive her. The pin was something I didn't want to look at. I told Aunt Sid to permanently remove it from my sight. When I opened the box I had to burst into tears. There were so many gifts coming to me late.

But the strangest part—it always makes me stop crying, as if someone's come and slapped me—is the fact that I don't have May. I stare at Aunt Sid's white walls, dumbstruck by a vision: I'm walking down the street and May isn't telling me where to go. I won't come home to her shelling five million peas. It's the craziest notion that ever came to me, that someday May would actually die. Sometimes I hear her on the porch fiddling with the lock. I'm waiting for her to yell at me. She's going to tell me to stop looking so sad.

What I know is Ruby did it for me. I'm not sure of a lot of things so far, but I know Ruby did the job for me. I don't believe in heaven or hell, or the flat gray space in between. It's all right for Justy, but not for me. We shall die, period. May's not watching me from heaven, if that's where she made it. I say that to myself over and over; I keep telling her, when I hear her on the porch — I call out, *"You are dead and gone."* I tell her, *"Beat it!"* I turn up the radio extra loud so I won't hear her feet stamping on the mat and her cigarette hacks.

Aunt Sid tells me how we're going to live. She says I'll have my baby and we'll be a family, eating breakfast out on the porch, with English muffins and orange marmalade, and she'll teach me what I need to know. She says, "Ruth, you are smart. Do you have any idea how smart you are? You can go to college and study whatever you choose."

"There's no way at this stage a teacher could show me long division," I tell her, and she says, "Nonsense."

I whisper, when she goes to make more coffee, that I want to be like Charles Dickens and write about all the good and strange people. I know I'll stay here for a while, but there'll come a time when I take my children and strike out. I don't know how or when, but I know I can't simply adopt another mother. Sometime I'm going to try my wings, see if they're strong enough. And perhaps I will write a fiction book about my life when I'm through with this, make up the end so Ruby and I go on a cruise to follow in Miss Finch's footsteps, and May marries the Rev after his wife kicks.

When Aunt Sid describes our future I want to run and hide. When it comes down to it, I don't know if I'll be able to walk out the front door. I don't know if I'll be able to walk into the college rooms with tall windows and everyone writing notes, learning tragedy from paperback books. Without May I'm empty. In my bones I'm so scared, but the mystery is in my heart — that's where I have the gumption.

ABOUT THE AUTHOR

Jane Hamilton lives, works, and writes in an orchard farmhouse in Wisconsin. Her short stories have appeared in *Harper's* magazine. For *The Book of Ruth* she received the 1989 PEN/Ernest Hemingway Foundation Award for best first novel.